Casting

By Thomas D. Haury

This book is dedicated to those warriors toiling silently to keep America safe from evil.

This is a work of fiction and not intended to represent any actual events nor to describe or represent any actual person or persons. Use of names and descriptions within this book are purely random and have no relationship to anyone past or present. Enjoy.

Published 2017

Prologue

Colonel Mitch Morgan poured himself another double shot of Jack Daniels Old No. 7 and read the letter for the third time.

Mitch,

I understand Tony is a grown man, but I am still his father and I am concerned that his welfare is not the top priority of his superiors, including you. Know this, if you do not respect me that is fine, but using Tony to get back at me will only insure our paths will cross again. I let the past go, you need to do the same or so help me God I will return to haunt your every waking minute. This is my solemn promise to you, do not take my words lightly.

Frenchy

The inherit threat was straight forward enough, just how Frenchy knew Tony was serving under his command and being used in an unorthodox way escaped him. Frenchy was as sharp as ever and obviously was still well connected within the U.S.

Army chain of command, that alone was reason for serious concern. The mission was militarily sound as far as Mitch could see and the odds were Tony and Jason would return to base shortly, so Frenchy's threat would be moot. But if anything happened to Tony, Mitch knew there would be no stopping Frenchy, Mitch was as good as dead. He lit a match and ignited the corner of the letter and dropped it into the steel trash can beside his desk. As it burned he downed the glass of Jack Daniels, and immediately poured another. It would be a very long, sleepless night reliving the nightmare that was Rong Di Ri.

Chapter 1

It was the summer of 1970 and Peter Lucas was standing

outside the one-hundred-year-old farmhouse that he called home.

He was 17 years old and quarterback of the Ft. Seneca High

School football team, who were the preseason favorites to win

the state championship in division III or single A as it was also

known. Pete wasn't tall enough to be recruited by the big schools

like Michigan or Ohio State, but he hoped to make it at some

division one university. The Raiders, as the Ft. Seneca team was

called, ran a Triple Option offense, which worked perfectly for

Pete. He was 5'9" tall and weighed only 170 pounds, but he was

extremely strong for his slight build. He had an impossibly thin

waist that measured just 27 inches, but his chest and upper back

mushroomed into a huge V shape. In fact when he went shirtless

as he often did while working on the farm, he resembled a

miniature Atlas that one could imagine holding up the entire world. He possessed blazing speed and quickness and his friend and tailback Ron Kruger was big at 6'1" and 210 pounds and fast as well. Together they made a great tandem. The team was scheduled to begin two-a-day practices the next week, the back-breaking torment of every football player who ever put on pads. Most of the players hated the mere thought of two-a-days. Pete on the other hand loved two-a-days, he was a self-proclaimed glutton for punishment with an unbelievable pain threshold. Pete also had an IQ that put him well into the realm of Mensa, though his scores had never been sent to that esteemed club, his acumen was special indeed.

Ft Seneca High School was located in the farm country of northwestern Ohio. Most of the students were farm kids and Pete was no exception. He was very handsome with a strong jaw, high cheekbones, dark brown hair cropped short, deep green eyes and a wide quick smile. He lived on his parents' farm along with about 200 head of Angus beef. Growing up outdoors on the farm; bailing hay, feeding stock and cleaning out barns, he was a hard worker and as reliable as the sun. This work ethic was instilled in him from an early age by his parents, and would dominate his overall attitude towards life in general.

Pete loved to hunt, mostly whitetail deer, rabbits and pheasants and had honed his shooting skills on groundhogs on the farm. Today was no different, Pete walked down the lane from the house carrying the rifle his dad had bought him on his 13th birthday. He continued on between the enormous red hay barn and the smaller machinery shed also painted a weather-faded red with a galvanized steel roof. He bent low and crossed under the single strand electric fence used to keep in the steers and across a twenty-acre pasture towards the treeline to the west. His chores were done, cows fed and watered, chickens fed, eggs collected and his fathers' hunting dogs fed and watered.

The air was hot and humid, a typical mid-western August morning following a steamy night when the temperature hovered in the mid-eighties. The sun was rising above a big oak tree in the pasture, Pete always wondered why you see a single large tree in the middle of fields and pastures, why that one tree? Shaking the thought from is head he crossed the pasture and slipped under the fence on the far side. Here he entered a forty-acre soybean field that he had plowed, fitted and planted the previous spring. Pete began to slow down, stalking his way towards the treeline at the far edge of the field. That tree-line marked the beginning of a wooded area on the Lucas farm where the Sandusky River, still a narrow stream at this point in its course that eventually would end at the shores of Lake Erie, snaked through bisecting the property into nearly equal east and west sides. The soybeans were only about two feet tall and still very healthy, bright green and smelled fresh in the morning air. In a month the plants would begin to yellow and dry out, at which time the beans would be ready to harvest and become feed for the steers, in good years there would be excess that could be sold on the commodities market to help defray the enormous cost of running a large farm. Half way across the field Pete began to crouch down as he walked slowly on, one hundred yards from the fencerow at the far end of the field he began to crawl, the ground was damp from last night's dew still clinging to the leaves of the beans. When he was eighty yards from the trees he could make out the shape of a large groundhog standing on his hind legs looking nervously around. Old Chuck.

Pete had tried to shoot Old Chuck for two years, but the groundhog was smart and always on guard. Pete had thought about using the dogs or poisoning the varmint, but he had realized that he had found an adversary. This was a challenge, like a good defensive football team. In his mind he wanted, no needed to beat this foe. It was his duty, like his brother Tony in Vietnam, to defeat the enemy. It was his destiny. To a high school kid on a farm in rural Ohio imagination helped to make things interesting, and kept life bearable. That was how he motivated himself to get up at 4:30 AM each morning so that his chores would be done by 7 o-clock and he would be free to hunt. It seemed to help him deal with everything going on in the world around him. He escaped into the hunt, everything else faded and the pursuit of the quarry became all encompassing.

Pete lay down in a prone position, resting the Remington 222 rifle on a large clump of dirt. Old Chuck ducked into his hole, but this time Pete waited. He decided to make today Old Chuck's last. Pete waited knowing that Old Chuck's den had more than one opening, but calculated that the one he was watching was the one Old Chuck would use. It was closest to the field and offered the best view of approaching threats. Pete waited there, lying in the field for nearly four hours. He was getting hot and starting to cramp up when he suddenly realized that Old Chuck was out of his hole and feeding at the edge of the field. Pete was furious with himself, how could he have missed the rodent coming out? He gathered his composure and began to focus on the target, but couldn't get a clear shot. Pete had been taught by his dad to never shoot an animal unless he was positive he could kill it with one shot. His dad had made him realize that it was morally wrong to inflict unnecessary pain on any living thing. If it was necessary to kill something, make it quick and as painless as possible. After what seemed like an eternity, in reality it was about ten minutes, Old Chuck was startled by a large redtail hawk soaring overhead. He scurried to the mouth of his hole, stopped and rose up on his hind legs.

Pete aimed and fired, Old Chuck fell backward into his hole. Pete jumped up, he won! He ran to the hole and looked in, he could just make out the hind legs of Old Chuck in the darkness. A feeling of pity, no; sadness; maybe, came over Pete. He was excited and sad and had a feeling like something was missing. He thought he would feel great, proud even, at besting his adversary. Instead he felt empty and unfulfilled. As the adrenaline subsided he realized that part of the experience was that he looked forward to each day's hunt. There would be no more hunting Old Chuck, he was gone.

Pete walked back towards the house, not paying any attention he walked right into the electric fence. After the initial shock, literally, he shook his head and headed for the back porch of the old federal style farmhouse. He stopped and scratched Buddy, his old Beagle, between the ears and thought about Old Chuck. He remembered the damage one of Old Chuck's holes had done to the five-bottom plow when one of the wheels had dropped into the hole and caused the hydraulic line to break. And the time that his sister Suzy's horse had stumbled when it stepped into one of the rodent's holes, almost throwing Suzy from the saddle. He realized that Old Chuck needed to go, but he knew he would miss the hunt.

Pete climbed the steps to the porch and opened the back door, the smell of ham and his mom's homemade bread filled his head. Pete walked into the kitchen still carrying his rifle. Joy Lucas had watched her youngest son come across the lawn and when he entered the kitchen she asked the same question she asked every day," get him?"

"Yeah," Pete said almost apologetic.

"Really? Wonderful, your dad will be thrilled. He's been after that whistle pig for years."

"Yeah," Pete said again and headed up the steep wooden stairs to his room.

Joy was confused, she thought he would be jumping up and down. Just then the timer on her oven went off and she rushed to check her bread. She did make a mental note to talk to Roger about Pete's reaction.

Roger Lucas was a solid five foot nine inch tall man seemingly built of granite. His body was compact and stout, at 205 pounds, but showed no sign of fat. His arms were thick, especially his forearms from lifting thousands of hay bales and feedbags. His shoulders seemed to blend into his chest, one big mass of muscle. He had jet black hair that was thinning on top, but few people would have known because he almost never removed the baseball hat that seemed permanently attached to his head. His green eyes were the common trait shared by all of the Lucas men. Roger had heard the shot from where he stood next to the aging Massy-Ferguson tractor he was once again working on. He had also heard Pete yell and he knew Pete had finally gotten Old Chuck. Roger smiled and thought "'bout time, he's been after that critter for two years."

Roger had a dread creeping into his mind, it had been three weeks since they had received Tony's last letter. Tony was his eldest son and the one Roger had always assumed would take over the farm when he retired. That was until Tony joined the Army and became a member of the 101st Airborne. Roger was proud of his son for serving his country, but he was worried about the politicians in Washington. They seemed to be leaving the military without a clear direction. War no war, fight or don't fight. Roger was angry now, his mind jumping from Vietnam and his son Tony to a war long over.

He was brought back to reality by a sharp pain in his left arm. The pain moved quickly up his arm and seemed to explode in his chest. He tried to kneel down and catch his breath. A sudden peace settled over him and all went black.

Joy Lucas was the perfect farm wife, an excellent cook, handy with first aid and tough as nails. She was five feet two inches tall and a little stocky herself, but she carried herself with pride and always had a warm smile for everyone she met. She had raised three boys and two girls, managed the finances of the farm and the temperament of her husband. Her brunette hair had turned a premature grey but she made no attempt to color it, she was honest to the core and proud to be exactly who she was. Joy was 52 years old and finally happy. She had just finished her college degree in business and her baby, Pete, would graduate high school in June. She looked forward to starting her craft store/market in the spring. Roger had agreed to build her a pole building out by the road over the winter, when the work on the farm slowed down a little. She could picture the sign on the door and the aisles of crafts and fresh produce. She smiled to herself as she baked, soon her bread would be earning her money not just ribbons at the county fair.

However, Joy, like Roger, had an uneasy feeling about Tony. He had written a letter a week for two years straight, until they stopped coming three weeks ago. Tony had said in his last letter that he was going "in country", meaning he was being sent to the front lines in Vietnam. She attempted to keep busy baking and making craft items to stock her store, but she could not shake the feeling of dread. Tony was Roger's favorite and she knew he was devastated when Tony joined the Army. Roger wanted Tony to run the farm, but Tony was as stubborn as his father and railed against what he saw as his dad's attempt to run his life. Joy feared that Roger blamed himself for Tony's decision to join the

Army and if anything happened to Tony he would not forgive himself. There was never a mention about their former life, the life Roger had left behind over twenty years before. Roger had made it taboo to even speak about it. She had tried at first to find out what had happened in Korea, but Roger slammed that door shut forever. The American government had been so appreciative of whatever Roger had done that they had bought him the farm they now lived on and even allowed Roger's brother Jean (John) to move nearby. They were taught to speak perfect English and given an unimpeachable background should anyone check. The children were all under the age of six so it was easy to have them adopt American ways.

Joy was roused from her thoughts by Buddy barking loudly. She looked out the kitchen window but couldn't see the little beagle anywhere. She called up the stairs to Pete, "Pete can you come down and see what's bothering Buddy?"

Pete came flying down the stairs and out through the back door, he had heard Buddy too and looked out his bedroom window. From the second floor window he had seen his father lying on the ground beside the old tractor. Buddy was standing beside him, pawing at him and barking wildly. Pete rushed to his dad's side and found him cold and not breathing, his mind raced, at first he couldn't remember what to do. Then the Boy Scout first aid training came flooding into his mind. He laid Roger on his back and began CPR. Joy who quickly realized there was something wrong, came running up from behind panting heavily she let out a cry of, "Oh God no!"

Pete turned to her and yelled, "call Uncle John!" and then added, "tell him to hurry, Dad's had a heart attack!"

Joy was stunned and it took her a second to control her mind, then she turned back towards the house yelling, "I'll get the truck, don't stop what you're doing!"

Pete kept up the rhythm but he knew his dad was in deep trouble. Then he thought to himself, "get the truck? What is she thinking, mom doesn't know how to drive!." Just then the old blue Ford pick-up came around from the right side of the barn and stopped no more than two feet from Pete and Roger. Pete lifted his lifeless father's body into the bed of the truck and jumped in after him. Joy threw the truck in gear and started off up the lane between the buildings and turned right onto the long driveway, which led to the road. She didn't even look, let alone slow down when she reached the road. She made a screeching left hand turn and stomped on the gas, it was five miles to town and the hospital was on the far side. She made the trip in less than five minutes. Pete didn't even notice all the horns and screeching tires, he kept up the CPR and prayed for his father's life.

Chapter 2

The Emergency Room staff was efficient and very competent for such a small town, they managed to get Roger's heart started and moved him to ICU. The prognosis however was not good, nobody knew how long he had been without oxygen and even with all of Pete's effort the damage was probably severe. Joy was as sturdy as ever and put up a valiant front, Pete was solemn and angry. He was supposed to fix the tractor, but he had forgotten. This was his fault, Tony wouldn't have forgotten.

The rest of the Lucas family, Suzy, Colleen and Henry had all arrived at the hospital. Suzy was 21 and a junior at Ohio State University, she was still home for the summer and working as a waitress at a local diner. Her blonde hair and fair complexion made her stand out among the rest of the family. She had bright blue eyes and very feminine figure, her curves were accentuated by her long legs and a beautiful smile. At 5' 8" tall she was a virtual Amazon among the stout farm women of the area. Colleen was 23 and had married her high school sweetheart, he had been drafted and was in Germany. She more resembled her mother at 5'3" tall and a healthy 130 ponds. Her brown hair and blue eyes added to the overall "girl next door" appearance. She worked part time at the hardware store and taught piano to some of the kids in town. She also played the organ in church on Sundays and was expecting her first child in December. Henry was the middle son at 23 and Colleen's twin, he was attending college at The University of Dayton. He shared Colleen's brown hair but had the green eyes of the Lucas men. He was a little taller than Pete at 5'11" and weighed a sturdy 220 pounds with a round belly and round face. Henry had never been interested in farming and was his mom's favorite. He was an academic and everyone figured he would be a teacher or professor someday.

The doctor came to the family and gave them the news, "Roger may never wake up. His brain had been starved of oxygen for a long time and there is no way to know what damage has been done." He said.

This was too much for Pete and he walked out of the waiting room. He had to get some air, had to think. He made his way outside and sat down on a low concrete wall outside the emergency room doors. He was convinced that this whole thing was his fault. Joy came looking for him, "how ya holding up?"

"I dunno, I don't know what to do."

"Pray", she said. "All we can do now is pray."

Pete hung his head and prayed, but he knew he had to find a way to make amends. He still didn't know what he had done wrong, but he was convinced he needed to do something. He couldn't fathom how this could happen without his being at fault, it seemed everything on the farm was connected to him. If he forgot to give a steer its medicine one time, it would die. If he forgot to water the chickens, they would turn on one another and one would be killed. Every time he forgot to do something, it was a disaster and his dad would say, "You're responsible for your actions. If you forget something, something or someone else suffers." He had forgotten to fix the tractor.

Joy went back inside and Pete's uncle John came out to sit with him. Pete loved his uncle and often talked to him about things that bothered him. John was six years younger than Roger and a little taller, he was slighter built but still very strong. He had the same jet black hair and green eyes as his older brother, but his face was longer and thinner than Roger's. John looked at Pete and couldn't imagine how he felt after finding his dad in the field. "We're all very proud of you," he said at last.

Pete was surprised, "proud of what?"

"Saving you're dad, you know, with the CPR and all,"
John said. "Hell, I don't even know how to do that, guess I need
to learn though. Your dad won't know what to do, he ain't used
to being beholding to no body."

"What?" Pete was thoroughly confused, "what are you
talking about? I am responsible for him being here!" Pete was
getting hot and he needed to vent. "If I had fixed the damn
tractor instead of shooting Old Chuck none of this would not
have happened! He would have been inside eating lunch with
mom, not out in the heat of the day beating on that rusted piece
of shit!"

John looked at him and smiled, "you shot Old Chuck?
Does your dad know?"

"What?" Pete was dumbfounded. "My dad's in there
dying and you're worried about a woodchuck?"

John smiled again, shook his head and pushed back the
baseball cap that he always wore. He waited a minute and then
said, "Pete, your dad eats too much greasy food and smokes like
a chimney. He knows its gonna kill him some day, but he ain't
'bout to quit. Doc told him to quit smokin' and eat better or he'd

have a heart attack Maybe now he'll listen, if it's not too late."
John's face grew solemn, he hadn't allowed himself to think of
losing his only brother until he said it just then.

Pete read his uncle's face and let out a sigh, "It can't be
too late, I can't take care of the farm alone. Tony..." his voice
trailed off. "Tony won't be back anytime soon."

This time John read Pete's thoughts, "your brother can
take care of himself, he'll be home soon enough. Your mom is
the brains of the operation anyway and your dad's gonna be just
fine." He got up and went back inside before Pete could notice
the fear in his eyes, there would be no way to save the farm if
Roger didn't pull through. Joy was the brain, but it took muscle
and animal insight to raise steers. Pete was an exceptional young
man, but he wasn't up to running a large farm yet.

Suzy came walking up, she had gone back to the farm to
get some things Joy wanted, a robe and slippers for Roger. It was
lucky she had gone, when she pulled up smoke was coming from
the house. Joy had not even thought of shutting off the oven and
had left the ham in. Fortunately all that was lost was the ham,
and the curtains were covered with soot. She sat down beside
Pete and put her arm around him, she began to cry. Pete held her

and wondered why he couldn't cry, he sat still and thought of Tony.

Pete's girlfriend Becky Getz came to the hospital to sit with him. Becky was a standout at everything she did, point guard on the girls' basketball team, shortstop on the fast pitch softball team and headed for salutatorian of the senior class. She would have been a shoe-in for valedictorian if it wasn't for Pete, he had never gotten a grade below 98% in his entire school career. What really pissed her off was that he didn't even study, she spent hours every day studying, and he would just show up and ace the test. It made her crazy, but it also made her want to know him better and resulted in their friendship and after a year of casual conversation she finally had to ask him to the Prom. He was just too shy to ask, she figured it out and began pushing the relationship, he was more than happy to let her dictate what they did and when. She considered it fair payback for his insufferable genius.

Becky was also very attractive when she tried, which wasn't very often. She usually wore jeans, t shirts and converse sneakers, her strawberry blond hair was almost always pulled back in a ponytail and she never wore makeup. Even with the tomboy look in full bloom, she was still good looking, with a very athletic build, 5'5" tall, and just 105 pounds. Becky was one of those girls that go unnoticed by most men until she decided to get herself all dressed up. When Pete had picked her up for the Prom in May he had just stood in her mom's foyer and stared at her for a long time. Becky thought there was something wrong, but finally Pete smiled and just said ,"wow." That night she was the most beautiful girl in the school and after that she couldn't hide her beauty behind the jeans and t shirts anymore. Every want-a-be ladies man at school hit on her, she was flattered, Pete was not and more than once he had to "have a talk" with one of the hallway Romeos.

Becky was crying and Pete was brooding, she looked at him and said softly, "I'm moving."

"What?"

"You know dad's been laid off and Ford offered him a spot on the line in Michigan, so he says he's gonna take it," she said while sobbing. Becky's dad, Mike Getz had been an assembly line worker at a local Ford plant for 16 years until the plant went to only one shift and his job went away. He had been laid off and unemployed for 6 months when Ford decided to add a second shift at a plant in Flat Rock, Michigan and offered the positions to the laid off workers from Ohio. It was a difficult decision for the family but one that had to be made, they decided to make the move before school started so their three children could start the year at their new school. Becky was the oldest, it would be hard for her to move for her senior year but in the end it had to be done.

Pete was devastated and just stared at the floor, he wasn't able to process this news along with his father's condition. Becky hugged him and continued to cry, after a half hour she kissed him on the cheek and said, "call me later, when you get home."

Pete looked at her puffy red eyes and said, "OK, I'm just not sure what's going on right now."

Becky smiled and said, "either do I, but we'll think of something", and then she stood and walked out of the waiting room leaving Pete alone with his thoughts.

Roger regained consciousness only briefly and rambled about war and Tony, he slipped into French at times which took the medical staff by complete surprise. The family took turns sitting with him, and Pete took his turn in the small hours of the next morning. Roger opened his eyes and looked as if the devil himself were standing there waiting to take him to the fires of hell. He began talking slowly at first but then the words seemed to be bursting from his lips, he began to detail a story Pete had never heard before. Roger spoke entirely in French, a language Pete had been taught since birth. He had been told it was to preserve the family heritage and that someday he may want to visit the family homestead in northern Ontario. Roger's story was a detailed account of a day in 1953 when as a Canadian soldier he and a small detail of men, along with U.S. Army Rangers saved South Korea from disaster. The story was fantastic and horrifying, the detail and descriptions given by the senior Lucas both scared Pete and enraptured him at the same time. At last came the part that completely tore Pete to pieces, Roger looked at Pete but in his delirious state saw Tony and said, "Tony, your real name is Antone Latelhaurie, you were born in North Bay, Ontario, this you need to know, but you can never tell anyone. Promise me you will never speak of this to anyone. Promise."

Pete did as he was told, "I promise dad."

Roger slipped back into unconsciousness. This affected Pete deeply, he had no idea if anything his dad had said was true, but why would he lie? Pete told his mom that his dad had talked about Korea just before he fell into the coma. She really didn't care, her whole life was unraveling before her eyes. Roger never did acknowledge Pete again and passed away two days after the heart attack. The funeral was hard on Pete and devastating for Joy. She was despondent and seemed to age overnight.

Becky and her family moved to Michigan and at first she wrote Pete every day and they talked on the phone twice a week, but after only a month the letters slowed and finally ended with one that said Becky had met a really nice guy at school and she needed to move on with her life. Pete didn't even reply, there wasn't anything else to be said. He took the news with the same stoic detached attitude he had felt in losing his dad, life went on.

School started and football season began, Pete played like a possessed madman. He made some mistakes and even got into a shoving match with Ron Kruger, one of his best friends, but his mental state was that of a suicidal maniac. He ran headlong into opposing defenses daring them to tackle him. Pete smashed the record for rushing yards gained and touchdowns scored. The

Raiders ran roughshod over the competition gaining recognition but also raising the ire of some of the opposing coaches when Pete would continue to pound the other team even after having a huge lead. The scouts were very impressed but being only 5'9" tall made it impossible for Pete to get any real consideration from the football powerhouses and in the end the best offer he received for a scholarship came from Kent State University. He considered it, but the anti-war troubles there and at other schools put him off. Pete was drifting, and he didn't even know which direction the shore was. It was now November and football was over and the days just seemed to plod along.

Chapter 3

Pete and his uncle John began the annual process of readying their traps for the upcoming fur trapping season. The Lucas' had continued to fur trap, a tradition handed down for generations. The first members of their family to come to the Americas had paddled up the St. Laurence with DeLesalle in the 1700's and had been trapping beaver, mink, muskrat, raccoon and fox ever since. Beaver were nearly extinct in Ohio before the family had been re-settled there, but muskrat, mink, raccoon and fox were still readily available.

The two men cleaned and oiled the traps, inspected wire triggers on the connibear traps and the pedal triggers on the leg-hold versions and tested the chains that were used to attach them to their stakes. There were nearly 1,500 traps in all and it took a full 12-hour day to prep them all for the three month long trapping season due to begin on November 15th. Ohio designated the start and end to the season but had yet to place limits on catches of fur-bearers except beaver. The Lucas family trapped a long stretch of the river that bisected their farm, as well as numerous ponds, lakes and creeks in the surrounding two counties. It would be a difficult year for the two remaining men, not having Roger to help this year would be a huge loss.

Pete took a chance and as they were trudging through the prep work and asked, " Uncle John, what was life in Canada like? I mean I know who we really are, dad told me before he died."

John looked at Pete and sighed, "your mom told me, she also told me not to talk to you about it."

Pete started to object, but John raised his hand and cut him off. "I will tell you everything I know, I think you guys deserve to know, but if you tell your mom I told you I will never speak to you again, understood?" John suddenly looked to Pete more like his father than he had ever seen him. The look was cold and severe.

Pete answered softly, "understood, sir."

John paused a few minutes, working all the time to free a rusted spring on a trap, then he began to speak slowly. As was their habit when speaking of important matters the language switched to French and Pete found it hard to continue to work. He forced himself to stay focused on his task and refrained from interrupting, even when he really wanted his uncle to repeat something or clarify a fact. He had learned from years of listening to lessons from his father never to interrupt, questions would sometimes be allowed at the end, or not. Such was the way of the woodsmen from the north.

The story John told was fascinating and extremely sad, at times Pete expected his uncle to break down, but the elder Lucas kept his composure throughout. His story began when John was just six years old. The Latelhaurie boys, Roger and Jean had a father named George that suffered from alcoholism like many First Nation men and a mother that had finally had enough of a husband that alternated between rage and stupor. The boy's mother simply walked away from their run down home and headed to the nearest town, met up with a man and never looked back.

George Latelhaurie came home from a three day binge to find his wife gone and his two young sons, aged 12 and 6, asleep in their beds. He woke Roger by rolling him out of bed onto the bare wood floor and proceeded to beat him bloody. The old man screamed at Roger to get up and get the furs they had stored in the shed loaded into his old truck. Roger woke Jean and the two boys loaded the truck with the furs and climbed in to wait for their dad. George folded himself into the drivers' seat and threw the truck in gear. They headed east to the largest town in northern Ontario, North Bay. There they headed straight for a fur trader that George knew would pay cash.

Roger knew enough to know his dad was going to get a fraction of what the pelts were worth and he was pissed off. He had done most of the work, his dad was too drunk most of the time to even get up and check the traps and now the old man was going to throw away a huge portion of their money just to get cash for more booze. When they got to the dealer's building he told his dad exactly what he was thinking, the response was a slap in the face and a vicious expletive laced rant. George went inside and came out less than five minutes later with a wad of cash in his hand. He ordered Roger and Jean unload the pelts into the dealer's building while he walked next door to buy a bottle of whiskey. The boys did as told and then Roger spoke to the dealer, "we won't be bringing you any more furs" he said in an icy tone. The dealer laughed at him.

When George LaTelhaurie returned to his truck with an open bottle, he ordered twelve year old Roger to drive them home. Roger climbed into the drivers' seat and put the truck in gear. Roger had been driving the truck for two years out on the reservation, their trap line was too long to do just on foot and the traps needed checked twice a day so he had learned to drive as a matter of necessity. Jean could tell his brother had changed, his jaw was set tight and he had the wheel gripped so tight his knuckles were white. By the time the trio made it back to their ramshackle home Roger had worked himself into a absolute rage. Roger jumped from the truck and met his father just as the old man got out of the passenger seat.

George looked at his son and saw his anger, and he laughed in the boy's face, "what are you going to do big man?" he laughed.

Roger hit him with a right cross so hard it knocked out two teeth, the second punch was a left to the abdomen knocking the wind out of the drunk. The third and final blow was to the back of the head and George crashed to the frozen ground, out cold.

Roger paced a few minutes letting the adrenaline subside, then he told Jean to go inside and grab all of their clothes and anything else he wanted to take with him. Jean did as instructed while Roger went to the shed and removed all of the traps and put them into the back of the old truck. He added their fishing rods, tackle and a canoe. Jean came out with the clothes and his stuffed bear. Roger had him put the stuff behind the seat in the truck and told him to get in. The final thing Roger did was go inside the house and grab has 4-10 shotgun, and shells from under his bed. He came out just as George was rousing and reached into his fathers' pocket and pulled out what was left of the cash. He took half of it and threw the rest in his father's face. Then got into the drivers' seat, put the truck in gear and pulled out of the drive.

George didn't try to stop him, instead he stumbled into the house rummaged under the sink and found a mason jar of moonshine and proceeded to drink himself unconscious.

Roger drove the old truck west to the tiny town of Lavinge and then turned north and in less than two miles the road turned into a dirt track, another mile and the track became little more than a trail with scrub and trees closing in on all sides.

Roger had been down this path many times, he hunted moose and trapped a small lake just ahead of his current location. He also knew there was an ancient house trailer abandoned on the west side of that lake. He had inspected it last summer while fishing for pike and had found that it hadn't been used in decades. He drove the truck as close as he could to the trailer but had to stop about 100 meters short because the ground was too soft and the last thing he wanted was to get the rusted old vehicle stuck. He maneuvered the truck until it was pointed back the way he had come and killed the engine.

Roger got out and told his little bother to stay in the vehicle until he made sure the trailer was safe. Picking his gun off of the rack behind the seat, he approached the trailer with caution but found it to be in the exact same state as it was six months before. The front door was ajar about six inches but Roger remembered he had tried to close it when he had left but it wouldn't stay shut. A quick recon of the premises revealed a very ratty old sofa, a sink with no running water and an empty ice box.

Returning to the truck, he had Jean help him unload their clothes and the two boys got started cleaning up their new home.

They cleared out all of the junk, piled it up and Roger lit the pile with a kitchen match. The fire was warm, even though it stunk from the various materials being burned. Roger left Jean by the fire to stay warn and set to work cleaning the wood stove, he had watched his dad carefully for years maintain the wood burning stove that kept their home warm during the bone chilling winters of northern Ontario. The sun was setting and the temperature was dropping like a stone. The stove cleaned and the chimney cleared of years of squirrel nests and debris, Roger placed some sticks Jean had gathered into the stove, wadded up an old newspaper they found in the house and lit another match. The fire sputtered at first but soon caught and Roger banked the box with a couple of birch log pieces he found stacked just outside the front door. He again left Jean to tend the fire, this one smelled much better, and went back out into the freezing evening. He did not have a flashlight so he waited a few minutes for his night vision to adjust, once he could see more than two feet in front of himself, he began searching for more firewood. A small pile of partially chopped wood was found behind the house and Roger carried a dozen logs around front and stacked them within reach of the door.

Next item of concern was the door itself, it had to close properly or the heat from the stove would simply escape. Roger spent a few minutes looking at the hinges and latch, he found that the top hinge was loose. The screws that had attached it to the door frame were almost falling out. Using his pocket knife like a screwdriver he managed to work them back into the frame although he could tell the wood was not solid and they would work their way back out again quickly. The good news was the door now closed, there was still a small gap but the latch now engaged. Roger stuffed one of his sweaters into the gap and their home was now fairly closed in and the stove was warming the place up quite nicely.

Jean watched Roger quietly, he thought his brother was amazing. It never occurred to the young boy that his older brother was scared to death. To Jean, Roger was infallible, he always knew what to do and he had always protected his little brother from harm. This new challenge would be conquered without difficulty, he had complete faith in Roger. It was an hour before Jean finally spoke, "what are we going to eat?"

"Tonight we will see if there is any canned food in the pantry, if not we will be hungry by the morning," Roger said softly. "Tomorrow we will go back to town and buy food and supplies. I will set some traps in the morning and we will have some fresh meat by evening."

The boys checked but found no food in the home, they laid their clothes on the floor next to the stove, Roger banked the fire so it would last several hours and they went to sleep hungry that first night.

The next day Roger was up at dawn, tended to the fire in the stove and headed out to the truck. He pulled his waders out of the back along with a hatchet and several connibear traps. These traps were spring loaded square traps designed to fit in the opening of the holes where muskrats burrowed into the bank along waterways. Mink were predators and hunted among other things, muskrats. Thus by setting traps at the entrances to muskrat holes, you could catch either animal. Muskrat and Mink are not highly valued for their meat but given the alternative of starving, it would do. He walked to the lake shore and began walking along the edge. He saw several "huts" or mounds of mud, reeds and sticks that muskrats build, similar to beaver huts but smaller, within 50 meters. Those would have their openings facing deep water so that even in mid-winter the ice wouldn't completely block the animals escape route if danger presented itself. On the shore he found telltale slides in the mud and snow that indicated where the rodents (muskrats were essentially large rats with better fur) had slid down into the water.

There was a thin film of ice on the surface but it was easily broken with the hatchet. Roger looked for holes along the bank, active holes would have a cloud of dirt floating in front of their openings from the animals either active burrowing or simply from their movement in and out of the hole. He found four promising holes within 100 meters of the house and set the traps. Then he trudged back to the house and changed into his work boots. He debated letting Jean sleep but decided it was too dangerous to leave him at the house alone. So he woke the boy and had him get dressed, they drank tea with water Roger boiled on the stove after scooping it out of the lake and added spruce tips he gathered from a nearby tree.

The boys drove to the tiny general store in Lavinge and bought beans, a bag of potatoes, a dozen eggs, bacon, coffee, some shells for the 4-10, two loaves of bread, peanut butter, soap, and a bag of rock candy for Jean. Pete paid for it and filled the trucks gas tank. He used almost half of their money and decided he would have to manage the money better in the future.

Once back at the house Roger assessed the house more closely, finding it had two bedrooms both of which were in poor repair but the boys were used to doing without. He found a back door off of what was left of the kitchen. A stone path led to a fallen down outhouse, another issue he would have to deal with soon. The biggest issue was making sure Jean got fed, clothed and to school each day. It was Sunday so he would have to figure out the school part tomorrow morning. There was only one school out here for Jean, the same one he had always attended, maybe he could catch the bus from the general store? It was worth investigating. Roger wasn't planning on going back to school himself, he had to earn enough money to keep him and his kid brother alive and away from their dad.

Roger was only twelve but he had the mind and soul of a grown man, he had been the man of the house for years already. He was a professional trapper, fisherman and hunter with more experience and grit than most men three times his age. He already stood 5 feet 6 inches tall and weighed a solid 160 pounds, with thick arms and wide shoulders. Most people automatically assumed he was closer to manhood than childhood, a hardscrabble life had burnished him into what seemed like hardened steel.

Roger checked his traps at dusk and was rewarded with two large muskrats, he re-set the traps and took the catch back to the house. Using the technique taught to him by his father, the same technique handed down through generations of French fur trappers, he skinned the animals, butchered them, and cleaned the meat using boiled lake water. He knew all about Giardia, the nasty stomach parasite that lived in standing water frequented by beaver, otter and muskrats, thus he boiled the water.

The meat was not tasty but it was full of protein and that was what mattered most, and with a steady supply of meat within walking distance the boys would never starve. Trapping season would last another two months giving Roger time to earn much needed cash, which he would use to among other things prepare himself for fishing season with tackle and gear sufficient for the job.

On Monday morning Roger drove Jean to the general store and was happy to find two other children waiting for the school bus. When it arrived Roger told the driver Jean would be there each morning for pick-up, the driver simply shrugged his shoulders and said "ok". It was a much simpler time and the entire population of the area knew George was a fall down drunk, finding out the family had moved didn't surprise the old man driving the bus and he wasn't one to spread rumors.

For the next 4 years Roger and Jean lived in the old trailer, "fixed it up pretty nice too" Jean added proudly.

On Jean's tenth birthday Roger took him to the general store to get some candy as a gift, once inside a voice from their past called out, "there are my boys!" George LaTellhaurie stood behind them smiling as if they had never had a cross word spoken between them. Roger's hands balled into fists but George continued to smile. He said, "I've kicked it Rog, I really have, once and for all. Nearly killed me but I haven't had a drop in months, you can ask anyone, its true. I swear."

Roger continued to be wary, he told Jean to pick out his gift and Jean did as told. Their dad just stood there smiling, he turned to Jean and said, "I am sorry for everything I've done, I want you guys to come home."

Roger finally spoke, "We have a home of our own."

"Where?" George asked.

Before Roger could answer Jean piped up, "North, by Cache Lake".

Roger shot Jean a nasty look and Jean quickly realized he had screwed up. George just continued smiling and said nothing. Roger paid for the candy and the boys headed for the old truck. George followed them out, careful to keep his distance from Roger who had now grown to his full five feet nine inches and had filled out to over 180 pounds. As the boys climbed inside the truck George appeared at the passenger window and leaned on the open frame. He spoke to Roger in a soft tone Roger had never heard from his father before, "I have changed son, you'll see."

Roger started the truck and eased it into gear, George leaned back and let the truck slide past him and watched it exit the parking lot and accelerate on the northbound Route 64. Jean watched as his father faded from view and worried he had somehow ruined everything.

The next day at school Jean was pulled out of class and asked to go to the head master's office. Once there he found his father smiling and talking to Mr. Tallman the headmaster, as Jean approached Mr. Tallman spoke." Your father was just telling me you and your older brother have been roughing it up by Cache Lake for a while and he wants you to come back home."

"Roger and I are fine and happy where we are," Jean replied.

"I know you think you are fine son but the Province of Ontario and in fact all of Canada has rules about minor children and safety" Tallman responded. George just smiled. "I am going to request that someone come visit your home and make sure everything is as fine and you say, if they agree you will be allowed to stay where you are if not you will need to either move back with you father or move into a children's home."

Jean didn't know what to say so he just nodded his head.

Tallman told Jean to go back to class and turned to George, "I imagine they will be back with you within the week, I am glad to hear you have cleaned up your life George" and the two men shook hands. Jean had started to walk away but heard what his head master had said, and it terrified him.

When Roger picked Jean up from the bus stop next to the general store Jean was quiet, "What's the matter little man?" he asked.

"Dad was at school today, he talked to the headmaster, they're going to send somebody to check where we live," he plead, then began crying. "They are going to take us back to dad's to live."

Roger had been worried what his father would do, now he knew the boys were in trouble. Roger had asked an elder from the Reservation a year before what would happen if his mom or dad tried to take the boys back. The man, a man respected by all, had told Roger that if either parent came forward and was deemed fit to care for them the boys would have no choice. He had also told Roger that once he turned 16 he had other options but Jean who was just 9 at the time would be placed into the parent's care and there was nothing he nor Roger could do about that.

Roger tried to calm Jean, when they got home they cleaned the trailer top to bottom, made sure there was ample wood stacked, the pantry was neat and staged to look as full as possible and then they waited. It was two days later when the boys returned from Roger picking up Jean at the bus stop when they found a dark blue sedan and a CMP Canadian Mounted

Police vehicle parked near the trailer. Roger's heart sank and Jean started to sob.

The "inspection" lasted just ten minutes and Jean was placed into the MP's back seat along with his clothes and other personal items. The MP spoke to Roger and was very blunt, "son what you have done here, with nothing but your wits and bare hands is nothing short of amazing, but the law is clear. Your father has been proven sober for over three months, has a decent job painting houses and has petitioned to have the two of you returned to his custody. Being underage your bother has no choice and I will take him to your father's home forthwith, however being as you are of age to choose for yourself you have the option of staying here. However you do need to re-enroll in school to do so, Your other option is to enlist as a hardship case in the army and see if they will have you, if that is your choice I will gladly offer a recommendation for you." His pride in what this teenage boy had accomplished alone in the northwoods of Ontario shone through his stern façade.

Roger asked, "Sir, what would you suggest I do?"

The MP replied, "Canada needs young men like you."

Roger nodded and then walked to where Jean was sitting in the back seat of the cruiser, he leaned in and hugged his bother and said, "I can't come with you little man, I just can't. I might kill him and then I would be in jail forever. I am going to join the army and as soon as you are old enough I will come and get you. Stay tough, and if dad screws up, beat his ass!"

Jean looked up at Roger who was smiling from ear to ear, Jean smiled back and said, "OK".

The two vehicles pulled away and the last Jean saw of Roger he was waving goodbye standing in front of that old broken down trailer.

"I lived with the old man for almost eight years and when I graduated high school your dad showed up at the ceremony, a month later my dad died from liver failure and I got a visit from an American. He told me I was being moved to America, my brother Roger had arranged it, and I would see him as soon as I got there. Sure enough we pulled into the drive of this old farm right here and your dad was standing in the driveway. Best damn day of my life." John said, finishing the story.

Pete didn't know what to say so he just kept prepping the traps, and in a moment the two men were talking football and hunting.

Chapter 4

One freezing cold night Pete had just finished feeding the steers and stepped from the barn into a complete whiteout, the only light coming from the large sodium fixture that hung on a pole midway between the machinery shed and the massive hay barn. Pete's mind instantly shot to Korea and his dad's story of the raging battle of Rong Di Ri. Pete stood still and could almost hear the screams of the wounded. The explosions and gunfire seemed to echo off of the buildings and pound in his head, then suddenly the wind eased and the white farmhouse materialized before his eyes and he was brought back to the present.

That night Pete decided he needed to find out more about what had happened that day in 1953, what had his father done that made the whole thing taboo to talk about? Why all the secrecy? Pete thought to himself, "its time for some answers."

Pete began his research at the school library but it was very small and had almost no information on the Korean War, short of a few history books and a couple of novels. The librarian, Lenore Granger, was a little surprised to see Pete. She was very short and very petite, with her hair pulled up in a bun atop her head and reading glasses that hung about her neck on a thin silver chain. Mrs. Granger knew who Pete was because like everyone else in football crazed Ohio she attended every game the school played, but she had never seen him in the library before. When she asked him if she could help he asked her if she had ever heard of a place in Korea called Rong Di Ri. She hadn't but she promised to do some checking and see if she could find anything.

"What is it you are looking for, exactly Mr. Lucas?" Mrs. Ganger asked.

"I was told there was a very important battle there in 1953 and I want to do a report about it." Pete lied about the report part but considered it better than having to explain that he promised not to talk about it with anyone.

"I'm afraid we don't have a lot of books on the Korean War, some of our local vets from the big War don't consider it to be worthy of much reading since we didn't finish the job like they did in Europe and Japan", Mrs. Granger apologized quietly.

"It was just a thought" Pete said somewhat dejected.

"I have a friend at the Library of Congress, I'll bet she can help you out but it might take a few weeks, when is your report due?" Granger asked.

"It's extra credit, so I just need it by the end of the term," Pete lied again and smiled as his hopes rose once again.

"Let me give Marge a call tonight, I haven't spoken to her in over a year so I need to catch up on her and her family anyways. What was that place called again?" she asked.

"Rong Di Ri, it was along the Bukanggang River, I'm not sure how the river's name is spelled but I was told it was a very important battle so if they have records of the war I would think they could find it." Pete responded, more than a little embarrassed that he had so little to go on.

"OK, but you're sure about the Rong Di Ri part?" Granger asked just being thorough and not being pretentious.

"Yes maam, I'm positive about that part," Pete stated.

"OK, I'll let you know when I know something," she said smiling.

"Thank you Mrs. Granger", Pete said as he walked out of the library.

"I had no idea he even knew my name" Mrs. Granger thought to herself as she placed the note to call her friend in the front pocket of her purse. In fact Pete hadn't known her name, but as she had moved to her desk to jot down the name Rong Di Ri, Pete caught sight of her name plate sitting on her desk Being more personal always seemed to help get things done, a lesson he had learned years before in elementary school.

True to her word Lenore Granger called Marge Temple that very night and after a full thirty minute report on all things Temple including an engagement (her daughter Adell to a banker from Georgetown) and a death (her Aunt Sophie). Lenore asked her friend for a simple favor, could she please check to see if there was any info in the Library of Congress about a Korean War battle at a place called Rong Di Ri and if so could she please either forward copies of the info or the title and author of any articles or books on the subject. She explained that it was for a student's report and that any info would be appreciated. Marge responded that she would love to be of help and would be in touch by the end of the week.

Chapter 5

Colonel Mitch Morgan was frantic, his signal sent to
Saigon was relayed to Forward Operating Base Scout :

Scout,

Where the hell are they? I need a report ASAP!

Col. Morgan

The report that came back via Saigon was terrifying and
yet succinct,

Col. Morgan,

Missing, Sir.

Maj. Lawrence Pierce

101ˢᵗ Airborne FOB Scout

Mitch Morgan was beside himself, what the hell had
happened? Two days ago all was going perfectly, three targets
hit, no-one had a clue what was happening, a total success. Then,
wham, a complete nightmare. They had not checked in as
planned, scouting patrols had no sign of them, nothing. Sweat
began to bead on the Colonels' forehead, his mouth went dry,
and he reached for Old #7.

Marge Temple entered the Library of Congress through the employee entrance just as she had every weekday for the past twenty three years. She hadn't missed a day of work other than vacation since President Kennedy had been assassinated in 1963. Even then she allowed herself only one day to mourn and then back to work. She was as everyday American as they came, 5'4" tall and full figured with chestnut brown hair and hazel eyes. She wore a black skirt and long sleeved white blouse and black low heels under a full length beige wool coat to keep out the frigid December wind. Her duties included logging in new arrivals and cataloging them properly, she was one of several new arrival clerks which given the vast amount of documents and other data arriving daily was absolutely necessary. The documents, books, artifacts and maps were then moved to their respective floors based on their catalog identification and filed accordingly by an entirely different set of employees.

At 11:30 AM Marge clocked out for lunch and entered an elevator and pushed the button for the third floor. Once the doors opened she stepped out into a large reception area, seeing a friendly face she walked to her left and approached Mark Fields, a man she had known for 18 years. He looked up from a document he was studying on his desk and smiled at her. "How can I help you today Marge?" he asked genuinely smiling.

"I have a friend in Ohio, a school librarian, who asked if I could research a battle that we fought in Korea in 1953 at a place called, let me see (as she dug a note out of her jacket pocket), oh yeah Rong Di Ri. Do we have any info on this battle? She says she has a student that wants to do a report on it and I told her I would look into it." Marge asked smiling back.

Fields stood and walked to a cabinet that had what seemed like a hundred drawers in it. Each drawer had a label. Some with a single letter but most with two or more letters on them. He pulled open a drawer labeled KOR and flipped through filing cards until he came to one labeled Rong Di Ri, on it was stamped Top Secret with a second stamp indicating the required clearance to access the documents. He looked at the card for a moment and then turned to Marge.

"Did your friend say how she came to know about this particular battle?" Fields asked with a concerned look on his face.

"She said a student had requested the info, Mark is there a problem?" Marge asked.

"Well, this set (meaning the documents) has a top secret stamp with a clearance level above what I have, so I can't help you." He replied.

"Really? I wonder what that is all about? Well, I'll tell Lenore I'm afraid I can't help her, I'm sure your clearance is way above mine." Marge stated the obvious and as she turned to walk back to the elevator she called over her shoulder, "thanks anyway Mark, see you Sunday at church."

"OK Marge, tell Bill I'll see him at the club tomorrow," Mark called back. After the elevator doors had closed behind Marge, Fields picked up the receiver on his phone and dialed the number written on the Rong Di Ri note card.

The phone rang twice and then he heard, "McSwain,"

"Mr. McSwain, this is Mark Fields at the Library of Congress, it says on this note card that I am to call you if anyone tries to access this record." Fields replied.

There was no need to identify which record, there was only one record that had that note attached, the one that no one had even known existed until today that is. "I will be there in fifteen minutes, do not move" and the line went dead.

Mark Fields was used to secrecy and he didn't even give the call a second thought. He returned to his seat and went back to studying the document on his desk. Fifteen minutes later he looked up expecting to see a Mr. McSwain but instead found himself staring at Elmore Craft the director of the CIA himself. Fields had seen the director on TV before but had never met the man in person and immediately started to feel flushed.

"Mr. Fields, please tell me who was trying to access the file." Craft said softly.

"Which file would that be Mr. Craft?" Fields replied.

"The file you called me about fifteen minutes ago Mr. Fields"

"I, I thought I spoke with a Mr. McSwain?" Fields stuttered.

"It pays to be discreet in my line of work Mr. Fields, now please tell me who tried to access the file? I am a very busy man." Craft relied coarsely.

"Marge Temple, she works in new arrivals, first floor, she said a school librarian in Ohio had requested info on a bat…" Fields was cut off by Craft raising his hand indicating for him to say no more.

"Thank you Mr. Fields, please return to your duties, and this conversation never occurred, understand?" Craft stared at Fields in a way that made him very nervous.

"Understood, sir." Fields stammered.

Craft turned and walked to the elevator, stopping to look back at Fields a give him one more stare to enforce the secrecy. Fields acknowledged the look by immediately looking directly down at his desk and he didn't look up for a full five minutes just to make sure the director of the CIA was gone.

Craft exited the elevator on the first floor and walked to his right, a hallway led to the rear of the building and an area that had numerous desks piled high with every sort of document created by man. He was appalled at the lack of organization, it all looked haphazard and messy. Elmore Craft was meticulous in every aspect of his life, including his attire. He was wearing a grey wool suit with a sky blue shirt and a royal blue tie. His shoes were polished a glossy black and he had a black topcoat over his left arm and matching black fedora in his right hand.

He walked through the clutter and came to a desk with a dark haired woman of at least fifty years of age sitting behind it. Her name plate read Margaret Temple. She had a document in her left hand and her reading glasses in her right. Craft put on his best smile and said "Mrs. Temple may I have a word with you?"

Marge looked up at the handsome man standing before her and smiled, "Excuse me, your name is?"

"Elmore Craft, Mrs. Temple and I really need to have a word with you in private if you don't mind."

Marge recognized the name instantly and her cheeks flushed, how could she be so dense as to not recognize the director of the CIA. "I'm sorry Mr. Craft I didn't recognize you at first, how can I help you?"

"Is there someplace we can talk privately," He insisted.

"Yes, of course, please follow me," Marge led him to a small office at the very back of the room.

Once inside Craft closed the door and turned to Marge with a cold look, "why were you trying to access the file on Rong Di Ri?" He asked gruffly.

"Oh, I have a friend named Lenore Granger in Ohio, sorry Ft. Seneca, Ohio, she is a high school librarian, she said a student of hers wanted to do a report on the batt.." Once again Craft raised his hand to stop the conversation as if even saying the word battle was forbidden.

"How do you know Ms. Granger?" Craft asked, much more gently this time. He sensed this was much less of a threat than he had believed.

"I went to college with her at Oberlin, we graduated together and we're sorority sisters." Marge added trying to be as open as possible to let Craft know she wasn't a threat to secrecy.

"Did Ms. Granger tell you the name of her student?"

"No, she didn't and I didn't ask because it didn't seem relevant. I didn't expect that a battle from the Korean War would be classified so I thought I could help her get some info for her student. As soon as Mark, I mean Mr. Fields, told me it was classified I left the third floor and that was that." Marge replied matter of fact tone.

"Fair enough," Craft replied and turned to leave but before he opened the door he turned and said," not a word to anyone about Rong Di Ri, understand Mrs. Temple?"

"What about Lenore? What do I tell her?" Marge asked.

"Nothing, I will speak to Ms. Granger." Craft replied and then opened the door and left without saying another word.

By this time Pete Lucas had become a complete loner, although he had never been much of a socialite. He hadn't even attended homecoming in the fall even though he was a shoe-in for Homecoming King, a title he had won in the secret balloting amongst students, but once it was known he wasn't going to the dance the runner-up Mike Douglas was made King in his place. He went to school, came home, did what he could on the farm and went to bed. He lay awake at night and his mind traveled to Vietnam and Tony. Tony had always sent Pete a Christmas card, but this year it hadn't come and Pete was getting worried. Next his mind moved to Korea and his father, and then back to the farm and his mom. He knew she was losing the battle with the bankers and that he had to try and get top money for the steers. It had been a hard winter already and it was still early, the steers would lose weight at this pace and that meant a lower selling price. He really didn't know what more he could do, so he would eventually close his eyes and fall asleep.

Lenore Granger was a creature of habit, she ate breakfast at the same diner every morning, arrived at the school by 8AM each day, had lunch in the school cafeteria and went home at 4:30PM every afternoon. She lived in a small bungalow in town on a quiet side street, the house was just three rooms, a small kitchen, living room and a single bedroom with attached bathroom. Her late husband Paul had passed away three years before after suffering a terrible case of pneumonia. They had no children and she had been an only child. Paul's niece Sarah lived in Cleveland and she occasionally traveled there to see her and her family on holidays, but usually days were spent at the school or with her two cats Shorty and Tiger. She arrived home after school on December 19th to find a handsome man in his late fifties sitting on her front porch with Tiger on his lap purring.

"May I help you?" she asked.

"Ms. Granger I presume, Marge Temple sends her regards" Craft said smiling.

"You're not her husband Bill, so exactly who are you?" Lenore asked a little more forcefully.

"My name is Elmore Craft, and Marge tells me you were seeking information about the Korean War." Craft replied.

"Your name sounds familiar, should I know you?" she asked quizzically.

"No not necessarily, but your request was out of the ordinary and raised some questions at the Library of Congress. We would like to help you out but the information you were seeking is, I'm afraid, classified." Craft said watching her for signs that might give him a hint as to her motives.

"I had a student request information on a particular battle in Korea, my library is quite small and so I couldn't help him. Marge and I go way back to college so I decided to call her and see if she could help. All she had to do was call and tell me it was classified and that would have been the end of it." Lenore said with more than a little disdain. Meanwhile she was thinking "how can a battle that happened nearly twenty years ago still be classified."

Craft caught the gender reference and now knew that the student was male. "I'm afraid once Marge requested the file it was out of her hands, she would have loved to call you and explain but our rules do not allow for that. I'm afraid we have some very strict rules when it comes to this type of information." Craft poured on the charm.

Lenore wasn't in the mood to be charmed and shot back, "How is it that a battle fought nearly 20 years ago is still classified and a simple request for the info causes the feds to send you all the way out here to tell me in person. Couldn't you have just called?"

"Phone calls are considered unsecure and as the info is classified we need to make sure it stays that way." Craft was getting tired of the old librarian's yammering and cut to the chase" if you would be so kind as to give me the student's name who made the request I will be on my way."

"I'm afraid our rules won't allow that," Lenore shot back using the Directors' own vernacular. "I can no more give out his name as you can give out your precious information, Mr. Craft."

"This doesn't have to get unpleasant Ms. Granger, we're all Americans here. All I want to do is interview the young man and ask him how he came to know about a classified battle. That's all. Nothing more I assure you."

"I'm sorry Mr. Craft but as you have said rules are rules, now if you'll excuse me," Lenore picked her cat off of Craft's lap and entered her home, shutting the door behind her.

Chapter 6

Colonel Mitch Morgan was out of his mind with anger. His team was lost and he needed answers, Major Pierce, his tour over, was now standing in the colonel's office and getting chewed up one side and down the other. The mood had gone from foul to unbearable in a matter of minutes and soon Pierce expected it to explode. Suddenly the outer office door opened and a beautiful young aide entered. She crossed silently across the Colonel's office and placed a folder on his desk and then just as silently exited the room closing the door behind her. Her appearance had created a pause in the rant that served to allow Colonel Morgan to regain his composure, he stared at his best officer and asked simply, "how do we get them back?"

"Sir, we have no intel as to where they are. They were in the north when they were captured or killed, we don't really know which, either way we can't ask for them back. If we do we would have to admit we were in the north and there is no way the administration would let us admit that." Pierce replied.

"Unacceptable" Morgan shot back.

"Sir, I'm afraid the facts are the facts, I cannot change them." Pierce answered while still standing at attention.

"Very well, Larry, keep your ears to the ground, I want them back and I will stop at nothing to achieve that, understood." Morgan growled.

"Understood Sir," Pierce said, adding "I want them back as much as you do sir."

"I'm sorry Larry, you have no idea how much Tony means to me, nor should you. His father and I have a history, or had a history I guess, either way I want Tony and Jason back and in one piece the rest of this goddamned war be damned!" Morgan snapped.

"I will do everything in my power to make that happen sir." Pierce stated, his eyes never wavering from the spot he had focused on upon entering the colonel's office over ten minutes before.

"Dismissed," Morgan barked as he turned towards the window that looked out over the parade ground at Ft Campbell, Kentucky home to his beloved 101st Airborne.

Pierce turned on his heel and exited the office, once in the outer office he smiled at the pretty young aide and upon opening the outer door placed his hat on his head and moved quickly onto the parade ground and crossed to the communications building, a nondescript building amongst all of the other nondescript buildings on the sprawling base. Once inside he quickly found Corporal Hughes who had a headset on and was obviously monitoring a conversation. Hughes suddenly became aware of his superiors' presence and removed the headset and began to stand and salute. Major Pierce put his hand on Hughes' shoulder and said, "at ease, Jim. Any word?"

"No, nothing sir." Hughes answered apologetically.

"Keep monitoring, I need intel and I need it yesterday," Pierce said quietly.

"Sir, yes sir."

Craft stood for a moment staring at the closed door and considered forcing his way in, but he realized that would be a very bad idea and instead stepped from the porch and walked to the dark blue sedan he had parked around the corner. He fired up the engine and pulled away from the curb, concentrating on his next move. He settled on a plan that could possibly cause extreme disruption, but might just be the best way to get the answers he needed.

The phone rang and Joy Lucas answered it on the second ring, "Lucas residence."

"Good evening Joy, this is.."

"I know who this, I will never forget your voice," she replied.

"Have you mentioned anything to your children about Roger's endeavors in Asia?" Craft asked.

"No, not a word," Joy snapped, but then she remembered Pete's conversation with Roger on his death bed, "but Roger did mention something to my son Pete on his death bed, just before he passed."

"What did Roger tell your son exactly?" Craft asked.

"I don't know and I really don't care, Roger is gone and the past is the past. Why are you asking these questions now?" Joy wanted to know.

"Just following up, making sure everything is in order," Craft lied.

"Everything is not in order, my son Tony hasn't written a letter in months, I don't even know if he knows his father has passed. Do you have any info on Tony?"

"No, I'm afraid not but I promise I will check on that first thing when I get back to my office." Craft assured her.

"Thank you for that, now is there anything else I can help you with?" Joy asked continuing to not use his name. She had been taught well Craft thought.

"No, that is all Mrs. Lucas, thank you" and he hung up the phone. Craft wiped the receiver with his handkerchief to eliminate fingerprints and left the phone booth. He walked across the parking lot and entered the Little Bavaria diner and found a booth near the back, slid into it and relaxed. After a hearty meal of potato pancakes and bratwurst washed down with a draft beer, Craft ordered a black coffee and asked the waitress where the local high school was.

"It's two blocks down, then left on Mill street, Mill dead ends right into the school parking lot. Are you going to the basketball game tonight?" she asked conversationally.

"Yes I am, thank you," Craft lied again. "Can I get my check? I don't want to miss tip-off"

"Here you are," she said laying the bill on his table. "I can take that whenever you're ready."

Craft paid the bill, left an appropriate tip and left the diner. He then drove to the next town west and checked into a motel for the night. He waited until 1:00 AM and then slid behind the wheel of his car and headed back to Ft. Seneca. Craft turned onto Mill street and immediately saw a possible problem. Mill street was only one block long and just as the young waitress had said the high school stood directly at the end of the street. Even worse was the fact that the whole area was lit up like an airport runway by no less than fifteen high powered sodium lights mounted on poles at least forty feet tall. "Not much chance of hiding in the shadows here" Craft said aloud.

He drove to the end of the short street and pulled into the parking area, he continued slowly along the side of the school and was pleased to find that the parking area wrapped around the back of the school as well, with an enormous football stadium standing directly behind the school. The grandstand for the stadium stood nearly as high as the school itself and ran from end zone to end zone, Craft estimated it must hold over 10,000 fans. That would amount to nearly every man woman and child in the entire township, and knowing how much people in Ohio loved their football he didn't doubt that the stadium was overflowing on Friday nights every fall. Craft pulled his eyes from the massive edifice and hung a left, he drove very slowly along the rear of the school to the end of the parking lot and there he finally saw what he was looking for. A loading ramp was built into the far back corner of the lot, next to the ramp was a large dumpster that was larger than his sedan and would work perfectly to conceal the car. As long as local law enforcement wasn't extremely observant and as long as no one had seen him pull into the parking lot he would not be detected.

Craft parked the car and waited three minutes to see if the local police had been called about a suspicious car entering the school lot, he calculated that in a town this small it would only take two minutes for a cop to respond to that call. Sensing the all clear, Craft exited the car and moved to the service door at the top of the loading ramp. He donned thin black gloves made of the highest quality leather, they provided him with perfect dexterity while eliminating any fingerprints. Pulling out two thin pieces of steel from the breast pocket of his jacket, within seconds he had picked the lock and slipped into the school. He didn't expect an alarm and was pleased he had guessed correctly when none was triggered upon his entry. He walked quickly but not hurriedly, moving through the back of the cafeteria where the loading dock was and into the kitchen. From there he made his way into the main hallway on the first floor of the three story school. He continued on noting the name on each door, most had a single teachers' name on them but a few simply said "Spanish" or "A/V" (short for audio/video) and when he had almost reached the front of the building he found the one he was looking for, the sign on the door read Main Office.

Craft reached for the door knob expecting to have to pick the lock but instead found it unlocked, he opened the door and quickly closed it behind himself. He made his way along a counter that separated the students from the office staff and found the small waist high swinging door that allowed access to the inner office. Once inside Craft pulled a small flashlight from his coat pocket and switched it on, being careful to not shine the light towards any windows and to not have it reflect off of any glass or metallic objects that might give away his presence. He crossed the office to a row of filing cabinets and quickly read the cards on the front of each drawer. It only took a second to figure out that the records were done by year not alphabet, he found the drawer labeled 1971 and opened it, smiling again at the fact it was not locked. Apparently student records are not a high risk for being stolen he thought.

Inside the drawer were nearly a hundred file folders all clearly marked with student names, flipping to the Ls he quickly found one labeled Lucas, Peter and removed it. Craft thought about reading it on the spot but decided he had been inside the school too long already and feared being discovered. He decided it would be easier to replace the folder the next day after he had read its contents and interviewed the youngest Lucas.

Craft slid the folder into a pocket that was sewn into the lining of his black trenchcoat, it was created especially for concealing documents and because the folder didn't have to be folded it created no noticeable bulge in the coat. The folder or document simply slid around his lower back and remained virtually undetectable. He then switched off the flashlight and slipped it into his pocket. Making his way back to the loading dock Craft slipped out of the back door locking it behind him. As he pulled out of the school lot and made his way slowly down Mill street, a police cruiser turned onto Mill from Main. The officer made no effort to stop him, it was merely a routine patrol, and Craft let out an audible sigh of relief. It had been years since he had done a B&E job but his heart was beating rapidly and his adrenaline pumping, it was exhilarating.

Back at his motel room Craft removed the folder containing Peter Lucas' entire school history and read it cover to cover in under twenty minutes. Something was wrong, "what is it" Craft asked aloud to himself. Pete had near perfect scores, maybe too perfect? No, the report from the state assessment showed extreme intellect and a photographic memory, so the grades were probably legit. He seemed to play only football, that's a little strange since he is obviously a very talented athlete, but no that isn't it either thought Craft. "That's it" Craft said aloud, "there aren't any acceptance letters to colleges. Now why wouldn't a superior student and a superior athlete have any acceptance letters from colleges? Because he didn't apply to any colleges that's why! But why not apply?" Craft didn't have the answer to that question, but he hoped to find out in the morning.

The following morning Craft arrived at Ft Seneca High School at 7:15 AM and walked directly into the principal's office, knowing exactly where it was located after his late night reconnaissance. Principal Bruce Peart was a pudgy man, bald on top with white hair forming a ring around his head. He had large brown eyes and a droopy look that was magnified by enormous

jowls and a triple chin. He wore a short sleeve white dress shirt,

dark grey slacks and worn brown loafers. In contrast Craft was

his typical impeccably dressed self, he wore a navy blue suit with

a white and blue pin striped shirt and a red tie. His trench coat

and fedora were perfectly placed as usual.

"Good morning Mr. Peart," Craft said while closing the

door. "My name is Elmore Craft, Director of the CIA." As he

pulled his credentials from his pocket and showed them to the

principal.

"W Well," Peart studdered, "How can I help you, Mr.

Craft?"

"I need to speak with one of your students, a Pete Lucas."

"Why would you need to speak with Peter? Has he done

something wrong? I mean he's top of his class."

"No, nothing like that. Pete requested some information

from the Library of Congress that was classified. He didn't know

it was classified mind you, but it was just the same. It came to

my attention and I wanted to speak with Pete in person to tell

him what I could about the information and explain why the rest

was classified. You see the info he requested concerned his

father Roger, who was in the Army at the time. I can't say any more, but given Roger was a national hero I felt I owed Pete an in person visit. Now can you please have Pete brought to your office?" Craft said politely.

"Of course Mr. Craft, I'll have him here in just a couple of minutes." Peart replied smiling.

"Mr. Peart, I must ask that you keep this confidential, I'm sure you understand I don't want this meeting publicized. Do we have an understanding?"

"Sure, mum's the word" the portly principal answered still swooning before his famous visitor. "Ill be right back with Peter, if you'll just excuse me for a minute." He said as he rushed from the office and down the hallway.

Craft removed the folder he had lifted the night before from his jacket and replaced it in the drawer where it belonged. He the moved behind the principals' desk and made himself at home. Removing his coat and hat and placing them on the corner of the desk, and taking a seat in the principal's chair. When Mr. Peart returned with Pete he was a little dismayed at losing his position to the Director but recovered nicely.

"Mr. Craft, this is Peter Lucas, Peter this the Mr. Craft Director of the C.I.A." Peart put extra emphasis on each letter of CIA.

Craft moved quickly to take control, "Thank you Mr. Peart, I would like a few minutes with Pete in private, if you don't mind."

"I'm not sure I should.." Peart began to object.

"It's OK Mr. Peart, I have permission from Joy Lucas and nothing will come of this I assure you," Craft said flashing his most genuine smile while ushering the Principal out of his own office and closing the door behind him.

"Now Mr. Lucas, suppose you tell me why you want information about Rong Di Ri?" Craft asked in a very conversational way.

"Why is the CIA involved, I mean this is" Pete was thoroughly confused.

"Pete, I'll explain soon enough but first I need to know why."

"My dad told me about a battle there when he was in the war, it seemed really intense, I wanted to know more about it."

"Did your dad say why the battle took place, or say anything about Ki Sun Pak?" Craft asked still smiling.

"No, he just told me about all of the wounded and dead and screaming women and about chasing some Reds, that's what he called them, for days. Then he told me the truth about who I am."

Craft sat bolt upright, "what, what did he say about who you are."

"Je suit e Latellhaurie" Pete answered.

"He taught you French as well I see."

"Actually my mom and dad both taught us all French, yes."

"Technically you are actually a Lucas, that is the name on your birth certificate, I've seen it in fact, your birth certificate I mean. But nonetheless, yes, you are your father's son and as such you deserve some answers but I'm afraid I can't give you everything you want. Some of what you'll want to know is too confidential for me to tell you, but I think I can give you a much better picture of what went on in Rong Di Ri. It will take a little time, are you available after school?"

"I have a couple of hours before I have to take care of the steers, can you come back after school?"

"This isn't the place for this conversation, how about meeting me at the Little Bavaria at 4:00. That's early enough there won't be anyone there for dinner and we should basically have the place to ourselves."

"Alright, 4:00" Pete said and stood to leave. "Thanks for coming all the way from Washington to talk to me."

"It's an honor Pete, your father was a true hero and I owe it to him." Craft said proudly. "Now no one can know about this meeting or the one at the restaurant, not even your mom, understand?"

Pete just nodded and left the office, his head swimming with questions and clouded thoughts.

The day ground on and Pete was anxious to get it over with, when the final bell rang he virtually sprinted for the door. He had taken the time to write down some questions he wanted to ask Mr. Craft and kept going over them in his mind. He ran out to the parking lot and flung open the door to the rusty old Ford pickup, fired up the engine and tore out of the lot. He shot down Mill street and had to slam on the brakes when he reached

Main. He made the right hand turn and stomped on the accelerator. He almost passed the restaurant because he was going too fast, again he slammed on the brakes creating an ear splitting squeal of tires. He turned into the lot next to the Little Bavaria and pulled alongside a large dark blue sedan. Pete jumped out and rushed to the door of the restaurant.

Craft watched in horror as the truck squealed its brakes and then launched itself into the parking lot, so much for a clandestine meeting he'd be lucky if the cops didn't show up after that display. When Pete entered the restaurant he simply shook his head and gave his best "what the hell are you doing" look.

Pete caught the look and realized he was the intended target, he instantly slowed down and tried to just relax. It wasn't even possible, but he really did try, not that Craft even acknowledged his attempt.

"Could you possibly have drawn more attention to yourself?" Craft asked sarcastically.

"I'm really sorry, I was, I mean my head is just, I'm not" Pete babbled.

"Enough already, OK, this is how this is gonna go, I'm going to tell you a story. I don't want you to interrupt me, understand."

"I under" Pete started to say.

"What did I just say? Don't interrupt me young man! I'm going to tell you a story, you are going to listen, when I am done I am going to leave and you may never see me again, although I think we will see each other sooner than we both suspect."

"But I have a list of questions," Pete started while pulling out a folded sheet of paper from his jeans pocket.

Craft took the sheet from Pete and crumpled it in his right hand, "never write anything down Pete, ever. You don't need to, you have a photographic memory. Always keep it in your head, where its safe and secure, didn't your father teach you that?"

"No, my father didn't have secrets."

"Oh really, did you know your father was in Army Intelligence in Canada? Did you know your father was a top flight operative? Your father had more secrets than most Pete, but he was truly a hero."

"You've said that twice now, what do you mean he was a hero?" Pete asked.

A waitress approached and both men ordered drinks, coffee for Craft and water for Pete, after she had moved out of earshot Craft began again, "Pete, I have a lot of information for you but you need to just sit back and listen. When I'm done talking things will be a whole lot clearer. I'm only here out of respect for your father and because I think you can handle the whole truth, OK?"

The waitress brought their drinks and asked if they wanted to order, Craft answered for both of them, "No thank you, the drinks are all we need right now." An older couple came into the restaurant and the waitress went to help them get seated.

"OK, so this is what I know and what I can tell you. Your father was a member of the Canadian Army and part of a special corps that is similar to the US 10th Mountain Division called the First Special Services Force. They specialize in mountain, artic and cold weather tactics including skiing, snowshoes, snowmobiles, snowcats and stuff like that. I mean these are very serious guys with a passion for survival, fighting and yes killing in the cold. He was also a member of the Canadian Intelligence Force, their version of army intelligence. In the early 1950s NATO stepped in to help South Korea fight off an attack from the north and part of the NATO force included your dad's unit. They were combined with some of the US force in Korea and were given a specific task, to protect a small village call Rong Di Ri."

Pete was now paying complete attention to every word Craft said.

Craft continued, "the commanding officer of the combined force was a Colonel by the name of Crabtree, an American with the 101st. Your dad and Crabtree had issues from the start, Crabtree was by the book all the way, your dad, well let's just say your dad wasn't, OK. A company of US Marines were stationed on the outskirts of Rong Di Ri as a buffer against attack. The rest of the force was placed just south of the town on high ground about a mile away. The Chinese and North Koreans wanted Rong Di Ri badly, you see it held a secret. Do you know anything about Asian cultures Pete?"

"Not really, I've read a lot about Japan and WWII but that's about it." Pete answered.

"Asian cultures place a huge value on honor, they believe that if you lose your honor you are ruined for life and it can even ruin the lives of your children and children's children in some cases. Rong Di Ri was the birthplace of Ki Sun Pak the most powerful man in South Korea in 1953, and home to his parents and his two younger sisters. The Chinese planned to attack Rong Di Ri, and take Pak's family prisoner. They then planned to make his mother and sisters into sex slaves and torture his father into denouncing Kim as an embarrassment to the family name. In short they planned to ruin Kim Sun Pak's good name and render him impotent in the eyes of his countrymen. If they had been successful the whole war could have ended up very different. Your father and a group of very brave men stopped that from happening, saved the Pak family from ruin and helped save South Korea." Craft stopped there for a moment.

"How do you know what the Chinese were planning and how do you know any of this," Pete asked.

"Well as to how I know what the Chinese were planning, let's just say we have our sources, as to the rest of it about your fathers' involvement and the battle itself, well that is an easier question," Craft grew a little more distant in his appearance.

"You were there, weren't you?" Pete more stated than asked.

"Yes, I was there. What your father did was crazy but also really brave. He took command and chased the Chinese all the way back across that frozen valley and eventually captured an officer that produced some very valuable intelligence." Craft said with obvious pride.

"So my dad was a real hero, but why couldn't he ever talk about it?" Pete asked.

"A couple of reasons, the first being the whole operation was classified to save the Pak family honor, after all; the South Koreans are some of our best allies. The second being that a true hero never really believes they are a hero, and finally Rong Di Ri changed your father forever. Something about that place caused him to become very angry about the way we were prosecuting the war, it made him less effective as an intelligence officer. So he was shipped home, but his constant badgering of the Canadian administration put him on the outs with Ottawa. Fortunately, he also worked for us at the time, so we moved him here to Ohio and created his new life. It was payment for services rendered." Craft stood and reached out his hand.

"So dad worked for the CIA?" Pete asked while standing and shaking Crafts hand.

"Pete what I have told you is highly classified so it needs to remain between us. There are still people looking for a crazy Cannuck that did so much damage in Korea, people can still get hurt so this secret is now yours to keep, understand?"

"I understand that much, but some things still are a little foggy for me." Pete replied.

"The fog will clear eventually but remember that some things must remain secret." Craft smiled and walked away having left a $20 bill on the table for the waitress.

Pete watched him leave, used the restaurant's bathroom and then exited much more calmly than he had entered.

True to his word, Craft called Army Chief of Staff, General Bruce Albion upon returning to Washington and requested a status report on Sergeant Anthony Lucas 101st Airborne. Receiving the request, General Albion forwarded the request to Fort Campbell and the noose tightened around the neck of Col. Mitch Morgan.

Chapter 7

Out of options, Colonel Morgan made the difficult
decision to change the official status of Sergeants Anthony Lucas
and Jason McBride to that of Missing in Action. He made the
formal change and then braced for the storm that would surely
come. The mission wasn't his idea but he had wholeheartedly
endorsed it to his superiors, now he would surely reap the ass
whipping he deserved.

It took less than 24 hours for his immediate superior to
haul him in and dress him down. Higher up the chain of
command the concern wasn't for the two soldiers but instead the
fear that their mission would be exposed and cause an
international incident. A formal reprimand was placed in his
permanent file and Colonel Mitch Morgan was assured his future
with the U.S. Army would never include a rank of General.

March 7th 1971 Joy Lucas finally gave in to the endless
calls from creditors and agreed to sell the farm, she cried for two
days, then vowed to never cry about it again. Pete was
devastated, he didn't know which way was up. He had been
drifting but at least he knew that each day he would come home

and see the animals. He could talk to them and take care of them. They needed him and he needed to be needed. He pleaded with his mom to reconsider, but she couldn't afford to keep the farm. She went so far as to show Pete all of the records, showing that the farm had been losing money for years. Roger had refused to listen, and she had hoped that her craft store would make the farm profitable, but all her hopes died with Roger. She would sell off the acreage and barns but keep the house and a few acres.

On March 11th a white car pulled into the driveway of the Lucas farm, it came to a stop in front of the walk that led to the front door. Two men clad in Army dress uniforms got out and walked up the walk. Joy Lucas watched them come, a feeling of total despair filled her soul. One of the two, a tall man with a cold expression knocked on the door. At first Joy couldn't move, her body refused to cooperate. Pete heard the knock and came into the living room. He looked at the door and saw the two men standing outside through the glass panes, then looked at his mom and realized she was overcome with grief. Slowly Pete walked to the door and opened it.

The officer who had knocked spoke, "is this the Lucas residence?"

"Yes", answered Pete.

"Is Joy Lucas at home?" asked the officer.

"She's very upset, we lost my father last fall and…"
Pete's voice trailed off as he felt his mom's hand on his shoulder.
Joy had come to the door and now looked quite calm.

"Please, come in officer," she said. "Can I get you
something to drink?"

"No ma'am, thank you ma'am" replied the officer. "I am
First Lieutenant Robert Lang and this is Sergeant Ben Hart. I'm
afraid we have some troubling news."

Joy sat down on the sofa, but showed no outward sign of
what Pete knew was terror welling up inside her. He couldn't
help but admire her strength and courage. She stared straight into
the Lieutenants' eyes and said, "let's have it."

Lieutenant Lang nodded and said, "Sargent Anthony
Lucas has been officially declared missing in action in the
conflict in Vietnam. I am sorry to have to bring you this news
ma'am. I can't provide you with much information at this time
because most of it is classified, but I can tell you your son was
doing his duty in service to his country at the time he went
missing."

"What do you mean went missing?" yelled Pete. "People don't just go missing!"

Joy stood and shot him a look that stopped him cold, she then turned to the Lieutenant and asked, "was he alone?"

"No ma'am".

"Did any of his unit return to base?"

"That's classified ma'am, I am not at liberty to discuss troop movements"

"Thank you Lieutenant, now can I offer you gentlemen something to eat?"

"No thank you ma'am, we unfortunately have another stop to make today." The Lieutenant said lowering his head and his voice. Pete now realized why his mom had been so nice to the soldiers, they were just the messengers and their duty was one Pete couldn't begin to comprehend. He now felt embarrassed at his outburst and tried to figure a way to make it right. As the men left, Pete held the door and saluted. It was a poor excuse of a salute, but the Lieutenant returned the salute anyway and smiled.

As Pete stood in the doorway watching the soldiers get in their car and drive away, he had a very strong urge to follow them. He began to think about Tony and how much everyone respected his older brother. An idea began to form, and Pete started to focus on that thought. A direction for his life was emerging in his mind, he was destined to follow his brother. He would become a Ranger, like Tony and his dad. He would hunt again, only this time he would hunt the enemy, but he would have to wait, Pete wouldn't turn eighteen until July. His fury would eat at him for months.

On March 15th at 4PM the phone rang and Pete answered it, "Pete, I heard the news about your brother, I'm sorry." Pete recognized the voice instantly.

""What do I do now?" Pete asked.

"I can help you, I can give you access to information that will make bringing Tony home easier, but it requires you working for me." Craft answered.

"How can you help?"

"You will have to trust me on that, if you're interested I can insure that you get to where you need to go, but its all up to you. Are you up to life as a soldier?"

"Yes, how did you know I was planning to enlist?" Pete asked.

"You didn't apply to any colleges, you're extremely intelligent, very strong, and very loyal. You're an Eagle Scout, and the son of Roger Lucas. It was all very evident to me." Craft replied.

"So I should enlist?"

"That is your decision, but if you do I will make sure you get what you need to help your brother, and your country." Craft added.

"How do I contact you?" Pete asked.

"You don't." and the line went dead.

In May 1971 the farm sold at auction to a man Joy had known since the creation of her new life, she retained the house and 5 acres for her garden but the rest of the 400+ acres, barns and other out buildings were sold. The steers and other animals were sold for slaughter except Roger's hunting dogs, a collection of beagles, elkhounds and blue tick coon hounds that had already been moved to John's place about a quarter mile away. She found the plans Roger had drawn up for her craft/produce stand, and Pete and his Uncle John built the building in the corner of the property where the drive met the road. Joy was stocking shelves and making plans. She kept herself very busy; partly because there was so much to do, and partly because she couldn't bear to think about Tony. When she did allow the thoughts to enter her mind, she would begin to cry and shake uncontrollably. She had heard horror stories about what the Vietnamese did to POWs and the conditions the troops were enduring. She would only allow herself short periods of grief, and then it was back to business.

Pete had made up his mind about joining the army, but had yet to tell his mom. When his draft card came in July, it made the decision even easier. He had a number that virtually guaranteed he would be drafted if he didn't go to college. He showed Joy the card after dinner on July 17th. She wasn't concerned, she assumed he was going to school so it wasn't a big deal.

"That means I'll be drafted for sure", Pete said.

"So, when you go to college you don't need to worry about being drafted." she replied.

"Yeah," added Suzy who was once again home for the summer, "College students are exempt from the draft."

"But I'm not going to college" Pete stated flatly.

"What?" Suzy nearly screamed.

Joy quieted Suzy with a look, and turned to Pete. "Why aren't you going to college?" she asked very calmly.

"Mom, I need to do this. I need to follow Tony and Dad, I need to know".

"You need to know what?" asked Joy, she was trying to stay calm.

"I need to know if I measure up, if I can be …"

"Be what? Dead!" screamed Suzy, she didn't look at her mom this time. "Pete we've already lost Dad and Tony, we don't want to lose you too!"

"Tony isn't dead!" shouted Pete, "He's MIA, probably prisoner in some camp somewhere in the jungle! Someone has to find him!"

"You! You think you can find him? Are you insane? Tony is gone, and you need to get that through your thick Lucas head!" Suzy was screaming at the top of her lungs now. "We all miss him, but he's gone!"

"Enough!" shouted Joy. "Pete is right, Tony is MIA and I will not give up on my son. He is alive and he will come home, but Pete you must understand that you can't go looking for him. If you join the Army you may end up in Germany or Korea like your brother-in-law Mike. And if, God forbid, you do end up in Vietnam you could end up MIA or dead yourself."

Pete was glaring at Suzy, his stare seemed to go straight to her soul. She turned away and said, "Tony is gone, I can't keep holding on." She began to sob, her whole body shaking. Pete got up and went to her, he wrapped his arms around her and held her. His strength was surprising and she quieted down after a few moments. She looked up at him and mouthed "I'm sorry." He nodded understanding and held her fast for another minute. She got up and went upstairs.

Pete returned to his seat and took a long drink of water. He looked at his mother and set his jaw tight. Before she could begin to speak, he said, "I'm enlisting tomorrow. I plan on becoming a Ranger and serving my country." His gaze was unflinching, and his mind was made up.

Joy Lucas knew that look and it terrified her. It was the same look Tony had when he announced his decision to join the Army against his father's will. She began to speak, but caught herself. She realized Pete needed her blessing, but he would do this even without it. She regrouped and began slowly, "Pete, if this what you need to do, fine. But don't expect me or your sisters or brothers to be happy about it. I think your throwing away your life. You can be anything you want, all you need is time to figure it out."

"I want to be a U.S. Army Ranger. That is what I want, if its not meant to be then time will tell. Je suit e Latellhaurie, I was born to do this." The look on Joy's face was of total astonishment.

Her reply was swift and with an edgy tone Pete had never before heard. "Where did you hear that name? You are forbidden to ever say that name aloud again!" She scolded him. "I'm asking you, where did you hear that name?"

"Dad told me before he died, he told me about Korea and a place called Rong Di Ri, he told me Tony's real name, he thought I was Tony." Pete answered somewhat unsure how his mom would react.

"Whatever your dad told you is never to be repeated to anyone, ever," she said sternly. "Your father made me promise to never discuss anything about our past and I will not dishonor his memory now by going against his wishes, you understand me?"

"Yes, I understand, was I born in Canada" Pete answered.

"Yes, but you have a valid U.S. birth certificate, you are an American citizen," Joy replied quietly.

"North Bay, Ontario?" Pete asked.

Joy nodded, but added, "not another word Peter, not another word."

Pete nodded his agreement, finished his water and carried his glass and plate to the sink. "I'm gonna get some rest, can I get you anything?"

"No, I just need time and my family," sighed Joy.

"I'm gonna find him Mom, I won't stop." Pete said softly and climbed the stairs to his room.

The way he said it somehow gave Joy a feeling of comfort. She knew it was an impossible task, but she also knew there was no point in trying to reason with Pete. He was her baby, but he was also a grown man with a stubborn streak the size of Toledo. The thought of Pete searching for his brother was ridiculous, but she was convinced that he would give it his all.

July 18th, 1971 dawned hazy and hot. Pete got up early, showered, shaved and dressed in blue jeans, a white cotton t-shirt and work boots. He left the house before Joy or Suzy awoke and headed into town. Pete was working at a local service station as a mechanic this summer and Jack Medley was glad to have him. He was reliable, honest and a hard worker. Jack paid him a little extra and considered it money well spent, but he knew it was only a matter of time until Pete went off to school. Everyone in town knew Pete, he was the quarterback of the football team and everyone also knew Kent State had recruited him. What everyone didn't know was that Pete had turned the offer down. Pete arrived at the garage at 7:00 sharp and began working on an old red Chevy for Mrs. Butler. Jack came in at 7:15.

"What time did you get here?" asked Jack

"7 o-clock like always," replied Pete.

"When you supposed to report to Kent?"

"I turned them down, I'm gonna enlist today."

Jack tuned around and ran right into the bumper of the old Chevy, which was on the lift and right at eye level. "Shit!" yelled Jack. After grabbing his head he stammered, "you're what? Are you nuts? You got shit for brains boy?"

"No, I'm following my brother into the Rangers," Pete replied softly.

"Bullshit! You ain't joining the Army, your Momma would kill you!

"She understands, its something I gotta do Jack."

"Bullshit! Your Daddy would kick your ass if he was here, what's John got to say about this?"

"My dad is dead Jack, and I haven't told Uncle John. I'm doing what I got to do, so just be cool."

"Be cool? What the hell does that mean, be cool? I'm supposed to just kick back and watch you throw away your future?"

"What future Jack? Wrenching on old Chevys, or working in some office? I'm not made to be penned up Jack and you know it. I'm an outdoors guy, I need to feel the ground under me and the wind in my face. I need to do this, for me and for Tony."

"Tony, what do you mean for Tony? You thinking of trying to avenge his death or something? They ain't gonna let you do that!"

"He's not DEAD Jack! He's MIA! Why can't anyone understand that! I'm gonna go find him."

Jack started to laugh, "you're gonna go find him? You gotta be shitting me."

"Jack, drop it."

"No, No really you're gonna go find him?" Jack was still laughing. "Oh please tell me where my brother is Ho Chi Mihn."

"Jack, for the last time drop it or I'll drop you!" Pete yelled.

Jack couldn't help himself, he kept laughing and walked away saying "Help me find my brover" in a poor Vietnamese accent.

Pete was pissed at first, but then he thought about it and realized just how ridiculous it sounded. He started to laugh to himself, what a fool. He also realized that he couldn't mention Tony again when talking about enlisting. He needed to make the case for joining on its own merits, not based on searching for Tony. He wasn't sure how he could pull it off, but he knew deep down that he had to do it. He was convinced that if he got to Vietnam he could find Tony. He had to.

Pete took his lunch at 11 o-clock and hopped in the old Ford truck, he left the garage and headed south on state route 53. He left town and rolled on past cornfields and fencerows. Fifteen minutes later he entered Tiffin, the largest town nearby and one where Pete knew there was an Army recruiting office. Pete had rode with Tony in June of 1967 when he had come to Tiffin to sign up. Pete remembered the recruiting officer telling Tony how much the United States needed strong young men like him. He also remembered that no one mentioned anything about Vietnam that day in 1967. The old Ford eased into the parking lot in front of the office, and Pete felt a strong sense of pride seeing the flag waving in the hot breeze. That was when he realized he didn't need any other reason to do this. He was an American, and proud of it.

Pete got out of the truck and headed for the door, before he got there he heard a voice say, "you sure about this?" It was Uncle John. Jack had called him and let him know what Pete was "fixing to do". "I'm not here to stop you, I'm just asking if you're sure."

Pete loved his uncle, and more importantly he felt that his uncle respected him. John had always treated Pete as an adult, while the rest of the family tended to treat Pete as a kid. John also knew, like Joy knew, no one could change Pete's mind once it was made up. But unlike Joy, John understood Pete and why he needed to prove himself. John had lived in his older brother's shadow his whole life and knew how Pete felt. Pete needed to prove to himself that he could be the man, not just Tony's kid brother. Deep down John hoped that Pete would slay this dragon, but on the surface he hoped to talk Pete out of going.

"Yeah I'm sure", Pete replied trying to be as convincing as possible.

"Hmm, that wasn't real strong" John said, "one more time, you sure about this?"

Pete caught on, "Sir, yes sir" Pete shouted this time.

John smiled, he didn't want Pete to go but it wasn't his place to stop him. "You're Mom's gonna be a basket case you know that."

"She'll be fine, Suzy might have a heart attack, but Mom will be OK."

"You're Mom hurts more than you know, she puts on a brave face but she's dying inside."

"I know Uncle John, but I need to do this. For me, not for Tony or Dad, for me. I need to prove myself. I …"

John cut him off by raising his hand, "enough said son, I understand more than you know. Let's get this over so we can both get back to work."

With that they both entered the recruiting office, a one story cinder block building painted a drab green with while trim, and Pete approached the front desk. There was a young male officer sitting behind the desk filling out some paperwork. He looked up and asked, "can I help you?"

"I'm here to enlist," stated Pete flatly. He was attempting to stand at attention, but his posture was wrong. The young lieutenant was taken aback at first, no one had enlisted for quite some time. The anti-war activists had created bad feelings among the young people and most recruits were drafted. He regained his composure and grabbed a form off of the desktop.

"I'm Lieutenant Mike Severs and I will be your recruiting officer, please fill out this form and sign it at the bottom. Are you eighteen?"

"Yes, I'm eighteen and graduated from Shawnee last year" replied Pete.

"Excellent, after you have completed the form we will need to schedule a physical exam. Once that's over, and assuming there's no problems we'll get you assigned a departure date."

Pete didn't say anything, he just filled out the form signed it and handed it back to the lieutenant. He was told to report the next day for his physical and sent on his way. John said goodbye to Pete jumped into his and pulled out of the lot. Pete jumped into the Ford and headed back to work. It seemed to him that there should have been more to it than that. He was making a life altering decision and all that mattered was a form and a physical. He was a little let down, but he was confident he was doing the right thing.

Chapter 8

Pete passed the physical and received his first orders, he was to report to boot camp at Fort Stewart in two weeks. He spent the time saying goodbye to his family and learning what he could about Army life. He was told to be respectful of everyone, yes sir , no sir and yes ma'am, no ma'am. Jack told him a secret to surviving, "just go along with everything. Don't make waves and don't complain, the drill sergeants are looking for troublemakers. Just keep under the radar and they won't bother you none."

On August 8th Pete said goodbye to his Mom, Suzy, Colleen and Henry. Joy tried not to cry, but it was no use. Suzy and Colleen were sobbing uncontrollably and Henry hugged his brother and whispered "take care of yourself."

"I will, keep an eye on Mom and Suzy for me. I'm counting on you."

"Who's the little brother here?" Henry replied.

Pete just shrugged and as he turned to board the bus, a hand grabbed his shoulder. Uncle John spun him around and asked, "where are you going? Nowhere without saying goodbye to Aunt May and me that's where." He hugged Pete and Aunt May hugged him and began crying. Pete pulled himself free from Aunt May and shook Uncle John's hand one last time.

"Thanks for everything. Take care of Mom for me."

"That will be an honor son", John said. "Keep your head down."

"Yeah", was Pete's reply.

Pete turned and boarded the bus, walked back three seats and swung himself onto the vinyl seat. He slid over to the window and gave a quick wave as the bus pulled away from the curb. Pete's stomach was in knots, he was heart broke leaving his family behind and worried about his mom. Added to that was the fear that he wouldn't measure up to the Army's standards. He looked around the bus, there were only four other passengers. An elderly black lady with her young granddaughter sat in the front seat opposite the driver. A young woman, no more than 18 years old who sat half way back on the drivers' side and a middle-aged white man sitting all the way at the back of the bus. Pete began a process that would serve him well the rest of his life. He decided to exercise his mind by memorizing where each person was and what they looked like. He gave the people names based on what they looked like and where they sat. For example, the lady with her granddaughter became Granny1C. The girl in the middle of the bus became Blonde11A. As the trip continued, people got on and off the bus and Pete continued his mind exercise. As the bus left the station in Lexington, Kentucky he noticed that the young lady who had started the trip with him was no longer in her seat. He felt a strange sadness, he hadn't even spoken to her, yet he missed her. He made another decision, he would make it a point to talk to anyone he found interesting from now on. He didn't like the feeling of emptiness he felt from never having spoken to Blonde11A.

In Knoxville, Tennessee several people got on the bus, one in particular caught Pete's eye. He was a young man with crew cut black hair, about 6 feet tall and carrying a duffel bag. He sat one row in front of Pete across the aisle. After Pete had cataloged the new arrivals and mentally deleted those who had gotten off, he leaned forward and spoke to the guy he had labeled GI2B.

"Where ya headed?" Pete asked the young man.

"Fort Stewart" the man replied in a thick southern accent.

Pete hadn't prepared himself for the southern drawl, and caught himself grinning at the sound of it. He controlled himself and responded, "me too, you going to boot camp?"

"No, I'm going to visit my granny" the young man snapped, "why else would I be going to Fort Stewart?"

Pete was startled. He hadn't expected this reaction. He started to sit back, but he decided that he hadn't deserved that remark and he said, "Hey, I just thought maybe you were on leave."

"If I was on leave, I wouldn't be headed back. I don't want to go in the first place. Damn draft, who the hell cares about Vietnam, I don't even know where it is. Bunch of slanty eyed gooks tryin to kill you. Who the hell wants to go through that?"

Pete was speechless, he had been completely confident in his choice to serve. There had been no doubt about it, this was the right thing to do. He was going to serve his country, help out the people of Vietnam and find Tony. But the first other person he met who was going to serve with him was completely against everything that Pete believed was right. Pete slumped back in his seat. He was suddenly very tired and quickly fell asleep. He awoke to GI2B shaking him.

"Wake up Yankee, this is our stop."

"Fort Stewart?" Pete said with a yawn.

"No, they ain't gonna deliver you to the door Sunshine", he said laughing.

Pete was glad to see his demeanor had changed, but he was confused as to exactly where he was. He struggled to his feet and grabbed his duffel. As he exited the bus, Pete was hit with extremely humid air that nearly took his breath away. He had never felt such heavy air, it was hard to breathe. He reached out and grabbed GI2B by the arm, "hey, what's your name?"

"Gomer", he said grinning.

"What?"

"Gomer, Gomer Pyle," he said imitating Jim Nabors.

Pete shook his head. "Wonderful, a smart ass hillbilly. Just what I need."

"Better than a dumb ass hillbilly don't ya think? Anyway, I decided that if I'm gonna be stuck here for six weeks. I'm gonna enjoy myself" he said. " Mike Moore, that's my given name."

"Who gave it to ya? You ought to send it back "return to sender" man." Pete joked. He added "just kidding, Pete Lucas" and extended his hand. Mike took it with a firm grip and shook it. "So how do we get to the base from here?"

A group of about two dozen recruits from seven states were milling around, some sitting on their duffle bags, others smoking cigarettes and talking amongst themselves.

"There's a bus. It'll be along here shortly. Where you from Yankee?"

"Ohio, and you hillbilly?"

"Jasper, Tennessee", he said. "What was your number?"

"What?" Pete asked, then realized Mike was talking about his draft number. "I enlisted."

"Oh for Christ's sake, you're a friggin lunatic! You actually signed up for this shit? Jesus, you're worried about a smart ass hillbilly, I'm stuck with a simple lunatic from O-HI-O no less." He was being over dramatic now, "what's next, you enjoy running long distances with heavy weights on your back."

Pete took this as a cue and started, "yeah man, 8 mile runs with 80 pound packs are my favorites. But only if you get to run in the pouring rain uphill and in ankle deep mud."

Just then the bus pulled up, the door opened and out stepped a man chiseled from solid granite. He took one look at the recruits and spat on the ground. The smiles disappeared from the recruits' faces and they immediately grabbed their duffels. The sergeant barked out orders and rules, the recruits stood at attention and did not move. Pete was focussing, he wanted to be the perfect recruit, but he was focussing so intently that he didn't realize the rest of the group had begun moving towards the bus. Mike ran into him from behind and knocked Pete down, before Pete could get up the sergeant was on him screaming at him to get to his feet and get in line. Pete was unnerved, embarrassed and angry. At first he blamed Mike, however then he realized it was his own fault. He remembered Jack's advice, "stay under the radar." From that point on he would follow that advice.

Basic training was just that, basic. Pete went through it without much effort, he was in such good condition from football and working the farm that the physical part was a breeze. The mental part was a little harder, although Pete had never been one to question authority. As a result, the drill sergeants didn't have to get in his face very often. He finished basic training in September and Joy, who had recently taken a drivers' training course, drove to Georgia to pick him up. Pete showed his mom around the base and introduced her to Mike. Both Pete and Mike had signed up for and had received assignment for Airborne training. Mike had decided that if he was going to have to be in the Army, he wanted to be as well trained as possible.

Mike Moore was as much a Redneck as there ever was, he loved nothing more than to be driving wide open along the "ridge", a narrow patch of asphalt road that ran from his parents' home to Red Run. Red Run was a wider patch of asphalt that ran to Tennessee Rt. 297 which connected the towns of Newcomb and Jellico Tennessee. He had a Roadrunner that he had bought brand new with money he had been saving since he was 10 years old. All he ever dreamed of doing was driving cars, and he was pretty good at it too. He had won some local races on dirt tracks and had hoped to move up eventually to races at places like Daytona and Bristol. That was before he had received his draft card, and the number that guaranteed his becoming a member of the U.S. Army. His smart-ass demeanor and quick wit made him a favorite among his fellow recruits and the target of drill sergeants. He had a comment for every occasion and kept everyone laughing, even the drill sergeants laughed as they made him do push-ups or pull double duty.

Pete went home on leave for two weeks before going to Fort Benning for Airborne training. While home, Joy fed him well and doted over him. Suzy came home from school on the weekends and even Henry came home once to see him. Uncle John came over and talked to him late into the night each night. The time passed quickly and before Joy was ready, Pete was back on a bus to Georgia. Pete arrived at Benning ready to learn, and he was rewarded with grueling days and nights. The training was intense and very serious, the sergeants were more vicious and intimidating than during basic training. The roadwork was longer and harder, the Georgia heat had given way to cold rains and ankle deep muck. The training course was through swamps and over mountains. The jump tower didn't even phase Pete, but some of the recruits couldn't overcome their fear of heights. Prompting Mike to comment, "What did they think "Airborne" meant, being shot out of a cannon?"

Pete wrote home every week, he would tell his mom what had happened during the week and how he was feeling physically. He did his best to keep the focus on what was happening, and that he was doing well. He made sure to include sore wrists and twisted ankles, so that she wouldn't suspect anything was wrong. He didn't want her to worry about him. His mental acumen made the training easier at times, but it often made him wonder why things were done the way they were. He considered making suggestions on how to improve various aspects of the course, but decided to keep his mouth shut and get along by going along.

Pete stayed under the radar, he worked hard and stayed focused. Occasionally letters would arrive without a return address, the first had seemed like total gibberish and Pete thought it was some sort of prank. The next day, another arrived and it seemed to be a letter from a relative except Pete didn't have an uncle Ed. Pete lay awake that night in his bunk and suddenly sat bolt upright, a code! Pete had read about codes and ciphers and had even done a term paper about the Culper spy ring ran by none other that George Washington himself. It was after lights out so Pete had to wait until the next day to begin trying to decipher the letters, it made for a sleepless night.

Pete skipped breakfast and waited for the barracks to empty out. Once alone he retrieved the letters from his footlocker and began the difficult task of deciphering the coded messages. He surmised that the original letter was the key, it had to be because it made absolutely no sense what so ever otherwise. Words were misspelled, the grammar was atrocious and even the punctuation was incorrect. While it was possible the sender was illiterate, Pete wasn't buying it. He only had about an hour a day of free time, except for one day a week when the entire company was given liberty.

Some of the guys were going off base during leave periods, but Pete decided it was better to stay put. The guys spent time with girls they met in nearby Georgia but when they asked Pete to go along, he would find an excuse to stay on base. This caused some of the guys to question his manhood and even whether or not Pete even liked women. Pete ignored them for the most part but Mike began to worry about Pete and called Joy one night to ask her if there was anything he could do to help. Joy had suspected all along that Pete was becoming more and more of a loner. She asked Mike to take Pete out and that he was not to take "no" for an answer.

Mike and two other guys Rick Dizt and Jim Muhr came to Pete's bunk one Saturday night, "Time to go out Pete" Mike said.

"No thanks," Pete said.

"Sorry man, orders. You're going like it or not"

"What? Whose orders?"

"Joy Lucas, the supreme commander" Mike said smiling, "and she said quote "don't take no for an answer"".

"Bullshit, you didn't talk to my mom. Did you? You bastard, you called my mom what are you 12 years old?"

"Hey man, she worries about her baby. Asked us to take care of you", joked Rick. This was a tactical error on Rick's part. Pete went into a rage that no one had seen before. He was out of control and looking to hurt someone, or something and Rick became the object of Pete's rage. Pete exploded on Rick with a fury Mike didn't expect and couldn't contain. The brawl lasted only about a minute, but Rick was busted up pretty bad with four cracked ribs and a broken nose. Jim had a slight concussion, broken nose and two black eyes. Mike was spared most of the rage and only suffered a cracked rib and two loose teeth.

For his part in the brawl Pete received a warning and was placed on the "shit list" for several weeks. This entitled him to do the nastiest jobs available on base. He would be awoke after just two hours sleep and made to drill in the rain alone, or he would be force marched throughout the night. Pete accepted his punishment without complaint and was taken off of the list a week early.

Pete used the solitary time while on the shit list to complete the deciphering of the code. He was correct that the first letter was the key, the series of misspelled words, bad grammar and punctuation had been used to highlight the cipher. The incorrect letters in each misspelled word would represent the correct letter in all future communications. For example the misspelled word shurt meant that every u in future communications would be an i instead. Without the key the communications were completely unreadable and as such encrypted. It was not a code that couldn't be cracked, in fact it was relatively simple, but it would serve to keep his bunkmates and most anyone else who happened upon the letters from reading them.

Using the key, Pete deciphered the second letter he had received and digested the material inside. He had no idea how Director Craft had gotten the intelligence, but the knowledge it gave Pete put him light-years ahead of everyone else around him. His fate was now sealed, he was headed to Vietnam. He would eventually head into North Vietnam, the letter said an operation involving him would be authorized to penetrate the enemy lines and strike at their core. What that meant Pete hadn't a clue but he accepted the fact that it would indeed happen, Director Craft had promised him help getting to Tony and Pete took him at his word.

Chapter 9

Rong Di Ri, Korea 1953

Dawn came stubbornly over the rugged hills, the
temperature was a bone chilling -10 degrees Fahrenheit and a
thick ice fog filled the valley below the ridge where members of
the UN force were gathered awaiting orders from HQ. The force
made up of members of the U.S. 101st Airborne and Canadian
members of the First Special Service Force had been waiting for
hours for their orders. This special forces group was a rekindling
of the WWII "Devil's Brigade" trained in hand to hand combat,
mountain warfare and ski patrols. The Devils Brigade had earned
their place in history in the Italian Alps fighting in some of the
harshest terrain and fiercest weather confronted by any army.

The UN force was commanded by Colonel Michael Crabtree a native of Bangor, Maine. Colonel Crabtree was a hard man and went strictly by the book, his men insisted that he would not take a shit without orders. Today was no exception, and so they waited in the freezing cold, meanwhile a battle raged in the valley below them. The rumble of grenades and artillery shook the ground and the screams of the dying drifted eerily up through the dense ice fog. The sun shone brightly up on the ridge making any hope of seeing through the white mist impossible. One of the Canadian troops, a Captain the Americans had come to call Frenchy because of his obvious French accent and his habit of berating them in the eloquent language whenever he got mad which seemed to be almost all the time, approached the Colonel.

"Any word from HQ Colonel?" He asked.

"None," came the reply.

"We cannot wait any longer, those men are being slaughtered down there," Frenchy implored.

"We will not engage the enemy without orders, that is final," the Colonel said staring straight into the eyes of the Canadian unit commander. This conversation had already occurred five times in the past ninety minutes and it was clear the answer would not change.

Frenchy saluted, turned on his heel and strode away. The Colonel was used to his Canadian counterpart questioning his authority and fretting over the planning of missions. He had witnessed the man's extreme valor and his ability to lead his men into a firefight. He considered the Captain a quality fighting man and a hell of a soldier but he chaffed at the constant questioning of his decisions.

Lieutenant Mitch Morgan was manning a 50 caliber browning automatic rifle and scanning the area immediately below his position when the Canadian captain approached him from behind. "Lieutenant, I need your weapon and ammunition" Frenchy stated flatly.

"My weapon sir? Why do you need my weapon?" questioned Morgan who stood a full seven inches taller than the Canadian.

"I do not wish to discuss my plans at this time Lieutenant, please stand aside and allow me to take control of your machine gun."

"Sir, with all due respect," Morgan began.

Suddenly a look of fury crossed the Captains' face, a fury the young Lieutenant had never before seen. That look froze the 22 year old in his tracks and made his blood run cold. Without a word Morgan stepped back two steps and allowed Frenchy to take control of the massive Browning 50 cal.

The captain hoisted the gun onto his right shoulder, grabbed a full ammo box by the handle in his left hand and walked over the edge of the ridge and into the icy mist. In a matter of seconds he was swallowed up by the fog. For the next hour the violence and explosions coming from the village shrouded in fog was more than many of the men waiting on the ridge could take. Several men begged their commanding officers to allow them to help, others became nauseous and vomited without even seeing the carnage.

At 10:07 AM February 2, 1953 the orders finally came to move in and reinforce the company of U.S. Marines who had taken up positions in and around the tiny village of Rong Di Ri. The men of the First Special Service Force moved quickly from their position on the ridge, swarming down the slope into the village, they were met by a small group of Marines gathering the wounded and dead in an attempt to save as many as possible..

Medics rushed to help them while the rest of the force pushed further into town. The thick fog and smoke from numerous fires mixed with a surreal orange glow from a raging fire in one of the buildings, created a scene reminiscent to many of their impression of hell itself. A single building stood untouched, surrounded by the Marine garrison

The soldiers were expecting to be met with hails of lead and the screams of Chinese soldiers rushing to engage them, instead the only screams were from the wounded writhing in agony and the wailing of villagers over the loss of loved ones. The NATO men made their way along the single dirt road that bisected the town, crouching behind any cover they could find. Commanders split the men into two groups and moved in opposite directions one north and the other south along the road. Scores of dead and dying Chinese and North Korean soldiers lay in the street, more were piled up in certain places obviously used as cover by one side or the other.

The men moved along, entering building after building, finding only dead villagers. The men shot or stabbed to death, the women naked with their throats slit, children shot in their beds. Hardened soldiers openly wept at the brutality, the senseless violence that they encountered. After clearing all of the buildings, the force regrouped on the western side of town beyond the village in a meadow that opened into the rest of the valley where a mile further on ran the Bukhangang River. There they met another small group of Marines walking slowly towards them from the valley below.

"What the hell took you so long?" asked one of them to no one in particular.

"Where is your commanding officer Sergeant?" Asked Colonel Crabtree.

"Dead sir, like most of the rest of our company, it wasn't for that crazy Cannuck we'd all be dead." He replied without caring if his statement was out of line.

"What crazy Cannuck?"

"The one with the Browning, he came out of nowhere, screaming in French and blasting Chinks and Gooks. They pissed their pants and took off running, he went after them and those of us who could, followed. We caught them down by the river and wiped them out, there must be four or five hundred of them down there."

"Where is the Captain now Marine?" asked Colonel Crabtree now fully aware that the crazy Cannuck was none other than Captain Latelhaurie.

"He's still chasing the remnants of the Chink army that crossed the river and headed northwest, that man is nuts he didn't even hesitate to hit the water. We took one look at that river and decided to call off the attack and get back here to tend to the wounded. We had no idea if you guys would ever show up, sir." The Sergeant said as he walked past the Colonel and headed toward town. The rest of the battered Marines filed past, all with a look of disgust in their eyes.

Lieutenant Draper of the Canadian contingent implored the Colonel to let him take a team to find his Captain and continue the assault on the Chinese Army. The Colonel was now enraged by the lack of proper following of the chain of command and not only gave the Lieutenant a direct order not to pursue the Chinese but posted sentries to stop anyone who tried. He ordered the village of Rong Di Ri sealed off and began the extraction of the wounded and dead Marines.

Colonel Mitch Morgan awoke with a sudden start as a cold chill swept over him. The nightmares had begun again the night he read Frenchy's letter and even though the crazy Cannuck had died almost a year before, he felt his presence every time he closed his eyes. The terrifying look in his eyes before he took the Browning and headed off into the ice fog still scared him even now, the death and utter devastation they found inside Rong Di Ri once they finally entered the village. The wailing women who had survived the assault, their looks of pain haunted him every night. The look of total disgust on the faces of the marines who had fought all night against overwhelming odds losing nearly half of their company never left his mind. "Damn you Frenchy," he thought. "I had almost forgotten that hell hole before you reminded me."

Pete received another letter, this one with specific instructions involving his immediate future. Pete had already intended to apply for Ranger training so when the letter stated "You will apply to become a Ranger" he said to himself, "no shit." The letter then went on to state, "when asked to become a sniper, accept." Pete softly said, "sniper, that's a new twist." The letter continued on to say Pete was to approach a Major Kim, a hand to hand expert, and say just one word, "Kashmir". Major Kim would take it from there. Pete read the letter again just to make sure he understood completely and then burned it using his butane lighter just as he had done with the first two. Using his photographic memory Pete had memorized the code, and then destroyed the key to keep anyone from finding it.

The next afternoon, during a break in training, Pete headed to the hand to hand training center, a large building made of cinder blocks with only small windows set high enough in the walls to keep anyone from seeing inside. The windows allowed light in to help create shadows and various light patterns that aided training. Pete entered the center from the west side through a steel service door and watched as a large black Sergeant conducted a class on disarming an enemy with a knife.

Pete quietly made his way past the class and approached a single desk where a Lieutenant was working on some paperwork. Pete stood at attention and waited to be acknowledged. The Lieutenant looked up from his paperwork and asked, "what can I help you with Private?"

"I am looking for Major Kim, sir." Pete responded.

"Is he expecting you, private?"

"I'm not sure sir, I was told I should come here and see him sir," Pete answered.

"One moment, Private Lucas," the Lieutenant said reading the label on Pete's fatigues to get his surname. He picked up the phone on the desk, pressed the number 5 and waited. He then announced Pete's presence and listened for a mere second before returning the phone to its cradle. "Major Kim requests you return at 1800, he will be in his office, through that door" the Lieutenant said while pointing to the door behind him using his thumb.

"Thank you sir," Pete replied while turning on his heel and then made his way quietly past the ongoing class. He had almost made it to the door when he heard the Instructor call out,"where are you going Private?"

"Pete instantly spun around and answered, "I am in "C"company sir, I am not part of your class this afternoon, sir."

To which the instructor smiled and said, "you are now Private, please show Bravo company how you pukes in Charlie company take on a knife wielding enemy." With that he charged Pete holding the knife above his right shoulder showing the intent of stabbing down towards Pete.

Pete shifted his feet to shoulder width, left foot slightly ahead of the right closing off his vitals from the oncoming threat.

When the Sergeant reached his position and began a downward motion with the knife, Pete reacted by dropping to his right knee, punching the attacker in the groin with his right hand while grabbing the attackers' right wrist in his left hand. The Sergeant groaned, and instinctively bent at the waist from the punch to his crotch, using the attackers' own momentum Pete pulled down on the arm with the knife while simultaneously lifting him by his crotch. The Sergeant, although he outweighed Pete by over 30 pounds was helpless to stop the ensuing body slam. Pete then pinned the Sergeant's right arm to the floor with his left knee and drawing his own knife held it to the instructor's throat.

Pete quickly released the Sergeant and stood at attention. The Sergeant stood slowly and fighting off the urge to pummel Pete, yelled "That is not the way we teach disarming in the U.S. Army, obviously you haven't been through my class yet Private! While your approach may yield positive results in some cases, our methods are proven effective! I look forward to showing you the proper method very soon."

"Sir, yes sir!" Pete barked, hoping that he didn't just open up a whole can of whoop-ass on himself.

"Dismissed, private," the Sergeant snapped and turned back to his pupils. He now had to critique Pete's defense without showing any sign of how he had been totally caught off guard by a brand new recruit.

Pete exited the center and returned to his unit in time to finish the day's training on weapon breakdown and cleaning.

At 1800 sharp Pete returned to the hand to hand center, he really hoped to not run into the same Sergeant he had embarrassed earlier. He opened the door and found the center completely empty, his own footfalls echoing inside the cavernous hall. He found the door behind the Lieutenant's desk and opened it, it opened to a short hallway with three doors. Each door was to an office, the first was empty with boxes piled on the floor and desk, the second was military grade spotless with not a shred of paper out of place but was otherwise unoccupied. The final door was to Major Kim's office, and the light was on. Pete approached the door slowly and reached for the knob, the door swung open and standing there was an Asian man no more than five feet three inches tall and weighing Pete estimated less than one hundred and thirty pounds. The Major just glared at Pete, a look of quiet anger on his face.

Pete swallowed and said quietly, "Kashmir."

Major Kim's expression did not change, he simply opened the door wider and allowed Pete to enter the office. Once inside, Kim closed the door softly and stood there eying Pete for several minutes. Pete stood at attention, trying to not move a muscle, waiting. Finally, Kim spoke softly in French, "I have waited a very long time for you to come, your training begins tomorrow. I have your schedule," he handed Pete a sheet of paper with times and dates, "memorize it, it will never leave this room. You have been chosen for a specific reason, a reason I do not know nor care about, I have agreed to train you as a debt to be paid. I will honor my debt, you will learn or die trying."

Pete looked up from the paper, his head spinning, confused as to what training he was to receive, what debt was owed, how he had been chosen and for what purpose. The confused look on his face must have amused the Major because he began smiling and chuckling softly. "I amuse you sir?" Pete asked keeping the conversation in French for now.

"You do not even know what you are being trained for do you? You have no idea who I am? You have no clue why you were chosen?" the Major mused.

"I know who arranged this, I agreed to do this to help my brother, beyond that I am in the dark, that is true, Major Kim." He replied.

"The dark is a good place, it is safer in the dark. You will learn to use the darkness, it will become your friend. Memorize the schedule and do not be late, I will not wait for you. It is easy for me to explain teaching a soldier, it is not easy for a soldier to explain being somewhere he is not supposed to be."

Pete returned his mind to the paper, it contained a schedule of dates and times covering a six-week period. Pete took several minutes to catalog the schedule, it seemed random at first but a pattern emerged and Pete used that pattern to permanently etch it into his memory. That was how his mind worked, he made patterns out of everything transferred those patterns to pictures and then stored the pictures in various catalogs or albums in his mind. In less than three minutes Pete handed the paper back to Major Kim.

The Major took it from Pete and placed it into a safe that stood just behind his desk. He closed the safe door and spun the combination lock. He turned back to Pete and simply said softly, "you have your orders Private Lucas."

Pete turned on his heel and exited the office closing the door behind him. The hand to hand center was eerily quiet as Pete made his way back into the main hall, a sliver of light pierced the darkness streaming in from one of the small windows. Pete caught a whiff of something, a scent he recognized, just as someone lunged from his right side. Pete reacted but a little too late. The attacker slammed a leather wrapped baton into his abdomen. Pete bent over from force of the blow the other end of the baton was slammed into the back of his head and all went black.

Pete awoke on the floor of the training center, his head throbbing and his stomach knotted up. He tried to stand, grew instantly nauseous and dropped back to his knees. He placed his head between his knees and waited for the nausea to pass. A minute later he once again straightened up and this time very slowly rose to his feet. He looked around but there was no sign of his attacker, "did that really happen?" he thought to himself. He slowly made his way back to his rack and rolled into it. Checking his watch he saw it was now 2130. He had been out for about three hours, why hadn't Major Kim found him? He had to have left the building at some point, did he leave a different way? Was Major Kim the one who attacked him? No, his money was on the Sergeant he had embarrassed earlier, this was classic payback simple as that, but it still didn't explain how he had laid there for three hours with no one noticing.

Chapter 10

Pete had already realized the schedule he had been given by Major Kim gave him very little free time and would interrupt most of his meals and a good amount of his sleep. He had no idea just how bad it would get by the end of his six-week course.

Kim was a master in both Tae Kwon Do and Aikido, he had also studied Jujitsu and Ninjitsu extensively but had not reached the level of master in either. The first training session began with teaching Pete to breathe. It was the most basic and in Kim's mind the most important lesson he could teach. Breathing properly focuses the mind, sharpens the senses and strengthens the body. Major Kim gave each command first in English, followed by French, Korean and Vietnamese, as a result Pete was learning martial arts and two new languages at the same time,

Pete was a motivated and willing pupil, but he was also headstrong and many times too smart for his own good. He would anticipate a lesson and try to run before he learned to walk. Kim continuously had to rein him in and slow him down, often by cracking him with a shaft of bamboo that Pete swore came out of the mans' body upon request. One second his hands were empty the next Pete was getting smacked across the gut or back with that damn staff.

The first six lessons were all about breathing, balance and controlling his thoughts, the seventh began as always with breathing exercises. After Kim and Pete had gone through the ritual, Kim began what Pete thought might be a sort of dance or stretching routine. Pete watched trying to memorize the moves. After Kim had gone through the routine once he began a second time, Pete joined in and soon they were moving as one. The movements were slow and smooth, gliding from one position to another. The hand movements were smooth and subtle, a turn of the wrist, a bend of the elbow, right hand below the chin, left across the waist. The leg movements were equally slow, smooth and elegant, bending at the knee while drawing the other knee up towards the chest. This was classic martial arts, learning the movements slowly at first, training the muscles and creating muscle memory so that when needed the muscles would simply react instead of needing conscious thought.

Kim told Pete to do his routine five times per day, "do not miss a session, if you do we will start all over." Pete just bowed and slipped away quietly. The training was as much mental as physical, Pete was being taught how to move effortlessly, silently and yet very quickly. His mind already razor sharp was being honed to an efficiency unrivaled in the world. He would be given puzzles, mathematic problems and physics equations to solve while doing his stretching and muscle training. The problems were to be done entirely in his head, his hands and feet were busy with their own work.

The third week Pete was introduced to actual kicks, punches and throws. This training was much more fun and raw. Pete and Major Kim sparred regularly with Kim always managing to just avoid killing Pete or at least severely injuring him. Pete pushed this to the limit, often going far beyond his capabilities to force Kim to respond. Kim would eventually respond and Pete would learn yet another move, kick or tactic he could add to his arsenal. Kim wasn't amused, he feared Pete was moving too quickly, so he introduced the art of Aikido to Pete in week four.

Aikido is a Japanese martial art that focuses on the more esoteric forms of fighting, using pressure points and the enemies own body to disable him. Pete was left writhing in agony several times after receiving a "tip" from Master Kim. Kim expected this to slow Pete down and make him take a more cautious approach, but instead Pete barreled on trying to learn everything and doing so the hard way.

Week six came along and Pete was allowed to merge all that he learned together into a single fighting system. Kim would attack and Pete would respond in whatever way he felt would remove the threat the quickest with the lowest chance of injury to himself. The final training session Pete met Kim in his office instead of the training hall. Master Kim was wearing his uniform instead of his workout clothes, and Pete was disappointed. He had hoped for one last thrilling session.

"I have paid my debt Peter, you are a very good student and I sense an even better man. Your father would be very proud of you." Kim spoke softly.

"You knew my father? The debt you paid, you owed to him?" Pete asked.

"Yes, he saved my family honor, now I have given you the tools to save your brother, my debt is repaid." Kim said smiling.

"Thank you Master Kim, will I see you again?" Pete asked fearing the answer.

"That is not a question I can answer, only time knows the truth. Never forget what you have been taught, add it to your military training and your own intellect and nothing is out of your reach." Kim replied.

Pete bowed and slipped silently from the room. He proceeded one last time down the short hallway and into the training center. This time his footsteps did not echo inside the empty room, not a sound was made as he moved effortlessly towards the door. He again smelled a familiar smell, and this time could hear his assailant breathing before the attacker even began his assault. Pete allowed him to come not changing his course or speed, at the last possible moment Pete dipped slightly and spun with blinding speed. His left leg catching the would-be attacker on the left side of his head. Before the man even acknowledged that he had been kicked Pete had slammed his right knee into the man's midsection and disarmed him. The leather wrapped baton was spinning in Pete's hands with such speed it made a whirring sound like a planes' propeller. He tilted the angle of his hands only slightly and the baton cracked into the attacker's left temple knocking him out cold.

Sergeant Adams, lay face down for several hours before coming to on the floor of the training center. He had to crawl to the phone on the desk and call for a medic. The Sergeant tried to file a complaint against Pete but Major Kim gave Pete an alibi for the time of the attack and the charge was dismissed without a hearing.

Chapter 11

Pete graduated from Airborne training in November and immediately applied for Ranger training. He was assigned to the 101st Airborne at Fort Campbell, Kentucky and began his duty as a private first class. Shortly thereafter he was accepted to Ranger training and began what would become the most intense training known to any army in the entire world. After arriving at Fort Campbell he was cleaning his weapon, when he was approached by a Lieutenant. Pete saluted as the lieutenant approached and stood at attention. The lieutenant asked, "Are you Private Lucas?"

"Sir, yes sir."

"The Commandant wants to see you in his office Private."

"When Sir?"

"Now soldier!" barked the lieutenant.

"Sir, yes sir" yelled Pete as he saluted and then rushed out into a pouring rain. He crossed the 300 yards to the Commandant's office in less than a minute and almost ran into an aide coming out of the door. The aide smiled and asked Pete's name.

"Private Peter Lucas ma'am", Pete replied.

"Careful Private, or you may have an accident," she said smiling again and overtly flirting with Pete.

Pete was embarrassed and removed his hat, stammered a bit and excused himself to see the Commandant. Colonel Mitch Morgan was a mountain of a man, 6'4" tall and weighing 245 pounds. He had black hair graying at the temples, piercing blue eyes and his face was creased with lines etched by years of hard work and hard living. He was known for being a man who fought hard and drank even harder, he was also very proud of the 101st and was its most staunch defender. Pete soon found that the Colonel was also secretive and hard to read.

"Private Lucas you any relation to Tony Lucas?" Colonel Morgan already knew the answer but wanted to see Pete's reaction.

"Sir, yes sir" replied Pete, adding "he's my brother sir."

"At ease soldier," Morgan gave the official order for Pete to relax. Then he continued "Private, Tony was the best I ever trained and I understand you're proving to be almost as good."

"Was sir, Tony is MIA not dead. He still is the best." Pete stated flatly.

"I didn't mean it that way son, I meant that I don't personally train anyone anymore" the Colonel replied calmly. Colonel Morgan was pleased to hear Pete defend his brother instantly and without question. That kind of loyalty was rare and Colonel Morgan was in need of someone he could trust without question.

"Oh, sorry sir. I guess I'm still a little touchy on that subject."

"No problem Private, I want him back almost as much as you do. He is a very good friend of mine as well as a damn fine Ranger." The pride in the Colonel's voice was obvious. "I have been told you can hit anything you shoot at, is that true Private?"

"I guess so sir, I've been shooting since I was 10." Pete answered. He wasn't sure where this conversation was heading, first Tony then shooting.

Colonel Morgan saw the look of confusion in Pete's eyes and decided to leave it there for a while. "How's your mom holding up son?"

"She's OK, she misses Tony and what does this have to do with shooting sir?" Pete was getting tired of the game and he still didn't know why he had been called to the Colonel's office in the first place.

"This kid's pretty sharp, he figured out the game almost before it began and shut it down. He might just be as good as Tony after all," Colonel Morgan thought. Then he said to Pete "OK, enough idle chatter, I've called you in to inform you that we think you would make a good sniper. You're used to working alone or in small groups, you don't socialize much and you can shoot lights out from extreme distance. We can train you in the art of sniping, from camouflage to stalking to finding your target. You interested?"

"I guess so sir, I'll do whatever is best for the Army sir" Pete said, amazed at how Director Craft had somehow arranged to have him "chosen" to become a sniper.

"Bullshit son, you either want to do this or you don't which is it?" The Colonel was still playing the game, he knew Pete would react to the directness of the question.

"Sir, yes sir. I would be honored to be trained as a sniper sir" Pete responded exactly as Colonel Morgan had thought he would.

"Very well Private, that will be all." Colonel Mitch Morgan then received and returned Pete's salute and Pete turned on his heel and left the room. Mitch Morgan was a little torn by using Pete, but he knew if he was half the man Tony was Pete would respond well. He needed a man he could send anywhere to do anything, that was Tony before he was captured in 'Nam. Now he needed Pete to finish what Tony had started. He had gotten word of Roger Lucas's passing too late to attend the funeral, the letter Roger had sent him prior to his death still haunted him.

Outside the Colonel's office Pete was deep in thought and bumped into the same aide he had almost ran into on the way in. "Beg your pardon ma'am." Pete apologized.

"If I didn't know better I would think your trying to run me down Private." she replied wryly. She was Missy James, a 21 year old 5'3" brunette beauty from Oak Grove, Kentucky. She was a civilian working on the base as an aide to Colonel Morgan and all the guys drooled over her. She was, to use Mike's phrase, 'built like a brick shithouse' and in spite of the clothes she was forced to wear on base her incredible body was obvious. Missy had shoulder length brown hair that literally bounced when she walked, dark brown eyes and a smile that lit up a room. She was exactly the type of girl Pete knew he didn't have a prayer with.

Pete smiled shyly and grabbed the doorknob to leave the outer office when Missy asked "Do you want to run me over Private?"

The way she said it Pete was almost sure she was coming on to him, but he wasn't much of a ladies' man and he didn't really know what to say. He only managed, "no ma'am. I would never want to hurt a lady."

Missy was only 21 but she had been hit on since she was 12 and she recognized that Pete was genuinely shy. She immediately fell for him, hard. But she also realized with him being shy she would have to lead this dance. "I'm sorry I've forgotten my manners, Missy James" she introduced herself.

"Pete," Pete stammered, "Er Private Pete Lucas". Pete shook her hand a little too hard and his palms were sweaty.

Missy ignored the obvious and tried to fuel the conversation. "Where you from Pete? I'm a civilian so we don't need the titles OK?"

"OK" Pete replied and added "Ohio."

"Ohio, well that's not that far at all. Do you go home much?" Missy asked.

"No, not yet. I've been too busy training to get home." Pete looked at his watch and almost cursed. "I've gotta go, roll call. Nice to meet you Missy."

"Bye, nice to meet you Pete, see ya soon!" Missy yelled after him as Pete was running towards his barracks.

Ranger training was absolutely miserable. Even Pete was exhausted and half dead by the third day. Mike was ready to quit seven different times, and would have if Pete hadn't been there urging him on. Pete would alternate between being a friend, consoling his buddy and being a taskmaster, screaming at Mike to get his ass moving. The instructors were so impressed with Pete that they recommended to Colonel Morgan that he be made an instructor upon graduation. Over 50 percent of the men who started the training dropped out or suffered injuries which forced them to be dropped from the program. Pete was more proud of his black beret than anything else he had ever accomplished. He was now a Ranger, one of the most elite soldiers in any army in the world.

Pete continued to master the martial arts, even when the rest of his classmates were sprawled on their cots exhausted beyond belief, he forced himself to go through the exercises. He would begin with the breathing exercises and that would put him into a trance-like state that Pete came to call the "Void", once in the Void he would shut out all outside noise, his mind would be set free to solve problems or contemplate complex thoughts unencumbered by the business of operating his body. His body worked seemingly separate from his conscious thought. The graceful fluid motions of the martial arts of Tae Kwon Do, Jujitsu, Ninjitsu and Aikido blended into a single system. Some of his classmates would sit and watch him mesmerized by the speed and grace of his workout. None however tried to keep up with him, a few did ask him to teach them but after a few sessions of grueling exercise they simply stopped showing up.

Joy couldn't make it to Pete's graduation because she was swamped with work at her business. Pete was upset at first, but he realized he was being selfish and besides Missy was going to be there. Joy was torn, she really wanted to be there but her shop was really getting busy. Pete assured her it was OK and she finally decided Pete would be fine without her. He was her baby, but he was old enough to do this without her help. She made sure to congratulate him several times on the phone and sent him a card with some extra money just in case. Pete didn't mention Missy to Joy, he didn't know if Missy really liked him or was just being nice. Pete still couldn't figure out what a girl like her would want with a farm boy like him.

Pete was honored to receive his beret and to hear Colonel Morgan read his name aloud as a U.S. Army Ranger. Missy was standing in the back of the large hall, smiling and looking absolutely perfect. The ceremony ended and Missy approached Pete and congratulated him, she was very formal and shook his hand. Then she leaned forward and said softly, "I'll meet you at 9:00 at Woody's in Hopkinsville."

Pete was thrilled and answered simply, "yes, ma'am."

Pete bummed a ride with two other new Rangers and arrived at Woody's a half an hour early. He was afraid if he were late, Missy wouldn't wait for him. Woody's was a bar and restaurant famous for cheap beer, good burgers and the best brawls around. Pete had heard the other guys talk about the place but he had never been in a bar of any kind in his life. He was dressed in jeans and a button down plaid shirt, but his hair cut and obvious swagger screamed Airborne to everyone in the place. He was not the only member of the 101st in Woody's that night, but he was the smallest. All of the other GI's were at least 6 feet tall and weighed considerably more than Pete. They all knew however that Pete was at least there equal, and most had seen his ferocious rage. They had knowledge the locals didn't, and a small Ranger seemed like a perfect target to some of the local tough guys.

One big guy, dressed in jeans and a leather jacket walked up to Pete and spit directly in his face. Pete was taken back by this, but decided to try and avoid a fight. He wiped his face with his sleeve and turned toward the bar. The big guy grabbed his shoulder and tried to spin Pete around. At that point Pete knew there was no walking away. Missy was just walking through the door when Pete grabbed the big man's hand and ripped it from his shoulder. Pete looked at Missy and said "I'm sorry".

Missy was a little confused about the reason for Pete apologizing, until the big man behind Pete smashed his beer bottle over Pete's head. Pete was a little woozy, but spun to face the man. The man was surprised that Pete was still standing and even more surprised when Pete said, "walk away."

"What? You puny little boy, who you givin orders to? I ain't in your piece of shit army!"

"Walk away!" Pete repeated louder this time.

"Fuck you, and your momma!" the man laughed as he said it.

This was another tactical error, Pete was willing to ignore the man until he brought his mom into it. Pete flashed red and yelled "walk away or they'll drag you out!"

The man didn't walk away, instead he swung his right hand in the direction of Pete's head. It never got there. Pete blocked the punch and threw a devastating right cross into the throat of his attacker. The man grabbed his throat and fell to his knees. Pete lifted his left foot and placed his boot on the man's face and pushed him over. Pete was about to turn and find Missy when a sucker punch came from his left side. It never made it to it's destination either. Pete's reactions were so fast that the intended punch was blocked and the second attacker was on the ground groaning holding his crotch and his bloody broken nose before anyone else could even figure out what was going on. At that point the rest of the 101st in attendance jumped in and the brawl was on. Pete slipped out of the melee and found Missy still standing by the front door. He grabbed her hand and yelled, "let's get outta here!"

They ran out into the parking lot and jumped in Missy's car. Missy fired it up and tore out of the lot just as the local police were arriving. Missy turned to Pete and said "you must really enjoy physical contact boy. First you try to run me down twice in one day, now you start a fight with a guy twice your size."

"First of all, I didn't try to run you over, second I didn't start that. He broke a beer bottle over my head!" Pete yelled. He was still feeling the adrenaline from the fight.

Missy laughed, then she turned to Pete and asked "he broke a bottle over your head? Doesn't that hurt?"

"Hell yeah it hurts! I got a golf ball size knot already"

Missy pulled the car over and said, "let me see that". Pete leaned over and let her look at the lump growing on his skull. "We better get some ice on that quick."

She started the car and drove to a small diner in the center of town. They went in and Missy asked for some ice and ordered a Pepsi, Pete just asked for some water. The waitress brought the ice wrapped in a towel and their drinks. Missy held the ice to Pete's head and said, "boy I can't take you anywhere can I?"

Pete laughed and said "ma'am you can take me anywhere you like, and I promise I won't ever complain."

Missy smiled, and thought "who is this guy? He still calls me ma'am. He drinks water and then he says he'll follow me anywhere." Then she asked, "who are you Private Pete Lucas?"

Pete looked her directly in the eyes and said, "I'm a farm boy from Ohio, who worked very hard to become a U.S. Army Ranger. I have a mom, a brother and two sisters in Ohio, a brother in 'Nam and a brother in law in Germany."

"No, No I don't mean who are you, I mean who are YOU." Missy asked again.

Pete was confused, he wasn't skilled in conversation in the first place and this was just plain weird. "I don't know what you want Missy, I told you who I am." Pete was a little upset, but more confused than anything else.

"What makes you who you are? That's what I want to know, why did you go through the hell to become a Ranger? Why do you still call me ma'am?"

Pete laughed, which made Missy laugh. "I call you ma'am because that is the way I was raised. Any woman older than you is to be called ma'am, and man older than you is to be called sir."

"Ok, first of all I'm not much older than you so drop the ma'am. And I mean now, I'm too young to be a ma'am. My name is Missy not ma'am."

"Is that your real name?" Pete asked.

"Yes that's my real name, why?"

"I just thought maybe it was a nickname or something, it sounds great for a little girl. But ..."

"But what? Are you making fun of my name?" Missy was getting defensive.

"No, No! I was just wondering what the rest of your family was like." Pete dodged the bullet and managed to completely avoid talking about himself. Missy talked about her family and her life for several hours. Finally, Pete looked at his watch and whistled. "I need to get back to base, I leave for training in six hours!"

"Leave, what do you mean leave?" Missy asked.

"Sniper school, I haven't had a chance to tell you. I'm going to sniper school at Fort Benning. I'll be gone six weeks. But I'll write you, if that's OK with you."

Missy was a mess, she was in love and wanting to spend time with Pete, and now he was leaving for six weeks. Leaving in six hours. She was an absolute mess!

Pete saw the confusion on Missy's face and took her hands in his. He stared straight into her eyes and said, "I promise I will be back in six weeks, after that I get two weeks leave. I will spend as much of that two weeks with you as you will allow me."

Missy caught her breath and took a tough girl stance, "I'll check my calendar, maybe I can squeeze you in some afternoon."

Pete was pretty sure she was kidding, but she was very convincing. He knew one thing for sure, he didn't stand a chance against her when it came to a verbal war. She would eat him up and spit him out. But, he thought to himself, "I would enjoy every minute of it."

Chapter 12

After graduating from Ranger training Pete went immediately to Sniper school, this was a relatively new training school designed to teach the art of stealth. The students were taught how to build a Gilly suit, the camouflage suit used by snipers. They learned how to stalk, the art of moving into position without being detected and how to escape detection while evacuating the area after the shot. The training is intense and very competitive. Pete really enjoyed the competition and the camaraderie shared by the select few who made it into sniper school. Mike was also chosen, but he was trained as a spotter. A spotter accompanies a sniper and acts as another set of eyes and as a bodyguard for the sniper, in the event something happens to the sniper, the spotter is capable of taking the place of the sniper. He carries an M-16 automatic rifle and another telescopic sight to help identify targets.

Snipers are a different breed, they have to like being alone or with one or two other people for extended periods. Sniping is very personal, a sniper spends hours or even days stalking his target getting to know them, their habits and their mannerisms. Killing is a part of war, the ugly part for sure, of that there can be no doubt. Sniping is killing on a one on one level and to be a good sniper a man has to be willing to kill his target while watching him through his scope. Most humans cannot handle the mental part of sniping, dealing with seeing the vivid image of another man's death by one's direct action zoomed in by a magnifying lens.

Stressing how difficult it is to live with what you've done was one of the ways the instructors used to weed out potential snipers. Using simulated kills with graphic images helped to insure the snipers wouldn't snap when asked to kill a real enemy. The soldier was taught to use what was called the moral authority or moral high ground to help justify his actions, this man wants to kill Americans thus he needs to die was stated with emphasis time and again.

All along Pete was writing his mom, keeping her informed of important dates and his progress. He was also writing Missy at least once a week. At first she hadn't responded and Pete thought about giving up, but three weeks after his first letter was sent her first letter had arrived. She explained that her daddy Earl, had intercepted the first two letters and kept them from her. He didn't want her getting involved with a soldier and refused to allow her to reply to the letters. Missy's momma, Emma James saw her daughter was in love and gave the letters to Missy behind her husband's back. Emma would check the mail before Earl got home from work and would hide Pete's letters from him. She would place the letters under Missy's pillow for Missy to find that night. Emma saw what Earl never would, Missy was head over heels in love with Pete and she was happier than she had ever been.

Pete and the other snipers were given their new weapon, a modified M-14 rifle called the XM21. It was heavy and had an extraordinarily long barrel, and was fitted with a new telescopic site. The longer barrel made the rifle more accurate at long range and the new site was required to allow precise aiming at distances of 800 meters or more. Pete loved this weapon, it was solid and felt good in his hands. It only took a few rounds before Pete was comfortable with the stock and the recoil. He was scoring high on targets and began to impress his instructors. The math required to make shots at extreme distances served to weed out still more of the class. Factoring distance, trajectory, wind speed and direction, gravity, even humidity became daunting when pressed to make a shot in a pressure situation.

A few of the guys started calling him Merlin, in reference to King Arthur's magician but others took to calling him the Samurai because of his constant training in the martial arts. Mike Moore just called him Yankee, unless he was pissed, then he called him asshole.

The more difficult shots included targets obscured by smoke, foliage or through glass or even walls, but the real showstoppers involved moving targets. The math became almost impossible once the target began moving, as such most recruits couldn't hit more than one out of ten moving targets at long range. They were instructed to wait for the target to stop moving before taking the shot if at all possible, when the target was stationary the snipers were all hitting at least nine of ten. Pete was the exception, he hit ten of ten consistently on stationary targets. However, the instructors were stunned when Pete hit seven of ten moving targets the first time he tried and as training went along the average approached the unbelievable ten of ten. What really set Pete apart from the others was his ability to simply disappear.

In every case where completing a simulated mission required absolute stealth, Pete was graded the highest of all students. This brought Pete praise from his peers, but some of the instructors thought he was getting cocky.

One instructor, Phil "Gunner" Gunther was especially concerned. He had trained Pete's brother Tony and saw similar qualities in Pete. Gunner was convinced Tony's cockiness had somehow led to his capture. He was not about to lose another star pupil because of what he called "ballooning", where a person's head gets so big it makes him stand out in a crowd. He pulled Pete aside and explained the concept. "If you start ballooning you'll get dead right quick! Understand! This ain't no joke boy, I seen it happen and that guy's MIA right now! You get a big head and you stand out in a crowd, that will kill a sniper faster than anything. The whole idea of sniping is to remain unseen, unheard and invisible. You got it boy?"

"Sir, yes sir" Pete answered, "who's MIA sir?"

"Did you hear anything else I said boy? If you can't stay hidden you die! You got a five shot, bolt action rifle. They've got automatics and heavy machine guns, you will get killed and get your spotter killed if you screw up! Do you understand me!" Gunner was screaming now and right in Pete's face. His face was deep red and his veins were bulging on his forehead. He was not going to let up until he was positive Pete got the message loud and clear. "This ain't no game boy, they will gut you like a pig and put your head on a stick! This enemy is sneaky, mean, nasty and determined! You must stay out of sight and be at least two steps ahead of them at all times! Got it!"

Pete was stunned, he had thought he was doing well, he knew he was the best in the class. At first he thought Gunner was just coming down on him to show the other guys that there were no favorites, but this was beyond that. He took the advice to heart and responded accordingly, "Sir, yes sir. I got it sir."

Gunner stormed off hoping inside that the kid really did "get it", if Pete was to survive he needed to be not just good, but invisible.

Pete had continued to practice his mind by learning to instantly assess a situation. He would walk into a room like the mess hall and identify everyone in the room. Not by name but by where they were and what they were doing. For example Private 1 pouring coffee, Lieutenant 2 seated at table 3 facing east 2nd chair from far end. By the end of his training Pete was able to assess a room full of people and categorize them in a few seconds. This single skill would prove more valuable than any other he learned in all of his training.

Chapter 13

After Sniper school Pete went home for a two-week

leave, and he brought Missy home with him. Joy was amazed at

the man who now stood before her. He was still only 18 years

old, but he was definitely a man. Pete conducted himself with

poise and military precision, Suzy was less impressed and razzed

him about his haircut and his beret, she was very impressed with

Missy however and even a little jealous. It was perhaps the first

time in her adult life when she wasn't the most beautiful woman

in the room. Pete ignored her and spent most of the time talking

with his Uncle John and Missy. He was completely taken with

her and she with him. He was considering asking her to marry him, but he still doubted that she would want someone like him. He was a simple farm boy from Ohio and now a soldier with low pay and an unsure future. She was the most beautiful woman he had ever seen and he just couldn't see what she saw in him.

Pete snuck out each morning to the small shed behind the house and did his workout, a half hour of peace, a half hour in the Void helped him ready himself for the journey he was about to undertake. The time came and Joy said goodbye. She knew Pete was headed for Vietnam and it terrified her, but she kept her chin up and prayed for his safe return, she even managed a prayer that Pete might somehow find Tony.

The car ride from Ohio to Fort Campbell was too short for Pete. He knew he was leaving Missy at a bad time. He loved her and she loved him, but they hadn't spent much time together and he was sure she would find someone else while he was in 'Nam. He was going on a twelve-month tour, he couldn't imagine her waiting a whole year for him.

Missy did her best to reassure him she would wait, she promised him three separate times. She told him she would wait forever if necessary, but he needed to be sharp and come home safe. She had seen so many soldiers wounded and killed that she couldn't express her fear for Pete. She was a nervous mess and had endured an upset stomach for most of the two weeks in Ohio. She knew even better than Pete just how dangerous Vietnam was and she was terrified he would never come home. She kept up a strong front, only crying a little when Pete said goodbye. He held her close and promised her, "I'll be home before you know it, if you wait for me I can get through anything."

"I'll be right here waiting," Missy answered through her tears.

"I love you Missy James" Pete said aloud for the first time.

Missy looked up and began to sob uncontrollably, "I love you too."

Pete held her fast, and waited as long as he could before he had to go. Missy watched him walk through the double doors leading out of the hall to the bus waiting outside. Pete stepped onto the first step, spun and waved to her, then disappeared into the bus. Missy was left with the other wives and girlfriends, all of whom were crying. She was sad, but Pete promised her he'd be back. And if there was one thing she had learned about Peter Lucas, he would keep his word, he had to.

Chapter 14

Charlie Company was flown from Kentucky to San Diego and from San Diego to Hawaii. The other guys with Pete were out drinking and partying all night, but Pete stayed on base at Schofield Barracks studying the maps they had been given. The land was strange and Pete wanted as much of a head start on evaluating the situation as he could get. He had requested and been granted his choice of spotter. He of course chose Mike Moore. He knew Mike was a knucklehead, but he also knew Mike was solid. He hadn't seen Mike get rattled when times got tough and he had confidence that if anything happened Mike would not screw up, he would do the job. Pete wasn't in this to just get it over with and go home, he still believed in the fight and was out to do his part to win it. After a two-day layover, Mike called it 'a two-day hangover', they boarded a flight to Saigon. The flight was long and everyone was tired when they landed, the rear door opened and the stifling, hot, humid air sucked all the rest of the energy they had right out of them. It was all they could do to get their gear and get off the plane.

Major Lawrence (Larry) Pierce met them on the tarmac and began barking orders immediately. The Company responded as Rangers do and made quick work of the tasks at hand. They were quartered in a series of tents on the Airfield for the night and were awakened at 04:30 for orientation. Pete and his company began a two-day Vietnam style basic training that consisted of local customs, some language, flora and fauna training and it was consistently stressed that personal hygiene was crucial. Some of the guys, including Mike went into the city to sample the local nightlife. Pete as usual stayed on base and continued to prepare for the job at hand. Mike came back and told Pete about the food and the women, trying to get Pete interested. It was no use, Pete was single minded in his determination to understand the enemy. He studied old mission reports and troop movements. He poured over topo maps and terrain studies. He was completely immersed. He also continued his personal workouts, the martial arts that Major Kim had taught him, as often as he could. A few of the others joined him using training they had received in private dojos which made the exercise more enjoyable.

Major Pierce addressed the company at breakfast 0500 March 4, 1972. "Men we have been given orders to proceed north to Firebase Scout and conduct recon patrols. Our mission is to locate, evaluate and help destroy VC supply lines in the area. Get your gear and we will assemble back here at 0600, the Hilos will be waiting."

The men ate in near silence, and went back to the barracks to collect their gear. All the partying and fun was over, today they entered the war. Pete had known the time was coming and had written letters to his mom and Missy in advance. He had agonized over the wording but finally ended up with, "I've got a job to do, may not get a letter out for a while, Love Pete."

Pete climbed aboard the Hilo and slid to the middle, if there was a need for fire he would not be of any help. His sniper rifle was all but useless in a firefight, he knew that. The slow rate of fire and bulky site made quick run and gun firing impossible. Pete would have to rely on his teammates to get him on the ground and away from the hilo safely. After that he could melt away and take care of himself. The ride north was longer than he expected and everyone, including the hilo's gunner was nervous. The gunner's eyes never stopped moving and he continuously swept his 20MM machine gun back and forth looking for any sign of the enemy. Pete thought to himself that a trained sniper could have a field day with these guys. He could shoot the pilot and there would be no way for the gunner to see him. The odds of the gunner looking directly at a sniper the instant he fired were astronomical, and if he didn't see the muzzle flash he would never find the shooter.

Fortunately for Pete no one shot at them and they landed at Firebase Scout, a small clearing hacked out of the jungle ringed by razor wire. There were tents in a rough semi-circle opening south with a larger mess tent in the center. The latrine was on the northeast side and the landing zone was on the extreme southern edge of the camp. Pete was amazed when the chopper never actually landed. They hovered a few feet off the ground and as soon as everyone was out, the crew lifted off and swung back south towards Saigon. The sound of the choppers was soon swallowed by the jungle and Pete, Mike and the rest of the team moved off to find their quarters. They were escorted by a quartermaster to several tents on the western edge of the semi-circle, this was home for the near future.

Pete found a bunk and threw his gear on it, he was tired even though he hadn't done anything all day. He started to sit on the edge of the bunk when a booming voice yelled "Attention". The entire team snapped to attention and Major Pierce stepped into the tent and addressed the men.

"Welcome to Firebase Scout, you will find all the comforts of home. We have lousy food, cold showers and holes in the ground to shit in." The men all laughed, except Pete, he was studying the Major. "You will be running continuous patrols probing the enemy's supply lines. They know we're here and they are trying to beef up their forces to take this position. Our job is to disrupt this build up and retain this position. We are not here to conquer North Vietnam, we are here to help South Vietnam, understand? You are standing on the northernmost point occupied by U.S. forces in South Vietnam. As a result we are the primary target of the V.C. So be very aware of your surroundings, when you are on patrol watch for traps and tunnels. The enemy has dug miles and miles of tunnels to use as supply lines and to avoid being bombed by our boys from above. They will eventually attack this position, we need to know when and where they will come from, how many of them there are and what they're bringing with them as far as firepower."

"Each squad will consist of an LT (lieutenant), a Sergeant and 6 Privates and will run two day patrols. The patrols will leave and return at different times of the day and night to keep the enemy off guard. We don't want them finding a pattern to our movements. At all times there will be at least two patrols out, the rest of the company will be charged with maintaining the base and guarding the perimeter. This all clear?"

"Sir, yes sir", came the reply from the assembled men.

"Privates Lucas and Moore please report to my tent at 1800 for your orders." Major Pierce said while looking directly at Pete.

"Sir, yes sir." Pete and Mike answered.

Major Pierce left the tent and the men began stowing their gear and getting settled. The first two patrols were assembled by their lieutenants and began being briefed on the mission ahead. Others were sent to take up guard positions around the perimeter, relieving members of Alpha company who would be air lifted back to Saigon tomorrow when the last of their patrols returned. Mike looked worried and Pete thought he could lighten the mood. "Hey hillbilly, how 'bout some cards?"

"What? You nuts? We are sitting here with a fucking target on our asses and you want to play cards?" Mike was agitated. "You signed up for this, not me. I was content to run the ridge in my Roadrunner and get drunk every night. We're gonna die here man, and nobody will ever find us!"

"Hey! No one is getting killed, and you'll be home driving that piece of shit of yours in no time." Pete was trying to get Mike to return to the light banter they usually enjoyed. But Mike was really scared and he couldn't hide it anymore.

"No man, this is it, we're dead." He was on the verge of crying now.

Pete got right in Mike's face and stared into his eyes. "I will not let you die here, you got me? We are a team and I will not die here! You and I will beat this thing, we are United States

Army Rangers and we will not fail." Pete's voice was low, but his message was clear.

Mike drew on Pete's strength and regained his composure. He still knew inside that he would not make it out of this place alive, but he also knew Pete would do everything humanly possible to keep that from happening. He gabbed Pete by the shoulder and looked down at the ground, avoiding Pete's stare. "Pete, just do me one favor. If I don't make it, don't leave me here."

Pete answered with the Ranger's motto. "Leave no man behind, those aren't just words Mike they're a duty. I will always do my duty, always."

Before Pete could add the obligatory "but like I said you're not gonna die" part, Mike interrupted him. Saying "It's 17:58 we need to be in the Major's tent in two minutes," Mike turned and grabbed his helmet and rifle and bolted out the door. Pete grabbed his helmet and followed.

Chapter 15

Major Pierce was a veteran commander with two tours
under his belt and a real respect for his enemy. He had learned
from countless encounters just how savvy and fierce the
Vietcong could be. He had witnessed them using animals as
weapons and rigging sophisticated traps out of bamboo and wire.
He was not as convinced as some of his superiors that regular
tactics would be successful in winning this war. He had been
Tony's commanding officer and had been responsible for
devising the mission in which Tony had been captured. As a
newly minted Major, he had convinced then Lieutenant Colonel
Mitch Morgan to send Tony and his spotter Jason McGrew into
North Vietnam to hunt high-ranking Vietnamese officials. They
had succeeded in killing several before they were apparently

captured 18 months ago. The operation was completely classified and only a handful of people had any knowledge of it. Pierce was still convinced that the plan was militarily sound, decapitating the enemy would eventually kill it. Sending in a couple of men could save thousands he had argued, and his superiors had agreed. Colonel Morgan had sent Pierce word that Pete was coming and that he was not in favor of repeating the mistake. But Pierce read between the lines and knew that what the Colonel meant was, "don't get caught this time".

At 18:00 Mike and Pete knocked on the door to Major Pierce's tent. The Major called for them to enter and they found him sitting behind a small desk made of some crates and a sheet of plywood. They saluted and he returned the salute and then spoke, "At ease men, gentlemen I have a mission for you." Pete and Mike looked at each other and then back at the Major. "We need to cover our patrols, they are getting pot shots taken at them by VC snipers and that can't stand."

"Yes sir," said Pete.

"I want the two of you to go out on your own patrols, but you need to shadow our guys and provide them with a safety net so to speak." the Major was searching for the right terminology.

"Your call sign will be Shadow and you will maintain radio silence for your own protection. You are expressly forbidden to use the radio for anything but to alert a patrol or this base of impending attack. Understand?"

"Yes sir" came the reply.

"Good. Private Moore please excuse us, Private Lucas and I have some other business to discuss." Major Pierce said as he stood and saluted Mike. Mike saluted and turned on his heel and left the tent.

"Private Lucas, can I call you Pete?" the Major asked. Without waiting for an answer he continued, "Pete, I knew your brother Tony." With this Pete almost jumped out of his skin, he had so many questions. Pierce sensing Pete's eagerness raised his hand and said, "I can't go into any particulars, but he was a helluva soldier."

Pete replied instantly, "He still is sir."

"Of course son, I'm sorry about that. We believe he was captured by the VC north of here near a village called Bong Hok. He and his spotter Jason McGrew were on a mission and somehow they were detected and captured. Or at least we hope they were captured" the Major replied.

Pete's eyes grew wide, "Tony was a sniper?"

"Yes, I thought you knew that much at least" said Pierce. "I thought Colonel Morgan would have let you know that much. He told me you were coming and I assumed he had told you what he could."

"He never told me Tony was a sniper, the Colonel had told me he trained Tony and Gunner told me he had trained a sniper who was MIA but I never put it together for sure." Pete replied.

"Well now you know, and I want you to know that I will not tolerate you doing anything to jeopardize the mission or my men. You will do your job and not spend any effort pursuing your brother, understand?"

"Yes sir, I didn't even know he was a sniper and I certainly didn't know he went missing near here," Pete answered. Now he couldn't help but wonder if Tony was nearby. All sorts of thoughts were clouding his mind.

"I didn't know what you knew, and I couldn't risk you going off halfcocked," Pierce replied and add, "That'll be all for now Private."

Pete saluted and left the tent with his head swirling. His emotions were out of control, he wanted desperately to just run out into the jungle search for Tony. He wanted to go to all the local villagers and ask them about his missing brother. He was overwhelmed at the thought of being in the exact place Tony had been just before he disappeared. He needed time to think, time to process this new information and get a grip on his emotions. He went to the tent, ignored Mike's questions about what the Major wanted and retrieved his gilly suit. He then went to the edge of the camp sat down and began adding local touches to the camo suit he would use to elude the enemy. He tried to shut out the thoughts and concentrate on his task, but it was no use. All he could think of was Tony in a POW camp somewhere nearby. It was eating him.

Then the jungle erupted around him. The VC were assaulting the camp and they were coming straight at Pete. He hit the ground and began crawling back towards the tents. "Get over here!" yelled a soldier from a foxhole about 10 meters to his right.

Pete scrambled to the hole and dove over the sandbags head first into the bottom of the hole. It took what seemed like an eternity for him to get back sitting upright. The two soldiers in

the hole with him were firing their M-16s towards the oncoming

enemy. Pete was shell-shocked at first and just stared at them. He

finally shook off the daze and yelled, "What do you need me to

do?"

One of the soldiers replied, "Where's you weapon

soldier?"

"I'm a sniper! My weapon is in the tent!"

"Shit!" came the retort, then just stay down and wait."

"Wait for what?" Pete replied.

Just then the shooting slowed down and within a minute

it stopped all together. "They're just testing our perimeter, Alpha

company told us they would come tonight and probe us to see

how we react. Seems they know our troop movements better than

we do," answered the soldier.

Pete sat dumbfounded, he realized all his training hadn't

prepared him for this. He was not in control of the situation and

that was very disturbing to him. His life was dependent on

others, as a sniper he was vulnerable when out in the open. He

needed to be in the jungle and invisible to survive. He also

realized that he couldn't help Tony, all he could do was his job and let the rest work itself out. "How long you think I need to stay here?" he asked the soldier.

"Don't know, but I imagine they exited the area as soon as they stopped shooting. If it was a small patrol they wouldn't want to get caught by one of ours coming back."

"Thanks guys," Pete said as he slipped out of the back of the hole and made his way to the tent.

The two soldiers didn't even realize he was gone until one of them turned around to offer him a stick of chewing gum. "Where'd he go?"

"I dunno, snipers are like ghosts they just appear out of no-where and then disappear again. My first tour there was this guy, Tony, he scared the bejesus outta me. He would just grow out of the jungle you know? I mean one second there was just jungle next second he's standing two feet from ya. Spooky I'm telling ya."

"Man, what you been smokin'?"

"I'm serious man, you'll shit your pants when one of those guys does that to ya. I was in a foxhole like this and this Tony guy just appeared right in front of me. He says "get ready they're coming" and two seconds later all hell breaks loose. You know come to think of it I never saw him again."

"Man you need to cut back, your losing it."

"Hey, fuck you. I'm telling ya its true. Just wait, you'll see."

Pete entered the tent and all of the guys were on edge. The gunfire had awakened them from a sound sleep and most of them weren't able to go back to sleep. Mike saw Pete come in and finally got to ask him about the Major. "So what did the Major want with you?"

"He knew my brother Tony and just wanted to let me know how much he liked him." Pete lied.

"That's all, why didn't he say that in front of me?" Mike asked.

"Maybe he was afraid I'd be emotional or something, I don't know you'd have to ask him."

Mike could tell Pete was uncomfortable talking about it and he was sure that Pete wouldn't have blabbed about his own emotional outburst earlier. He decided to let it go for the moment figuring he would have plenty of time to discuss it while they were on patrol. He laid down on his cot and slowly gave in to his fatigue. He slept fitfully and was shook awake at 0400 by Pete.

"What the hell?"

"SHHH, We need to go" Pete whispered.

Chapter 16

"Now? What time is it?" Mike asked a little too loudly.

"0400, now get your ass up or I leave without you" Pete answered in a whisper. " And for God's sake keep it down."

"Shit, 0400 and he's pissy too," this time Mike whispered.

Mike gathered his gear and slipped out of the tent, Pete was waiting about 20 meters away. Mike walked over to Pete and said, a little too loudly, "Why so early?"

"Keep it down," Pete whispered, "you're supposed to be a sniper."

"I am a sniper, and I'm better than you any day." Mike whispered this time.

"In your dreams hillbilly, we need to get out of here now, before the clouds break."

"What?"

"There's a quarter moon, if the sky gets clear our silhouettes will stand out like neon lights, let's move," and Pete moved off to the west slipping through the razor wire and into the jungle. Mike followed Pete through, but got his shirt caught on the wire and ripped a hole in it.

The two men worked their way into the dense jungle, Pete carefully stepping to avoid any traps. Mike following Pete's every move knowing that Pete had already made sure the path they took was clear. They traveled about a kilometer before they stopped for Pete to check the map and get his bearings. Mike sat down against a huge tree and whispered to Pete, "where are we going?"

Pete realized he hadn't even briefed Mike on their patrol before they left. "Sorry man, I was so wrapped up with this first patrol I forgot to show you." Pete slid over beside Mike and showed him the map. It was a topographical map of the area showing the various elevations, rivers, trails, villages and roads. Pete pointed to a small creek or river on the map and whispered, "listen."

Mike held his breath and he heard the unmistakable sound of running water. He smiled and looked back at the map. Pete then pointed to a hill that was the headwaters of that small river, and pointed to his right. Mike turned and through the canopy, the dawn was just illuminating a dark lump, the hill on the map. Mike was amazed at Pete's ability to move through the jungle and be able to find a spot on a map. Mike knew if he were to lose Pete he would never get out of the jungle. Pete then pointed to a trail cutting across the side of the hill, it then crossed the river and headed down the valley alongside the river for several hundred meters before cutting east towards the Rangers' base. "Wait a minute, you mean there is a trail and we just humped a "click" through the dark and nasty?"

"Easy big boy, we don't ever want to be on a trail or road," Pete answered.

"Oh I forgot you love hiking through thick jungle," Mike said sarcastically.

"No, I like staying alive. The trails are watched and full of traps, the roads are mined and swept by patrols. We love the dark and nasty because it keeps us alive." Pete replied. "Now, we need to get into a position that lets us watch this trail and the river, and is in the thick and nasty."

Mike looked at the map with Pete and they both saw the place at the same time. "There" they said together.

"Let's go, we need to be in position before Charlie. If he gets there first we'll still get him, but only after he gets one of our boys." Pete said as he was moving out.

The two snipers moved together slowly and silently, they slipped down hill towards the river and then cut back to the right and up the hill Pete had pointed out earlier. By the time they would be in position the sun would have moved far enough south to no longer be illuminating the hillside thus leaving them in the "thick and nasty" and safely out of sight. They made their way about two thirds of the way up the slope and found a massive tree to use as cover. Pete found a position between two of the trees enormous roots, which provided a perfect gun rest, as well as extra cover. He was able to see about 75 meters of the trail, at a distance of about 250 to 325 meters. The hill they had just left had several clearings and Pete had an excellent view of all of them. The valley beyond the river opened into a marsh of rice paddies, it was very open but the grass and raised sides of the paddies provided a lot of cover for troops moving through them. Pete's main concern was to the right of the river, he had only two small openings in the jungle on that side. Both were still pretty overgrown, and Pete figured that any enemy sniper would approach the trail from that side. Or, Pete just realized, they might come right down over the hill to where he was lying.

Mike had taken up position just right of Pete and he was restless as cat in a kennel. He was continually moving and shifting his weapon, turning his head and wiping the sweat from his face. Finally Pete whispered, "Hillbilly, calm down you're gonna get us both killed. Do me a favor, slide around behind me and watch our ass."

"What? You want me to watch your ass, why is it gonna do tricks or something?" Mike was smiling now.

"Just don't want a Charlie enema, cover the hillside behind me, I got the valley. If you make contact, remember don't move. Just speak slowly and quietly what you see. This guy is looking for movement, he won't see you unless you move. Got it."

"Right, don't move. How long am I supposed to be a statue?" Mike asked while taking up the position Pete had asked him to take.

"Until dark, then we become the predator, for now we play the role of spider."

"Quit it, you know I hate spiders and snakes." Mike said.

"Pay attention, and be still. The hunt is on" Pete replied.

At around 1600 Pete caught movement on his right, "I knew they would come in from that side" he whispered.

"You got contact?" Mike whispered back.

Pete had forgotten Mike was even there until he heard his voice, "movement on the right side, stay alert there may be some above us as well."

Mike was scared, he was not happy being a sitting duck for the North Vietnamese army. He was sweating and his bowels were beginning to rumble. "For Christ's sake Mike don't shit your pants," he thought to himself.

Meanwhile Pete was calm as could be, he was completely relaxed, absorbed in the hunt. After about ten minutes a figure slipped silently onto the trail. Pete quickly realized it was an American patrol he had seen earlier, and they were now moving down the trail towards camp. He began to relax when he caught movement ahead of the patrol. The contact was almost 300 meters ahead of the patrol, too far ahead to be the point man. Pete whispered to Mike, "American Patrol, but they've got company."

"Should I warn them?" Mike asked. "The Major said only in event of an attack on a patrol or the base."

"No, there's only one that I can see so far" Pete replied. "A sniper I'm guessing."

"You got a bead on him?" Mike asked.

"Not yet, just a minute."

Pete was scanning the area where he had seen the movement, he couldn't make out any human forms. Another movement, and Pete was zeroed in, it was a pig. " It's a pig, a damn pig." Pete laughed.

Mike began to laugh, then Pete saw something else and he zeroed in again. This time it was a human and he was armed. The man was at the edge of the jungle, where the rice paddies began. Pete was over 600 meters from the man but through his scope he could clearly see a rifle in the man's hands. He wasn't wearing a uniform, he was wearing a camo suit, a sniper. The man was taking aim at the American patrol, Pete caught himself watching and realized he needed to react. His training took control, he aimed and took a long breath. Held it for a second and then exhaled, as he exhaled he slowly slid the trigger back. The explosion from the rifle caught him and Mike both by complete surprise. Pete didn't feel the recoil at all. He watched through the scope as the sniper slumped over his rifle. Pete had killed a man, the enemy, but a man none the less.

The American patrol took cover in the jungle beside the trail, and Mike was on the verge of puking. "What the fuck! What the fuck!" Mike said, again too loud.

"Damn it Mike, quiet down," Pete whispered. "The pig was spooked by a sniper, he was bearing down on our guys. I had to take him out." He expected to be sweating and nervous, but he was calm. He didn't even have any regrets like he did when he shot Old Chuck.

"Holy shit, you killed a VC sniper?" Mike asked.

"Yea, slide on around here, easy and quiet." Pete said.

Mike slid around the massive tree and joined Pete between the two roots. Mike used his spotters' scope to view the scene. The American patrol had advanced to the area around the sniper, and were on the radio. "Scout this is Team 7, Scout this is Team 7, you read?"

"Team Seven, this is Scout."

"Scout, it's nice to have a shadow, over"

"Roger Seven, over."

Chapter 17

The patrols were for three or four days, and most of the time Pete and Mike spent lying motionless in the jungle or worse yet in the rice paddies. Mike was convinced that Pete was looking for the worst possible place to set up that he could find. In fact that was exactly what Pete was doing, he figured that if he didn't want to be there neither would the VC. Pete and Mike were very successful in shadowing the Rangers' patrols. It had been two months and they had killed a total of three snipers and were very popular with their fellow Rangers. They were also getting very popular with the enemy. The rumors of a Shadow, silent death from out of nowhere, were passing through the villages and tunnels.

Pete was determined to continue his workouts, even getting Mike to join him occasionally. When out on patrol he would wait until long past dark to remove his gilly suit and begin the breathing exercises that marked the beginning of each session. On nights with a bright moon he would have to skip the training altogether and Mike would notice a change in his friend's demeanor. Pete would be more anxious and on edge, the saving grace for this was that there were very few cloudless nights in Vietnam.

On May 6th 1972 Pete and Mike slipped out of camp at 0230 in a pouring rain, and began a patrol heading more north than west. They had not yet patrolled this area, and several teams had reported coming under fire in the area. All of the patrols had been attacked with more than snipers, usually running firefights that lasted for 30 minutes or more. Mike was concerned that they were walking into a full company of the enemy, too many for a sniper and his spotter.

They had traveled over three kilometers when Pete signaled a halt. Mike slid up beside Pete and took in the scene. They were on the edge of a small village, there were six huts with two small gardens and some bamboo cages with chickens in them. "What are we waiting for?" asked Mike.

"It's not what you see Mike, it's what you don't see." Pete replied.

"No fires, no guards, no people," Mike answered. He had gotten much better at accessing situations. He and Pete had spent two full months in the jungle and he was beginning to feel comfortable.

"Right, no people; but chickens," Pete thought aloud. "I think we need another view of this."

Pete began to circle around to the right with Mike following his every step.

They came to a small opening between two of the huts. The other four huts were across a small courtyard from the two on their side. They remained ten meters inside the jungle, just close enough to see into the village but hidden from view. Pete kneeled down and became so still Mike was sure he wasn't breathing. After several minutes Mike saw something odd on the opposite side of the courtyard. He was sure he could make out the outline of a gun barrel.

"I see a gun on the far side, between huts 1 and 2", Mike whispered.

"I got a human form, just to the left of hut 1," Pete answered.

"Ambush", Mike whispered again.

"Yea, ambush" Pete whispered, "We gotta change the play."

"You mean warn our guys?"

"No, I mean we have to go on offense," Pete replied.

"How do you propose we do that? One M-16 and your pea shooter ain't gonna do much against a heavy machine gun" Mike sounded skeptical.

"Stay here, I'll be right back," Pete said and slipped off to his left.

He moved slowly and carefully. By the time he had gone twenty feet Mike could no longer see him. Pete was at his best while completely alone, so wrapped up in the hunt he lost all connection to anything else. He moved slowly but made better time than Mike could imagine. After only twenty-five minutes, Pete was in position behind the machine gun nest. He was able to see that there were two men manning the machine gun and two more behind each hut with automatic weapons.

Pete slipped a grenade from his belt and slowly pulled the pin, he then lobbed the grenade towards the big gun. It landed directly under the gun and exploded before either of the men manning the gun could react. Both were killed instantly. The other four men were confused, they didn't know what had happened. They hadn't seen the grenade, but they gave into fear and began shooting wildly into the courtyard.

Mike dove to the ground as bullets whizzed all around. He had not been able to see Pete, but he had seen the grenade sail under the gun. He now knew Pete was behind the enemy, which meant he couldn't shoot back for fear of hitting Pete. So he laid there waiting, not sure what to do.

The enemy soldiers realized they were shooting blind and began to whisper in Vietnamese. After a moment the two behind hut #2 joined the two behind hut #1 and again began speaking. They were clearly arguing and that made Pete's job easy. He pulled the pin on a second grenade and waited as long as he dared before lobbing it towards the soldiers. One of the men saw the grenade emerge from the jungle, but he was too startled to speak. He just pointed and it was too late. The grenade detonated and all four men were killed.

Pete stayed concealed, while making his way back around the village to Mike's position. Mike was still lying flat on his stomach, watching the courtyard when Pete whispered, "ready to move?"

Mike bit his lip to avoid yelling out, turned towards Pete and whispered, "One of these days that shit will get you killed boy."

"Nah, but those guys never saw it coming," Pete laughed.

"No shit, man I saw that first grenade come in and boom." Mike said. He was smiling too, but he was just glad Pete was on his side. He just shook his head and followed Pete into the 'dark and nasty'.

Another two months passed with endless patrols and continuing success. In July they began a patrol that took them to the same small village where the attempted ambush had occurred. They determined that the village was clear this time and continued the patrol, moving east away from the village parallel to the trail. After traveling about a kilometer Pete caught movement ahead. He signaled Mike to stop by slowly raising his hand, and together they slowly knelt down. When kneeling, or lying prone on the ground they were invisible. Their camo was extremely convincing, Pete's suit was actually alive. He had successfully transplanted small plants and moss onto the canvass panels where they had rooted themselves, drawing nourishment from the mud and water Pete was daily immersed in. The area they found themselves in now was more open with tall grass and low bushes. Pete had maneuvered them along a small depression to minimize their exposure. The movement had been ahead and slightly to the left of their position approximately 1000 meters.

Mike had gained much of Pete's ability to notice even slight movement that didn't belong. They could ignore swaying grass or the wind in the trees while focusing on movement that wasn't random. Pete had explained it to Mike one starless night lying in a pouring rain watching a VC patrol move through the jungle. "Notice how their movements are planned, each step, each turn. They aren't fluid like the wind or smooth like a wave. Their more mechanical, they have to think and react. Nature just moves." Mike was often amazed at how Pete was always in control, he envied Pete, and admired him at the same time.

The two silent predators lay in wait, watching the grass, waiting for another glimpse. Just before dark Mike noticed a strange shape in one of the trees right at the edge of the jungle. He whispered to Pete, "I got something in one of the trees."

"Give me a bearing." Pete responded.

"11:00, large tree, branch about half way up" Mike replied.

"Got it, can't be sure yet" Pete was looking through his scope at the strange shape. It was almost dark and the tree served to make the shadow even more obscure. Pete watched the shape until it was too dark to even see the tree. Then he slowly lowered his scope and sat silently for over an hour.

Mike had fallen asleep by the time Pete was ready to move, "Wake up Mikey," Pete whispered while nudging him slightly.

"Morning already" Mike said sleepily.

"No, time to see what's in that tree. I'm a little nervous about being out here in the open. Lets swing around to the right and get into the D.N." Pete said as he began moving slowly towards the glowering darkness.

"I don't like the looks of that" Mike whispered back.

"I know, but I like the grass less, too open and that tree dweller has me concerned." Pete continued to move towards the inky black outline now just 20 meters ahead.

Mike was sweating like crazy now, it was hot but that wasn't why he was sweating. Pete was concerned about the "tree dweller" as he called it, when Pete got concerned Mike was downright terrified. Nothing had rattled Pete before and Mike didn't even know what the hell was in the tree, if anything. Mike was confused and not paying attention, he stumbled and fell just as they reached the edge of the thicket. It sounded as if a mortar had exploded right behind Pete. Mike fell breaking a small sapling and let out a loud "Shit!"

Pete hit the ground and laid perfectly still for a minute, then whispered "Mike, Mike you hit?"

"No, I just fell. I'm sorry man, I just fell" Mike couldn't stop apologizing.

"Shhh, forget it Mike. Let's get back away from the clearing." Pete was pissed but tried not to show it. He moved quickly away from the clearing and deep into the dense undergrowth. Finally, he stopped beneath a huge tree and sat against its trunk. "We will have to wait a while before moving back out to the edge for a look at what's in that tree."

"I'm so sorry man" Mike was still apologizing, "I just fell. I guess I wasn't paying attention. I didn't see that root across the path."

"What root?" Pete spun around to face Mike.

"The root I tripped over, the reason I fell" Mike answered.

"There wasn't no root, I didn't step over a root" Pete seemed to be getting angry.

"Hey man, I'm telling ya I tripped over a root or a log or something." Mike was adamant and getting too loud.

"Shhh, Jesus Christ!" Pete whispered. Even though he whispered so softly a person three feet away couldn't have heard him, Mike understood Pete was really upset.

"I'm telling .." Mike began. Pete covered Mike's mouth with his left hand and raised his rifle with his right. He placed the barrel on Mike's shoulder temporarily until he could get his left hand from Mike's mouth onto the stock of the rifle. He raised the butt to his shoulder and peered through the scope. The scope gathered in what faint moonlight there was filtering through the canopy and outlined a shape moving through the dark. Pete followed the shape as it steadily moved towards them. Mike was terrified, so afraid he was unable to move a muscle. He wanted to turn and face whatever was coming from behind, but he couldn't move.

Pete didn't move, to Mike it didn't even seem as if he was breathing. Mike's heart was pounding in his head and his stomach was tied in knots. He knew he had screwed up, now he was going to pay with his life. What the hell was he doing here! Why did he let Pete talk him into being a Ranger! A sniper! What an asshole! Who the hell is this idiot with a rifle next to me! Mike's mind was in overdrive and he couldn't slow it down. "Damn it Mike! Get a grip! Nobody talked you into anything! You're a goddamn pussy!"

Mike confronted his fears and regained his composure. His breathing slowed and his mind cleared. Pete was still focused on something.

The shape moved quickly and quietly, too quickly and too quietly! Pete knew what it was, but he didn't know exactly what to do about it. He didn't want to say anything to Mike for fear that Mike would freak out and do something stupid. He still needed to find out what or who was in that tree and if he squeezed the trigger any hopes of that were over. Still the shape approached, steadily, silently until it was only about 30 meters from them. Then it stopped and began to look around, sniffing the air as if trying to locate its prey. A breeze had begun blowing from behind and was carrying the scent towards Pete, he could now smell the beast. It was 350 pounds of muscle and teeth, and it had been tracking them by scent until the wind had shifted. They were being hunted by the real lord of the jungle, a tiger! Pete was in awe and terrified at the same time. He watched as the beast struggled to find the scent, it began to circle to the left in an effort to find them. As it moved it continued to sniff the air, but as it moved it actually was getting farther away. Pete watched as it eventually disappeared from view some 300 meters to the west, heading steadily away from them.

The whole process had only taken about five minutes, but it seemed like and eternity to Pete. He was spell bound by the power and grace of the huge beast and by the way it was able to move through the jungle without making a sound. Finally he lowered his weapon and leaned back against the tree trunk.

Mike moved quietly beside him and sat staring out into the darkness. After a couple of minutes he couldn't wait any longer and asked Pete, "Did you see them?"

"There was only one," Pete whispered back.

"Only one, why didn't you shoot him?" Mike asked.

"'Cause I still want to know what is in that tree."

"Maybe that guy was the one in the tree," Mike said.

"Nah, there wasn't enough time for it to get across the clearing, two separate bogies" Pete answered.

Mike had caught the terminology, "what do you mean it?"

"We were being tracked by a tiger," Pete replied calmly.

"A what? A tiger, you gotta be shittin' me!" Mike exclaimed, again too loudly.

"Shhh, damn it Mikey you're gonna get us killed if I don't kill you first myself."

"What's the difference, I'd rather be shot than eaten by a fuckin' tiger," Mike replied.

"Let's move," Pete said as he rolled to his right, "I need to see what's in that tree, before it climbs down and disappears."

The two men worked their way slowly along the edge of the jungle, just far enough inside to be hidden, close enough to the edge to keep track of their target. At 0320 they were directly across the clearing from the target, the tree in which Mike had spotted the strange shape. The clearing was only about 250 meters across at this point, and Pete didn't want to chance crossing so close to the target.

"We'll set up here and wait for light" Pete whispered. "Get some sleep, I'll keep watch."

"I slept a little earlier, I'll take the first watch" Mike answered, "besides, you can't shoot what you can't see."

"Fair enough" Pete replied, "wake me at 0530."

"Now I'm an alarm clock?" Mike cracked.

Chapter 18

Pete grinned and closed his eyes; he was asleep in minutes. He woke up and was sweating; it was hot, real hot. Pete looked around and realized it was nearly noon. Then he realized Mike was no longer next to him. Pete wanted to stand up and look for Mike, but he remembered he was at the edge of the clearing. He very slowly sat up and surveyed the area. The target tree was visible, but the shape they had seen the night before was gone. Pete still couldn't find any sign of Mike, except the faint evidence of a trail leading from Pete's location through the tall grass heading towards the tree across the clearing. Pete was pissed; Mike had gone after the tree dweller alone! "Damn it Mike, we're a team" Pete whispered to himself.

At first Pete thought he was mad because Mike had gone off alone, then he realized he was more upset that Mike would find out what was there before he did. Pete realized how stupid that sounded, and the anger passed. He began moving slowly towards the tree but after Pete had gone 50 meters his anger had turned to fear. What had Mike found and could he handle it? Was he alright? Pete realized how much Mike meant to him, Mike was his best friend. He had never had a real best friend before; at least not one like Mike. Pete began to move faster, then his training kicked in and he slowed back down. "Whatever he found, whether he is fine or not, getting yourself killed won't help him one bit" Pete thought to himself.

It took Pete two hours to cross the clearing crawling most of the way on his belly, his navigation was a little off and he ended up about ten meters north of the tree. He slipped quietly into the jungle and began working his way around the tree keeping approximately 10 meters distance. About two thirds of the way around he came across a fresh track, a single footprint, and the sole was smooth and had veins visible in the impression. "This guy has leaves wrapped around his feet, pretty slick" Pete thought. Just then Pete caught a movement out of the corner of his eye. His movements were smooth but extremely quick, dropping his right knee to the ground and turning to square his shoulders to the target. He snapped his rifle to his shoulder and just as he began to pull the trigger he realized it was Mike.

Mike hadn't seen Pete until he moved, and he didn't even have time to yell "don't shoot." When he realized Pete recognized him, Mike just dropped to his knees and then slumped forward.

Pete was beside himself, first Mike went off alone, and then he almost got himself shot, by Pete no less! Pete covered the 20 meters to Mike in a second and began berating him, albeit in a whisper. Suddenly Pete realized Mike wasn't responding, and Pete flashed back to his dad beside the tractor. "Mike, you alright buddy?"

No answer.

Pete rolled Mike over and began checking for wounds. He couldn't find any at first, but then he opened Mike's shirt and found a gun shot wound under Mike's left arm. He pulled out the small first aid kit from Mike's pack and pressed gauze against the wound, it wasn't bleeding all that much. Pete wondered if that was good or bad, maybe it hadn't hit anything vital, or maybe he's already lost most of his blood. Mike's shirt wasn't that bloody, so Pete chose to be positive. He wrapped a bandage around Mike's chest to hold the gauze in place and keep pressure on the wound.

Pete pulled the radio from Mike's pack and spoke calmly, "Scout this is Shadow, Scout this is Shadow you read?"

"Shadow this is Scout, go ahead"

"I need a Medivac now, over"

"Position?"

"6 clicks North, Northwest of Scout"

"No can do Shadow, proceed to Evac LZ Bravo 2"

"That's three clicks from here! He'll never make it!" Pete screamed into the radio.

The voice came back calm and authoritative, "Proceed to Evac LZ Bravo 2, radio when in position." It was Major Pierce now on the radio.

Pete recognized his voice and his meaning, there was no sense endangering a hilo and its crew to try and save one man. Pete was on his own, and this was one mission in which he could not afford to fail. "Roger Scout, Shadow out," Pete replied. Then he replaced the radio in Mike's pack. He checked the bandages, picked up his rifle and slung the strap over Mike's neck and under his right arm. That way it wouldn't fall off Mike's limp body. Pete picked up Mike's M-16 and stood Mike up as best he could. Pete then slung Mike over his shoulder like a sack of potatoes and headed off towards the evacuation landing zone the Major had given.

Pete was only 5'9" and after three months in the jungle he had shrunk to 150 pounds. Mike was 6' and weighed 190 pounds, of what was now dead weight, it was all Pete could do just to walk. He didn't even try to stay hidden, he just walked, trying not to stumble over tree roots and uneven terrain. Pete was in a daze, he couldn't imagine what would have caused Mike to go off alone. He was walking for hours before he even realized he hadn't checked his direction since starting out. He set Mike down and leaned him against a tree while he checked his bearing. Something moved to his left and Pete swung the M-16 towards the movement. A man dove for cover and the jungle erupted in gunfire. Pete returned fire, then pulled a grenade from his belt and lobbed it towards the enemy. The explosion killed two of the attackers and several others writhed in agony, Pete used the confusion to grab Mike and make a run for it. He left the area with the enemy firing blindly at the position he had just evacuated. He continued on for another 90 minutes before once again lowering Mike to the ground and leaning him against a tree.

This time he took a few minutes to make sure the area was clear and then began studying the map. After getting his bearings he pulled out a candy bar and ate his first food of the day, it was 2230. He drank half of his canteen and poured some in Mike's mouth as well, Pete knew he needed to get Mike out of the jungle fast. He was about 200 meters from the LZ, a clearing on top of a hill, but that 200 meters would be the worst. The hillside was extremely steep and covered with thick vegetation. Pete would need to climb the hill with Mike on his back and in total darkness. He needed to be in position just before dawn, and make sure the area was secure before calling in the Evac. Pete gathered up his gear, lifted Mike onto his shoulder and began the climb.

It was agonizingly slow going, Pete had covered only one hundred meters in the first two hours. He had to pull himself up the hill using trees and vines, several times his feet slid out from under him and both he and Mike tumbled down the hillside. On one of these falls Pete slid down sideways and slammed his ribs into the trunk of a tree, Mike then slammed into Pete crushing his ribs against the tree. Pete gasped for air. He managed to move Mike enough to get himself clear of the tree. He could barely breathe, the pain was staggering. Each breath caused a stabbing pain, trying to cut off whatever air was getting in. Something told Pete to relax and as soon as he did the breaths came more easily; however he still had cracked several ribs, and needed to get Mike up the hill.

He struggled to his feet and found the M16, using it as a prop Pete pulled Mike first up to a seated position, and then standing. Just as Pete was beginning to try and hoist Mike over his shoulder again, he heard someone talking. He looked around, searching for the source of the voice, and finally realized it was Mike!

"I can walk, I can walk," Mike was whispering.

"OK, OK easy hillbilly," Pete was grinning from ear to ear.

"I can walk," Mike continued over and over.

Together the two battered rangers slogged up the hill and collapsed at the top. It was now 0400 and Pete pulled the radio from Mike's pack. "Scout, this is Shadow, over."

"Shadow this Scout, go ahead," came the call back.

"At LZ Bravo 2 requesting Evac ASAP, over"

"Roger Shadow, ETA 1 hour, over" This was code for one hour after sunrise.

"Roger Scout, ETA 1 hour, Shadow out" Pete replaced the radio in Mike's pack and took a quick look at the bandages around Mike's chest.

The wound had begun to bleed badly from all of the effort to climb the hill. Mike had once again lost consciousness and he was having a hard time breathing. Pete was hurting too, but he knew they weren't home free yet. Pete still had to make sure the site was secure enough to land a chopper and get out without getting shot up. He lifted Mike up once more and carried him out into the middle of the clearing, it was pitch dark and Pete was confident they would remain unseen. After placing Mike on his good side and covering him up to keep him warm and to camouflage him from sight, Pete proceeded to check the perimeter. He came across several areas that seemed to have signs of recent activity, each of them had clear views of the landing zone. He first considered possible American patrols waiting for Evac, but then he noticed some scat beside a tree near one site. The scat contained traditional Vietnamese food. While it was possible Americans were eating Vietnamese food while on patrol, it didn't seem likely.

Pete began setting traps for would be attackers. He had to improvise, first he bent a small sapling over and tied a piece of monofilament fishing line to it. The other end of the line was looped around a stick and shoved into the soft earth some 10 meters away. Pete placed a grenade next to the stick with the pin almost all of the way pulled out and tied the end of the fishing line to the pin. When someone ran into the fishing line the stick would pull out of the ground, the sapling would snap back upright pulling the line taught. This would finish pulling the pin on the grenade and activating the trap. When Pete was done setting four of these traps he felt much better joining Mike in the clearing. He lay next to Mike, motionless, invisible for what seemed like an eternity. At 0630 Pete heard the unmistakable sound of a chopper coming in hot from his left, right out of the rising sun. He quietly pulled a thin wire and activated a green smoke grenade, the signal of all clear to the chopper pilot. As the chopper approached the pilot and co-pilot began looking for the patrol.

"I don't see anything, you?"

"No, but we got green smoke,"

"Yea, but who put it off? I don't like this"

Just then the radio cracked to life, " Evac 21, this is Scout, you got them yet?"

"Negative Scout, we have green smoke, but no sign of the patrol."

"Evac 21, they're there, get them the hell out of there."

"Negative Scout, there is no sign of them"

"Damn it Evac 21 they're snipers! You won't see them until you're on the ground! Now get down there and get them! That's an order!"

"Roger Scout, we're going in," the pilot switched off the radio and looked at the co-pilot. He was not happy about the situation, but he swung the chopper around and swooped in low across the clearing. Just then an explosion rocked the jungle off to their right and another to the left, Pete's traps had slowed the enemy's advance. The chopper began to pull up to evacuate the area when the co-pilot spotted Pete.

Pete had sat up and had his rifle trained on a target to the chopper's right. The co-pilot turned to the right just in time to see a VC slump over a heavy machine gun. Pete had shot him before he could get a shot off. He shouted, " There they are", pointing towards Pete.

The pilot still couldn't see Pete because he was once again hidden. The co-pilot guided the pilot in and Pete emerged seemingly out of nowhere before the pilot's eyes. Pete lifted Mike into the chopper, but before he could get in the machine gun on the right was opening up on them.

"Go!Go!" Pete yelled and he dove to the ground. He still had Mike's gun over his shoulder and his own rifle was lying on the ground beside him. But the radio was in Mike's pack, on Mike's back.

Chapter 19

The chopper took off low to the left, taking a few hits but escaping without any major damage. Now, it was Pete's turn. The VC thought they had the advantage, he was alone and out in the middle of an open field. They were dead wrong. Pete was alone and in the middle of an open field, but he was the predator not the prey. The chopper was the focus of the enemy fire giving Pete some time to maneuver. As the hilo made its swing back over the jungle to the left of the clearing, the gunner in the back of the chopper finally had an opportunity to open up on the VC. He laid down a heavy barrage all along the edge of the jungle as the pilot hurried to get out of range of the enemy fire.

Pete used this time to get away from the landing zone, but instead of heading away from the enemy he headed directly towards them. He covered some thirty meters before the chopper had cleared the area. This would have seemed like a suicidal move to most men, but Pete knew that not even the VC would expect it. The gunner on the chopper didn't hit any of the enemy, but his fire gave Pete the break he needed. The clearing was covered in tall grass and low bushes, the grass was nearly chest high and some of the bushes were nearly three meters tall. This provided Pete with plenty of cover to move much faster than normal, in the open snipers may take an hour to move one meter.

When he finally stopped moving and took up his position, he was less than fifty meters from the tree line. The VC patrol had regrouped and began talking heatedly in Vietnamese. It became obvious to Pete that only a few of the soldiers had seen Pete not get on the chopper. They were arguing that the patrol should move into the clearing to capture or kill the American.

The rest of the patrol, as well as the ranking officer had not seen Pete dive to the ground. They were against heading out into the clearing, fearing that the chopper or other U.S. aircraft would catch them out in the open. Pete smiled and thought, "I'm not the only one that likes the thick and nasty."

After several minutes and the persistent endless chatter of the men who had seen Pete, the officer decided to get a closer look. He was confident that if American help were on the way, it would have arrived by now. The enemy patrol fanned out in an arc and began to slowly advance towards Pete's position. This was exactly what Pete had expected them to do, he just hadn't expected the delay.

The enemy were spread approximately five meters apart as they moved through the tall grass. Pete had positioned himself tight against a clump of thorny bushes on the opposite side of the approaching men. As expected the two men closest to Pete's position went on either side of the bushes rather than trying to go through them. They were convinced that they would find the American either wounded or dead right where the chopper had landed. They moved right past Pete and headed slowly towards their target. As they finally came to the spot, one of the men located the place where Mike had been lying. Seeing the blood he was convinced he was correct and that a wounded American was near by.

The officer wasn't so sure, he knew that the chopper had been called in to evacuate wounded. His take on the situation was that the wounded men had been loaded onto the chopper. He remained convinced that no Americans remained in the clearing, they had all gotten on the chopper.

One of the men who had seen Pete drop to the ground noticed something strange. There seemed to be evidence, grass bent the wrong way; that the American had gone toward the east. Directly towards the position they had just come from. Just as he turned to call his commander over for his opinion a bullet ripped through his back, killing him.

Pete had watched the patrol pass and had been content to let them move on by. Then he watched with concern as the soldier discovered his trail. He reacted instantly, rising up from his hiding place and opening up with Mike's M-16. The Patrol was caught completely off guard. Pete's initial volley killed four of the seven men and wounded one. The remaining two men dove for cover, they had no idea where the bullets were coming from. One of the soldiers jumped up and tried to run, in his confusion he ran directly at Pete, reading this as an attack Pete shot him dead.

The last uninjured soldier crawled towards the edge of the clearing. Pete was able to track his movement by watching the grass wave wildly as the soldier moved hurriedly away. Pete was not concerned with him in the least, he was obviously no longer a threat. The rest of the patrol was another matter. Pete knew he had hit most of them, but he wasn't sure how many if any were still alive. So Pete did what he was trained to do, he slipped back into the tall grass and slowly made his way east to the edge of the jungle.

On board the chopper the pilot was reporting what had happened and their ETA to the field hospital. " We've got one wounded, chest wound, corpman's working on 'im. ETA ten minutes, over."

"ME356, roger that, one wounded. We'll have emergency crew waiting at the pad, copy ETA ten minutes."

Another voice came over the radio, "ME356 this is Scout over."

"Scout, ME356, go ahead."

"I read one wounded, status of the rest of the team, over."

"Still on the ground Scout, we were taking fire and had to go."

" That's unacceptable! How long does it take to get one man on board? Damn it ME356, go back and get him!"

"Negative Scout, we're coming home. Man we have won't make it if we turn around."

"Scout to Shadow do you read, Shadow respond!"

"Scout, this is ME356. Your man doesn't have a radio. It's on the wounded guy. I'm afraid he's on his own," the voice came from the gunner on the chopper.

Chapter 20

Major Larry Pierce was furious, he slammed the radio on the table and yelled, "How fucking long does it take for one man to get on a chopper? Son of a bitch!" He turned to his aide Corporal Jones and shouted, " get me the team leaders, NOW!"

Corporal Timothy Jones was not used to seeing Major Pierce angry, in fact he hadn't ever seen the Major this upset before. He hesitated a moment. Then realizing the Major was about to explode again, this time all over him, he sprinted for the door of the tent. In less than two minutes four team leaders, all Lieutenants, were standing in front of the Major's desk. They were all a little nervous, Corporal Jones had told them the Major was, "more pissed than I've ever seen 'im." In the two minutes it had taken them to assemble Pierce had regained his usual cool composure.

"Men, I need volunteers, we have a man alone some ten kilometers from here. He has no radio and a VC patrol is breathing down his neck. I need a team to go out and bring him back. We're Rangers, we leave no man behind."

Lieutenant Mike Roth spoke up first, "How did we get one man stranded out there Sir?"

"He's part of a two man team, the other man was wounded. The wounded man was evacuated ten minutes ago, the chopper was taking fire and couldn't wait." The sarcasm in the Major's voice when he said the last part was obvious.

"Couldn't wait Sir? What the hell? One man and they couldn't wait!" Roth was equally appalled.

"Never mind Lieutenant, we need a team to go get him," the Major replied.

"A two-man team," Lieutenant William "Bones" Bonner was thinking out loud. "Holy shit, that's Shadow!"

"Shadow! Fuck! My team's in Sir," shouted Roth. "They saved my team twice, once when they took out a machine gun nest waiting to ambush us, and last week they popped a sniper who had us pinned down in a fucking rice paddy."

"Sir, I'd like to take my team in as well," replied Bones. "Shadow picked off a sniper that wounded Willy."

The other two Lieutenants offered their teams as well, everyone had great respect for their silent angels. Having a shadow made all the men feel better, and more than once had saved their lives. Major Pierce thanked them all for their willingness to come to the aid of a fellow Ranger. In the end he selected Roth and Bones to each lead their teams in a two-pronged maneuver. They would approach the target area from separate vectors, their orders were to find Shadow and kill any VC they encountered. The Major was ready to take the fight to the enemy.

The two patrols assembled in less than fifteen minutes and at 0655 they headed out in search of the lone soldier they all owed their lives to. Lieutenant Roth's team headed due west, crossed the river near the spot Pete had killed his first sniper. Then they swung northwest towards the evac point. They would have to go to the last known location and hope Pete was there, or at least they hoped to find a clue that would lead them to him. Bones lead his team due north, after several kilometers they would turn west and approach the evac point along the same path the VC patrol had taken to attack Pete.

For his part, Pete wasn't waiting for anyone to come. In fact he didn't even consider the possibility. He was in complete control of his situation and in no way felt any bit uneasy. He made his way slowly through the jungle. Looking for traps and any sign of the enemy. The VC were very skilled at making traps out of sharpened sticks, mines or even using animals as weapons. Pete stayed off of the trails and watched for signs of human activity. He was still focused on two things. First he needed to find the tree dweller and eliminate him before he preyed on any more Americans. Second, he couldn't figure out why Mike would let him sleep and go after the guy alone. Mike wasn't the sharpest tool in the shed, but he wasn't stupid either. He also wasn't sure enough of himself to go after a VC sniper alone. It just didn't make any sense.

Pete found the area where he had found Mike, and began looking for the tracks he had found the day before. Eventually he found the sign, the impressions of leaves being smashed into the ground. He could make out the veins in each leaf; the sniper had wrapped his feet with leaves to cover his tracks. Pete took a minute to locate the direction his prey had taken, once established, the hunt was on. This was what Pete did best, hunt. He followed the tracks north to a point where they abruptly turned to the east. Pete stalked his rival slowly. It would sometimes take him an hour to cover fifty meters. The jungle was extremely thick and he couldn't break cover. He didn't know where the VC sniper was, but he knew he would find him. He had no choice, this man had shot Mike, Pete's best friend. Pete tracked the elusive enemy all day and by dusk had only traveled one thousand meters.

The two American patrols made much better time, covering eight of the ten kilometers to the target area by nightfall. Both patrols radioed the base, no sign of VC or Shadow. Unlike Pete, who continued to move after dark, the two patrols settled in and waited for first light to approach Pete's last known location.

Pete continued his hunt, although moving even slower. He felt he was getting very close, the night was clear and a bright half moon filtered through the jungle canopy. This light was more than enough for Pete to operate. He had become very good at spotting the trail left behind by his target. The slightest hint of a bent leaf or a slight impression on the ground was like a neon sign to the Shadow. This guy was good, but Pete was in a league of his own. By 0330 Pete knew he was nearly on top of the enemy, he slipped under a large fern and allowed himself a little sleep.

He awoke at 0540, it would be light soon and he wanted to be in position before sunrise. He climbed a huge tree he had found before going to sleep. Using large vines that grew up the trunk of the tree as climbing ropes he hoisted himself and his rifle into the tree. Snipers were specifically taught to avoid trees as roosts because if spotted there is no escape, but Pete wasn't interested in escape, only in completing his mission. He had hidden Mike's weapon at the base of the tree, an M-16 was of no use in sniping. He reached an enormous branch a full ten meters off of the ground and lay prone along its girth. He was at the edge of another clearing. This one had several large rice paddies in the center. The paddies were filled with water and tall green shoots sprang from the flooded fields. There were earthen berms along both sides of the clearing and between each of the fields. These held in the water needed to grow rice as well as being used as paths for the villagers who tended the fields.

Pete scanned the clearing and the opposite treeline for his man. This was the enemy's hunting ground for today. A day Pete intended to make the hunter into the prey. No movement yet, but the day had just begun.

Lt. Roth's patrol reached the edge of the clearing known to the Americans as EVAC LZ Bravo 2 at 0630. One day to the minute of when Mike had been air lifted to safety. The American patrol found the remains of four VC where one of Pete's traps had been set.

"Jesus, these poor bastards didn't know what hit 'em," one soldier said.

"One bad assed Ranger, that's what hit 'em," replied another.

"Holy shit!" added Lt. Roth, "I'm glad I'm on their side."

"Man," was all another man had to say, shaking his head and turning away.

They pressed on, keeping to the edge of the jungle. At the site of Pete's second trap all they found was a single bloody shoe. These men were used to seeing carnage, but it never got any easier. After another 100 meters the patrol came across the VC heavy machine gun still pointed out into the clearing. Two Vietnamese soldiers lay dead beside it, each with a single bullet to the head. Pete had shot the second man after diving to the ground below the chopper, allowing it to safely get Mike out of the area.

"Fuck, these guys aren't human! No one shoots that damn good," a soldier said. Then he spat on the ground beside the fallen VC.

"This may be the most amazing thing I've ever seen," added Lt. Roth.

"Hey, LT, over here!" yelled the patrol's point man, Private Mitchell Holt. Mitch was a natural tracker and always wanted to be on point. He was a dyed in the wool soldier, and loved everything about Army life. In short, most of the guys thought he was nuts. But they all admired his courage and relied heavily on his ability to assess a situation. He had continued out into the clearing and located the landing zone.

The rest of the team fanned out and approached the site slowly. They had their weapons against their shoulders, sweeping the area with their eyes. The last thing any of them wanted was to get caught out in the open by an enemy patrol. Once they all arrived at the target area they just stared at the devastation. A total of five enemy soldiers lay dead, gunned down, most hit only once to the head or chest.

A few of the Americans spread out and surveyed the area. Nearby they found the sixth victim, the one who had ran directly toward Pete. Again, he only had been shot once, in the head.

"Holy God, Almighty," whispered Sergeant William "Bud" Jamison. Bud was on his third tour of duty in Vietnam. The rest of the men including Lt. Roth held him in the highest esteem. "Sarge" as they all new him was a true hero having earned a Purple Heart and the Bronze Star for valor.

"Ever seen anything like this before Sarge?" asked Lt. Roth.

"Nossir," answered Bud. "I've never seen nothin' even remotely come close to this,"

"Sarge what happened here?" a soldier asked.

"I have to get a better look around, but my best guess is that someone caught these guys out here completely by surprise."

"Yeah, but who? A chopper maybe, or another one of our patrols?" Asked the Lieutenant.

"Nossir, there ain't a chopper gunner in the world who could shoot like that. They just spray lead everywhere and hope they hit somethin'," Bud answered. " No, this was done by someone with more skill, a marksman."

"You mean a sniper. You're sayin' Shadow did this? One man killed all these men. that's impossible Sarge!" argued Lt. Roth.

"I told you, I ain't never seen nothin' like this before. But you asked me what happened, and I'm tellin' ya what I see. Like I've said before, snipers are weird, they just grow out of the jungle."

"Come on Sarge, there has to be another explanation!" one of the men argued.

"Maybe he can tell us!" yelled a soldier from the edge of the clearing. He was pointing toward a clump of bushes a few meters in front of him.

There, crouched down, was a young VC soldier. He appeared to be at most sixteen years old and scared beyond belief. He was muttering to himself and rocking back and forth. Two Americans moved slowly towards him, fearing he may be wired with explosives, or waiting to throw a grenade. He looked at the Americans and began to cry and babble in Vietnamese.

Lt. Roth brought his South Vietnamese translator over, all patrols had a translator assigned to them, and asked him to translate what the boy was saying.

"I can't really say Sir, he isn't making any sense," said Lt. Trang of the South Vietnamese Army. "He keeps repeating the same thing over and over. Something about a ghost rising out of the ground."

"What'd I tell ya sir? Ghosts. Them damn snipers are ghosts, or at least shadows," replied Sarge.

"Alright Sergeant, secure the prisoner and let's get the hell outta this damn turkey shoot. This place is the last place I want to be if the VC come looking for these guys," ordered Lt. Roth.

"Yessir," answered Sarge. "OK men, lets move, we got anything on Shadow's trail Mitch?"

Mitch had been studying the landing zone and had found some interesting clues. He was pretty sure he now knew what happened, but he still didn't know how. "The way I see it Sarge, after the chopper took off 'ole Shadow moved this way, due east" Mitch began.

"East, no that can't be right Mitch. The enemy patrol and the big gun were both coming from the east," interrupted Lt. Roth.

"First of all he had taken out the machine gun already, and I know it doesn't seem right. But I'm tellin' ya he went east, over to those bushes." Mitch was pointing to the bushes 30 meters away. "He sat and waited for the patrol to pass him by and wham!"

"He didn't want to fight at all though did he Mitch?" added Sarge.

"No, he was content to let them go on by. But this guy here" Mitch said pointing to the one soldier found lying ten meters from the rest, "this guy spotted him and forced his hand."

"You're close Mitch, but I see it a little different. Either way I need a direction and you're saying east, that right?" Sarge asked.

Mitch wanted to know what the veteran sergeant saw differently and began to ask, "Sarge…"

"Mitch, he went east right?" Sarge interrupted.

"Yessir, east," answered the Private. He would have loved to debate Sarge on the merits of his case, but that would have to wait. Sarge wanted to get out of the clearing as soon as possible. As always, Mitch took the point and led the team out of the tall grass and into the dense jungle.

Once safely inside the cover of the jungle, Lieutenant Roth called for the radio. "Scout, this is team five over."

"Team five, this is Scout go ahead."

"We've found the LZ, Shadow has exited the area heading 090. One prisoner, ten dead enemy, awaiting orders."

"Team five, this is Scout. When did you engage the enemy?"

"We didn't sir, the prisoner is a sixteen year old boy. The only survivor of his patrol; keeps muttering about a ghost."

Major Pierce smiled, "damn Lucas you're good," he thought. "Roger team five, come on in. Team three is heading toward your location on vector 270. They should intersect Shadow and bring him in."

"Roger Scout, team five heading in."

Chapter 21

Lt. Bones Bonner had his team at the eastern end of a large rice field. The field was broken into several paddies. He had his men begin to spread out. The intention was to move down either side of the clearing using the earthen berms as cover. Just as the men reached the first barrier a burst of machine gun fire erupted from the opposite end of the field. The American patrol dove for cover behind the mound. They were safe, but they were now pinned down. If they began to move or try to flank the enemy the big gun would rake their position. Pete watched this all unfold, but he couldn't respond, not yet at least.

He knew that the VC sniper was somewhere on the opposite side of the opening. He had to wait for a mistake.

After being pinned down for twenty minutes, Lt. Bonner was ready to move. He ordered several men to provide cover for the rest, using their M-16s to send a hail of bullets towards the enemy. The machine gun at the opposite end answered their fire. Bones led the rest of the men in a flanking move around the northern side of the field. This movement caused the mistake Pete had been waiting for. The enemy sniper adjusted his position to try and get a bead on the advancing Americans. Pete spotted the movement and zeroed in on it. It took several seconds to locate the target in his scope. First, he found the rifle and followed the barrel up to where the shooter's head should be. Only when he got to where the enemy should be all he could see were leaves of a large tree.

Pete used his best estimate as to how far back on the rifle to aim. He didn't know what type of rifle it was, nor what the stock looked like. He simply guessed that the man should be about eight inches back from the point on the gun he could see. Then he drew a breath let it out slowly and fired. The report from Pete's gun was completely lost in the melee that was going on in the field. Pete watched the rifle for signs of movement. He chambered another round, but before he could fire he saw the rifle slide slowly off the tree branch and fall to the ground. After seeing the weapon fall, Pete turned his attention back to the field.

Lt. Bonner had his team nearly half way down the North side, the enemy had several men hiding behind a berm just twenty meters ahead of the Americans. Pete was amazed to see that most of the Americans didn't have their automatic weapons with them. They had left them behind for the men providing cover. Instead they had all drawn their sidearms, 45 caliber pistols. Pete wasn't sure how to respond. He wanted to fire on the enemy closest to the patrol, but he didn't have a real clear shot at any of them. There was a large tree blocking most of his firing lane. Instead he decided to do something more risky. He took careful aim and fired.

Lt. Bonner was moving very slowly along the side of the mound, trying to keep his head below the apex so that it wouldn't be exposed to the enemy. He was leaning against the muddy wall of the paddy, his head just inches from the wet ground. Suddenly the ground directly in front of his face exploded, covering his face with mud. He froze, as did the rest of his team.

"Where the hell did that come from?" one of the men whispered.

"Lt. Bonner slowly raised his hand to quiet his men. He was looking up into the trees some distance away. He spotted a slight movement. Raising his field glasses to his eyes he nearly fainted, he could see Pete and recognized the hand signals. Pete was warning him of the men directly in front of his position, using his arm as the mound Pete clearly showed Bones where the men were. Then he watched as Pete laid back down on the branch and took aim.

Bones wasn't sure what Pete was aiming at now, but he was sure it wasn't at the men in front of his position. The lieutenant gathered his men and prepared his assault. If the machine gun wasn't there it would be easy. They would simply rush the enemy, over the mound and take them by surprise. But with the big gun taking that option away things got more dicey.

Pete recognized the lieutenant's situation and began correcting it, he took his time and made sure he had his target locked. He couldn't get a good shot at either of the men manning the machine gun, but he had a perfect shot at the gun itself. He once again took a slow breath, let it out and fired. The 7.62MM slug slammed into the mechanism feeding the Russian gun, destroying it. The shrapnel from the impact wounded one of the men operating the gun and the other soldier dove for cover. The big gun was out of commission.

It only took a minute for Bones to realize that the machine gun wasn't firing anymore. He calculated that Pete had taken care of his main concern, now he needed to act quickly. The lieutenant gave the signal and his entire advance team rushed the enemy position. The VC were trying to regroup themselves, they had lost their cover fire and didn't know why. Suddenly eight Army Rangers stormed over the top of the barrier, killing three of the enemy and taking the other four prisoner. The three Rangers who had been providing cover fire, rushed up the South side of the field and met up with the rest of the patrol. They had used most of the team's ammunition and were getting worried. The few remaining enemy soldiers fled the area taking the wounded machine gunner with them. Lt. Bonner ordered the men to follow him, and he led them to the area where he had seen Pete. To his surprise, Pete was no longer in the tree.

Having realized the threat was over, Pete had begun working his way to the other side to find his real target.

Bones called for the radio and a soldier produced it quickly. "Scout, this is team three over."

"Team three, this is Scout go ahead."

"We have neutralized a VC patrol, 5 enemy dead, four prisoners. Sighted Shadow earlier but no sign now. Over."

"Return to base team three, Shadow is obviously not in need of assistance. Scout out."

"Roger Scout, team three coming in," Bones placed the radio back in the soldier's pack and shook his head.

"Well boys, we came out to rescue Shadow, and he rescued us. Lets get moving, we can make the fire base by nightfall if we don't run into any more Charlie," Bones said.

"What do you mean, Shadow rescued us Lt?" One of the soldiers who had been providing cover fire asked.

"You don't really think you guys took out that gun, do ya Leon?" asked Bones.

"I don't know, you think it was Shadow?"

"I know it was buddy, I saw 'im. He was in this tree and nearly blew my head off over there," Bones pointed to the mound where his team had been positioned.

"He shot at you sir? Why the hell would he do that?" asked another soldier.

"To get my attention Rick, and he got it alright. Then he told me about these guys here being on the other side of the barrier," the lieutenant said pointing at the prisoners. "I saw him taking aim at something down towards that damn gun, so I figure he took care of that as well. Now let's move before Charlie comes back with more of his friends."

Chapter 22

The two teams made their way back to Firebase Scout, leaving Pete to his business. The clearing was eerily quiet after the firefight, it would be hours before the villagers would dare to venture out to their fields to check their crops. Pete made his way around the Western edge of the clearing, checking the gun position to make sure no-one was hiding there to ambush the Americans. He pressed on, his movement painfully slow to avoid detection. It was nightfall before Pete arrived at the edge of the jungle on the South side of the clearing. He slipped into the thick

vegetation and felt relief, he could move more freely now. The

sky had filled with clouds and it began to rain lightly.

Pete needed to know for sure that the VC sniper was no

longer a threat. He slowly approached the area where he had seen

the rifle fall from the tree. It took him several hours to find the

exact spot, in the dark the jungle took on a menacing appearance.

He stepped slowly and then felt something strange under his

boot. He was standing on something metal. At first he was

paralyzed by fear, the feeling of metal beneath his boot sent

shock waves of panic through him. In his mind all he could

envision was a mine, a life altering if not ending mine. He slowly

knelt down, keeping his weight firmly on his left foot. Any loss

of pressure on the detonator and he was dead. He reached down

with his left hand and almost fainted at the touch of the rifle's

sights. Pete immediately rolled onto his back and pointed Mike's

M-16 into the tree. There, about five meters off of the ground, on

a large branch lay a very thin Vietnamese man in a hand made

camo suit. He was staring blankly at the ground. A small wound

was evident on the left side of his neck. Pete had been slightly

off in his calculation, and had hit the sniper in the left side of his neck. The bullet had passed through the man, cutting his windpipe and making it impossible for him to even scream for help.

Pete grabbed the rifle, hoping to have a chance later to examine it. He slung it over his left shoulder, next to his own and carried the M-16 at the ready. For the next twenty-four hours Pete was a Ranger first, sniper second. He needed to get back to the firebase. He was almost out of food and water and the ribs he had cracked while carrying Mike were threatening to mutiny if he didn't get some rest. Pete used his sense of direction and made tracks straight for the base. He traveled much more quickly than he would have under normal conditions. The thought was that the men manning the machine gun would have reached their base and a new patrol, possibly much larger would be heading toward Pete. He needed to make time, there would be other opportunities to hunt, but only if he got out of the way of the stampede.

Chapter 23

The two Vietnamese soldiers who had escaped the battle

in the rice paddies reached a village some three kilometers north

of the rice fields, at the western edge of the village was a small

hooch, inside the hooch was a trap door. The door led to a tunnel

that took the men several hundred meters to another door.

Beyond that door lay the base, a full brigade of North

Vietnamese soldiers had gathered here to begin an assault on

American positions to the south. The wounded man was treated by two women using bandages and herbal tea and local medicine. The metal fragments from the gun and Pete's bullet had cost the man his right eye and left several lacerations on his face. The uninjured soldier was debriefed by General Lim Tok and two of his Colonels.

"What has happened to your men?" asked the General.

"We set up an ambush outside of Men Soh, we were in position when an American patrol entered our trap" answered the soldier. "We had them pinned down in the rice field, and Li Bot was going to shoot them like fish in a pool."

"I ask you again, where are your men?" the General's tone was more agitated now.

"Killed or captured by the Americans sir, I don't know what happened. Just when Li Bot was supposed to start firing, I watched his rifle fall to the ground. Then the machine gun that Hu was using to keep the Americans pinned down just exploded. He was hit in the face with shrapnel. I helped him up and saw the Americans rush my men who had gone forward to attack the Americans. They knew exactly where my men were. They are using spirits to see behind barriers and kill our snipers and destroy our big guns." The soldier was nearly hysterical, and kept blabbering on about shadows and spirits.

The General dismissed him and turned to his two deputies, "We need to know what the Americans are up to, this spirit or whatever has cost us men and time. Radio Colonel Poh and see if he has any news of this American new weapon."

"Yessir!" replied both men in unison.

Colonel Li Poh was a ruthless, cutthroat, evil, deceitful and absolutely brilliant man. He ran a detention center for American POWs just inside North Vietnam. He used a unique method of gaining information from his prisoners. He would dress as an average soldier and hang out near a special cell (a metal cage ten feet square and four feet high) reserved for new arrivals. He made no attempt to speak to the prisoners and if they asked him for anything he feigned ignorance of English even though he had graduated from the University of California Irvine just ten years earlier. After several days in the cell the men would feel comfortable enough that Poh couldn't understand anything they said. The prisoners would begin talking amongst themselves. Planning escapes, which never would happen, and discussing other things Poh found much more interesting. He made it a point to put men from different units together hoping for information about American forces such as troop strength and locations of bases.

He had received General Tok's inquiry and was curious himself. He had not heard any of his prisoners mention anything about a so called spirit or new weapon that could see through or around barriers. He had one prisoner that might know, but he hadn't even gotten the man's name rank and serial number from him over the two plus years he had been here. All he got was "hammer". Colonel Poh had been amazed when the prisoner had immediately identified Poh as an officer and never accepted his inability to speak English. If anyone here knew about this weapon it would be him.

"Good morning Hammer, how are you today?" Poh asked as nicely as he could manage.

Hammer just stared back at Poh, he didn't even seem to acknowledge his presence.

"I know you can hear me, and I know you want to go home," Poh said with feigned tenderness. "I can arrange for you to go home if you help me with a small problem I have."

Hammer didn't even blink.

"I am hearing word of a weapon system or spirit, a sort of ghost, helping the American patrols. This person or weapon can see through or around barriers. All I need from you is a name of a person or a weapon system and you can go home. I speak true, you have my word." Poh was really trying to sound sincere.

"Hammer!" shouted the prisoner, surprising Poh with the power of his voice.

Poh recovered from the initial shock and thrust a bamboo staff through the metal bars of Hammer's cage. The bamboo slammed into Hammer's midsection knocking the wind out of him. He would have fallen over if he wasn't already on his knees because the cell was so short he couldn't stand up. Colonel Poh was now sure, with this outburst, that Hammer knew something. The prisoner hadn't even spoken for almost six months until just now. Poh had Hammer removed from his cage and began trying to get the information he needed.

First he tried a soft approach, allowing Hammer to bathe and shave. Followed that by giving him a good meal of pork and rice. He told Hammer that if he just gave him the information he needed, he would be treated this way at all times and arrangements would be made to send him home. Hammer ate the meal, bathed and shaved and never even made eye contact with Poh. He simply limped back to his cage and waited for the door to be opened. As he began to climb in, Poh smashed his bamboo staff across Hammer's lower back. The pain was incredible, but Hammer kept moving, trying to get into the cage. Poh again slammed him with the bamboo, this time hitting him on his right leg just below the knee. Hammer heard the bone break and the ensuing pain coupled with the pain from the first hit overwhelmed him. He blacked out momentarily, when he came to he was lying on the floor of his cage. His leg twisted in an abnormal position. The entire camp shuddered at his scream when he wrenched it back into place.

Colonel Poh smiled at the sound, he would break this Hammer and get what he needed. The General was well connected and if Poh could deliver the goods, he would be rewarded handsomely. Poh had a few other tricks up his sleeve, and he would use every last one if necessary. Tomorrow was another day.

Chapter 24

Mike Moore had arrived at the field hospital in bad

shape, the bullet had punctured a lung. Fortunately, it hadn't hit

any other vital organs, and for the most part it hadn't bled nearly

as much as it should have. He was stabilized and moved to a

hospital in Saigon. After several hours of surgery where a large

section of his left lung was removed due to the damage the

sniper's bullet had caused, he was in recovery when he awoke to

a pretty blonde nurse wiping his brow.

"Where am I?" he asked.

"Saigon, you're doing great," answered the nurse. "I'm Jeanie, and you've been through a lot in the last day or two Private. So relax and take it easy, the other nurses and I will come by and check on you periodically."

"Pete! Where's Pete!" yelled Mike.

"I don't know private, you came in with a couple other GI's from the field hospital in Leim. What's Pete's last name?"

"Lucas, Private Peter Lucas," Mike whispered as he slipped back into a stupor.

He awoke again an hour later, this time he felt a searing pain in his chest. He was gasping for breath, and waving his right arm. A nurse reacted immediately, calling for help and rushing to his bed. She helped him to relax and began checking his vitals. A doctor arrived and asked the nurse what had happened.

"He was gasping for breath and flailing his arm around, his BP and heart rate are high but not through the roof."

"OK private, what are you feeling?" asked the doctor.

"Where's Pete? Private Peter Lucas, where is he sir?" Mike asked.

"I haven't treated a Private Lucas today son, says here on your chart that Jeanie couldn't find him anywhere here at the hospital. How are you doing son?"

"I gotta find Pete, he saved my life! The tree dweller. I saw him and instead of just callin' for Pete I turned my head to get him. I screwed up and the tree dweller hit me." Mike was rambling on and the doctor could not make anything of what he was saying. "Pete, gotta move so he won't find Pete. If I get him movin' Pete'll get 'im."

The doctor gave Mike some more sedative and the wounded soldier gave in to sleep quickly. A note was added to Mike's chart saying that he needed a psych evaluation. The doctor wasn't sure what Mike was talking about, but he decided to try and find Pete. He was able to get Mike's unit from his records and radioed the firebase.

"Have you guys got a Private Peter Lucas there?" asked the doctor.

"He's out on patrol sir, what do you want with him doctor?"

"I've got a patient, Private Michael Moore. Keeps asking for him, saying something about a tree dweller. It's pretty weird, but this Private Lucas, he's OK?"

"As far as I know sir, he's a sniper and Moore was his spotter. They came under enemy fire, Moore was hit and Lucas hauled him 3 clicks to an LZ. You need to let Private Moore know Lucas isn't a Private any more, he's being promoted to Sergeant and if I have anything to do with it he'll receive every damn medal this Army has to offer," added Major Pierce.

"I'll let him know Major, by the way Private Moore is gonna be fine at least physically anyway," the doctor replied.

"Roger that Doc, I'll let the men know. Tell Private Moore I'll see him soon back at Campbell. Scout out."

The men were relieved to hear that one of their own had made it back from the dead. The company had taken more casualties than it cared to admit, and their tour had another seven months to go. The stories of the Shadow were all around the camp, growing to ridiculous proportions as they were embellished each time they were told. The written reports filed by Lieutenants Roth and Bonner were hard enough to believe, let alone the wild tales being told by men who weren't even there.

At 0430 on July 18th, Pete's 19th birthday he slipped quietly into camp. The sentries on duty didn't even see him. He quietly slipped off his camo suit and headed to the showers. The cold water revived him for a moment, and made him feel alive. He had spent six days in the jungle, the last three alone and he had loved it. He dressed quickly and went to the communications tent, there he found Corporal Jones listening to the Rolling Stones. Jones nearly had a heart attack when Pete walked through the door.

"Where did you come from? Does the Major know you're back? Where have you been? We've been lookin' for you everywhere!" the Corporal was talking a mile a minute.

"How's Mikey?" Pete asked when Jones took a breath. Pete quickly realized he hadn't been proper and corrected himself, "I mean how is Private Moore sir?" he asked while saluting the officer.

Corporal Jones quickly returned the salute and caught his breath. "Private Moore is going to be OK, he had a collapsed lung and some internal injuries, but they patched him up down in Saigon. He'll probably ship out to the states later this week."

"Thank you sir, I need to get some sleep. If the Major needs me I'll be in my bunk," replied Pete. He turned on his heel and slipped out the door. The corporal realized that he didn't even hear him leave.

"No sound, amazing, he didn't make any sound," Jones said to himself.

Pete slipped into his tent and found his bunk in the dark. He rolled into it and fell asleep instantly, he slept for twelve straight hours. When he awoke, he straightened his bunk gathered his gear and headed for the Major's tent.

He knocked on the door and heard the familiar, "Enter!" from within.

"Private Lucas reporting for duty Sir!" Pete stood at attention before Major Pierce.

"At ease soldier, I would like a full report as soon as you can get me one understand."

"Sir, yes sir,"

"I have heard remarkable things from some of the men, your fame is growing Pete," the Major added.

"Fame sir?" Pete questioned.

"Yes fame son, you wiped out an entire enemy patrol single handedly. You took out a machine gun and alerted a Lieutenant to an ambush. These are pretty famous stories here at our little outpost in the jungle."

"There was one survivor of the patrol sir, a boy and I took out the gun not the men operating it sir. They escaped and will probably be returning with more men." Pete was noticeably upset with himself.

"Pete, what you did was courageous, but you're a sniper. You can't chance being seen. Private Moore is proof of what happens if you get exposed!"

"I don't know what happened to Mike, I was asleep, when I got up Mike was gone. The tree dweller was gone too, so I went looking for Mike..." Pete was rambling.

"Wait a minute, tree dweller?"

"Mike saw something in a tree the night before he was shot. We couldn't get into position before dark, so we settled in and waited for first light. Mike was supposed to wake me just before dawn. I woke up around noon and Mike was gone. By the time I found him he had been shot." Pete had his wits about him again and was speaking slower.

"That's what Mike was talking about, he was rambling on about a tree dweller and getting hit because he turned his head instead of just getting your attention by calling to you."

"So he got hit right next to me, and I didn't know?" Pete felt even worse.

"Yeah, he said he didn't want the guy to find you, so he moved towards the guy to flush him out. He figured if he got the guy moving, you'd get him."

"I did, but not until the firefight in the rice paddies," Pete said flatly.

Major Pierce was in awe, and a little uncomfortable. This young man in front of him had killed nearly two dozen men and it didn't even seem to affect him. He had just turned nineteen today and yet he seemed as old as the jungle itself.

"Get something to eat Pete, or should I say Sergeant Lucas," the Major said smiling.

Pete looked at the Major confused, "Sergeant, sir? I don't understand."

"Hey, don't look a gift horse in the mouth son, pay's a little better, not much, but every little bit helps."

"Thank you sir," Pete said quietly.

"It'll be official when we get back to Saigon, we don't do ceremonies out here," Pierce added.

"Understood sir," Pete said, saluted and turned to leave.

"Sergeant, after you eat see me for your next assignment."

"Yessir," Pete replied as he exited the tent.

Pete crossed the yard and entered the mess tent, as he did everyone inside stopped talking and looked at him. He was the smallest man there, yet everyone knew he was a real hero. Everyone except Pete, he didn't know what to make of the men's reaction. Lieutenant Bones Bonner stood up, walked over to Pete and saluted. Pete saluted and then Bones shook Pete's hand and said, "It's an honor to serve with you Shadow."

Pete was floored, he didn't know what to say so he didn't say anything. He just shook the lieutenant's hand and nodded. Bones returned to his seat and Pete walked slowly to the chow line. He hadn't eaten real food in a week, and he wasn't sure he wanted to start now. He managed to eat some bread, potatoes and a bowl of noodles. His stomach had shrunk so much that it was all he could do to force the food down. He drank milk and a glass of juice, but the juice didn't compare to the fresh stuff he had picked himself in the jungle. Pete had changed since the first time he entered the jungle, he was more in tune to nature. He could find food everywhere, fruits, plants and even wild peppers were all around. He had been trained to survive. He would slip into a village and grab some rice without being seen, he could eat insects and other animals if necessary. He knew he needed good food to be strong, but he found it less and less appetizing.

Chapter 25

After eating Pete returned to Major Pierce's tent. He knocked and once again heard, "Enter" from inside. The Major had a map sprawled across his desk and he was bent over it and talking to Corporal Jones. He turned a saw Pete standing just inside the door. "Come on over Pete," he said. " Tim and I have been pouring over this map, seems we have a slight problem."

"What's that sir?" Asked Pete.

"We are being targeted by the VC from just across the border, they are moving more and more men and material into position. I need intel. I also need to slow them down a bit. If we could remove a few of their commanders, especially a few specific Generals, that might do the trick."

"You want me to enter North Vietnam, hunt down generals in the North Vietnamese Army and kill them, that right?"

"Yes, that's correct. Only one problem, we're not supposed to be in North Vietnam. So if you get caught...."

"I'm on my own," Pete finished the Major's sentence.

"Exactly. So you in?" Pierce asked, already knowing the answer.

"Yeah, I'm in. As long as I get to go alone" Pete replied.

"Wait a minute soldier, I can't send you in without a spotter. What if you get in trouble?" the Major shot back.

"Then you'd have two men in trouble instead of one, besides Mike is on his way home and unless I miss my guess this needs to happen ASAP." Pete argued.

"These men are all Rangers son, any one of them can act as your spotter," Corporal Jones replied.

"No sir, Mike went through sniper school and he was exposed by a sniper. These guys are the best in the world at what they do, but they don't do what I do, Sir" Pete answered.

"Very well Sergeant, you've made your point," Pierce said. "Here's a list of the officers we need eliminated for this thing to work." He handed Pete a small notebook. "There are bio's and pictures of each of them. Our latest intel says that a full division of VC are massing here, Pierce pointed to a town just seven kilometers north of the border. Their leadership will be nearby, but were hearing about a huge tunnel complex. If the Generals are in the tunnels, you may not get a chance at them."

"They have to come out sooner or later sir," Pete stated.

"I don't know, they may just run the entire offensive from underground" the Major said.

The strategy session went on for an hour, Pete listened to the Major and his aide detail what they knew about the area. He then borrowed the map and returned to his bunk. He spent several more hours committing locations and names to memory. He would carry the map with him, just in case, but opening a large map in the jungle was equivalent to lighting a signal fire. Pete would only open it as a last resort. He went to the quartermaster and obtained as many rations as he could carry, along with ammo and some other goodies; a couple of anti-personnel mines and four grenades.

He also took a small crate into the jungle outside the razor wire and buried it, placing supplies into it so he could access them without having to enter the camp if necessary. He covered the lid with leaves, grass and other debris. Before heading out he sat down and wrote letters to Missy and his mom.

In the letter to Missy he asked her to check on Mike, and to make sure Mike's parents were given all the support they needed. He assured her he was fine and that he would write again as soon as he could, but he didn't know for sure how long that might be. The letter to Joy was very different. He told her about Mike and asked her to contact his parents and let them know how much honor Pete felt having served with their son. He was more honest with his mom, writing "I feel at home here, the jungle is alive and I feed off its energy. The wildlife is amazing, I even saw a tiger recently. The patrols are only three or four days long and I spend most of my time sitting or laying in one place. It is hot though, real hot and the bugs can bother you if you let them."

He never mentioned any fighting and of course didn't write anything about his new mission.

At 0330 the next morning Pete slipped out of camp, unnoticed as usual and began his mission alone. He felt so alive he had to slow himself down at times. He moved silently but quickly through the jungle. Keeping to the densest forest, he managed to cover nearly five kilometers the first day alone. For a sniper that was equal to running a four-minute mile.

General Tok was pacing in a side tunnel that he used as his office, the delay caused by the failure of the last two patrols was driving him crazy. "We need to reduce the American patrols, as long as they operate far from their base we cannot get our people close enough to strike! The ambushes were supposed to cripple the Americans, instead they have delayed my offensive."

"I'm afraid I have more disturbing news General," added an aide who had just entered the room. "Your son Liu was a member of the patrol destroyed by the Americans at Kon Djirang, we recovered all of the bodies except Liu's. He is missing, either captured or … missing sir."

"Very well Li, tell Colonel Poh I need information NOW!" General Tok did his best to hide the fear and anger he felt. Liu was his only son, just sixteen years old. The boy had joined the North's army against his father's wishes, saying he needed to prove to his father he was worthy of his name. The General turned to the earthen wall of his dark office and lowered his head. He thought about Colonel Poh and his prisoners, and an idea came to him. He summoned another aide and gave him a written message, with instructions to deliver the message to the commanding officer at the American base.

The message was given to a local villager, a woman, who frequently went to the base to sell rice and local fruit. She gave the message to Major Pierce and waited for a reply. Pierce opened the note and read:

Commander,

I would like to offer an exchange of prisoners, I have two American POWs and you have five of my men. Please respond quickly, my prisoners will be moved soon.

General Liu Tok

Peoples Army

Major Pierce was taken aback, two Americans for five VC. That was a very attractive offer, too attractive it would seem. He needed to call his CO and get direction on this. He asked the woman to wait, and crossed the compound to the communication tent. He raised his CO on the radio and read him the offer. Then he expressed his concerns. "Either these guys aren't what they appear, or they have info very valuable to Charlie."

"Agreed Major, I need to take this to HQ. I would recommend you get busy interrogating your prisoners, I can't see HQ passing on two American POWs. I think they would jump at a 20 for two swap," came the reply.

Major Pierce crossed back to his tent and handed the woman a message to be carried back to General Tok. It read:

General Tok,

We need to know the names of these two prisoners. After verifying that they are indeed American, a time and place can be arranged for the transfer.

Major Lawrence Pierce

The South Vietnamese interrogators used by the US Army were brutal and at the same time inefficient. They only managed to get the location of a single tunnel entrance from the prisoners. They did not even interrogate Liu Tok, saying he was too young and emotionally damaged to be of any value.

General Tok was pleased with the American response, he contacted Colonel Poh directly and said, " Poh, I need a list of the American prisoners you have at once. Also, what have you learned about the enemy from your interrogations?"

"A list sir, what need do you have for a list?" Poh dared to ask.

"Colonel, you do not question my authority. I need the list and information about this weapon," the General was stern in his tone.

Poh realized his error and replied quickly, "sir, I will provide the list immediately. I have been interrogating a prisoner that I think has the information you desire."

"How long have you held this American?" the general asked.

"About two years sir, he has only spoken one word since being captured, "hammer". I am sure he is keeping secrets sir" Poh responded.

"Two years! Poh this spirit thing is new! How could anyone in your prison for two years have any new information!" the General was furious. "Get me a list, this "Hammer" will be one name, I need a second."

"A second sir?" Poh asked meekly.

"There is to be a prisoner swap, I told the Americans I have two American POWs to trade for my men. This "Hammer", who is obviously of no use to us will be one of them. Choose a second, make it an officer, I need someone with value to make it irresistible for the Americans."

"But sir, I know Hammer has information." Poh pleaded.

"Nonsense! Get me another name and information about this spirit or whatever it is, NOW Poh!" The general shouted and slammed down the receiver.

Major Pierce nearly screamed when he read the names, Air Force Captain William Paul and Hammer! He held his composure just long enough to reply to the note with a time and place for the transfer. The woman exited the camp and Major

Pierce shouted, "Son of a Bitch! Hammer! Thank God!"

Chapter 26

The two American POWs were blindfolded and placed in

a truck, they had been told they were going home. Both of them

assumed that they were actually being taken somewhere to be

killed or tortured. Hammer's shattered leg was infected and hung

loosely blow his knee. The men rode for hours in the truck, along

rough roads that jarred their teeth and sent shock waves of pain

through their tortured bodies. Finally, they stopped and several men lifted them from the truck and set them on the ground. Captain Paul was able to stand and walk unassisted, Hammer could stand only by leaning on the Captain.

Two days after receiving the names, at a bridge separating North and South Vietnam, Major Larry Pierce stood on the South side with half of his company deployed along the river. An equal number of North Vietnamese faced them from the opposite side.

General Tok stood beside the two battered Americans, he turned to them and said in English, "gentlemen, its time to go home."

As they started across the bridge with Captain Paul aiding Hammer, five VC soldiers left the south side and headed toward them. They passed each other, neither group saying anything and continued to their comrades. The VC soldiers reached the other side first, and the Americans were worried that the enemy might shoot the POWs on the bridge. General Tok however was an honorable man and simply loaded his men onto the truck and headed north into the jungle.

One of Pierce's men, Sergeant Bud Jamison rushed onto the bridge, hoisted Hammer onto his shoulder and carried him back to the Major. As he set him down, he couldn't believe his eyes, "Tony?"

"Sarge! Man am I glad to see you!"

"Soldier, where the hell have you been?" asked Pierce jokingly.

Tony saluted, then said "Sergeant Tony Lucas reporting for duty sir!"

"Welcome back son, we'll talk later. Let's get these men outta here boys! Captain, I'm Major Laurence Pierce 101st airborne." Pierce said to Captain Paul. "I've notified the Air Force, they'll have someone waiting for you at the field hospital in Liem. A chopper will be waiting for you at our base, we'll get you the hell outta this God forsaken jungle ASAP."

As the men of the 101st slowly backed away from the bridge and headed for their base, a silent figure was crossing the same river just three kilometers to the west. The Shadow had arrived in North Vietnam.

Mike Moore arrived at Fitsimmons Army Hospital in Colorado and was treated with care. He was soon able to walk and it was now clear to the doctors that he would make a full recovery. His parents drove to Colorado to see him. It was a joyous reunion, one the hospital staff was grateful to see for there had been many more sad homecomings than happy ones. Mike's dad, Jack had kept his beloved Roadrunner in perfect condition. Mike was happy, but he couldn't help worrying about his buddy. Pete was still in the thick and nasty. Major Pierce had let Mike know Pete had taken care of the "tree dweller" and that he had made it back to base unharmed. Mike sat up in his bed, with his family all around him. A Purple Heart hung from his uniform, it would soon be joined by a Bronze Star. But Mike wasn't interested in staying in the Army, he was ready to go home.

Back at Fort Campbell, Missy was a wreck. She had processed Mike's Purple Heart medal and his pending Bronze Star. She had also processed Pete's rank advancement to Sergeant, a little tidbit he had left out of his last letter. She had also heard, in the words of Colonel Morgan, "he's been nominated for every damn medal the Army has to offer." Meaning he had been in some real fighting and not even mentioned it to her. She knew he was trying to protect her, but didn't he think she would find out? She was Colonel Morgan's aide for crying out loud!

An urgent communication came in for Colonel Morgan, when he read it he shouted "Hammer! Holy shit, Hammer!"

Missy ran to the Colonel's door, "Sir? You alright sir?"

"Missy, they got Hammer! Sonofabitch! I can't believe it!"

"Hammer, sir?" Missy was at a loss.

"I'm sorry Missy, he was here before you. Hammer was his call sign. He's a sniper, Sergeant Tony Lucas," the Colonel replied.

"Tony! Oh my God Tony! When, where, I need to call Joy!" Missy cried.

"Whoa! Missy how do you know Tony and Mrs. Lucas? He was in Vietnam before you started here."

"I've kinda been seeing Pete, sir." Missy admitted.

"That's against the rules young lady," Colonel Morgan replied. But he was too happy from hearing about Tony to make a big deal about it now. "Nevermind, not a word to Mrs. Lucas you hear me. There is a formal method for notifying family. Understand?"

"Understood sir, does Pete know sir?"

"I don't know, he's on a mission at this time," the Colonel answered. "Besides, you're not supposed to be involved remember?"

"Understood sir, I'll be at my desk if you need me." Missy said and walked back out into the outer office. "Tony is alive, Pete will be thrilled," she thought. But the part about Pete being on a mission worried her, Mike was in the hospital in Colorado. Who was with Pete?

Pete was alone, but completely focused. He was hunting again, and this time he had specific targets. It was a twist on the original game plan and Pete loved a challenge. The prisoners Bones had captured gave him a starting point, a single tunnel entrance in a hooch on the edge of a small village. Pete was on his way there when a strange sound caught his attention. It was a vehicle, a truck or something heavy, and it was close. Pete worked his way closer and found a new road had been cut through the jungle. The truck he had heard was now some 300 meters west and moving away, but there were dozens of North Vietnamese troops walking down the road. Most were just walking not paying any attention, but a few were scanning the jungle for movement. Pete watched them pass by and then followed them. He stayed well back, sometimes completely out of visual range of the retreating army.

Pete knew that sometimes commanders would leave a few men lagging well behind the main force to act as a buffer. He was not at all interested in running into even a few VC, his mission was clear. Gather intel on troop strength and movements, and kill the officers on his list. He would be a true sniper now, one shot, one kill. He had to do this the right way, to be caught inside North Vietnam was not an option. He managed to sneak to within earshot of the main encampment. In doing so he gathered data on the number of men, guns, trucks and other material in the camp. The hooch from the intel was at the far western edge of this new camp, disguised as a village. The jungle canopy hid most of the camp from view from the air, but the new road should be very visible. Pete noticed the road continued on past the camp heading northwest.

General Tok had brought the prisoners back to the camp, and taken his young son down into the tunnels. In his office, he hugged Liu and asked him about his captors. "How many men at the camp Liu? I need you to draw the camp, where things are, what defenses they have."

But Liu was still in shock, he had never seen men killed, all of his comrades gunned down by a ghost who rose out of the ground. He could not help his father, he was an emotional mess. He simply muttered over and over, "a ghost, they use a ghost. It killed all of the men in my unit, rising out of the ground, it had black eyes and spat fire."

General Tok was disgusted, he had his son back but what good was that if he was a mental patient. "Take him away, and get me Colonel Poh. I need information."

Colonel Poh had news that the General found more interesting, "Shadow is a sniper unit sir, a helicopter pilot we recently captured revealed this information. Apparently this particular sniper unit is considered very highly by the Americans."

"They should be Poh, they have cost us much in men and time. Good work Poh," the General replied and put down the receiver.

"Snipers will not stop our offensive," Tok told his aide. "Assemble the men, we will begin our move tonight."

"Will we not wait for General Deng sir?" asked the aide.

"No, he will catch up. His men are not carrying any heavy guns," the general answered.

Pete had moved back away from the camp to a location some 700 meters from the hooch. He used a small notebook to draw the camp and document men and materials. He then pulled out the notebook he had been given containing his targets. The first page was on a General Deng, he was highly thought of by the American intelligence agencies. His leadership and military mind were both highly regarded, thus he made a formidable opponent. The second page was on General Tok, he was considered more of a renegade, less conventional and thus very dangerous. According to the bio, Pete was looking at his troops and forward operating base and for this reason he instantly became Pete's primary target.

At 2300 the camp Pete had been watching began to come alive, by 2330 the division began moving out. "Holy shit, their going to attack!" Pete thought. His first instinct was to try and warn Scout, but then he took a deep breath and relaxed a little. This many men would not travel quickly, he had some time. "Time to find General Tok and ruin his night," Pete smiled to himself. There was very little light and Pete had a difficult time picking out any target, let alone one man in an entire division. The enemy began to move along the new road, heading southeast. They used a few trucks and carts to haul the big guns and extra ammo, however; most of the men traveled by foot. Pete watched intently, trying to spot the General amongst the throng. As the huge numbers of men slowly dwindled to a hundred or so, an old Renault staff car pulled up outside of the tunnel entrance.

"Of course, a General wouldn't travel by foot you idiot!" Pete whispered to himself.

After several minutes three men emerged from the hooch and climbed aboard the Renault. Pete pulled up his scope and identified the man in the passenger seat as General Tok, the other two were obviously his aides. The staff car pulled out and started down the road, Pete needed to move quickly if he was to get a chance at the good General. He slipped back into the dense jungle and began to run towards the river. The best chance he would have at taking out his target was on the bridge, if they really were attacking across the river into South Vietnam. He figured that the Air Force wouldn't bomb the enemy inside the North, so he would wait for them to cross the border before calling in the cavalry. Pete ran the six kilometers to the bridge in just under an hour. He had hidden his radio, additional food and "goodies" on the North side of the river where he had crossed the day before. He would first verify the enemy's intent, hopefully kill the General, then proceed west to get the radio and call for air support.

He settled in some 800 meters west of the bridge, there he found a small mound covered with thick bushes where he could lay in wait. The cover was so good that a small tree snake never even noticed Pete as it hunted in the bushes. The reptile slid silently along a branch inches from Pete's face, its tongue flicking in and out, smelling the air for prey. The snake passed and Pete continued to watch the bridge. The clouds had gathered even thicker and it began to rain, lightly at first but then picking up to a total downpour. The enemy wisely used the weather to their advantage and began crossing the bridge causing a firefight to break out with South Vietnamese soldiers on the southern side. The fighting became intense and the North began sending mortars into the South's position. After less than twenty minutes the enemy's force had overwhelmed the border guards and the bulk of the Northern force began crossing the bridge. It was just before dawn when the jeep first entered Pete's view, the only light coming from the new morning's predawn sky.

The math racing through Pete's head was staggering, angles, trajectory, wind speed, even the earths' rotation all being computed through trigonometry and all of without a conscious thought. As if this were a pop can at 25 meters he was aiming at, Pete calmly steadied his weapon. He slowed his breathing which in turn reduced his heart-rate making him more relaxed and allowing his weapon to become completely still.

His scope pulled in the meager light and allowed Pete to identify his target. Now he used a trick taught to him by his mentor Gunner, keeping both eyes open while sighting. Gunner had said that this was crucial, allowing a marksman to see anything or anyone that may be approaching the target. Because of the extreme distances snipers were shooting at, "you gotta make sure nothings gonna come between you and your mark" he had said. So with both eyes open Pete watched, and as he had hoped, the furious thunderstorm delivered. A flash of lightning shot across the sky, bringing with it a forceful clap of thunder. Just as the thunder began Pete slid the trigger back. None of the more than a thousand men even heard the report from the XM21 rifle. General Tok was killed instantly, his driver was also hit by the slug after it passed through the General's head. The jeep veered left and plunged into the river. A mad scramble ensued, with several dozen men jumping into the river to try and save the General.

In the mean time Pete slipped away to the west, found his hidden stash and pulled the radio from its pack. "Scout, this is Shadow over."

"Shadow, Scout go ahead."

"Charlie has crossed into SV, one star less. Request air support at the bridge. Count one division, mortars, 50 cal. over."

"Roger Shadow, planes enroute. You clear?"

"Roger Scout all clear, headed north." Pete ended the transmission and replaced the radio in its pack. He again stashed the pack and grabbed some more food. He also took with him the bag of explosives. Just in case.

Chapter 27

The Air Force F4 Phantom attack planes streaked in out

of the gloom, dropping bombs and strafing the enemy with

20mm cannons. The loss of life was staggering, but the enemy

continued heading south.. They abandoned the road and crossed

the countryside under cover of the canopy. They stopped

altogether during the middle of the day, waiting instead for the cover of darkness. Once the sun set, the mass of men and equipment made swift progress towards the American base. They stopped again just before dawn, a mere kilometer from the base. Again they would wait for nightfall, this time to attack.

Major Pierce had understood Pete's message completely. He had called Saigon and asked for reinforcements, but the response had been too little too late. By the time he had a commitment from HQ to send two additional companies, he had already given the order to abandon the base and huge Chinook helicopters began arriving. To the untrained eye it would have appeared that reinforcements were coming in fast and furious. In reality, for every man that got off the chopper three got on. The men who got off the Chinook circled around the chopper and rejoined the line of men getting on. Major Pierce knew that there were spies in the camp, acting as locals or even as South Vietnamese troops. He would let Charlie see what he wanted to see. By the time the VC arrived most of the men would be safely evacuated.

In Liem, Captain Paul and Tony Lucas had arrived at the field hospital. The Air Force Captain was given a full work up and cleared for immediate transport to Saigon. Tony was not as lucky. His leg was really messed up, the infection was threatening to cost him his leg. The doctors pumped him full of antibiotics and pain killers, he was sedated and his leg operated on. After four hours of meatball surgery he was sent to recovery, there was still not much the doctors could say. He would probably lose his leg if the infection couldn't be stopped soon. They placed him aboard a chopper and he was flown to Saigon to the same hospital Mike had been at two weeks earlier. Eighteen months of captivity had caused his legs to lose most of their muscle and he had a bad respiratory infection as well.

Joy Lucas was busy baking bread for her little store when the white car pulled into the drive. She saw it and her legs buckled. "Oh God no! Not Pete, not my baby!" she cried.

"Mom, what's wrong?" came a call from Suzy in the front room.

Joy couldn't answer, she was shaking all over and about to pass out. Suzy began to head for the kitchen when she heard a knock on the front door. She looked towards the kitchen, then turned and opened the door leading to the front porch. Two men dressed in Army uniforms stood on the porch. Suzy realized her mom had seen them pull up. She did her best to act brave and said quietly, "May I help you?"

"Is this the Lucas residence?" ask the Lieutenant.

"Yes, I'm Susan Lucas."

"Hello ma'am. I'm Lieutenant Ross Hargrove and this is Sergeant Phil Gunther. Is Joy Lucas home?"

"Yes, I'm Joy Lucas," came the answer. Joy had steeled herself once again, and was standing in the doorway just behind Suzy.

"Ma'am the Sergeant here has come all the way from Fort Benning to give you some good news, Sergeant."

"Ma'am," Gunner said, tipping his hat to Joy, "I'm gunnery sergeant Phil Gunther. I trained both of your sons. They are two of the finest the U.S. Army has to offer."

"If you have news please give it," Joy interrupted. "I'm not getting any younger."

Gunner smiled, " Gunnery Sergeant Anthony Lucas has been returned as part of a prisoner exchange…"

"Oh my GOD!!!" screamed Joy and Suzy together. They began hugging each other and the two soldiers. Joy was crying and Suzy was sobbing uncontrollably, neither could speak they were so overcome with emotion.

"He has some injuries, his one leg is pretty bad I guess. The docs operated on him in Saigon, he's recovering. He'll be back in the states by the end of the week." Gunner added.

Joy calmed down long enough to ask the men inside and offer them some fresh bread and her homemade jam. They sat at the kitchen table and talked about Tony and the war. Gunner was a two-tour veteran and wasn't very interested in talking about his time in Southeast Asia. He did enjoy talking about Tony and how good he was at his job. He wasn't specific, but he made Tony out to be a real hero. When Joy asked about Pete, Gunner changed. He became more solemn and not as open.

"What can you tell me about Pete, Gunner?" Joy asked.

"He's a little different," Gunner replied slowly as if he was choosing his words very carefully.

"Different how?" asked Suzy. She always knew Pete was weird.

"Pete is all alone, there is no one in his class." Gunner added. He continued, "I can't explain it but Pete is almost, well he's like a ghost."

"A ghost? Explain yourself sergeant." Joy said flatly,

"I mean, he can just disappear. I've trained hundreds of men ma'am. I ain't never seen anyone like Pete. He gives a whole new meaning to stealth."

"OK, I thought you meant he was gone, or missing or something," answered Joy.

"Naw, he's fine as far as I know" replied Gunner. "We better run, I gotta be back on base tomorrow. Got a new batch of guinea pigs comin' in."

"Thank you for coming all this way men, we really appreciate it and I'm sure Tony will as well," said Joy.

As the soldiers drove away Joy and Suzy began calling everybody to spread the good news. Uncle John was ecstatic when Joy called him, but he quickly asked about Pete. Joy told him that there was no news on Pete, except that he was fine last anyone knew and that she would let him know if she heard anything. Joy continued her calls and John continued to worry. Pete was a quality young man, but he wasn't half the physical presence Tony was. He was also concerned how Tony would react when he learned about his dad and the farm. Joy was too happy to even care about tomorrow, her son was alive and coming home.

Tony awoke from surgery in severe pain, but the medical staff was efficient and treated him with great care. He was feeling better several hours later when two officers approached his bed.

"Sergeant, how are you today? I'm Captain Lewis and this is Captain Meyers, we're with Army intelligence. We need to debrief you. You were a POW for a long time, can you tell us what happened?"

"You want to know what happened? I was in a steel cage for two years, sir!" Tony said with more than a little disdain.

"We have no record from the North Vietnamese saying you were ever in their custody. Then suddenly they offer you in a swap. Very suspicious don't you think Sergeant?" Captain Meyers asked.

"Holy shit! These guys think I went AWOL or worse turned on them," Tony thought.

Lewis continued, "Why do you think the North kept us guessing as to your status Sergeant?"

"Probably because I didn't even give them my name, rank and serial number, sir" Tony said flatly.

"Why did you not identify yourself to them soldier? If we had known, we could have worked for your release" said Meyers.

"I was not authorized to give them any information. My mission was classified, and I was operating under the mission directive, sir. I gave them my call sign. If they had intended to contact the Army and notify them of my capture they could have used "Hammer" as identification."

"Hammer, your call sign, that is all you gave the enemy in over two years?" asked Lewis.

"Yessir, Colonel Poh who runs the prison or camp or whatever you want to call where I was held. He would dress as a regular grunt and just hang around near the cells. He pretended not to know how to speak English, but I saw through him right off" Tony answered. "He would just sit and listen to the prisoners."

"There were more than just the two of you?" asked Meyers.

"Hell yes, sir. At any given time there were probably twenty or so of us," Tony said. "They would separate the men based on rank and branch of service. Putting Air Force with Marine or Army. Then ol' Colonel Poh would just sit around and listen. Because nobody knew anybody else the guys would talk. What unit you in? Where were you stationed? That kind of stuff. Poh learned a lot about our troop strength and base locations by simply listening."

"Interesting, but you gave him nothing?" asked Meyers.

"Hammer, I gave him my call sign," repeated Tony.

"You didn't talk with the other prisoners?" asked Lewis.

"Only when I was sure Poh wasn't around, but he figured out I was onto him pretty quick and moved me to a cell away from the others. The only guys he would put in with me were the ones he was through interrogating. I wasn't sure if they had broke or not, so I didn't say anything to them."

"So this Colonel Poh, did he interrogate you?" asked Meyers.

"Yeah," Tony said softly while looking down at his leg. "He did his number on me a couple of times, keeping me awake for days, beatings, stuff like that. Then just before I was released he changed. He pulled me into his office, fed me a real meal. Told me I could go home if I told him about a secret weapon. Something he called a shadow."

Meyers and Lewis looked at each other, then back at Tony, "continue" said Lewis.

"He said this weapon could see around obstacles and killed without warning. I didn't know what the hell he was talking about, so I couldn't tell him anything if I wanted to." Tony added.

"Did you want to, tell him something I mean?" asked Meyers.

Tony rose up in his bed, he had had enough. His physical presence even after two years of captivity was daunting. Tony stood six feet four inches tall and weighed 230 pounds when he entered Viet Nam, his time as a prisoner had reduced that weight to 160 pounds. "No Sir!" was all he said.

The two Captains were convinced Tony hadn't turned, in fact they had never really suspected him in the first place. He didn't have any real tactical information for the North to use, and in the tow years since his capture the entire situation had changed. "Relax soldier, we're not questioning your patriotism," said Meyers.

"Aren't you?" scowled Tony.

"No, we just need to know what you know about this prison where you were held. Any idea where it's located?"

"Yeah, it's about twenty-five clicks North of the border outside a village called Hok. It's just northeast of the village, less than a thousand meters. There are two main buildings, the office where Poh sleeps and does his interrogations and a second that is a barracks for his men. The prisoners are held in cages about ten feet long, six to ten feet wide and four feet high. Do you know what it's like to not be able to stand upright for months at a time?"

"No Sergeant, thankfully I don't. Any other info on the camp?" asked Lewis.

"No but my spotter Jason, Jason McGrew, any word on him sir?" Tony asked longingly.

"I'm afraid I'm not familiar with the name, but I'll check on his status and get word back to you" the Captain replied.

"Thank you sir." Tony said sliding back down onto his bed.

The two Captains left Tony and took the information he had provided back to Military Intelligence. A copy of their report made it's way to Colonel Morgan. He omitted most of it in a communication to Major Pierce. In the communication Colonel Morgan simply stated:

Additional target identified, bio will be forwarded forthwith.

Major Pierce received the communiqué and scoffed, "additional target, we're on the move and he's adding targets. If that bio comes in Timmy, leave it at the drop site for Shadow if not, oh well."

Corporal Tim Jones acknowledged the order, "yessir."

Sure enough, on one of the last choppers to arrive to take Rangers from Firebase Scout an envelope carrying Colonel Li Poh's bio was on board. Corporal Jones took the envelope and a second one from Major Pierce and placed them in a plastic bag. He placed the plastic bag in an empty ammo box and carried the box into the jungle some fifty meters. There he found a wooden crate buried next to an enormous tree. He brushed away the dirt and leaves from the lid and opened the crate. He placed the ammo box next to three others that were already there. He was curious as to what was inside the other boxes, but his fear of being outside the camp outweighed his curiosity. He replaced the lid and covered it with dirt and leaves, doing his best to camouflage it.

When he returned to the base he found it virtually deserted. There were no more than twenty Rangers left including Major Pierce and himself. They would attempt to hold the base, but failing that, they would destroy it before retreating into the jungle. A much larger force made up of regular Army and Green Berets were moving into position just a few kilometers south of the base. The plan was to draw the enemy into a fight for the base, then attack from the flanks, pinning them between two pincers. The northern side of the base had been heavily mined, creating a barrier for a retreating Charlie. The Rangers knew they were bait, and to a man they weren't real happy about it. They made themselves very visible, giving the illusion that many more men occupied the base than actually were present.

Chapter 28

The leading edge of the enemy force reached the

northeast corner of the camp at 0100 the following night. They had been told by local villagers that there had been a lot of activity the last two days, many helicopters had came and gone. Colonel Phen, who had taken over for the late General Tok took this to mean that the Americans had reinforced the camp. He sent half of his men around the north side of the camp and ordered them to attack from the west upon hearing the battle begin. He led the rest of the men along the eastern side and prepared to attack from there. At 0300 they assaulted the base. The enemy ran headlong into a hail of 20mm and 50mm machine gun fire. Scores died in the first wave. The troops on the western side began their attack just moments after their comrades to the east. They too met stiff resistance from within the base.

Colonel Phen ordered his artillery to bombard the camp with mortars. The shells rained in and several Rangers died. The rest fought on, their courage under fire extraordinary. Major Pierce held his men together, running from one side of the base to the other. Re-supplying them with ammunition and urging them on. A shell landed just feet from his position on the western side, killing him instantly. Corporal Jones witnessed his death and ordered the men to fall back to positions near the center of the camp. There they manned mortar tubes and answered the enemy's artillery barrage.

Colonel Phen ordered another wave of soldiers to attack the weakened Americans. They penetrated the outer edges of the base, and began attempting to scale the razor wire and fencing surrounding the inner complex. The western force reached the razor wire as well, with the Americans gunning them down by the dozen now that they were out in the open. As the dead piled up, the men following were able to use the bodies as cover. It wouldn't be long now before they breached the inner compound.

Corporal Jones ordered the charges be set and then ordered his men to exit the camp. A tunnel of sorts, sand bags and earthen mounds had been made running from the innermost section of the base leading all the way to the southern edge of the camp. The remaining eleven Rangers ran into the trench and detonated the explosives they had planted around the camp. The explosions went off all around, confusing the enemy soldiers. Some thought they were being bombed by airplanes, others just ran back towards their own lines. In the confusion, many men following up the initial charge fired at the retreating men, mistaking them for Americans. Colonel Phen realized the

Americans had rigged the camp and tried to order his men back to their positions outside the camp, but the confusion was too great.

The Rangers exited the base and raced through the jungle to a prearranged location. There they met an advance party for the flanking force. Corporal Jones gave them the intel they were waiting for, and the order to attack was given. An hour after the initial attack, Colonel Phen had his men back under control and regrouped outside the base. He ordered his men to move in, expecting at least a small amount of resistance. When he reached the center of the camp, he was faced with the reality of the situation. The Americans were gone, only eight American bodies were found. He had lost nearly two hundred men, but at least he had the base.

As dawn broke two A4 fighters streaked over the base, seconds later their bombs exploded. The North Vietnamese soldiers scattered for cover. Then seemingly out of nowhere, mortar shells began exploding all around the base. As the enemy tried to regroup, the Green Berets attacked from the east, followed immediately by the Army from the south and west. Colonel Phen ordered a full retreat out the northern side of the base. His men ran straight into a massive mine field. By the time they had regrouped just two kilometers south of the river, they had lost another two hundred men. His army was in trouble, and he was trapped. If they tried to cross the bridge during the day, the American planes would cut them to pieces. The colonel set up a defensive position in the thick jungle in a valley between two large hills. He would have to wait for General Deng to reinforce his beleaguered men, before attacking the Americans again.

The American force chased the enemy north out of the camp, but when they reached the area where Colonel Phen had stopped, they also stopped. The American leaders did not want to attack the enemy in such a defensible position. They took up position on the far side of a large clearing. They remained inside the forest far enough to keep from being seen. In the meantime helicopters of Rangers returned to Firebase Scout to collect their dead comrades and reconstitute the camp. The loss of Major Pierce was palpable. He was considered a good leader and an even better man, but as always, no Ranger was left behind.

Chapter 29

Pete had moved steadily North after leaving the river. He

worked his way back to the camp where General Tok had

initiated his attack on the Americans. He found the base empty, except for a few villagers eager to get back to their lives. He waited for sundown, and then slowly approached the hooch containing the tunnel entrance. Once there he debated for a second whether or not to enter. Finally he silently slipped through the doorway. He found the entrance open, with no signs of a guard. "The entire force must have gone forward," he thought.

He climbed down a homemade bamboo ladder and entered the main tunnel. It was dark except for a faint glow somewhere ahead. He hugged the wall on the left side, moving slowly and quietly towards the light. About fifty meters from the entrance he came upon a small side tunnel, he slid through the narrow entrance and entered what had been a small office. It was pitch dark and musty. Pete waited by the entrance for his eyes to adjust, after a moment he could make out a desk, chair and some papers on the desk. Pete moved to the desk and looked at the papers, most of them were maps of the area and documents written in Vietnamese. Pete removed his pack and slid the papers inside. Then he placed an explosive on top of the desk and laid a grenade on top of it. He tied monofilament fishing line to the pin and pulled the pin until it was just barely holding on. Then he slipped back into the main tunnel. He placed a second explosive and grenade in a small niche along the wall, and connected the fishing line to it as well. Pete then stretched the line as tight as he dared and tied the end to a root poking out of the side of the tunnel. The line was a little higher than Pete wanted, it was closer to waist high than ankle high but in the dark he thought it would still work. His booby trap was complete, now he needed to get out before anyone caught him.

As he worked his way back towards the entrance inside the hooch, light spilled into the tunnel. Someone was in the hooch, and they had a torch! He heard talking and then yelling in Vietnamese. The light and the men holding it started down the ladder. Pete backed up and began looking for somewhere to hide. He found a small depression in the wall and smashed himself into it. There was more yelling and several men rushed past him carrying a wounded man. Pete realized they would hit his trap in seconds. He pushed himself out of the depression and bolted for the ladder. Standing between him and the ladder was a slight figure, the young man just stood there as Pete rushed past him, his eyes wide with fear and astonishment. The two soldiers tripped Pete's trap just as Pete reached the ladder. He vaulted up the shaft as the tunnel exploded. Pete ran from the hooch into the jungle. Several villagers saw him, but they did not know what had happened. The ground shook and a slight trench formed where the collapsed tunnel had been. Liu Tok died crying aloud, "the ghost! It's the ghost!"

Pete ran deep into the jungle before stopping to get his bearings. "I am stupid! What was I thinking? You're a sniper you idiot!" he kept thinking. "Alright, asshole, from now on no more heroics. Just do your job. I need to find General Deng, and then I can get away from the border. There should be less heat the farther inside North Vietnam you get. Now move soldier!"

Pete moved north again, this time he stayed close to the new road. If Deng was in the area his men would travel via the easiest path. After covering another two kilometers Pete watched as an enemy scout moved quickly along the road. Within minutes more and more soldiers passed by, "this should be Deng's unit" Pete thought.

Pete wasn't sure how to handle this one, it was broad daylight and there wouldn't be any storm to cover the report from his rifle. He decided to try and let the army pass him and then take the General from behind. This would be tricky, because the General's car would be in a convoy of trucks and other vehicles. Pete surveyed the area and found a spot where the road curved to the right. He climbed a large tree and sat on an enormous branch. The branch was so large he could sit with his knees pulled up to use as a gun rest.

It took a full hour for the force to pass by and Pete still hadn't caught sight of the General, finally a full ten minutes behind the last of his men, the General's car, along with several other trucks came into view. The car was similar to the one General Tok had ridden in, an aging Renault with a convertible top that resembled the staff cars used by Generals during the second World War. The General's car was located between two trucks in the convoy, making a difficult situation even worse. The right hand bend in the road was Pete's saving grace. He had correctly figured that the General would be riding on the passenger side of the vehicle, not driving. The truck following the General blocked Pete's view of him until the road swung to the right. Pete had the road in his sights, as the General's car entered his view, Pete acquired his target. He had a very limited window of opportunity. The road returned to its original path just 200 meters after the curve.

Pete relaxed, took a deep breath, held it for a second and let it out slowly as he pulled back the trigger. Six hundred meters away General Deng's head snapped abruptly to the left and his driver was suddenly covered with blood and human flesh. The driver slammed on the brakes and the truck behind slammed into the rear of the Renault. Men were screaming at each other and several men were pulling the General from his seat. They all took cover behind the vehicles and stared west into the jungle. Pete sat motionless, his breathing slowed to almost a stop. A patrol of enemy soldiers were sent into the jungle to search for the man or men who had killed their beloved commander. Pete sat on his branch, and watched the patrol advance. They came about three hundred meters towards Pete, before giving up the search. Even if they had looked directly at Pete the odds of them identifying him as a human, let alone an American soldier were astronomical. His camo suit was so alive now that he actually had insects living on it. His face painted with grease paint, his helmet alive with an air plant and moss. He was invisible in plain sight, just another part of the jungle that surrounded him.

After nightfall, he made his way down the tree and into the blackness of the forest. He had slept the afternoon away, sitting on his branch. Several birds had inspected the sleeping Ranger, but none of them feared him. He smelled like the earth, and felt like a tree. The wildlife knew he was different, but they didn't know what he was. His calm exterior and lack of obvious malice calmed the creatures, but in the wild not everything is as it seems. Once on the ground Pete moved slowly but steadily north, his next target was a Colonel in charge of intelligence for this region of the North. He was supposed to be headquartered in a city called Hihn some twenty kilometers northwest of this location. It would take Pete a week to get there, unless something unforeseen happened.

Back at Firebase Scout the Green Berets had peeled off from the main thrust of Americans and circled back south of the Firebase. They eventually returned to their base some thirty kilometers south of Firebase Scout in Liem. The army soldiers that had pushed the North Vietnamese out of Firebase Scout, also slowly slipped back to the south leaving a company of men two hundred strong to act as a buffer with the enemy. It had been decided by HQ not to pursue the retreating North Vietnamese, but rather to regroup and restore the situation to its original state. The belief was that the enemy would cross the river back into North Vietnam, licking their wounds. As a result, most of the soldiers began the long hot trek back to their base outside of Da Nang. Those remaining on station were resting quietly little more than five hundred meters from the enemy.

The following night General Deng's forces crossed the river into South Vietnam and met up with Colonel Phen. Colonel Shen Zeng had assumed control of the arriving force and together with Phen planned their next move. They decided to split up and flank the Americans. A small force would attack the enemy head on, drawing their fire and attention. The rest of the division would circle around the major group of Americans and attack the base again, from the same positions as the original attack. They based their decision on the principal that most people would not expect a second attack from an enemy at the same place as the earlier defeat. Also, they assumed that the defenses would not be fully repaired from the first attack, making it easier to storm the base. Once they had the base, they would push north into the rear of the American army pushing them towards the river.

Again they waited through the day for the cover of darkness, and an hour after sundown the two North Vietnamese armies began to move. They spilled out of the jungle valley they had used as cover and Phen's men headed east around the American unit and down to the same staging area they had used two days earlier. Zeng's men headed west, again avoiding contact with the American buffer troops. They took up positions on the west and northwest sides of the base. Phen sent his most trusted aide, Colonel Zhu, with one hundred men to the southern edge of the camp blocking the escape route used by the Rangers in the last firefight. When everything was in place, Phen gave the order and mortars began slamming into the base. The Rangers inside the base were not ready for such an onslaught. It only took a few minutes for them to be fully operational, but those few minutes were costly. Twenty-five were killed in the first three minutes. Fifteen of those were sleeping in their tent when a mortar landed directly on it. The men on sentry were caught off guard by the ferocity of the attack. By the time the Rangers began answering the artillery with their own mortars, the enemy had advanced to the outer edge of the camp.

The American gunners manning the machine guns laid down a wall of lead, slowing the enemy advance. The new commander of the base, Major Thomas Lipinski, was not prepared. He reacted slowly to the threat, and then made several poor decisions. First he ordered his men to shell the enemy's artillery, which was still inside the jungle. Most of the rounds landed harmlessly in the forest, a waste of resources and time. Second, he ordered his gunners to wait for the enemy to breach the razor wire before opening up. Had this been a small-scale attack, it would have been a smart decision. Let them get close, and then wipe them out with little hope of retreat. However this was a major assault, involving over a thousand enemy soldiers. Letting them in opened a floodgate that couldn't be closed.

The Rangers were forced to attempt to use their escape route, out the south end of the camp. There they met Colonel Zhu and his men lying in ambush. The Rangers fought their way through the enemy and into the jungle, but in the process they took heavy casualties. Of the four hundred and six men in the camp prior to the attack, only three hundred and sixty six made it out alive. Another eighty-three were wounded. Lieutenant Bones Bonner was killed as was Private Mitchel Holt. Sergeant Bud

Jamison was wounded in the left shoulder, yet kept fighting and helped carry Mitch's body. He had no intention of leaving his young friend behind. Lieutenant Mike Roth showed extreme courage by attacking headlong into Colonel Zhu's line, breaking through to give the Rangers their way out. Corporal Tim Jones was the last of the Rangers to fall that day, hit in the back while rushing into the jungle. He was scooped up by Pete's former classmate Rick Dizt and carried towards the evacuation point. Corporal Jones had radioed for evac prior to their exiting the base, and the choppers were already in the air.

Air Force A4's were also on their way, they devastated the area immediately around the base. As the Rangers were reaching the LZ, the enemy caught up to them. A firefight began, this time the Rangers were ready and the outcome was more to their liking. The enemy failed to advance any further, and a plane streaked across the treetops. A second later two bombs filled with NAPALM exploded in the jungle surrounding the enemy. Dozens were killed instantly and many more burned. The North Vietnamese retreated back to the base to regroup with their comrades.

Colonel Phen ordered his men to push north from the base, hoping to pin the majority of the American force between his and Colonel Zeng's army and the river. The A4's that attacked the base, were ordered to also provide cover for the Company of regular army personnel left north of the base. Upon the Rangers evacuating the base, the Army unit was left stranded between a large enemy army and the North Vietnamese border. HQ ordered the trapped men to move out, heading east first then south. The air support was used to shield the movement by dropping NAPALM and straifing the enemy lines. Two hours later several B52's arrived and laid down massive amounts of ordinance. The combination of these two tactics gave the soldiers time to evacuate the area without even engaging the North's forces.

The overall effect of the battle was that the North now had a substantial foothold in the South and Pete was now much further behind enemy lines than he knew. Pete was oblivious to the devastation happening forty-five kilometers south of him. He continued to head north, using the night to make better time. He stayed in the thick and nasty as much as possible. The terrain he covered was some of the most difficult anywhere on earth. The plants were thick and some had defensive mechanisms, thorns, razor sharp leaves and stinging nettles. The insects were insane, biting flies and mosquitoes; worms that burrowed into the flesh and leaches were among the worst. Pete did his best to ignore the hardships. He focused on the hunt and on his surroundings. Eight days later he had arrived, his body would recover, but his mind was showing signs of trouble.

Chapter 30

For Pete the mental challenge was far more difficult than the physical. Being alone in a foreign land was hard enough, but being alone and without any hope of rescue was an anvil on his shoulders. If he made a mistake the consequences were too daunting to contemplate. He would be disavowed by the army and rejected as an agent of the U.S.; left to fend for himself. Pete had already decided that if he were caught he would go out fighting, even though he knew there would be no hope. He carried a five-shot bolt action rifle and a Colt semi-automatic 45. No match for even one well-armed VC. But he had vowed to never be captured, at least his mom would be able to have a funeral. Unlike the daily grind of not knowing that weighed on her with Tony's situation. He had watched her agonizing each morning, then watching the evening news each night, hoping to see some glimpse of her eldest son.

Pete sat in a tree, overlooking a small river, and contemplated his life. He felt at home here in the jungle, yet he missed his home on the farm. He thought about Missy, his Mom, his sisters and brothers and felt even more alone. He sat quietly remembering his dad, the strongest man he had ever known, lying helpless on the grass beside the tractor. Finally, thousands of miles from home, Pete began to cry. He let it all out, all of his pain. The anger over losing his father too soon, the fear of losing his older brother and the loss of the family farm. Waves of sadness washed over him. He shook all over and began to feel light headed. He took in a deep breath and realized he hadn't had any food or water since climbing to his arboreal roost the previous morning. He slipped his pack from his shoulder and found a bag of nuts he had saved. As he ate and sipped water from his canteen, he surveyed his surroundings.

It was just after dawn and the sun began to make inroads into the darkness of the canopy. The forest's inhabitants began to stir as well. Birds were flitting from branch to branch and the cacophony of sounds made Pete smile. He did love the jungle, and he was where he needed to be. A large bird with bright red feathers on it's neck landed just feet from Pete. The bird noticed him and began quizzically turning its head this way and that to try and figure out what exactly he was. Pete watched the bird for signs of fear and found none. He was just new to the bird, not alarming, just unknown. He very slowly pulled out a nut and even more slowly reached out his hand. He set the nut on the barrel of his rifle, which being camouflaged looked like a branch or a vine. He slipped his hand back inside his suit and waited. It was nearly four minutes before the bird finally hopped onto the barrel of his gun and took the nut in its beak. It lingered only a few seconds, then flew off to find another meal.

Pete watched and listened for another hour, soaking up the beauty and majesty of the place. At 0730 he raised his field glasses and got to work. He had chosen this particular tree for a reason. The small river it overlooked was the main "highway" in this part of Vietnam. Traffic flowed along its quiet surface continuously. Pete was interested in one particular cargo. His next target was Colonel Phen Nyguen, an intelligence officer in the North Vietnamese army. He was considered a high profile target due to his web of spies and operatives in South Vietnam. This target had no doubt been added by Director Craft. In fact Pete's next target after Colonel Nyguen was to be Major Su Lien of the South Vietnamese army, a spy working for the Colonel. The bio Pete had for Colonel Nyguen was very specific, he used the river to move quickly from the interior of the country to the border area near Dong Ha. There he would clandestinely meet with his spies and receive information and pass along orders for his operatives.

The previous night Pete had cut several branches from the tree, providing an unobstructed view of the river in two areas. One view was upstream from his position and the other downstream. Pete's view was limited by several other large trees between the two openings; he would have a clear line of sight for ten to twenty seconds at any given time depending on the speed of the boat carrying his target. He watched the boats traversing the river, looking for his man. The bio listed two separate boats that the Colonel used. Pete watched for the listed craft, but scrutinized as much of the traffic as possible. He had no way of knowing how old the intel was or if it was accurate in the first place. He watched the river all day, occasionally sipping water from his canteen, but never taking his eyes off of the river. As darkness fell he relaxed and stretched out onto the branch. He was still amazed at the size of the trees in Southeast Asia, he could lay flat out and not fear falling off. Pete lay there looking up at a starlit sky, the noise began to rise again as the night creatures emerged to take over the jungle.

Missy was there to welcome Mike home, or at least back to Fort Campbell. Colonel Morgan and Missy stood in the bright sunshine of an August day and waited while Mike and seven other wounded Rangers made their way onto the parade grounds. Once the men were assembled an honor guard presented the colors and a military band played. Then Colonel Morgan called the men one by one and presented them with the various medals they had earned. Mike received his Bronze Star and his parents were beaming with pride. Tony Lucas received a Purple Heart, Bronze Star and Silver Star and had been recommended for the Medal of Honor.

When Missy heard Tony's name called she was elated and terrified at the same time. Tony's leg below the knee was limp and may never recover to full strength, the infection had nearly forced it to be amputated. Any longer and the doctors feared for his life. Mike wasn't sure what to think, was this really Pete's brother? Once he saw Missy crying and then found Joy in the audience he was sure of it. Then he realized Tony's little brother had somehow done the impossible, he had brought him home.

"Who is this guy?" Mike thought. "He saved my life, his brother's life, and he's still over there!" It was all he could do to keep from breaking down. After the ceremony they all retired to the mess hall for drinks and goodies. Mike found Joy and they shared a long hug.

"I owe him my life" Mike whispered to her.

"So do I son", Joy answered as Tony came up to them on his crutches.

"Mike Moore, this is my oldest son, Tony," Joy introduced them.

"Sergeant," Mike said saluting.

"Private, I've heard a lot about you from my mom. You served with Pete?" Tony asked the obvious.

"Yessir, I am, or was his spotter," Mike stammered.

"You still are Private, or so I'm told. Pete has refused a new spotter for now." Tony replied quietly.

Mike's expression said it all, he realized Pete was all alone and shared Tony's agony of knowing what that meant. He waited for Joy to excuse herself to talk to Missy, before continuing the conversation. "He's all alone? What the hell is going on?"

"Don't know for sure Mike, but my guess is he's been sent to finish what I started. I'm madder than a bald faced hornet about it, but there's nothin' I can do now." Tony said looking down at his battered limb.

"I'll bring him back, I promise, he saved my ass. Least I can do is return the favor." Mike said defiantly.

"No you won't son," came a voice from behind. It was Colonel Morgan. "You will report to your unit commander as ordered, and before long you will be back home with your family. We all want Sergeant Lucas home safe and sound, but he has a job to do and he will do it."

"Sir, I meant Private Pete Lucas sir." Mike replied unknowingly.

"They have kept you in the dark son," answered the Colonel smiling. "We're talking about the same young man, Pete has been promoted." The Colonel walked away shaking his head.

"Sergeant, jez, now I'll have to salute him. For Christ's sake, not bad enough I owe him my life, now I have to salute him too." Mike was pouring on the sarcasm.

Tony laughed and began to realize why Pete picked Mike to team up with. When it gets bad a good laugh is like a miracle cure. "You keep saying Pete saved your life, care to talk about it?"

"Not really, but what the hell," Mike said smiling. He told the whole story, embellishing and exaggerating nearly all aspects. Except when it came to his last minutes with Pete. He became much more serious and looked as if he would break down at any moment. "Your little brother is the most amazing man I've ever met. He laid there beside me, not moving, just waiting. We heard the chopper coming, and then the enemy machine gun opened up. Pete jumped up, aimed and shot the gunner in less than one second. I can't even imagine how he knew where to shoot, but the gun stopped firing the second Pete shot. He dove back to the ground and waited again. Then when the chopper came down, he picked my fat ass up and literally threw me into the chopper. The machine gun opened up again, Pete told the chopper to go, and just as we lifted up I saw him fire again. He took out that damn gunner. As we swung around, the chopper's gunner let go. But I still don't know how Pete got outta there alive."

"If half of that is true Private, Pete is a real hero," Tony said beaming with pride.

"As I live and breathe Sir, it's true." Mike said flatly.

"Hey, are you two gonna join us?" called Joy from a table nearby. Seated with her were Suzy, and Mike's parents. Directly beside Joy on the right sat Missy. She was smiling but Tony could see she was dying inside. He went over and sat next to her. Joy was happy, Tony was home and it warmed her to see Mike would make a full recovery. She had learned to put fears of what Pete was doing aside, Tony had made it home and so would Pete. They all chatted and made small talk. The gathering broke up and the families headed for home. Tony said goodbye to his mom and little sister for now, he would be back in Ohio the next week for an extended leave.

As they pulled away, he turned to Missy and said, "I know you need to talk, how 'bout we go find somewhere quiet?"

At first Missy thought he was being rude, but then she looked into his eyes and saw the same pure honesty she had seen in Pete. "I'd like that Sergeant" she replied.

They proceeded to a small opening between two buildings where there stood a large oak tree. Tony eased himself down and sat leaning against the trunk of the oak. Missy sat cross-legged on the lawn facing him. Tony looked at her and smiled, Pete had picked a winner. She was beautiful and sweet.

A southern belle, she was most certainly that. "So, what can I do for you?" He asked.

"Is Pete gonna be OK?" she asked longingly.

"I don't know Missy, I haven't seen Pete in over three years. He was a sixteen year old punk when I left. They tell me he's a hell of a man now. I can't imagine what has happened since I've been gone. My dad's dead, we lost the farm. He must have grown up fast."

"I know you don't know the Pete I know, but you know Vietnam. Is he gonna be alright?" she pleaded.

"I can't lie to you Missy, that place is as close to hell as I want to get. I mean the … " he couldn't finish.

Missy surprised him again by standing up and walking over to him. She sat next to him and put her arm around him. He wasn't sure how to react. She took his head and laid it on her shoulder, and held him close. Tony felt her embrace and melted into her. He was home. It took a total stranger, his brother's girlfriend no less, to make him realize how lucky he was. He had wanted to help her, to ease her pain, but she had turned it around on him. He sat there and soaked up her embrace.

"He will make it," he finally said. "He saved Private Moore and from all accounts a bunch of other guys owe him their lives. The Rangers will not leave him behind. You can take that to heart."

"I know, leave no man behind," Missy said dryly.

"That is more than just a slogan," Tony said defiantly. "They will risk their lives for one another, they will bring him home. I guarantee it."

"Good," Missy said equally defiant. "And when he gets here I'm gonna kill him."

"Yea, me too," smiled Tony.

"I got first dibs, that good for nothin' brother of yours has been keeping secrets." Missy said jokingly.

"I don't know, he owes me for travelling thousands of miles and not even waiting to say 'Hi' when I was released." Tony joked.

"Well, we'll double team him when he gets back," Missy replied.

"Yeah," Tony said leaning his head back down onto her shoulder. Tony closed his eyes and his thoughts snapped back to his first meeting with Colonel Morgan after returning from

'Nam. The Colonel had informed him that he had been recovered due to the efforts of another sniper team. He had asked for the names of the men to whom he owed his life. The response took his breath away. He was incredulous. It couldn't be possible, Pete, his baby brother. He was a sniper, he was a Ranger. He had saved my life! Life was cruel and beautiful and strange and completely insane!

The story Tony was told was beyond belief. He had already heard most of Mike's story from the Colonel a week earlier, although hearing it from Mike had made it more real. Pete was considered by Colonel Morgan and the brass to be the perfect sniper. Tony was furious when he found out Pete had been sent to North Vietnam. Although he was secretly hoping his brother would kill Colonel Poh before he came home. Tony knew his chances of seeing active duty as a sniper again were virtually zero, Pete would have to finish the job. Tony just wanted Pete to come home. He held out hope that somehow Jason, his spotter, would also come home. Jason had been his best friend for over two years and Tony went to sleep each night dreaming about his buddy.

The last night they spent together in the jungle of North Vietnam was permanently etched in his mind. It was raining buckets and the two Rangers were moving slowly through the thick undergrowth when suddenly several figures jumped them. Tony had fought several men killing one and wounding another with his knife before being smashed in the back of the head with the butt of a rifle. When he came to, he was in a cart pulled by a water buffalo. His hands and feet tied behind his back. Within hours he was in Colonel Li Poh's prison and he never saw Jason again.

Chapter 31

Pete spent three days in the tree, watching the river. He had spotted several boats matching the description of Colonel Nyguen's. However; he had yet to identify anyone on board one of those boats. The day dawned cloudy, a mist covered the jungle and it was difficult for Pete to even see the river. The fog lifted somewhat by 0930 and Pete began scanning the river in earnest. He had fed his bird friend again first thing this morning. He would miss the little guy when he had to move on. At 0955 he noticed a patrol boat entering his upstream view. This wasn't unusual, but he paid special attention to them. He thought that maybe the Colonel had given up taking commercial craft for more capable military transportation. But as he scanned the vessel he found once again his target was not aboard. As he began to move to the downstream viewing area, he caught the corner of a second boat following the patrol boat. This boat was a commercial vessel and fit the description perfectly.

"He's got an escort," Pete said softly to himself.

He scanned the boat front to back with his binoculars, no sign of the Colonel. But he was convinced that this was the one.

There was a small cabin just aft of the cargo hold, and it blocked the view of the rear deck. He watched it until it passed into the area hidden by the trees. He quickly shifted his position to lying prone on the branch. His rifle aimed at the edge of the downstream opening. It was about a minute between when the boat left the upstream opening until it entered the downstream window. Pete had the lens covers on his scope open and he was sighting in the target area. The bow of the patrol boat came into view just as a driving rain let loose; Pete was in the zone now and nothing could shake his concentration. A breeze was blowing slightly in Pete's face, he didn't mind, a cross breeze would have caused much more trouble. The patrol boat passed, Pete scanned it again just in case, no sign of the target.

The bow of the second boat entered his scope and Pete began to search it. He covered the front half quickly, no sign. As the small cabin came into view, he found several men inside taking cover from the rain. One by one he eliminated them as potentially Colonel Nyguen. The boat would be out of visual range in less than ten seconds now. His open eye, the one not looking through the scope, once again spotted something. There was a small table set up on the rear deck, an umbrella sheltered the table from the rain. Seated at the table was a man, a slight man with a drink in his hand facing the rear of the boat. Pete focused on the man and quickly identified him as his target. He took aim, inhaled, exhaled and fired. The boat was just leaving Pete's visual range when the Colonel fell backwards. The force of the impact knocked him and his chair over backward as if he had been leaning back on the chair and lost his balance. In fact his men assumed that was what had happened until they saw the gaping wound in the back of his head and heard the muted report of a single shot from somewhere far away in the jungle. They had to look closely to find the entry wound in his left eye.

Pete closed the lens covers on his scope and laid his head on his left arm. He drifted off to sleep; it would be a long wait for nightfall. He didn't dare travel during the day; the darkness was his friend; the thick and nasty his salvation. As he slept his small friend returned, the little bird with red feathers. It perched on the barrel of his rifle, adding to the illusion that this was just another tree branch in the Vietnamese jungle. He slept soundly for the first time in a week, when hunting he only slept for short periods not wanting to miss his prey. Even when sleeping he was so in tune with his surroundings that any slight noise or sudden silence woke him immediately. This afternoon he slept without worry, tonight he would begin another hunt.

The steady rain cooled the day and by evening the jungle was eerily quiet. The usual din of insects and birds were drown out by the monotone of falling water. The jungle didn't stop its constant movement for a little rain, but it did modify the way it went about its business. The rain made life a little easier for the reptiles and amphibians; more difficult for the insects and birds. But all in all life and death went on. Pete awoke just after dusk and slowly raised himself up to a sitting position. It took him fifteen minutes to achieve this. Not because he was ill or injured, but because he wanted nothing, not even the insects to notice. Nothing served as an alarm in the jungle more than dead silence. Humans moving through the jungle caused the wildlife to freeze, the animals, birds and even insects would become invisible. Pete needed to remain invisible too. He needed to be invisible to humans and wildlife both to survive. The North Vietnamese were very aware of their jungle, they knew its secrets and its nuances. A sudden change in behavior by the wildlife would be recognized instantly.

After sitting upright, Pete scanned the area below his tree

for signs of activity, human and non-human alike. After several

minutes he was confident that the coast was clear and he began

his decent to the forest floor. Once on the ground it took a while

for his legs to stretch out and his back ached. The ribs he had

cracked while carrying Mike screamed at him to lie back down.

However, he needed to move now. His next target was the spy

Colonel Nyguen had inside the South Vietnamese army, Major

Lien. The Major would be a more difficult target. He was

stationed in Dong Ha, a larger population area. More people

meant less cover; less cover meant more danger. Complicating

the matter was that he was a South Vietnamese officer, which

meant that if caught Pete would cause a huge political firestorm.

The only advantage was that if he were caught, Pete would

probably be spared the torture and eventual death he would face

in North Vietnam.

Pete made his way east, staying in the deep jungle as long

as possible. Eventually he came to an area of extensive farms and

open land. This would be his major test. He was still in North

Vietnam and needed to negotiate several kilometers of this

dangerous terrain to reach the border. From there he would cross the DMZ and be able to breathe a little easier. As usual he waited for darkness before moving out and kept to the thin trees and bushes on the edges of fields. The time seemed to drag on and it seemed to Pete that he would never get through. By dawn the next day he had traveled less than half the distance. He found a small ravine separating two fields and slipped into its tall grass and scrub bushes. In no time Pete realized he wasn't alone. A huge snake was coiled under a fallen branch just ten feet from his feet. He wasn't sure, but it looked to be twenty feet long. The snake didn't move, and neither did Pete. It was a Python and Pete marveled at its size, it had a lump some six or seven feet from its head. "Last nights' dinner", Pete thought, "Good, he won't be hungry at least."

The day dawned hot and the temperatures soared, the ravine remained shaded providing some relief. By late afternoon the snake was getting hot, its meal nearly digested, and began to stir. Pete watched it closely, he wasn't sure what he would do if it tried to add Ranger to its diet. As it uncoiled and stretched out the full size of this enormous reptile became apparent. The monster was easily twenty feet long and a foot in circumference and Pete was mesmerized by it. The python slithered along the bottom of the ravine then turned abruptly and began to approach Pete's position from below. He watched in wonder and fear as the giant moved steadily closer. Pete was sitting with his back against the earthen wall of the ravine, with his legs pulled up towards his chest. The snake slid itself between his feet and his backside, as if his legs were a bridge and the snake a river running beneath them. Pete sat helpless for five minutes as the entire snake passed under his legs. The stress was more than Pete had felt since entering Vietnam. Once the snake had vanished from view, Pete relaxed and slowly drifted off to sleep. He would not sleep soundly though, this place was too dangerous, too exposed.

Chapter 32

Tony was getting around better, but still needed crutches. He went to an exercise class twice a day to strengthen his legs, even the good leg suffered severely from lack of use while he was imprisoned. The class was full of soldiers that had been wounded or injured in Vietnam. No one spoke of Vietnam, instead they talked about home and cars and girls. Tony realized how lucky he was, most of the men in the class were missing limbs or had been badly injured. He considered his situation only a minor setback, never considering that he may not walk unassisted again.

Missy visited Tony every day and they became very close. She realized there was more than an ordinary attraction between them and she was unsure what to do. She considered not visiting Tony, but that didn't seem right and she really enjoyed being with him. Tony felt the attraction as well and did his best to discourage it. He even hinted that Missy should visit less often, although his effort wasn't convincing. Finally Missy had to make a decision.

"I think I have a problem Tony," she said during a visit.

"Can I help?" asked Tony not sure what she meant.

"I'm falling in love with you," Missy replied quietly. She said it while looking down at the floor, not knowing what his reaction would be she was afraid to look him in the eye.

"I've been feeling this coming for a while," said Tony. "I don't know what to do. I think you are the most amazing woman I've ever met, but you're Pete's girl."

"I can't wait for Pete, I love him, but you need me now." Missy began to sob.

Tony held her tight, "I think we should let this play out a little and make sure we know what we're feeling is real. If it is, Pete will understand and everything will work out. If not we'll know for sure and you and Pete will still be together."

"I can't do that to Pete," Missy continued to sob. "He is the most honest man I know, how can I sneak around on him. Especially with you! He went to Vietnam to bring you home, now I'm gonna leave him for you. This is wrong!"

"If it is we'll know soon, and Pete will understand either way." Tony tried to comfort her.

"And if he doesn't understand?" Missy asked. "You lose a brother and I lose the first man I ever loved."

"Then maybe we shouldn't see each other any more."
Tony responded.

"I can't do that," Missy replied. "I love you too. This is
screwed up, Tony!"

"Yeah, that much is true. Just know this, I care about you
Missy and if you need to wait for Pete I can live with that. If not,
I want to see where this will go." Tony said still holding her
tight.

Missy turned to face Tony and kissed him deeply. They
embraced for a long time and the romance began in earnest.
Missy began spending lunch at the hospital and every evening
they spent hours together. After two weeks, Missy felt she
needed to write Pete. She wasn't sure what to write, she certainly
wasn't going to write a Dear John letter, but she needed to let
Pete know Tony was in her life. The words came agonizingly
slow and she cried for hours after writing it, it took her two days
to work up the courage to mail it.

Pete was only half way through his list of targets and still
in North Vietnam. He again waited for nightfall to move from his
hiding place. The ravine had fallen into heavy shadow before the
surrounding fields, and Pete had moved into a position from

which he could see his path before it became dark. Clouds had gathered during the day and Pete sensed the rain long before it actually came. When it did come, Pete emerged from his refuge and moved quickly across the open terrain. He used the rain and near total darkness to cover him as he walked, jogged and even ran at times. He covered the rest of the distance to the border during the rainstorm, some six kilometers, and swam across the river before dawn. Once in South Vietnam, Pete relaxed a little. He still traveled only at night and kept to the densest cover, but the stress was noticeably less.

Pete finally came to the outer edge of Dong Ha and began his stalk. His target was usually very visible around the town, making the job more difficult. Shooting him would be easy, get away afterward would be much more difficult. Pete noticed in his Bio that the Major had a mistress in Bok Whey a village several kilometers southeast of Dong Ha. He thought the Major wouldn't be quite as conspicuous when traveling to see her, making Pete's job a little easier. Pete slipped around Dong Ha and made his way to the tiny village of Bok Whey. The village was so small Pete nearly missed it while trying to stay in the thick cover. He found a large tree, climbed into its expansive canopy and waited. The intel had Major Lien arriving each Tuesday and departing Wednesday morning. It was Sunday night and Pete settled in for a long wait.

He slept uneasily through the day Sunday, watching the villagers go about their daily lives. They tended their fields, fed the chickens and buffaloes and worked their way through the day. Pete realized that they lived much like he had lived on the farm. The difference being the lack of machinery, but the work was basically the same. The children worked alongside their parents, although they would occasionally manage a game of tag or chase a chicken around the courtyard. Pete felt a connection to the people, a bond based on hard work and love of the land. It would be hard to leave this place when the time came.

As night fell, the villagers retreated to their huts and the smell of fires filled the air. He had camped his entire life, first with his dad on hunting trips and later with the Boy Scouts. The smell of a campfire made him smile and think back to good times spent with his dad, Tony, Henry and Uncle John. Sitting around a campfire listening to stories of the good old days told with flair and exaggeration by the two elder Lucases. He smiled to himself and fell asleep dreaming of home.

Monday was less pleasant. It began raining early and continued all day. He wasn't sure, but it seemed as if ten inches of rain fell on the tiny village that day. No one ventured out all day, and Pete was chilled and miserable. Even the wildlife took the day off for the most part, an occasional insect flew by, but the birds and mammals just hunkered down and waited for the rain to end. His position some six hundred meters from the village was comfortable in that he could change positions from sitting to lying without worrying about being detected. As the absolute darkness of a rural night descended upon the area, the rain subsided, finally ending completely at 0130 Tuesday morning. Pete slept once the rain stopped and awoke at dawn, the villagers were hard at work and everything was back to normal. At 1120 the unmistakable sound of an engine could be heard approaching from the northeast. A jeep came into view and riding in the passenger seat was Major Yan Lien. Pete watched as a young woman, he estimated not more than eighteen years old, came to meet the jeep followed by two young children. Not only did the Major have a mistress he had another family.

Pete watched as the reunion continued, the kids hugging their dad and the young woman doting over her man. The family walked slowly to the third hut in the village and went inside. A few minutes later the two children came out and ran off to play at the edge of the courtyard, climbing onto the jeep and pretending to drive it. An hour later the Major came out and lit a cigarette, obviously having enjoyed his mistress's company. Pete decided that he would wait until the Major headed away from the village before taking his shot. It would be too traumatic for the kids to witness their father's death.

He didn't consider not killing the Major, he was a traitor and, as such his fate was sealed. Pete was also disgusted with the man, he was a pig, using his mistress for sex and bearing his children then returning to his other family as if nothing had happened. But this wasn't personal, it was a job, the Major was the target and the target would be hit. As darkness fell Pete lowered himself from the tree and eased his way around until he was some seven hundred meters north of the village. He found a position on a small hill overlooking the trail that served as a road to Bok Whey. The distance was good at over six hundred meters, the angle of fire even better with his position some thirty meters higher than the trail. He would be facing the west, meaning the wind would be in his face and the sun at his back. He was concealed in a thicket of thorn bushes and had a large opening to acquire his target.

The morning dawned bright and there was a strong breeze blowing from the west. At 0710 Pete heard the jeep long before he could see it, the sound carried by the wind. He lay prone in the thicket using his pack as a gun rest. The jeep came into the opening and made its way across his field of view. Pete followed its path and just as it was about to leave the area he inhaled, exhaled and pulled the trigger. The Major slumped forward, and the jeep accelerated. The wind pushed the report from the rifle east into the jungle which swallowed it. Pete once again closed the lens covers on his scope and laid his head on his left arm. Sleep came easily, and he stayed there until his beloved darkness once again covered the land.

Chapter 33

Pete awoke to the sound of a commotion just down the hill from his hiding place. Two animals were wrapped in a struggle of survival. It was dark and he couldn't make out exactly what was going on but he recognized the squeals and shrieks of a pig and the deep groans of a predator. Potbellied pigs were everywhere in Vietnam and a full grown boar with tusks was a formidable opponent. He instantly realized that only a tiger would attempt to take on such a large meal. Pete quickly and quietly rose from his prone position and backed his way out of the thicket. He continued to back away from the area until he reached the edge of the forest. Once inside the forest he moved quickly north and then west toward Dong Ha. Pete expected to be able to hook up with a U.S. patrol or even come across a U.S. base along the way. He found neither. He pressed on west toward the Ranger forward base Scout, eating fruit and other plants he found along the way. Twice he entered small villages after dark to grab rice and vegetables that the locals had stored in baskets or left out to finish ripening.

As he approached the coordinates where Scout had been he found a changed landscape. The place was crawling with VC and the base itself was in ruins. He dodged VC patrols it seemed like every hour and made his way around the southern edge of the former base. Coming north along the western edge of the camp he found the buried crate left for him. He took several minutes to make sure it wasn't booby trapped before opening the lid. He found an extra ammo box had been placed in the crate. Ignoring it initially he pulled a box from the crate and opened it. This box contained rations and candy bars, Pete unwrapped a chocolate bar and devoured it. He slipped his empty pack off of his back and loaded the entire contents of the box into it. He lowered the empty box back into the crate and removed a second box.

This one contained clean underclothes and toiletries such as toothpaste, soap, bug repellent and a new toothbrush. Pete quickly added the clean clothes to his pack and put the bug repellent (which Pete considered useless) back into the box. He lowered the second box into the crate and removed the last one he had left for himself. Opening the ammo box Pete found, amazingly enough, ammo for his XM-21 sniper rifle and his 45.

Also in the box were several letters from Missy and his mom. He slipped the letters and the 45 caliber ammo into his pack, the rounds for his rifle he placed into the belt he wore around his waist and several more were placed one each in the pockets in his fatigues. The reason for only one round per pocket was simple, a single round had nothing to bang against to make noise, two rounds banging together amounted to a trumpet blast signaling your position to the enemy.

Pete stared at the final box in the crate for several seconds before slowly lifting it from the crate. Booby trap? A grenade wired to the lid would be deadly. He held the box by its handle for a moment, and then slowly lowered it to the ground beside the open crate. He smiled to himself, "fool, they would have booby trapped the crate and taken the other stuff if they'd have found it. This must be from Major Pierce." Still he opened the lid slowly and peered inside. Two envelopes were all that occupied the box. He slid the envelopes into his pack and replaced the box, closed the crate and covered the lid with leaves and dirt. He would read the letters later, now he needed to evacuate the area before another VC patrol came along. The route he chose was very familiar. Moving west across his original hunting grounds he picked up the small stream he and Mike had first located on their initial patrol. Then north over the hill and past the headwaters of the stream, down the northern slope and into a valley filled with rice paddies.

Pete slept in a tree overlooking the valley once the sun broke the horizon and lay still all day as the locals tended to the green shoots sprouting from the flooded fields. Once night again crept across the countryside, the Shadow passed silently along the edge of the valley and back into the jungle on the northern side. From here it was just four kilometers to the river separating the two countries. Half way to the river a North Vietnamese patrol passed quietly along a narrow path just two meters from him. The enemy soldiers were on alert and seemed to be looking for someone. Did they detect his presence? Pete wondered.

After the patrol passed, Pete remained hidden for a full thirty minutes. Just as he was beginning to rise up to proceed, a movement caught his eye. Suddenly he could make out three, then four, five and finally eight figures emerging from the bush. It was a U.S. patrol. "That was who the VC were looking for", Pete thought. He was relieved that he had not been detected and he felt compelled to make contact. However making contact without being killed was very complicated. The patrol was obviously behind enemy lines and doing everything possible to keep from being detected. In the end it was better to avoid contact and let the patrol finish their mission while he finished his own.

Another half hour passed before Pete again began the slow process of rising up to resume his forward progress. This time he was able to get up and cross the trail without any contact and press on north towards the river. He stopped just short of the river and climbed a tree to wait out the rapidly approaching day. Once settled in he slid his pack off his back and pulled out a package of crackers. The smell was wonderful and the taste would have passed for a French pastry to him. He savored each bite and took his time eating each thin wafer. He had been in the jungle alone for seven weeks now and without regular food for six. He had shrunk to one hundred and thirty five pounds and suffered from several parasites. He had stopped trying to avoid being bitten by insects and ravaged by leaches and boring worms. Without realizing it he was losing some of his physical ability while gaining mental acumen about his surroundings.

He pulled the letters from his pack and opened the first; it was from Colonel Morgan and contained an additional target. The bio was for a Colonel Li Poh and contained the usual information. Pete pulled out his book that contained the other bios and opened the three metal rings used to retain the pages. He turned to the last page and added the new information behind it, closed the three rings and closed the book. After replacing the book in his pack, he opened the second letter. It was from Major Pierce and was hand written on paper torn from a legal pad. The letter began simply:

Sergeant Lucas, (Pete still wasn't used to the title and smiled when he read it)

The bio sent by Colonel Morgan, 101st Airborne U.S. Army, is of a man that needs to be eliminated as a matter of principal. This target is, in my opinion, evil. There is a military reason for his elimination, he is part of the enemy intelligence gathering community. However, his termination is also warranted for his brutal treatment of American POWs.

At this point, Pete put down the letter and pulled his book back out of his pack. He quickly opened it to the back pages and scanned the bio. There was no mention of POWs in the bio, just that he ran a company of troops based just northeast of a tiny village in North Vietnam. He had attended college in the U.S. and was considered a rising star in the North Vietnamese army. It discussed the Colonel's habits, travels and the strength and makeup of his troops. A map of his camp, and a picture of the Colonel were also contained but no mention of POWs.

Pete returned to the letter from Major Pierce.

The information found in this bio came primarily from Sergeant Tony Lucas.

Pete nearly fell out of the tree. He read on.

Sergeant Lucas was recovered in a prisoner swap on July 25th, 1972 along with Captain William Paul USAF. This swap was a direct result of your actions Sergeant, the five POWs captured during patrols you shadowed on July 17th and 18th were the impetus. Sergeant Tony Lucas has been sent to the rear to receive medical attention, all indications are that he will be OK. The Colonel whose bio you now have was the commandant of the prison camp holding our men. Your mission is clear. God Speed Shadow!

Scout

Pete was floored. He wanted to scream out loud and jump up and down! Tony was alive, not only alive but headed home! "Mom will be so happy, thank you," Pete whispered as he looked toward the heavens.

The day passed, but Pete couldn't sleep. He was excited and his mind raced from home to Tony to Colonel Li Poh. Pete decided to save the Colonel for last, he wanted to complete his main mission before hunting the man his commander had called evil. As he lowered himself from the tree, a sudden weakness came over him. The lack of sleep and his poor diet was catching up with him. He made his way to the river and struggled across, keeping his pack dry by holding it above the water with one hand while swimming with the other. This took all of the energy he had and it took a massive effort for him to scale the opposite bank. He crawled into the jungle and used a tree to pull himself upright. He then staggered to the location he had buried his radio and other supplies. He sank to the ground beside a large tree and pulled the radio from its pack.

"Scout this is Shadow, Scout this is Shadow, over."

No response came.

Several minutes later he tried again, "Scout this is Shadow, Scout this is Shadow, over."

Again no response. He replaced the radio in the pack and returned it to its hiding place. He drank some water and ate a tin of sardines. He was sweating profusely and his mind was a blur. His only salvation was the absolute remoteness of his location. He gathered himself enough to move away from his stashed radio and supplies and found a tree with huge vines covering its trunk. Using the vines as a ladder, he scaled the tree and found an abandoned monkey nest cradled in a fork some ten meters from the ground. He collapsed onto the bed of leaves and branches and fell into a fever induced stupor. Pete had malaria and he was in real trouble.

Chapter 34

Tony returned to the only home he had ever known on September 25th 1972. He was very nervous about how it would feel being there with his father gone and the farm in someone else's control. But Joy greeted him with a hug and a kiss and the rest of the Lucases quickly made him feel right at home. His sisters took turns offering him food and drink, asking him if he was comfortable and generally making a fuss. Uncle John and Aunt May came right over and they too doted over him. Tony was grateful, but also a bit overwhelmed. He did his best to be polite and thanked everyone for all their help.

It was a full three hours before John could get Tony alone and ask him how he was. "Son, how ya holdin' up?" came the question.

"I'll be better once everyone relaxes a little," Tony replied.

"Yeah, I'll bet. But you need to realize how it's been for them. First your dad, then you, then Pete. It's been a long two years" John said quietly.

"What the hell happened Uncle John? I mean, man, how did we lose the farm?"

"It was as good as gone before your old man passed Tony, Roger wouldn't admit it, but it was."

"That bad huh?" asked Tony.

"Yeah that bad, your mom showed me the books. Your old man was good with animals, but he was lousy at runnin' a farm." John said smiling. "But, your mom is really doing it up with her little store."

"Looks that way," answered Tony.

"What do you hear about your bother Tony? No bullshit son, the truth."

"He's in Vietnam Uncle John, I really don't know much else."

"I said no bullshit dammit!" John said, his voice rising slightly.

"I don't know anything," Tony continued.

"Listen boy, you may be an Army Ranger but I can still whip your ass if I need to," John was getting hot. "Now I know Pete's a sniper, he told me that much. And you are too, aren't you?"

"Yessir, I am," Tony replied softly.

"Now spill it boy, or I will forget about your leg and rip you a new one." John was staring directly into Tony's eyes.

"Let's go for a ride, mom can't hear this," Tony said while grabbing his crutches.

The two men slipped out the door and got into John's Ford truck. He fired it up and pulled out of the drive. They drove about a mile before turning down an old two-track lane running along the creek that bordered the old Lucas farm. The lane led back to a small grove of oak trees where the Lucas boys had spent countless hours hunting squirrels and cutting firewood. John stopped the truck and Tony hopped out and made his way to a huge stump and plopped down on it.

"You're right Uncle John, I was a sniper, and a damn good one at that. I was so good at it the army decided to use me as an offensive weapon. The only problem was, I thought I was better than I really was. Jason is still missing and it's my fault. He was my responsibility, I screwed up and he's paying for it." Tony said his voice cracking with pain.

"You've paid for it too son, don't beat yourself up." John answered.

"With all due respect Uncle John, that's bullshit." Tony shot back.

"Maybe, but it's the truth. Listen, you did what you could, as well as you could. There's no shame in that. You are a hero son. Live with it." John replied forcefully.

"Hero, give me a break. I didn't finish the job, some hero, they had to send my little brother to finish what I couldn't." Tony was angry, "He's in that god forsaken hell hole because I couldn't do the job! Do you have any idea how that feels? My nineteen year old brother may die because I wasn't capable of doing my damn job!"

"What the hell are you talking about?"

"They sent him to finish what I started, he's not in South Vietnam Uncle John!" Tony screamed, " He's in North Vietnam! Alone!"

"What? No, that's bullshit. He's just a kid," John said in disbelief.

"It's true, and it's all my fault," Tony said softly and hung his head.

"Well, there's nothing we can do about it now Tony." John's mind was racing, he needed to help Tony, not beat him up. "You did what you could, and regardless what you say you are a hero; to me and your Aunt May anyway. Pete is a solid young man, he'll get through it, just like you did."

"I am here because of Pete, Uncle John," Tony replied. "He helped capture the guys I was swapped for, who's gonna help Pete? I'm stuck here, with this worthless leg! I can't even walk, how the hell am I supposed to help him?" Tony cried.

"Have faith son, I do," John answered. "Somehow, some way, he'll get home. I know it sure as I'm standin' here."

"You don't know Uncle John, you've never seen that place." Tony replied and pulled himself up. "Let's go, mom will be worried."

They climbed back into the truck and headed back to the farmhouse. Before long the Lucas women were fussing over Tony all over again.

Chapter 35

A figure appeared in his mind, he made it out to be an
enemy soldier and he searched frantically for his weapon. The
figure fled and he gave in again to the fever. Pete was sweating
profusely and having horrible delusions. He was reliving the
events of the past six months in terrifying stereo. His mind
rambled from one startling image to another, in no particular
order. He writhed in pain and convulsed from loss of control of
his muscles. The image of the enemy soldier re-appeared and
again he flailed trying to find his weapon. The image fled once
more and he slipped back into fitful sleep.

Pete came to, in the early morning hours of a clear
September day. He attempted to sit up, but couldn't muster the
strength to do so. He reached down with his left hand and found
his canteen, managed to get the cap off and drank lustily from it.
The water was sweet and felt cool going down his throat. He
tried again and this time managed to get to a seated position
leaning his back against the tree. Took another drink and using
his right hand pulled his pack to his side. He pulled out a ration
tin, opened it and devoured the contents. He didn't even take

time to see what it was he was eating. It didn't matter, he was starving, and it was food or at least something that passed as food. He scanned the area around his position and found himself in a large tree, sitting in an old monkey nest. He didn't remember how he got there, or exactly where there was. He was still groggy and soaking wet from sweat.

A movement on his right prompted him to quickly find his rifle, he grabbed it and spun to face the threat. A large form screamed and fled into the canopy. Pete was still trying to get his wits about him when the form reappeared. Pete stared at the form and it slowly came into focus. It was a large monkey, easily two feet tall standing on a limb and clutching another limb with its left hand. Pete was startled and mesmerized at the same time. The creature was beautiful and its eyes were so full of emotion. Pete felt a connection to it, a kinship that was strange and yet strong. He stared at the primate for a long time and it stared back, he was still weak and had to lower his rifle to keep from dropping it. The monkey watched him carefully and slowly sat down, still grasping the small branch in its left hand.

The two strangers stayed this way for nearly an hour, before the monkey suddenly jumped from its limb into a tree behind Pete and was gone. Pete was trying to stay alert in case the big stranger returned, but his fatigue took over and he fell asleep again. The monkey returned while Pete was asleep and watched quietly from his perch in the neighboring tree.

Pete woke again the next morning to find the canopy empty around him, but his strength was coming back. His memory was also returning and the news of Tony's return to the living filled his mind once again. Pete wasn't sure how long he had been out of commission, but he had a feeling it had been several days. In fact it had been nearly seventy two hours and he was in desperate need of more water and a bath. He finished off his canteen, ate another tin of sardines and some more crackers. Then he began the long process of trying to get down out of the tree.

It took a full hour to get himself upright and his pack and rifle onto his back and secured. After doing so he noticed he was once again not alone. The monkey had returned, and was watching him closely from the neighboring tree. Pete had a feeling this master of the canopy had been his guardian angel, watching over him while he battled the infection coursing through his veins. They once again stared at each other for a long time, this time Pete smiled at the creature and began to lower himself down. It may have been wishful thinking, but Pete could have sworn the beast smiled back.

Pete hit the ground feeling reborn and strong. He quickly returned to the river and waited by its banks for nightfall. Once darkness fell, Pete stripped and slipped into the cool water. He took a long bath and washed his sweat soaked clothes. Back on shore he pulled the new underclothes from his pack, the ones he had removed from the crate five days earlier, and put them on. The only good thing he had found about having been sick was that all of the parasites had left his body; apparently they didn't like being exposed to malaria any better than he did. Once dressed and clean, Pete filled his canteen, making sure to add the tablets that purified the water. They made the water taste funny, but it was better than having diarrhea for days.

Pete decided he needed some protein, so he pulled some fishing line from his pack and tied small hook he had made from a wire ring on the sardine can he had eaten earlier. The other end of the line he tied to a fallen tree branch, his fishing pole was complete. All he needed now was bait. This was the easiest part, there were thousands of insects in the jungle and finding one was easy. He quickly found a caterpillar and impaled it on the hook. A quick flick sent the hook skyward and it arched down into the slowly flowing stream. It took only two casts before a strong tug signaled a bite. Pete pulled and after a short fight he landed a nice fat fish. He checked the river three times for signs of the enemy before he committed the heresy of starting a small fire. The risk of starting the fire was huge, but he decided he needed the meat and sushi wasn't on his list of edible items.

The fish cooked quickly and Pete extinguished the fire immediately afterwards. He savored the flavor and texture of the meat, it was wonderful and very filling. He finished every last bite and buried the bones and remnants of the fire just in case anyone might come across them. He hadn't seen nor heard any signs of human activity in this particular area of the jungle neither in his first crossing into the North or since re-entering the country a week before. He began to feel safe here, and he found that very comforting. There was at least one place he could relax a little if things got bad.

Chapter 36

Pete gathered his pack and rifle and set off north, the next target on his list was nearly fifty kilometers inside North Vietnam and would be his toughest test yet. General Bihn Vok was commander of the North Vietnamese communications center in the city of Wihn. His center coordinated all of the communications coming in from the front and directed those communiqués to the proper authorities in the rear, and visa versa. The U.S. Army had detected the center and General Vok, but because of a huge SAM site and political wrangling in Washington nothing could be done about assets in North Vietnam. The city of Wihn was ringed with Russian SAMs and the potential of losing more pilots kept the Americans at bay. The intel indicated that without General Vok, the coordination of information would be disrupted, it seemed the General didn't trust anyone with the whole system except himself. Thus he was the only one capable of coordinating the entire network.

Pete had committed the entire bio to memory and was once again hunting the enemy. His body was strong again and for the first time in a long time his mind was strong as well. He had come to grips with the fact that he was alone and without any hope of rescue. He realized that his radio was useless unless he moved farther south or east to get into range of a large U.S. force. He felt reborn after almost succumbing to the fever that wracked his body for five days and nights. The jungle seemed more alive and energetic too. The wildlife was active and vibrant. He caught glimpses of monkeys in the canopy occasionally, and wondered if one of them was his guardian angel. He was in awe of the natural world around him, and felt compelled to take care of it as much as possible.

He ate more frequently and consumed nearly twice as many calories as before his illness. He was convinced his weakened body was the reason he had fallen ill. He still took no precautions against parasites or mosquitoes, other than using the water purification tablets in his drinking water. He could deal with bugs and worms, leaches and spiders but diarrhea was not an option. He made sure to drink plenty of water, dehydration was also not an option. It was easy to get plenty of fruit and even vegetables in Vietnam, rice was everywhere and there were thousands of edible plants. The real premium was on protein.

Fish was the easiest form, and Pete tried to stay within range of a water source at all times. He concentrated on catching fish that he could cook quickly on a tiny fire, avoiding the larger meatier fish that would take longer to cook and because much of the meat would go to waste anyway.

It was now October and Pete had been in the jungle alone for three months. His hair was nearly over his collar and he had to mend his clothes regularly. He shaved nearly every day, partly to keep parasites and insects from inhabiting any beard that would grow and partly because he couldn't stand the itching caused by new growth. It would take nearly two weeks to cover the distance to Wihn and there were literally thousands of North Vietnamese between him and his target. The mission was clear, but the execution of the mission was still vague. How to kill a man in a busy city where you cannot be seen in public without being immediately spotted, captured and most likely killed? This question rolled around in Pete's head for days on end.

Colonel Mitch Morgan was beside himself; he had gotten word of a weak signal from Shadow eight days ago, but since then nothing, not a peep. He knew Pete had been successful up to now, taking out four targets. He also knew that the young man had now been alone in the jungle for way too long. The plan had been for Pete to return to base after no more than two weeks, no matter whether he was successful or not. Pete had radioed Scout about the raid, then nothing for two months. This was not acceptable. Colonel Morgan had no idea Major Pierce had not given Shadow the order to report every two weeks. In fact Pierce had not given Pete any orders at all, simply "here are the targets, do whatever you have to do to complete the mission."

Morgan called Missy into his office and asked her a direct question, "Missy James, are you still in contact with Pete Lucas?"

"I haven't gotten a letter from Pete in three months sir, I probably won't ever get another one," she replied her head down tears beginning to flow.

"Why would you say that young lady? We have no information that anything is wrong with Pete," asked the Colonel.

"I sent him a letter a month ago, it was a terrible thing to do, but I couldn't bear him not knowing."

"You sent him a Dear John letter?"

"No not really, I told him the truth. I told him I was spending a lot of time with Tony and that I was feeling confused. I asked him what I should do." Missy began to sob.

"He didn't reply?"

"No, Sir."

"Missy, you can stop beating yourself up for now. Pete hasn't gotten your letter. He hasn't been in contact for almost two months. I don't know where he is for sure, but I know he is still out there, that much I am sure of." Colonel Morgan was confident and reassuring to Missy.

"Yes sir, I know he's gonna be OK. He has to, he promised me he would come back. And I promised him I would wait. Oh god what am I doing?" Missy cried.

"You are going through what every other GI wife or girlfriend goes through, it is a horrible strain. Not knowing, expecting a knock at any time. I suggest you talk to your momma, she'll have better advice than I can ever hope to give you." Colonel Morgan added. He was at a loss trying to help her, his own marriage had ended in divorce ten years earlier. Katherine couldn't take the stress of waiting for that knock; she had found solace in another man's arms. Morgan considered it fair; she had been through hell with him. He was gone as much as he was home and when he was home he drank to forget what he had seen and what he had done half a world away. No woman should have to go through that, but he missed her more than she would ever know.

Missy excused herself and Colonel Morgan went back to pacing and worrying. What the hell was going on over there? Why didn't Shadow check in? There hadn't been any confirmed kills for nearly a month now, who was next on Shadow's list? This became a focal point for the Colonel and he began trying to think like Shadow. "If I were him who would be next?" he thought to himself. The bios were spread across his desk and he was deep in thought when the knock came.

"Enter," Tony heard the Colonel say and he proceeded to enter the office of his commanding officer. "Sergeant Tony Lucas reporting for duty sir"

Colonel Morgan looked up at Tony, then returned his gaze to the bios on the desk. Tony stood at attention for ten full minutes before the Colonel looked up again and said, "at ease, Sergeant." Tony relaxed and waited for the Colonel. He waited another five minutes before the Colonel finally looked up again and leaned back in his chair. The bios were still open on the desk and the Colonel seemed to be struggling with an unseen demon.

"Tony, I want your opinion on something but I don't want to mess up your recovery."

"I am going crazy with nothing to do but physical therapy sir, anything to break up the day would be welcome." Tony replied.

"This isn't just anything son, it is a mission plan, Shadow's mission plan," the Colonel replied watching Tony for a reaction.

The reaction was swift and direct, "what the hell is Pete doing over there, sir? You knew what happened to me and Jason! Damn it sir, he's too young!"

A raised right hand quieted the Sergeant; the Colonel sat up straight and looked Tony in the eye. "I wouldn't have sent him if he wasn't ready," answered Morgan. "He is more ready than any soldier I have ever known. He may be the perfect sniper, smart, silent and ridiculous with a rifle. Have you seen his scores? Your brother is not the kid you left behind son, he is a man and one helluva soldier."

"You know what I mean sir, the mission is impossible. There are thousands of VC and just one of him. If he pops one of theirs' deep behind the lines, they'll turn out the entire country looking for him like they did us. We evaded them for four days, but there are just too many of them. They walked arm in arm towards us until they literally stepped on us, we had no chance and neither does Pete," Tony said softly. "They'll torture him, and if I know Pete he knows that. So he'll open up on them, and they will kill him."

"You sound very certain of that Tony, you know something I don't?"

"I spent two years in a steel cage sir, I know more than you can even imagine," Tony answered flatly.

"Yes, I suppose you do. But I know that Shadow has already hit four targets and we're not seeing any mobilization at all, in fact they don't seem to know what they're looking for. Look at this intel, you see any effort by Charlie to find Shadow?"

Tony studied the intelligence and then the bios on the Colonel's desk. He paid specific attention to two of the bios, those of General Vok and Colonel Li Poh. "This guy is next, he said finally pointing to the picture of General Vok."

"What makes you so sure?" asked Morgan.

"He's the second farthest in country, making him perfect. He can be hit, and when the VC expect Shadow to head back for the border he'll move further away from it. The next hit will be on General Trang; here, Tony laid another photo on the desk. He will be much easier than Vok because he is confident in his own safety and because he won't be in a city. Then comes Whey Poh southeast of Trang and headed in the right direction. Pete will save Poh for last, close to the border and very out of the way. I assume that this is what you wanted from me?" Tony asked.

"Yes, that is exactly what I wanted. I want to try and have a team ready for extraction as soon as possible. You're saying the best spot will be the crossing where you were returned to us?" asked the Colonel.

"No, I said that Poh would be last. Pete will head east after the hit and try to get to Da Nang. He knows we have a large presence there, and he will hope to be able to make radio contact while still in the North."

"That doesn't seem right, why wouldn't he just cross the river where he crossed the first time and get back into the South as soon as possible?"

"Because, he already knows we lost Scout and he couldn't make radio contact from there. The best shot he has is Da Nang. That is where he'll go." Tony was adamant.

"I hope your right Tony, your brother's life may rest on where I position this team," answered Morgan.

"Da Nang, sir. That is where I would go, and that is where Pete will go." Tony never even considered another option, he was positive.

Chapter 37

Pete continued his track north, skirting villages and towns, sticking to the thick jungle as much as possible. Crossing open areas only in the dark of night, he made his way north to the outskirts of Wihn. General Vok had his communications network concealed in an old warehouse near the center of the city. It looked like any of the fifty other buildings surrounding it, remnants of the French rubber industry that had been the main source of employment and revenue in the city. The general rarely left the building, except to go home once every week or two to visit his family who lived in an apartment on the north side of town. The apartment was also very non-descript, in a building set on a hill with several other flats each having a small garden and a view of the city. There was nothing to advertise that a General in the Peoples Army lived there and that is exactly the way Vok liked it.

Pete waited until 0200 to approach the edge of the city, the night was very dark and the city was blacked out. The North Vietnamese worried about the US bombing their cities so they kept them dark at night much of the time. He slipped between buildings and down deserted alleys, avoiding several patrols that guarded the city. Pete soon realized that the war was not as evident here, there seemed to be much more of a normal pace to life. It took him three hours to find the right building, then another thirty minutes to decide where to set up his surveillance. He chose a rooftop nearby that had a large overgrown garden growing on it. It seemed as if the owner had abandoned it, or at the very least let it go untended for quite some time. His camo suit worked nicely here to keep him hidden from prying eyes. He needed to watch the movements in and around the target, the execution was still vague but getting clearer by the hour. The rooftop provided a good view of the main entrance on the south side of Vok's building as well as the entire west side. The west side had two large overhead doors for loading and unloading as well as another small door for employees. The hope was that Vok would use one of the two entrances to come and go. Pete didn't have time to find out if there were other entrances on the east or north side of the building because the dawn was coming fast and he needed to hide.

The overgrown garden was a perfect hiding place during the day, the vegetation kept the hot sun from baking him and the elevation allowed for a slight breeze to reach him. The first evening he found out that he wasn't alone on the roof. At first one, then several, finally a dozen thin, flea infested rats emerged from a small hole in the masonry at the northeast corner of the roof. They scurried along the ledge that rimmed the roof and crossed the four feet of open rooftop to the edge of the garden directly in front of Pete's face. The first two climbed right over Pete and headed for the overripe fruit lying on the roof behind him. The third rat stopped a few inches from Pete's outstretched left arm and began sniffing the air. Rats have an extremely good sense of smell, and this one was convinced he smelled something other than a rat. He approached Pete's arm and carefully sniffed the sleeve, he backed off slightly and then pounced on Pete's shoulder. Pete almost jumped up, but realized the rat was chasing something. It was a large beetle that had made Pete's camo suit his home. The rat scurried away from Pete with his dinner in his mouth, chased by two other rats that were trying to steal it from him. The rodents continued to forage for food in the garden, several times Pete thought he would have to fight them off but each time they found something else to occupy themselves. The fleas they left behind were another matter. They were relentless.

Biting Pete and making it nearly impossible for him to keep still, this was the worst he had encountered yet and he had no idea how long he would have to stay here.

The next two days were more of the same. The fleas were not going anywhere and the rats were getting more aggressive. They had begun chewing on his suit and taking pieces of it back to their nests. Pete decided that the fourth night would be his last on the roof, if he didn't get a shot at Vok he would have to find another way, maybe at Vok's apartment at the north end of the city. At 0110 the small door on the west side of the building opened and two men stepped out onto the loading dock. They were talking and smoking cigarettes. The glow from the cigarettes wasn't enough for an identification so Pete simply watched as the men continued their conversation. This was obviously nothing more than idle chatter as both men seemed relaxed and enjoying their smoke. Two minutes passed and one of the men tossed his cigarette butt off of the loading platform and turned toward the door. The other man stopped him and the first produced something from his shirt pocket, he handed the object to the other man and headed back indoors. The light streaming from the door illuminated the man left outside for an instant and Pete was pretty sure it was General Vok, but he wasn't positive. There couldn't be a mistake, if he hit the wrong man he wouldn't get another chance at Vok.

Another minute passed and the man walked to the edge of the platform and tossed his cigarette onto the ground. Unlike the first man he didn't immediately turn to head back inside, instead he reached into his shirt pocket and pulled out another smoke. He then raised his right hand and used the lighter the first man had given him to light the cigarette in his mouth. The light from the butane lighter was just what the doctor ordered as far as Pete was concerned. He used it to positively identify General Vok.

The process was the same as always for Pete, he inhaled, exhaled slowly and evenly slid the trigger back. General Vok had no chance, his chain smoking had killed him long before he could have developed lung cancer. The report from the rifle was deafening in Pete's ears. He was certain that the entire area would be crawling with police and soldiers in no time. But after five minutes with no sign of anyone even stirring he rose up slowly and made his way down off of the rooftop the same way he had came nearly five days before. Sliding over the ledge on the west side of the building his feet found the drain pipe, hand over hand using his feet against the wall to slow his decent he lowered himself the thirty or so feet to the ground. Once on the ground Pete moved quickly to an alley west of the building and clinging to the wall of buildings he slipped quietly to the edge of town. There he found the small river he had crossed to enter Wihn and slid down the bank and into the water.

He swam and floated the river for nearly a kilometer until he reached the northern most edge of the city. There he scrambled up the bank and crossed a narrow street and entered a garden. It was nearly dawn and he needed to hide until darkness returned. He found a thicket of small bushes and squirmed inside. He didn't sleep much because the gardener was very active in her garden and he was afraid of being discovered. He didn't want to have to kill the woman; she was not a target. But if he had to, he knew that there wouldn't be any hesitation. As darkness finally came the gardener headed inside to enjoy a hard earned meal. Pete slipped from his sanctuary in the thicket and helped himself to several pieces of fruit and a tomato; and then moved silently north out of the city and soon was back in the thick jungle. He found another small river and stripped naked, washing his clothes and even his camo suit to rid them of fleas.

He found that the rats had done more damage than he thought to his camo, ripping several holes in it and stealing at least a dozen of the canvas panels that create the non-uniform image that is the basis of camouflage. He couldn't do anything about the missing panels, but he had to repair the holes and re-plant the plants and moss uprooted by the ravenous rodents.

Pete stayed here beside the river for two days, eating well and fixing his damaged gear. He had not been able to eat much during his week in Wihn and he was afraid of getting weak again. So he made sure to take in as many calories as he could and used the water from the river to wash away the last remaining fleas and other pests he had acquired on the rooftop. He was now convinced he hated rats more than anything else he had encountered in Vietnam.

On October 11th he once again headed north, this time he would be able to stay in his beloved jungle all the way to the target. The thick and nasty was exceptionally thick here and it took Pete seven days to navigate the fourteen kilometers to a tiny village hacked out of the jungle. Surrounding the village were several fields used as training facilities for artillery, marksmanship and conditioning of troops. There were large barracks which housed the new recruits and smaller quarters for instructors and officers. On the eastern edge of the camp were several batteries of anti-aircraft missiles also known as SAMs or Surface to Air Missiles. They appeared operational, but Pete figured they were also probably for training purposes.

He watched the training from a massive tree some six hundred meters away, noting who came and went. He was amazed at the poor quality of the training, lack of equipment and poor conditioning of the recruits. It was nothing like he had experienced in his days at Fort Stewart. But he had to admit that the enemy was certainly holding their own, however; he was convinced that if the US were to attack North Vietnam the story would be completely different. Fighting a defensive war was much more difficult than when you were on the offensive. The US air and armor power were ineffective as defensive weapons, but everything changed when you turned that power loose.

General Trang was not only the commander of this training base he was the head of recruitment and training for all of the ground forces in the North Vietnamese army. He had several aides that carried out his ideas and provided him with recruits, but he was the man in charge of the pipeline that fed the human wave of soldiers used by the field commanders. What they lacked in equipment and training they made up for in sheer numbers. This facility and several others like it churned out more new soldiers per month than the US produced in a year. Much was being made of the loss of US personnel in Vietnam back home on the news, but the losses taken on the other side were truly staggering in comparison.

Pete slipped in closer to the base after dark each night and made precise notes concerning troop numbers and the base layout. He figured this data was already in US hands but it wouldn't hurt to pass it along to HQ just in case. At around 0400 each night Pete would make his way back to his arboreal roost and watch the sunrise. He was lying prone on the large branch he called home on the third day when he noticed something moving on the branch directly in front of him. He had been looking through his scope and not noticed it until it was just inches from the end of his rifle barrel. The long thin tongue flicking in and out sniffing the air for food, his movements slow and calculating, a large snake approached. Pete quickly recognized this as not just any old snake, it was a green tree pit viper. Extremely poisonous and not too friendly, this particular type of snake has a really bad reputation as being ill tempered. It is best known for falling out of trees onto unsuspecting victims.

Pete wasn't sure what to do, so he just froze. He held his breath to try and hide the heat associated from even the most basic of bodily functions. The snake slowly advanced avoiding the cool rifle barrel and looping itself over the stock just in front of the sniper's right hand. Pete felt the cool scales of the snake as they slid over the back of his hand pushing the head with its flicking tongue closer to his face. Pete had closed his eyes and pressed his face into his left arm to shield it from the viper. The snake sensed no malice from the lump it was traversing and sensed no food present as it continued moving towards the trunk of the tree. The feeling of the large snake slithering over his right shoulder, onto his back and down the back of his legs made Pete want to jump out of his skin. He held his breath for as long as he possibly could, then slowly let it out and quickly took in another and held it. The snake had moved on and was now negotiating the thick tree trunk by spiraling its way down. Pete heard the rush of branches and a light thump as the snake fell the last ten feet onto the jungle floor below him. He was unnerved by the experience and couldn't relax for several hours.

Finally, at 1630 he was back on task and scanning the base. He had identified the building used by the senior staff but had not seen General Trang since arriving three days before. Suddenly there was hurried movement in the camp and troops rushing into formation. A vehicle pulled up in front of the building and out stepped General Trang.

He spoke with several officers and a Caucasian man that had been riding in the back of the vehicle and then turned and walked towards the assembled men. He walked in front of the men and addressed them, they responded on cue with shouts and pro-government slogans. The address lasted for over ten minutes upon completion of which the men rushed to various areas to prepare for inspection. The general went inside the building with several other officers, and didn't re-emerge for nearly an hour.

Pete was tired; the incident with the viper had cost him vital sleep. He was used to sleeping for an hour or two around midday but today he couldn't even close his eyes without seeing that tongue. The general's arrival had made matters even worse; he now had to stay alert in case the target attempted to leave. His mind wandered wondering who the white guy was with the General, Pete guess a Soviet advisor but he really couldn't be sure. "A camera would be wonderful right now" was his next thought. He was roused from his doldrums by a large explosion to his right. It was the artillery firing down range, practicing for what would undoubtedly be a demonstration for the general. This was the opportunity Pete had been hoping for, on cue the door to the office opened and out stepped the General and his staff. They strode quickly toward the artillery range and met up with the head instructor just behind the line of cannon and mortars.

The instructor spoke to his recruits then saluted the general. He turned towards the guns and raised his arm, as he shouted instructions he yanked his arm down. This was the signal to fire, and the men responded with a barrage of fire. The general watched through field glasses as the rounds landed all around the intended target, with several direct hits. The general smiled and applauded the men. Next the men demonstrated the speed and ease with which they could reload and re-aim the guns, taking aim on a second target. The instructor's arm went up and he shouted orders, as he yanked his arm down the artillery again gave forth a thunderous explosion. Lost in the noise and confusion was the report of a single shot 7.62 MM rifle. Pete's shot hit its target and General Trang was killed instantly. The confusion and scramble after his death showed Pete that he had nothing to worry about. There would be no search party, almost no one even suspected that an enemy sniper was anywhere nearby. The Russian advisor Major Evgeny Kolskoff recognized the sniper's marksmanship and made a hasty retreat to the relative safety of the office. Pete closed the lens covers on his rifle and drifted off to a very uneasy sleep. His dreams filled with a cool feeling on his hand and a flicking tongue.

Chapter 38

Tony was now walking with a cane and back on the base

at Fort Campbell, he had been given a position as a small arms

instructor. A position he was on one hand grateful to have and on

the other hand took as an indication he would never return to the

field as a sniper. He wasn't sure what his future was with the

Army or with Missy. She had kept seeing him all along but he

sensed she was being very cautious with their relationship. He

wanted to ask her to visit Ohio with him, but he was afraid of the

answer she would give. Instead he went to rehab each morning

before heading to the range to instruct young men on the finer

points of field stripping their weapons.

Missy was still torn, she thought she loved Tony but

knew she loved Pete. She was afraid her feelings for Tony were a

combination of misplaced longing for his brother and pity. She

found herself missing Pete more as Tony's health got better, she

wanted desperately to talk to Pete and find out how he was and

where he had been for the last three months. She talked for hours with her mom about Pete and Tony and what she was going through, her momma's advice was strait forward and honest.

"If you're in love with Pete, wait for him however long it takes. True love is not something you decide honey, it just happens. You can't control it any more than the weather, it will do what it wants and you just have to go along for the ride. But follow your heart sweetheart, if you listen to your head you'll end up regretting it later." Emma James told her. "This isn't a race, take your time and be sure. This is a decision you can't afford to mess up, or it will haunt you the rest of your days."

"Thanks a lot momma! No pressure, just my entire future hanging on one decision, you're a lot of help! I've loved Pete from the moment I saw him, but Tony needs me and he's here, now. I don't know where Pete is and if he'll ever come back." Missy shot back.

"True, but if he does come back you can't avoid him, he's Tony's brother. You'll see him all the time, birthday parties, weddings, Christmas. You ready to deal with that?" Emma asked.

"I don't know momma? How did I get into this mess?" Missy cried.

"Love is always messy sweetheart, if it weren't it wouldn't be so powerful," Emma replied.

"Well I could do without it at this point," Missy added. "Who needs this, nauseous all the time, worrying and crying."

"Yeah, but the pain is worth it once you've got the one you love. You're daddy is my true love and I knew it the first time he smiled at me. I wouldn't trade all the pain he has caused me for anything, cause when he holds me tight and kisses me I still get light headed" Emma said musingly.

"I don't feel that way with Tony, I mean I feel good when I'm with him and were holding hands and all. But there isn't any feeling that way, all lightheaded and starry eyed" Missy said.

" How about when you were with Pete?" asked Emma.

"I didn't get to really spend enough time with him momma," Missy answered.

"That's bull girl, you spent time with him in Ohio at his momma's place, so was it special or not?" pressed Emma.

Missy thought back to the trip she and Pete took to Ohio before he left for sniper school, the way she felt when he told her he was leaving right after they got back to the base. The way that she felt watching him board the bus taking him to the airfield on his way to Vietnam. The way she felt when he told her he loved her and asked her to wait for him. The way her head spun when he kissed her goodbye. She had forgotten that feeling until now.

She looked at her momma and started crying again, through her tears she whispered, "I love Pete momma."

Emma James replied, "I know honey, I've always known."

Pete was headed southeast on his way to Bong Hoi, a city near the coast that also hosted his next target General Whey Poh. The General was in charge of coastal forces along the border between the North and the South. His men controlled the river traffic and the ports, which meant that he controlled the logistics in the region. The rivers of Vietnam served more like highways, moving men and materials to the front and casualties to the rear. His operational capabilities were admired by the U.S. brass; thus his place on Pete's list.

It took Pete a full three weeks to travel the forty kilometers to Bong Hoi, his travel restricted by the terrain, weather and the fact that this part of North Vietnam was much more heavily populated than areas further from the coast. Not that it was teeming with cities or even humans, but there were enough people to make Pete's life very dangerous. He kept to the jungle as much as possible and used the dark of night to cover his movements. His diet improved with the increase in human activity, food was more plentiful and of better quality. In one village he found a chicken roasting on a fire unattended, unable to resist he helped himself to a wing and two drumsticks. He could only imagine the alarm caused when the cook found her dinner partially absconded.

The enemy patrols were still small and not on high alert, but Pete was sure that would change when he was through with his next target. Up in the center of North Vietnam no one was suspecting an enemy sniper, but here in the border region it would be figured out instantly. Pete needed a plan for exiting the area safely before he could even begin planning the actual shot. He figured that if the VC were paying any attention his pattern would be clear once Whey Poh was dead. Hit a target and head north, next target head south, next north again. This had worked up to this point, but they would recognize this and once the General was shot they would cover all areas north of the city. Also, they would cover the southern exits because that is the shortest path to safety. Heading west would make sense, as long as it followed again soon with a move south toward the border, so they would block this path as well.

The only paths that Pete found possibly safe were east to the coast, but there was nowhere for him to go from there, and west with a turn northwest shortly after leaving the city. This seemed safe, but Pete really worried about the enemy completely shutting off the western exits from the city immediately after the General's untimely demise. A seed of a thought entered Pete's mind, what if he got a ride out of town? After all, the General was in charge of logistics. He would try to find a ride, but if one couldn't be found he would have to try the western exits.

It was early December when Pete arrived outside the city of Bong Hoi, a small city with low buildings and a bustling port. General Whey Poh had his headquarters in a building on government docks upriver from the commercial center. However nothing moved into or out of this area without his knowledge, nothing that is except a shadow. The General had been warned of assassination attempts by agents of the South and possibly by American agents, but he ignored them for the most part. He had been made aware of the deaths of General Vok and General Trang, but he blamed their own men. The fact that Major

Kolskoff had witnessed Trang's assassination did little to dissuade him of his certainty that these were acts of internal operators. There was no way that an agent from the South, let alone an American could operate in North Vietnam for that long without being detected.

He had his finger on the pulse of his country, if anything or anyone moved he knew about it immediately. He had been the one who detected an American team sent into the North two years prior and had them captured in a week. One of the men was scheduled to meet the American press in Hanoi this week. He would be ordered to tell them he was captured inside North Vietnam or be killed. The Americans wouldn't try that again, the outcry from their own citizens if they were found in North Vietnam would be disastrous to the American administration.

The General kept a flat on a hill overlooking the docks; here he kept a mistress that served him fine meals and French wine. He missed the French, or at least their food and especially their wine. He had to make special arrangements now to get his wine, an exercise he considered a nuisance. His official residence was in Hanoi where his wife and two daughters lived, but he only went home occasionally to see them and meet with party heads. He sat quietly looking out over the docks drinking his wine on an evening that was pleasantly without rain.

Pete watched him sip his wine from a point almost directly across the river, he observed the General for two days planning for his escape unconcerned about the actual shot. He could take the shot at any time, the General showed no signs of taking any precautions. His security consisted of two bodyguards and an aide that traveled with him at all times and even stayed in a flat adjoining the one the General was sitting in this very moment. No, the shot would not be the problem. Getting away would be the problem, unless he could find that ride. On the third night Pete silently left his hiding place on the hillside above the river and made his way down to the docks. He slowly worked his way around several small buildings at the edge of the harbor and noticed a large boat moored to the jetty, its name was the Montang. He lowered himself onto the deck of the boat and slipped quietly inside the cabin. Here he found two berths for the crew and a small washroom, heading toward the front of the boat he found the wheelhouse and stairs leading below decks.

He tiptoed down the stairs and found the hold empty except for a crate filled with rope and other accessories used on the boat. At the rear of the hold he found the engine room, or more aptly put the engine closet. The room was barely big enough for the engine and a small cabinet that stored spare parts. Pete was looking for a hiding place, a place to stow away, in short his ride out of Bong Hoi. He opened the cabinet and found it empty, this was perfect as long as the boat would sail when he needed it and as long as no one looked for spare parts for the engine. Pete left the boat quickly and returned to his hiding place above the river. He watched the next day as the boat, his ride; was loaded with cargo and prepared to cast off. The crew was busy making ready, stowing gear and supplies. It was getting late and Pete realized that his ride was either going to set sail that night late or wait until morning. The crew disappeared below decks and all was quiet again on the jetty, it was 2330. They were waiting for first light. Pete focused on the General's flat, there was a faint light coming from the parlor. The General was enjoying a bedtime glass of Port. Pete's shot interrupted the General in mid swallow, and the ensuing shattering of the glass as it hit the floor awoke his mistress. She ran into the parlor and finding the General dead rushed next door to his security team. By the time they assessed the situation and sounded the alarm

Pete had already reached the jetty and was crouched down behind some crates just a few feet from the Montang. The alarm and commotion awoke all of the personnel on the boat and they rushed onto the deck. They all ran to the railing on the starboard side and were looking up towards the General's flat and jabbering in Vietnamese. Pete used the distraction and slipped onto the deck and into the cabin, quickly making his way below decks and into the engine compartment. He opened the small cabinet and stuffed himself inside along with his rifle and pack.

The night was long and the cramped cabinet was hot. Pete heard a commotion on deck and several sets of footfalls running down the stairs. He heard men yelling and figured a VC patrol was searching the boat, he just hoped they wouldn't open the cabinet. As it turned out the patrol questioned the crew and when they ascertained that the entire crew had been sleeping on the boat when the General had been shot they took a quick look around and left the boat. Pete then heard the engine fire up and felt the boat start to slowly accelerate and then list slightly to port. The cargo wasn't evenly spread out in the hold, but apparently the crew didn't mind the list and they headed upriver towards Mihn.

Pete waited for nightfall and then climbed out of the cabinet, he had felt the boat stop several times and heard men talking loudly. The VC were searching boats along the river and he had been lucky so far not to be discovered. It was time to get back into the dark and nasty where he felt safe, but he still needed to get off the boat undetected if possible. As he entered the hold from the engine room he noticed several boxes with packing that were open, looking inside he found explosives, grenades and ammunition; all the makings of a large explosion.

He needed to get away from the boat long before the explosion or else he would either be blown up or captured quickly by the VC coming to investigate. So he decided to rig one of his special traps. He pulled some monofilament fishing line from his pack and rigged a tripwire across the aisle between two crates near the stairs, this one he was able to place ankle high making it virtually invisible. He connected the monofilament to the handle on an ammo case he emptied, making the case relatively light. The case he balanced dangerously on the corner of one of the crates. Below the crate he placed a dozen land mines. The ammo case was bound to land on at least one of them, setting it off and with it the rest of the cargo. It would be a hell of a blast; Pete was hoping he would never know if it even went off.

Pete then made his way slowly up the stairs, as he peeked out of the door he could make out the captain in the wheelhouse. Concentrating on navigating the river, the captain rarely looked back into the cabin. Pete slid out of the door and into the main cabin. He crouched low and quietly made his way down the hallway toward the back of the boat. He peered into the berths as he passed them and found everyone inside asleep; quickly he crept to the doorway leading to the deck and saw a man standing on the rear deck looking back toward the stern of the boat. Pete slipped through the doorway and crouched behind a crate on the deck just feet from the deck hand.

Moments later a voice from the front called out and the deck hand answered, he turned around and walked right past the crate Pete was crouched behind. Continuing on he walked around the side of the cabin and headed toward the bow. Pete moved quickly to the stern, grabbed a line that was attached to a cleat on the transom and tossed the free end into the water. He grabbed the line firmly and lowered himself into the river, the strong current and wake of the boat threatening to rip his arms out of their shoulder sockets. Pete relaxed his grip on the rope slightly hoping to allow the line to slide through his hands slowly so that he gradually got further from the boat. Reality struck him when the rope was ripped from his hand almost instantly and he found himself floating in the river. The current was fairly strong and it took him ten minutes to make his way to the western shore. At that point he hauled himself up onto the bank and entered the jungle, quickly finding a very thick, overgrown area and settled in for the remainder of the night. Unfortunately he had no idea exactly where he was, that would have to wait until he could get a bearing from some sort of a landmark.

The Montang continued on its way, upon returning to the stern the deck hand found the loose line trailing behind the boat and pulled it aboard. Not wanting to get in trouble for failing to secure the line he didn't report it to his captain. The next morning a patrol boat pulled alongside the Montang and ordered her captain to stop and allow them to search the boat. The captain complied while complaining that he had already been searched twice the previous day. The patrol ignored his complaints and boarded the vessel, several armed men entered the cabin and checked the berths. Two more men continued forward and began to descend the stairs, when a wave caused by a passing boat rocked the Montang abruptly. The ammo case fell from its perch on the crate and landed on not one but four separate mines.

The ensuing explosion engulfed the boat and the patrol boat moored alongside. All hands were lost and another patrol boat nearby misread the situation and set off after the boat that caused the wave. To the commander of the patrol boat it seemed that the boat he was now chasing had fired on the two vessels. Before the innocent boat even knew what happened a hail of cannon fire had ripped through its hull, destroyed it's engine and killing three of its crew.

Pete was oblivious to the whole incident; he was currently trying to figure out just where in North Vietnam he was. He knew that he was northwest of Bong Hoi, but just how far northwest he didn't have a clue. He left his hiding place and moved slowly southwest until he came to a small stream. Following the stream he came to an area that seemed familiar, after some thought and a quick survey of the area he realized he was on the outskirts of Wihn. This was the stream he had used to rid himself of those horrible fleas. The knowledge of where he was comforted him somewhat however it also worried him that

he was once again two weeks away from the border.

Chapter 39

In Hanoi a press conference was beginning, the communist government had allowed several international press agencies to set up cameras and microphones in a conference room in a dreary brick building across from the headquarters of the Peoples Army. The assembled media had been told they would get to see captured American spies and ask them questions. A short thin man in a North Vietnamese dress uniform entered the room and gestured for the men and women to be seated. He walked to a podium that had been set up to the right of four steel chairs that faced the now seated reporters, and began to address them in English.

"Today you will witness the crimes of America against the Vietnamese people. The men you will meet today are criminals, spies for the American government, sent to harm the wishes of the Vietnamese people. These spies were all captured inside North Vietnam, where the American government says they do not operate. They lie! These men will tell you the truth!" he shouted.

With that he motioned to his right and two more Vietnamese soldiers entered the room, ushering in four obviously non-Vietnamese prisoners. Three of the men were white and the fourth was black, all were obviously not in good health and seemed bewildered. The soldiers placed one man in each of the four seats, then saluted the man at the podium and backed away from the seated prisoners and took up positions against the wall behind them. The reporters had a distinct feeling that the prisoners were not comfortable with being there, but once the first man began to speak they became willing participants in the propaganda for the North Vietnamese.

Each of the men spoke slowly and carefully; everyone could tell that they had rehearsed their statements. When the microphone was placed in front of the third man he spoke quietly and calmly, he gave his name as Jason McGrew. He told the story of his capture in North Vietnam and that he was a spy for the American government in Washington. He spoke very softly and the officer snapped at him to speak up. Jason suddenly snapped his head towards the officer and screamed "Hammer!"

The reaction was swift from the two Vietnamese soldiers standing behind the prisoners, they immediately grabbed Jason and drug him from the room. He didn't resist and was thrown into a cell down the hall from the conference room. He knew he had cost himself his chance at release, they had told him and the others that if they cooperated they would be sent home soon after the press conference. He didn't believe them for one minute. He was certain that they would be tried as enemies of the state and shot by firing squad. Jason just felt he needed to let HQ know that he was still alive and that he had not betrayed his country. It was worth the trouble if his mom and dad got to see him one last time. A brief moment of clarity for a mind shattered into pieces.

Jason had not fared much better than Tony in prison, he had been wracked with dysentery and beaten severely. His left arm was messed up in the shoulder because they had chained his arm above his head for so long that permanent damage had been done to his rotator cuff. His body was weak and he suffered from delusions and flashbacks. He almost welcomed death at this point, at least the pain would end and he hoped he would find peace. He often thought of Sarah, his girlfriend, whom he adored. The guards regularly told him no one was waiting for him any longer, that he was all alone. They told him his parents were dead, his lover was now a whore in America. His comrades had abandoned him and went home to have their way with his girlfriend. After two years Jason didn't know what to think, he just wanted it to end.

The press conference continued without him, the men had finished their statements and the press began asking questions. The men would turn and look at the officer to see if it was OK to answer a question; if he nodded yes they would answer. If he shook his head no they would avoid the question by saying they were American spies and apologized for harming the people of Vietnam. After several questions were avoided this way, one reported asked to speak with the soldier who had been removed from the room. The officer in charge grew angry and ended the press conference, saying " these men have told you all you need to know, the Americans are liars! They come to our country to rape our women, kill our children and steal our land!"

With that he ordered the two guards who had returned to the room after depositing Jason in his cell to remove the prisoners from the room. Once that was complete he motioned to the back of the room and a door opened behind the media seats. "Please follow Major Dongtau and he will show you the way to your cars, they will take you back to your hotel." He then turned to his right and exited the room through the same door the prisoners had used. Once in the hallway he walked directly to Jason's cell and turned to face him. He smiled a devious smile and spoke softly, "you caused much trouble today McGrew, your outburst has cost you dearly. The others will go home tomorrow, you will never leave Vietnam alive."

Jason just smiled back, he had finally given in to the reality that he was never going home and it had somehow set his mind free. He could now relax and be himself, the smart assed, wisecracking, fun loving nut that had made him the perfect choice as Tony's spotter. As the officer walked away Jason yelled out, "hey rice boy, does your momma know you grew up to be a five foot tall, slanty eyed pig fucker?'

The officer spun around and rushed back to the door of the cell, his eyes wide and his face turning red. "I will teach you who is boss, American scum!" He shouted back. "You will die tomorrow, and I will still be alive!"

"Yeah, but you'll still be five feet tall and a pig fucker! If you were half a man you would kick my ass, but then again you are half a man aren't you!" Jason shot back,

The officer turned away and walked quickly down the hallway, he was hot and the American had gotten him even hotter. He had a problem now, the American had already spoken to the press and they had his name, rank and serial number. If he were killed it would look very bad in the international press. This whole press conference had been called to curry favor in the international court of public opinion, killing this man could erase any good will gained today. "Damn Americans, they are rude, arrogant and sneaky like snakes" he thought.

The press conference was shown all across the world and in Boston Massachusetts a family cried aloud at the site of a missing son. John and Mary McGrew had almost lost hope they would ever see their only son after Tony had returned home with no idea what had happened to him. The site of him on TV brought out all of the emotions at once, unbelievable joy that he was alive, fear that he was still a prisoner, pride that he had not allowed the enemy to break his spirit. The phone rang constantly with news from the entire congregation of St. Michaels parish, everyone had seen Jason on TV and wanted to let the family know. It was a very long night for the McGrew family both in Boston and in Vietnam.

Tony Lucas had seen the press conference and was out of his quarters and in Colonel Morgan's office before the elder Ranger could even get briefed himself. The two men worked all night on a plan to get Jason out of that prison and back to the states. Neither of them knew that the man they were trying to rescue was not the man they had known before. Two years in prison had messed up Jason McGrew's mind to a point of no return. He was suffering from what would later be called Post Traumatic Stress Disorder and it would plague him for the rest of his life. Jason had died in Vietnam, his body was still very much alive, but his soul was long gone.

Chapter 40

The manhunt that ensued after General Whey Poh's assassination was unlike anything Colonel Morgan had ever seen. The VC were scouring the countryside with every available man. The reports were so bad that the Colonel didn't dare show Tony, or even his superiors for that matter. He had briefed the Joint Chiefs the week before as to the success of Pete's mission and his apparent ability to stay under the radar. But the VC weren't using radar anymore; they were literally beating the shit out of the jungle trying to force him into the open. Of course neither the VC nor Colonel Morgan had any idea that Pete was a hundred kilometers away and moving further away each day.

Pete made steady progress south from Wihn towards his last target near the village of Hok. Colonel Li Poh was unaware that anyone even knew who he was let alone that they would be targeting him for assassination. He conducted his cruel business as usual, beating captured prisoners and playing tortuous psychological games with their minds. He hadn't even given a second thought to the sniper called Shadow after General Tok had requested the information. After all, the General was dead and as such he was in no position to help the Colonel's career. Li Poh hoped that his hard work would soon lead to a promotion and a transfer to Hanoi, he was weary of the jungle and the incessant insects.

Pete arrived at his destination in mid-January 1973, it had been a very long trek through the densest of the thick and nasty. He lost count of how many patrols he had avoided during that time, it had to have been over fifty. The rain fell constantly this time of year and he was suffering from another fever, this one not as bad as the first but still bad enough to make him miserable. The chills would cause him to shake uncontrollably at times, making it difficult to stay concealed. He would simply try and focus his mind, after a minute his body would respond and the tremors would stop. Pete surveilled the camp and was amazed at what he saw, ten cages with at least one prisoner in each. The cages were not tall enough for a prisoner to stand upright, so they either sat or laid down almost all of the time. The guards really didn't have to guard anyone very often; the prisoners were only allowed to leave their cages when they were taken into the small building where Colonel Li Poh had his office. Pete didn't even want to think about what went on in there, instead he tried to find out which of the VC was the Colonel.

The natural instinct of wanting to rescue the prisoners was overwhelming; however Pete knew he couldn't help them. Even if through some amazing luck he managed to kill all of the guards and get them out. It was nearly 15 kilometers to the radio, and most of the prisoners weren't in any condition to walk let alone run. The whole group would be recaptured within hours, including Pete. No, he would have to rely on the governments of the two countries to solve the prisoners' fate, he had a mission to complete. He tried to put out of his mind what might happen to the men in the cages once Colonel Poh was dead.

He had been watching the camp for two days and still hadn't seen any sign of an officer. He began looking at the guards through his scope, just in case. After about twenty minutes he focused his scope on a guard sitting near one of the cages, he was almost certain the guard was actually Colonel Poh. He slowly pulled the black book from his pack and turned to the picture of the former Cal Irvine grad, sure enough it was him. "Well you son of a bitch, you might have made a good sniper in another life Colonel. Hiding in plain sight like that, pretty slick I gotta admit." Pete whispered to himself.

He watched the Colonel for several hours until he exited the camp via a small footpath on the eastern side. Pete was on the northwest side of the camp and the Colonel was out of sight after taking ten steps into the jungle. Pete kept watch and waited, it was nearly an hour later before the Colonel returned to the camp via the same footpath. The following day the same scene played out, although this time Pete knew what to watch for and quickly found the Colonel masquerading as a guard. He again sat near one of the cages and observed the goings on inside the camp. At nearly the exact same time as the day before he stood up and walked slowly to the eastern edge of the camp, looked around discretely and then ambled down the footpath and out of Pete's field of view.

Now that Pete had his target's pattern down, he needed to find out where that footpath went. He also knew that being a prisoner camp there was a real good chance the entire area immediately surrounding the camp was heavily mined. He proceeded to make a huge arc around the camp keeping a distance of at least five hundred meters from it, hoping that the minefield would not be nearly that large. As he moved he used a compass to track his position and he ended up directly east of the camp near a small stream just before dawn, climbed a tree and slept the morning away. He awoke at 1300 and slowly lowered himself to the ground, keeping low to avoid detection he searched for the footpath leading to the camp. At 1330 he was still looking for the path when a movement to his right made him freeze in his tracks. The object came closer and after a minute the Colonel came into view not more than fifty meters away. Li Poh walked slowly and looked around constantly, not nervously, but as though he were looking for something. He approached the stream and waited a moment, then carefully stepped into the water and waded across to the other side. Once across he disappeared into the thick vegetation on the opposite bank. Pete kneeled down and waited.

It was nearly ten minutes later when the Colonel re-emerged on the bank of the stream and once again waited a moment before wading across and continuing back towards camp. As he passed Pete he was still looking around and Pete could have sworn he looked directly at him. The Colonel obviously didn't recognize him as an American soldier, or even as a human because he continued walking at the same leisurely pace. After the Colonel passed and had been swallowed up once more by the thick jungle, Pete relaxed and settled in where he was. After dark he would cross the stream and find his ambush point, the Colonel's habit of pausing at the stream would be the perfect opportunity for Pete's shot.

It seemed like an eternity before darkness finally engulfed the jungle that night, but Pete waited patiently for it. He watched a pair of small lizards fight over a frog, only to have one of the lizards snatched by a hawk a moment later. Life and death were ever present in the jungle, one creature's predator is another creature's prey. When darkness finally came Pete rose up from his hiding place and slipped silently onto the footpath, he moved very slowly in case the path was mined with only the Colonel knowing the safe route. He found no mines and slowly made his way to the stream, it was shallow and slow moving at this point although Pete could here the sound of rapids in the distance downstream. Standing at the crossing point Pete scanned the area for large trees that could be used as a roost but found none. The area was mainly low, thick bushes and swamp. The stream ran nearly north and south at this point, with the camp northwest of the crossing meaning that the path had to make a bend somewhere between the camp and here. Pete continued to look for a place to set up, he was convinced that this would be the perfect place to make the shot but he needed a line of sight to this spot from somewhere else.

He did the unthinkable and pulled out a light stick from his pack, these are plastic tubes with chemicals in them that when bent the chemicals combine and the stick glows as a result of the chemical reaction. Pete was about to do the equivalent of firing a signal flare, but he needed a line of sight and he couldn't see a hundred meters in the dark. The light stick would allow him to move away from the crossing and still be able to locate it from a distance. If he could see the light stick tonight, he could see the man tomorrow. The danger was obvious, if he could see the light so could anyone else nearby. He was banking on the fact that there wasn't anyone else nearby.

Pete took a long deep breath and snapped the tube, the light wasn't really all that bright but in the jungle at night it seemed like Las Vegas. He set the stick on a branch off the side of the path some two meters, hoping that the Colonel wouldn't be able to see it during the day. The chemicals would be long past creating any light by then but plastic tubes don't grow in the jungle, if he saw it, the Colonel would immediately recognize it as American and sound the alarm.

Shadow moved quickly away from the light, wading into the stream and heading downstream until the current picked up and water started to get deeper. He then scaled the riverbank and moved into the jungle. He walked a few steps and then turned to try and find the light, sometimes he could make out where it was sometimes all he saw was blackness. He felt the ground in front of him begin to rise and he hoped the greater elevation would bring him better luck. After negotiating the jungle for nearly twenty minutes he came into a small opening in the undergrowth. A huge tree stood in the middle and around it were piles of stones. This was some kind of an old structure and the jungle was in the process of reclaiming it. The opening proved to be very timely, Pete turned back towards the river and could just barely make out a faint glow. He moved a little to his left and the light seemed to get brighter.

A small group of bushes clung to the edge of the opening beyond which the hillside dropped off sharply towards the stream. Pete crawled between two of the bushes and laid down prone. He opened the lens covers on his scope and located the light, easily making out the plastic tube. He was calculating the distance to the target when suddenly the light was gone! He searched with his scope to try and find out what was happening. If the enemy found that light he was in real trouble, and he knew it. He set down his rifle and pulled his pack from his back, opened it and grabbed his field glasses. The glasses are not as powerful as the scope meaning more overall area is shown at one time and they allow both eyes to focus on the subject at the same time.

It took him several minutes to catch a glimpse of the green glow, he zeroed in on the position and found several individuals fighting over it. It was another minute before he could finally relax, the individuals were in fact monkeys who had been drawn to the light like moths to a flame. Pete now feared that one of the monkeys would try to eat it and get sick or even die. The troop of monkeys moved on and Pete watched the light dance from tree to tree, eventually it fell to the ground. The monkeys had finally gotten bored with it and given up trying to eat it, discarding it like unripe fruit.

The bad part about this whole incident was that Pete had lost track of where the crossing really was. He wouldn't have much time later to identify his target and take the shot before Colonel Poh had disappeared into the thick and nasty once more. He had hoped to use the glow stick to get range and location fixed so that all he had to do was wait, now he wasn't sure exactly where to focus on. It was 0330 and still extremely dark so Pete closed the lens covers on his scope and drifted off to sleep with the green dancing light filling his mind.

He awoke at 1110 and found the jungle alive all around him, the droning of insects wings, the chirps and screeches of birds and the smell of flowering plants. He slowly stretched his legs out and pushed himself up onto his elbows, the jungle floor is not always a comfortable bed. He reached under himself and pulled two large branches out, it would be considerably more comfortable by not lying on those any longer. A major drawback to finding your position after dark was that you couldn't always tell what you were sitting or lying on until it got light. Pete recalled one night sitting on what he thought was a log, only to have a large snake move out from under him as he sat down.

His position made more comfy, the wait was on and Pete soaked up the scene. He wanted to make sure he remembered all of the beautiful and wondrous things he had seen in Vietnam, he was sure he would never forget the horrors he had seen. They would haunt him, he was sure of that. A light rain began to fall and the jungle hushed in response. It was nearly 1230 when the rain finally subsided and the sun reappeared, the effect was to create a sauna. The hot sun evaporating the new rain raised the humidity to nearly 100 percent.

Pete concentrated on the area he thought the path crossed the stream and after ten minutes he detected the trail through the underbrush. Further to his left he could see the stream as it wound its way through the small valley. Using the stream's natural tendency to flow downhill he was able to predict where the stream and the path he had previously detected would intersect. He focused on that location; double checked his scope and rifle, got into position and waited.

He lay prone in the dank, wet foliage. His camouflage so complete that even the fat pig browsing the leaf litter and underbrush not more than five meters to his left did not detect his presence. He had been there in that position for over three hours and didn't even notice the pig. The focus, the total concentration was on his quarry. This was it, the last of his elusive targets. After this last mission he would go home his year tour nearly up, he caught himself trying to remember what home looked like. It seemed as if it were another lifetime, ancient history that he had read in a book or a story he had heard told by a stranger. He had no vivid memory of life before, no vision other than the hunt.

He forced himself to focus on the quarry, and his concentration was quickly restored to its almost maniacal clarity. He had tracked and stalked him for three days and nights. He wanted this one. The other missions were a matter of duty, necessary, even insignificant. This one he wanted for Tony and in his own mind he considered it justice. He hadn't allowed himself to consider his own feelings; anger was as deadly as a bullet. His training came to the fore and took over whenever stress was exerted on him, he was exactly as advertised, the perfect killing machine.

Finally, his prey came into view precisely where Pete had determined he would and the situation unfolded exactly as he had envisioned it. The river was narrow and shallow, the perfect place to cross. The trail was well worn and free of traps. The prey stopped to survey the crossing. Pete took in an even breath, held it for a second, let it out and smoothly pulled the trigger. The XM21 rifle recoiled, but he never even noticed. The bullet exited the barrel traveling at 2,800 feet per second, crossing the seven hundred and ten meters to the target in just one third of a second. The slug entered the left eye and upon impacting the back of the skull flattened out, creating a gaping hole. Death was instantaneous, and Colonel Li Poh was dead before he hit the ground.

Pete closed the lens covers on his weapon and laid his head on his left arm. He drifted off to sleep, content that his camouflage was so effective that the entire Vietnamese Army could pass by him and never even know he was there. As it was, no one even came looking for Colonel Poh until after he didn't return for dinner. Pete watched from his hillside refuge as several guards from the camp came into view along the path. They found the Colonel's body and became very nervous. Two of the men grabbed the Colonel, one taking his legs the other placing his arms under the armpits of the dead man and together they carried him back towards camp. Pete knew a manhunt would begin immediately, so he rose up out of his hiding place and headed southwest into the dense jungle.

Chapter 41

Tony wasn't aware of Pete's comfort zone, the place he considered a safe haven just inside North Vietnam. The place where he had stashed the radio and other supplies, the place where his guardian angel had watched over him in the fall, his Eden in southeast Asia. That was where Pete was headed, not Da Nang as Tony had asserted. Pete had considered the idea, but he was sure that the area would have been even more treacherous to cross now than it was in August when he had been hunting the South Vietnamese traitor Major Lien. The plan now was to pick up the radio, hope that it was still working and head south into South Vietnam and hope to make it to Liem. Pete knew there was a large base there with a hospital and regular army personnel. He hoped to be able to make it all the way without assistance, but if necessary he wouldn't hesitate to call for EVAC. His mission was complete, he just needed to get back home alive.

It only took Pete five days to reach his safe area, only it wasn't as quiet any more. He dodged patrols constantly, and the traffic on the river was nearly continuous. Pete found his radio and didn't even check to see if it was still functional. He just threw it in his pack and headed to the river. At the river Pete had to wait six hours before the river seemed quiet enough to cross, even then a patrol boat came around a bend upriver just as Pete was climbing the far bank. He dove into the undergrowth and the patrol slid quietly by on the river's surface. Pete worried about his guardian angel, had it escaped before the crush of humans entered it's domain?

Tony and Colonel Morgan paced the Colonel's office waiting for news. Missy knocked and entered without waiting for a reply. She gracefully crossed the distance between the door and the Colonel's desk and handed him a report. As she did Tony couldn't help but stare at her, and she did her best to ignore his gaze. Tony had come to grips with her decision to end their relationship and wait for Pete, but her beauty still enthralled him. He had been a little upset when she told him, but he wasn't as emotional as she was. He understood her reasoning and had moved on. His leg had continued to improve, but he would walk with a limp for the rest of his life, a constant reminder of his time in Southeast Asia. Missy had been a wreck before telling Tony, but afterward felt relieved and happy again. She quickly exited the room and exhaled heavily.

Colonel Morgan had focused on the report and did not even notice the tension between his two most trusted aides. He read it quickly and handed it to Tony. There was still no official word from Hanoi on the status of Jason McGrew. Colonel Morgan had urged the State Department to contact Hanoi about Jason after the botched news conference. The press had begun badgering the administration and the State Department for more information on the men interviewed and the North's claims that they were captured in North Vietnam. Colonel Morgan had kept the lid on his covert mission so far, but he wanted Jason released quickly hoping that would end the press inquiry.

Neither Tony nor the Colonel knew how badly Jason's psyche had been damaged. In his cell in Hanoi, Jason rocked slowly back and forth, his mind flashing between childhood scenes of ice skating and baseball then back to the horrors of Vietnam. He would hallucinate about insects and snakes, women and evil little men with sharp teeth and dark eyes. His rare lucid moments were filled with pain and misery, his captors taunting him and filling his head with more horrible images. Release from prison would not free Jason McGrew from the demons in his mind. The only freedom he could expect was waiting at the end of his earthly life. Until then he would endure more pain and suffering than any man should.

John Lucas called Tony every Saturday to check up on his progress and see if he had any news about Pete. John had his own demon to slay, the one created the day Tony confided that Pete was alone. It haunted him night and day, he didn't dare share this demon with anyone. Releasing it would be disastrous for the rest of the family and maybe even for Pete. No, this demon was his to fight alone. Pete was special, a gift from God, to John. He was the son John and May never had, their two daughters were beautiful and precious, but he had always wanted a son. May had such trouble delivering the girls they decided not to try having a third child. Instead John had kept a close relationship with Pete, filling in where Roger hadn't had the time to devote to his youngest son. He couldn't bear losing his son in a war halfway around the world. So he did the only thing he could do, contact Tony and pray for news.

"Tony, how ya holding up?" he asked.

"I'm getting around a little better, doc says I'll always limp a little though. When they fixed the breaks, the leg ended up a little shorter than the left one." Tony answered.

"That's great, but are they gonna force you out of the service?" John asked, hoping the answer was yes.

"They haven't said one way or the other, but I'm hoping they'll let me stay on at least for a while, 'til I can get used to being back in the states and all." Tony replied.

"Any word on your brother?" came the inevitable question.

Tony hated this question, John asked it every week and every week Tony had to give the same answer, "no, nothing yet. But as I keep saying that is actually good news. He should be in contact soon though."

That was something Tony had never said before and John jumped on it with both feet. "Why, you know something you're not saying?"

"Uncle John, you know I have to be careful here. I've already said too much, but hopefully soon. I have to get going, I have a meeting with the Colonel at 1200. Take care of yourself and keep an eye on mom for me," Tony said and didn't even let John say goodbye before hanging up the receiver.

John was excited and a little apprehensive, soon, what did Tony mean by soon? He would try to wait until next Saturday, but he may have check back with Tony sooner.

Chapter 42

Major Kolskoff was intrigued by the American sniper

running amok in Vietnam, he had warned the Vietnamese after

witnessing General Trang's execution, or assassination or

whatever it was to be called, he didn't care but it bothered him

that he wasn't sure what to call it, that this was a serious threat.

The morons didn't listen to him at first, but after General Poh

was shot they wised up quick. He was consulted on ways to

catch the killer, but apparently they we too late in setting the

cordon around Bong Hoi and the American, he was sure this

sniper was the American they called Shadow. Word of Colonel

Poh (no relation to the General) being killed filtered through to

him and he knew the American was no longer in the North.

Kolskoff spoke in Russian to make sure the Vietnamese

officers in the room could not translate the conversation," He is

obviously very good, can you kill him?"

"Yes Major, I am sure" was the reply, "but he is back in

the South, can I pursue him there?"

"Yes, Igor you may," Kolskoff answered. "I feel Director Craft's hand on this and I want to take away his prized possession." Kolskoff was, as were many members of the Red Army, KGB as well as a commissioned officer.

"Very well Major, I will track him from his last kill" Igor replied and left the room.

Major Kolskoff hated Vietnam, he hated the heat, the constant rain, the bugs, the food and the people. His "hosts" were idiots, not much above livestock on the evolutionary tree in his opinion. They lacked intelligence, culture, tradition and frankly they stunk. He missed the Bolshoi, the Kremlin and his family. At first he had looked upon this posting as a reward for his hard work in East Germany where he had helped root out a group of dissidents. However, he now looked upon this posting as a curse, he could not wait to be recalled to Moscow even if it meant a desk job at the Kremlin or another of the various buildings occupied by the military of the Soviet Union. Igor had been with him in East Germany too, his aide de camp was more precisely his personal assassin. Igor was a skilled marksman and seemed to carry out his duties with uncommon glee. Kolskoff realized his man was probably a psychopath, but as long as he was the Major's psychopath it was acceptable.

Pete moved slowly south through the area where Firebase Scout had been. He found it was a changed landscape. Napalm had burned much of the jungle canopy and left a surreal alien scene. There were fewer animals, and the entire area seemed empty to him. He moved extremely slowly, sometimes covering less than a hundred meters in an entire day. Patrols constantly passed by, and he found more and more mines and booby traps. He narrowly missed setting off one trap when he slipped on a rain soaked log and came within inches of a pit filled with sharpened tipped sticks. The stress on his body and his mind were beginning to take their toll, he was weak and the parasites had once again invaded his body. Boring worms, leaches and mosquitoes gnawed at his flesh, bacteria and disease wracked his body from the inside. He had a lesion on his left forearm from a cut he had gotten weeks earlier that refused to heal and was now dangerously infected.

On January 24th 1973 Pete reached an area outside of Liem that he thought was at least close to a U.S. base. He had never been to any base in Vietnam other than Scout and the

Airbase in Saigon, so he wasn't exactly sure how far from the base he was. But he felt he was close enough to try the radio. Pulling it from his pack he became suddenly distraught. The radio was in bad shape, it had been through hell and it looked like it had taken a direct hit from a mortar. It hadn't of course, but it didn't look functional. Pete never the less switched it on and was stunned when it came to life. He cued the mic and said in a whisper, "Scout this is Shadow, over."

No answer.

He repeated the call again, this time a little louder, "Scout this is Shadow, over."

The response came back, "Shadow, this is Red Three. Scout is no longer here, what's your location?"

"Red Three, this is Shadow. I need EVAC, ten clicks south/southwest of Scout, over."

"Rodger Shadow, can you give us a better fix on your position?"

"No, I'm not doing so good sir, I need EVAC," then a long pause. "Shadow out."

"Shadow, this is Red Three. Shadow, this is Red Three over! Shadow, help's on the way."

Pete slid down and sat against a tree. He was completely exhausted even though he had only crawled and walked fifty meters in the past eight hours. He was about to give up when he heard a noise above him. He couldn't see it, but he knew that sound anywhere! A chopper! And it was close. He forced himself to stand and stumbled towards the sound, but it continued to get farther away. He made it several hundred meters before he could no longer hear the chopper any more. He found himself now near a clearing and in the distance he could make out a hill through the mist. He decided to spend the night near the clearing, hoping a chopper would fly close enough to see smoke if he popped it. He rested throughout the night and moved just before daylight to a spot some five meters inside the trees, straining his ears for any sound resembling a rotor.

Word of Shadow's contact raced through the communications network and reached Admiral Lindsey Hunt, commander of the USS Kittyhawk battle group in the waters just off the shores of Vietnam. He was waiting for the news ever since Colonel Morgan had told him about his missing man. Admiral Hunt was keenly aware of those special few in the Special Forces, the SEALs were his version , but he respected the Rangers as much as anyone. He had a SEAL team waiting to extract Shadow just off DaNang per Colonel Morgan's request. The problem was, Shadow was nowhere near DaNang. In fact he was so far inland that the SEALs wouldn't be able to use a boat to get to him at all.

He quickly contacted the team leader, Captain Robert Miller, and recalled the team to the Kittyhawk for a planning session. SEALs pride themselves on planning, it is the precise planning of each mission that allows them to be so successful. The original extraction had been planned for two weeks and rehearsed many times. The new plan wouldn't be as detailed and raised the stakes tenfold. When Captain Miller arrived, he was ushered into the Comm and he and the Admiral went over the new mission.

Pete waited by the clearing all day, no choppers came. He began moving slowly along the edge of the clearing and came upon a scene of devastation. There were dead VC just inside the jungle, most very young with mortal wounds from gunfire and shrapnel. He found a sack with rice and some vegetables in it. It was the first real food he had eaten in days. He ate it heartily, even though he was surrounded by death. He could see more dead in the clearing and realized they were Americans. He quietly slipped out into the open and checked each man for signs of life; he found none. He did find food, a radio and an M-16 with ammo. He waited an hour and ate again, drank thirstily from the canteens he found and began to regain his strength. He retreated to the jungle and found a tree to roost in for the night. The next morning he ate some more and drank the clean water. He shaved and washed his hair for the first time in at least a week. Invigorated he once again slipped out into the open and scavenged more food, water and some clean socks. Returned to his roost and waited for nightfall.

Chapter 43

Colonel Morgan called Tony into his office urgently, he didn't mention Pete to Missy. She hadn't talked about Pete for months, but he was pretty sure she was still Pete's girl. "You got everything right but the most important part," he told Tony sarcastically.

"What do you mean sir?" Tony asked completely unaware of any of the developments in Vietnam.

"Pete is near Liem not DaNang, he contacted Red Three two days ago. He was still looking for Scout, poor bastard doesn't have any clue what has happened since he left the camp six months ago."

"Liem, shit, what the hell is he doing there? That doesn't make any sense! The SEALs, they can't do an extraction in Liem! Fuck!" Tony shouted.

"Keep you pants on son, Admiral Hunt tells me his boys can get Pete but he needs a better location. Red Three reported that Shadow was faint and commented that he needed EVAC. What do you make of that?"

"He's in trouble Colonel, otherwise he'd just walk out of the jungle into one of our camps and catch a chopper to Saigon."

"That's what I thought too, I've asked the Admiral to have his team ready to go the minute we get a fix on Pete. Until then we have to wait and hope he can somehow figure out exactly where he is."

"And if he can't? We just gonna leave him there? Fuck that! I'll go get him myself!"

"The hell you will, this is out of your hands son. We'll get him back, but your job is done. You gave us your best shot, now we have to play the hand we've been dealt. Dismissed."

The way the Colonel said it took Tony by complete surprise. "He thinks I screwed this up! He's blaming me for Pete not being where he should be!" Tony thought.

"Sir, he should have been in DaNang. There is no tactical reason for him to be in Liem!" Tony blurted out.

"I said dismissed Sergeant," the Colonel said flatly and sat down at his desk.

Tony stood silently for a second, then saluted, turned and left the office slamming the door as he did so.

Missy was startled by the door slamming and tried to ask Tony what was wrong, Tony just glared at her and stormed out of the office. He was furious and confused. He jumped into his truck and left the base and headed for town. Once there he started drinking and didn't stop until he was completely stoned. He stumbled out of the bar with the help of a bouncer and was summarily dumped onto the gravel next to his truck. A young waitress from the bar took pity on the drunken soldier and drug him into the passenger seat of her car. She drove him to her small apartment and with great effort helped him inside and onto her couch. Twelve hours later he awoke with the worst headache of his life and a pretty young lady smiling at him from her kitchen. She welcomed him back to the living and they began a conversation that lasted well into the afternoon.

Tony told his hostess everything, all of the horror and pain; the loss of life and even the loss of Missy, his latest heartbreak. She listened with rapt attention. After a long time, Tony stopped talking and just stared at her. He hadn't even noticed how beautiful she was, how her dark brown eyes shone brightly against her fair skin. How she appeared to be mesmerized by his story. He finally asked with obvious embarrassment, "I'm sorry but I don't think I even asked your name?"

She replied softly, "Tracy."

"Tracy, I'm Tony and I can't believe I just told you my life's story. I guess I just needed to get it all out."

"I'm glad you did, I had no idea anyone could have such a life," she said again very softly.

"Please tell me about yourself," Tony pleaded.

"Not much to tell, " she answered. "I was born and raised right here. My momma and daddy divorced when I was 12, I lived with momma until last summer. She kicked me out when I …" She stopped mid-sentence.

"When you what Tracy?" Tony asked. "You've heard all the horrible stuff I've done and had done to me. Nothing you did could have been all that bad."

"I got caught with some weed and a couple of tabs of acid, the cops took me home to my momma instead of busting me. She slapped me right in front of them and told me to get out of her house. I haven't seen her since. I was already working at the bar and slept in my car for a couple of months til I could get this place. It ain't much, but it's home now," she said apologetically.

"This place is nice," Tony tried to comfort her. "I live on base, in a barracks with a bunch of other guys. To me this place is a palace."

"Thanks, but I know it's a dump," she said quietly.

"Are you still getting high?" Tony had to ask.

"No, I really wasn't even when I got caught. The stuff belonged to my boyfriend, but he had been busted before. So I said it was mine to keep him from getting in trouble. Then he turned around an' left me when he found out I didn't have any place to live, he was kinda living with me and momma at the time." Her embarrassment was obvious, shacking up was still not accepted in rural Kentucky.

"Hey, I'm not one to judge," Tony replied. "Besides, I was the skunk who tried to steal my brother's girl while he is in Vietnam. How about we forget the past and just start over."

"I'm not sure that's possible," Tracy answered flatly.

"I'd like to try, if you will." Tony said and pulled her onto his lap. He placed her head on his shoulder and held her tight, his strength comforting her and giving her reason for hope.

"OK I'll try, but I've got to get ready for work. I get off at midnight, will I see you then?" She asked, hoping that he wouldn't leave her too.

"I'll ride in with you, get my truck and head for base. I'll be back at midnight to pick you up, and this time I'll drive you home." He said with a smile.

Nightfall gave Pete the cover he needed to move once more. He needed a good fix on his position and to do that he needed landmarks. The area he was it was relatively featureless, just low hills and jungle everywhere he looked. He assumed he was northwest of Liem and so he headed in a southwesterly direction. He moved very slowly and at times nearly had to back track to avoid the VC and various other obstacles. He came across a large village the next evening and began searching for anything that would identify it. He slipped into town and searched the carts and crates for any signage that would tell him where he was. Nothing appeared to give any clues until he found a map rolled up and stuffed in the basket of a bicycle. He grabbed the map and slipped silently out of town between two huts and into the familiar safety of the dense forest. He found a large tree, climbed into its upper reaches and slept until dusk.

After waking Pete listened closely for any sound that would indicate human presence nearby, after several minutes he was satisfied and pulled the crumpled map from his pack. It was a pretty old, worn map but he was able to make out the basic forms of rivers and towns. He had found a smaller river the day before just a kilometer to the west, and the village he had procured the map from sat on the bank of a much larger one. Using these two rivers and the map he was able to find only three possible places he could be. Then he pulled out the topographical map he carried from Firebase Scout and tried to eliminate areas and get a firm bearing on his position. The topo map allowed him to use large hills and swamps to fill in the blank areas of the other map. Ten minutes later he was sure that he was near the confluence of the Huong and Hirti rivers. This proved to be good and bad news at the same time. The good news was he now knew where he was and could give that info to Red Three. The bad news was he didn't see any way for a team from Liem to get to him without confronting half the V.C. troops in the area. A chopper evac was probably out too, just too big a risk of losing the bird and crew to get one guy. "The best way is the river, but how?" Pete whispered to himself. "Just make the call and let them figure it out," he finally decided.

"Red Three, Red Three, Shadow, over"

"Shadow, Red Three, got a fix on your position?"

"Roger that Red Three," Pete answered, translated his coordinates and then asked, "Can I get a ride or do I need to walk out?"

"Shadow maintain radio silence and stay put, we'll get back to you."

"Negative Red Three, I'll call you, I can't have a radio chirping at the wrong time," Pete responded.

"Roger that Shadow, Red Three out."

The radio went silent and Pete lowered himself from his roost. The coordinates he gave Red Three were several kilometers away, just in case Charlie was listening. Now he wanted to move even farther away, away from the coordinates and away from the village where he had found the map. Both were potential hazards until he was sure if help would even be coming.

Tony arrived on base in time to get chewed up one side and down another by Colonel Morgan. He hadn't gone unnoticed at the bar, in fact the Colonel had been there with a couple other officers and witnessed his breakdown. "You can't hold your liquor can you son!" He bellowed, "you gonna crawl into a bottle and give up soldier?"

"No sir! I'm not an officer, Sir!" Tony screamed back.

Colonel Morgan flushed red and lunged for Tony, the audacity of this Sergeant to attack his manhood was not to stand. Tony expected the attack and even with his bad leg not only managed to avoid the Colonel's onrush but used the Colonel's own momentum to send him sprawling onto the floor of the office. Morgan was up in a flash and this time more in control, he approached Tony with his fists raised and his teeth clenched. Tony stood completely still and made no attempt to defend himself.

"Come on son! Let's have a go of it!" the Colonel taunted.

"No sir, I have no desire to fight you."

"Coward! You're not man enough to stand up for yourself, left your little brother to finish your job! Your pathetic!"

"My brother will finish what I started, and if you don't get him killed he'll come home in one piece. After that you and I will go at it sir, then we'll see who's a coward, sir." Tony was in total control of his emotions and cool to the point of being cold.

Colonel Morgan lowered his fists and stared blankly at what had been one of his best friends, "what the hell happened to you? You were the meanest, nastiest soldier I ever knew. Now your soft, and not even willing to fight to defend your honor!"

"I don't have to defend anything from you sir, you were my friend until you used me, Jason and Pete. For what? I've gone over the reports a thousand times, there hasn't been any gain from our operation! Your premise was wrong, they just keep filling the void with bodies. They don't have any brilliant military minds, just thousands and thousands of bodies that they keep throwing at our guys. You can't win if the people you're trying to help don't want you there. That is the problem, sir, nothing else." Tony bowed his head and turned to leave.

"Don't you turn your back on me soldier!"

Tony turned back towards his commanding officer, saluted, turned back towards the door and left.

Colonel Morgan was devastated. What the hell had happened, where was the Tony Lucas he had known before Vietnam? He slumped into his chair and stared blankly out the window, watching the sun set over the Kentucky hills.

Missy opened the office door and carried in an urgent communication, her confused look was lost on the Colonel as he snatched the paper from her hand. He had no time to babysit her now. "Dismissed" was all he managed to grunt.

Missy turned quietly and headed for the door, but before she could reach it the Colonel called her back. "Young lady get me Admiral Hunt, ASAP!"

"Yes sir," she responded immediately. Missy wasn't exactly sure what had just happened but knew enough to stay clear of the Colonel when he was angry.

A moment later Morgan's phone beeped, "Admiral Hunt is on the line sir," Missy's voice came through the intercom, and then the phone rang. Morgan picked it up and spoke directly to the head of the USS Kitty Hawk battle group. "Admiral, there is a new EVAC location for your team, can you still provide support for this old friend," the despair in Morgan's voice carried half way around the world.

"It would be an honor Colonel, what is the location?" replied the Admiral.

"It's a little more tricky I'm afraid"

"Always is Mitch, always is," came the reply.

The coordinates were given and the Admiral asked for a few hours to get a plan together. He called Captain Miller to his wardroom. He now had to ask for volunteers, this EVAC would be a hundred-fold more dangerous than the one planned for the coast outside DaNang. The Huong River is a major water route cutting across Vietnam from the port of DaNang into the hinterland. As it wends its way west then south it gets narrower and faster moving, splitting into several branches. The main branch reaches southwest and is met by the easterly flowing Hirti River. It was three kilometers up the Hirti River that Pete had given as his location.

Chapter 44

The rivers and coastline were the Navy's domain, that was the reason Mitch Morgan had contacted his long lost friend Admiral Hunt in the first place. His swift boats plied the rivers and coastline of Vietnam controlling the flow of people and goods along the way. The Rangers' contemporaries in the Navy were the SEALs, known as the most lethal fighting force on earth. Colonel Morgan often disputed that claim, offering his Rangers as the obvious choice for the title, but he never questioned the SEALs ability. In fact he often commended them on their prowess for being the sharks of the sea, even if his Rangers were the lions of the land.

Captain Robert Miller was a massive physical specimen, six feet three inches tall and nearly two hundred and forty pounds. He was tough, nasty, mean and brilliant. His I.Q. was off the charts and his ability to think clearly in the midst of chaos was considered his best trait. His team of SEALs were handpicked, he had trained these men, taught them everything they knew about fighting, surviving and weapons. SEAL training is legendary for its brutality, misery and hardship. But most of all it is legendary for producing the finest fighting men in the world. Seaman Eric Vargas, a quiet latino from Los Angeles was in charge of the boat, weapons and gear. Lieutenant Mac Faulk, a black man from Valdosta, Georgia was in charge of explosives and communications. The final member of the team was Walter "Chief" Holcolmb from Columbus Ohio. Chief was the smallest man on the team at just under six feet and very wiry, only weighing one hundred and sixty pounds. Chief was short for Chief Warrant Officer, his rank, and also because he had a penchant for trying to run the show whatever the situation.

Captain Miller ran through the plan several times to work out any bugs, this wasn't going to be a walk in the park by any means. The initial entry into DaNang harbor and up the Huong would be relatively easy. The U.S. and its South Vietnamese allies controlled DaNang and the surrounding area, but the VC were still very active. Once they moved ten to fifteen kilometers up the river everything would change, the control over the river and surrounding countryside was mixed at best. There would probably be running gun fights along the river, and a possible major confrontation. That is why they would have an escort of two other swift boats for part of the journey. But once the river split into several branches, the escorts would drop off and wait for the lone wolf to return. The risk to a larger expedition was too great to be justified, a small team in one small boat would be far less noticeable and thus more likely to succeed.

The team gathered its gear and headed to the boat, each man carried an automatic weapon, pistol, knife, several grenades, ammo, a small amount of food and water. The boat was equipped with a 20mm cannon mounted on a swiveling platform on the deck and two large outboard motors to power it up the river. Additional food, water and explosives were also stowed on the boat. They prepared to depart as a nervous Admiral Hunt waited for word that Shadow was in place. The news came at 0110 that night.

"Red Three, Red Three, this is Shadow, over" came the whispered call.

"Shadow, Red Three, are you in place?"

"Roger Red Three, have you found a ride for me?"

"Roger Shadow, squids coming in tomorrow, small team, be ready"

"Read you Red Three, Shadow out."

Squids, the Army term for Navy personnel, was often used as a derogatory phrase but in this case Pete considered it to be just code. He wasn't much for the inter-forces sniping that was common amongst the branches of the military. He found it really kind of ridiculous, but at times it could be really funny.

Captain Miller received the "go" from Admiral Hunt and launched the swift boat into the darkness. They met up with their escort just outside the harbor and the three Navy boats moved slowly upstream. The darkness helped cover their movement, but each of them knew they were being watched. All traffic in and out of DaNang was monitored by both sides, being invisible here was impossible. There was no obvious sign that this was anything but a normal patrol, "nothing to see here, move along," was the hopeful image being presented. The swift boats patrolled this river all the time, nothing new for the enemy to see.

Dawn broke as the boats made their way fifteen kilometers upstream from DaNang. The morning silence was broken by the unmistakable sound of incoming fire. Several explosions erupted behind the last of the boats, mortars lobbed at them from somewhere behind the wall of green along the shore. Then small arms fire came crashing in from the port side. The gunner on the boat closest to the shore opened up with his 20mm and ripped apart the green veil that blanketed the riverbank. Screams of pain punctuated the thunderous sounds of gunfire. All the while the three boats kept moving and soon the gunfire abated and all was quiet once again. Another kilometer and a suspicious boat came around a bend in the river, it was angling towards the swift boats and then accelerated abruptly. Lt. Faulk read the threat and lifted a grenade launcher from its place along the starboard gunwale, aimed and sent the explosive projectile hurtling towards the oncoming boat. The impact was intense and obliterated the small boat, the secondary explosion confirmed the suspicion that the boat was carrying explosives intending to sink one or more of the U.S. boats. The huge explosion worried Captain Miller and he ordered the group to speed up, putting distance between the explosion and his team as fast as possible. They were now traveling at nearly 20 knots and were thus ahead of schedule.

Reaching the split in the river, Captain Miller released his escorts with the provision they return once he radioed that he had his package. The escorts acknowledged his order and turned about, revving their engines and exited the area at an impressive pace. The roar of their engines helping to mask the low drone of the team's engines running slower now cutting into the main branch of the river. This part of the river was much narrower, only about 30 to 40 meters wide, and shallower. The water moved faster and the engine had to work harder to keep them moving forward. It was now near 0930 and hot, the sun glare off the water intensified the rays baking the men.

There was absolutely no cover for the team as they plowed ahead into the ever more uncontrolled region. All four men were on pins and needles, scanning the shore for movement. An hour passed with nothing more than an occasional bird sailing overhead. The heat and sun causing fatigue to set in, the constant drone of the engine the rhythmic slap of the waves against the bow of the boat lulling the crew into a trance. A single report from a rifle and the ringing of the hull as it glanced off into the water shattered the lull and brought the team to instant life. Chief manned the gun swinging it back and forth scanning the jungle. No other shots were fired and the boat plowed on into the onrushing current.

Colonel Morgan received word of the rescue attempt ten hours after it had begun. The time difference between Southeast Asia and Kentucky was the major factor in this delay, but another reason was that Admiral Hunt was in the midst of a full out scramble on the Kittyhawk. The call had come in for air support from a group of Marines being overrun by Charlie, and the pilots of the USS Kittyhawk were obliged to help. The jets screamed off the deck of the carrier, rocketing into the wind and then banking hard left and streaking towards the distant battlefield. Flight operations on a carrier are always chaotic at best, but rough seas and the obvious distress of the Marines put the entire ship on edge. Only after all the planes were launched and the ship began to switch to recovery mode, that is bringing the planes back aboard, did the Admiral get to the communications room and send out this message.

"Colonel Morgan,

The team is away, set out 0130, if all goes as planned should return in 24 to 36 hours.

Admiral Lindsay Hunt."

Mitch Morgan was on edge; he paced his office and cancelled all appointments. Missy didn't know what was wrong, but she knew something big was going on. The Colonel was moody a lot anymore but this was different, he was really tense, even nervous. She had never seen her boss so agitated. It was time she found out what was going on, so she did the obvious, she called on Tony. She found him at the range, where he was every day, instructing soldiers on the use and maintenance of their weapons. She ignored the leering of the men, all of whom would love a chance at her, and walked straight up to Sergeant Tony Lucas. Looked him right in the eye and said a little too loudly, "What the hell is going on soldier!"

"I don't know what you're talking about miss, but I'm busy right now," he said calmly.

"Don't give me that shit Tony! Something's up and I need to know what it is, now!" She yelled.

Tony grabbed her by the arm and rushed her out of the range hall and into the bright sunlight. "What the hell is your problem Missy? What are you raving about?"

"Colonel Morgan is really nervous about something, you guys had a major blow-up two days ago. What was that all about?" She asked.

"That was nothing, I got drunk in town and the Colonel was at the bar. He tried to read me the riot act and I wasn't having any of it. I told him he was the drunk, not me and that was that. I haven't spoken to him since." Tony explained.

"That can't be what's wrong, he's really nervous, pacing and looking at his watch. He even cancelled all his appointments today, all of them! Something is going on, are the guys in some kind of trouble? The guys in 'Nam I mean," she pressed the issue.

"Its Pete," Tony lowered his voice and his eyes.

"What do you mean? What's Pete? Tony dammit what the hell is going on!" She was getting louder again.

"Missy, Pete is in trouble, he needs evacuated from behind V.C. lines and the Colonel blames me." Tony said nearly in a whisper.

"They're going in to get him, right? No man left behind, right?" Missy was crying and pleading.

"Yes, they're going after him, but it's not gonna be easy. He isn't where I thought he would be, he shouldn't be where he's at, it doesn't make sense." Tony babbled.

"How can it be your fault, you're here and he's over there? That doesn't make sense." She countered.

"Colonel Morgan asked for my opinion where Pete would be when it came time to evacuate, I had it all figured out, I was so sure. Colonel Morgan had a team ready to grab him, but when he radioed in he was sixty kilometers away in Charlie controlled land." Tony confessed.

"You did your best right? I mean you didn't intentionally give the Colonel bad information, right?" Missy asked, sure of the answer.

"What the hell is that? Of course I did my best, he's my brother for God's sake!"

"Then it's not your fault," she said.

"Tell that to your boss, I'm through with him and his Army, just killing time until my discharge comes through," Tony said angrily.

"I'm sorry things didn't work out, with us I mean, and the Army," Missy apologized.

"I'm over it, I found another girl, I'll be fine once I'm off this base for good" Tony said flatly.

"Another girl, who is she?" Missy couldn't help but ask, a little jealousy sneaking into her tone.

"I've gotta get back to work, take care of yourself," he replied and left her standing in the sun alone.

Chapter 45

When Missy got back to her office Colonel Morgan was even more upset, he demanded to know where she had been. She told him, and what Tony had said. He scoffed at Tony's explanation that he did his best and even said that he would push for Tony's discharge to get him off the base as soon as possible. Calling Tony a bad weed and in need of being removed from his base.

Missy was sad to see her boss so lost, he had no control over the situation and it was killing him. She was however disgusted at his behavior towards Tony, someone she knew had been one of his best friends before Tony went to Vietnam. Tony was right, this war was hell and tearing everything apart, even friendships and careers.

The SEAL's boat slid slowly through the murky water, a cross between coffee and cinnamon color, carrying silt from the terraced fields further upstream. The four SEALs still on edge, still scanning the continuous green wall that passed on both sides of them. One kilometer short of the site where the two rivers would meet, Captain Miller ordered Seaman Vargas to nose the swiftboat into an eddy along the right bank of the river and then kill the engine. The four men worked astonishingly quickly and in complete silence to first pull the boat into a small inlet and then to cover it in branches and vines until it was virtually impossible to recognize as a boat. In order to tell the boat from the surrounding jungle you had to be within five meters and even then you had to be looking for a boat to see it.

Confident in his team's success at hiding their only ride to safety, Miller ordered his team to move out, into the dense jungle towards a rendezvous with a Shadow. He didn't know anything about the man the Army called the Shadow, and really didn't care to, all he knew was that the Admiral had originally ordered his team to grab this Shadow a week earlier outside DaNang. After that mission was scrubbed, the Admiral then asked his team to volunteer for this mission. Miller never even contemplated saying no, and he knew the Admiral didn't expect a "no" answer when he asked. This is what SEALs did, and that was that.

A kilometer later the team could make out the confluence of the two rivers, now they veered right and headed up the right bank of the Hirti River. It was the same murky brown and the thick and nasty was still thick and nasty. The men moved quietly through the jungle with Chief leading the way, he was so thin he could slither between vines and underbrush the others had to force their way through. The SEALs moved steadily towards the coordinates they had been given by Red Three, being careful to avoid enemy patrols and traps. By 1130 they had reached a point roughly a kilometer away from the final coordinates and Miller signaled a halt. The team needed a break and he needed to survey the area, while the men slipped their packs off and kneeled down on the ground to rest. Captain Miller pressed on a little further to gage the last distance to the target.

What he found alarmed him, a camp of at least fifty enemy soldiers was less than two hundred meters from his team's position and directly between them and their target. After assessing the situation his slipped slowly back from the edge of the camp and headed back to his men. The plan was going to have to change a little, they would have to go around the enemy camp and that would take precious time. When he reached the team he didn't even wait for questions, he merely gave the hand signal to move out and headed northwest around the obstacle.

For his part Pete had begun his move towards the Evac point the day before and was getting close to being in position as well. However, he too had came upon an obstacle, his wasn't quite as large but was ever more dangerous. The first hint was a sudden silence in the canopy, then an almost imperceptible sound, a very faint sound. A very deliberate, very calculated footfall. Pete was being stalked. This time it wasn't a tiger, it was much more deadly, this time the stalker was an enemy sniper. Pete could tell this man was very good at his craft too, anyone else would have never heard him. But this sniper was stalking the Shadow and without knowing it he was following Pete into a slow motion trap.

Pete had not chosen the location at random when he issued Red Three the coordinates, this particular spot offered several distinct advantages to a predator like the Shadow. The location was in the crotch of three ravines that converged where two tiny streams met to form a larger one, the larger one then passed several hundred meters through the third ravine and then tumbled some fifteen meters over a waterfall into the Hirti river. This convergence of water covered any slight sounds made by someone approaching, allowing even regular men to move along its banks without being heard.

It also made it so that anyone close to the water couldn't hear anything but running water, the approaching enemy would be unheard even if they weren't silent. The SEALs would need this advantage, for an entire team to move undetected through the jungle was asking more than Pete was prepared to risk. The steep walls of the ravines made shooting anyone in the bottom difficult, because to get a clear shot one had to almost be hanging over the edge of the ravine. That meant being exposed, and if you are exposed you die. The final advantage the location offered was a secret that Pete had found accidentally while desperately trying to avoid a patrol earlier in the week. The waterfall hid a small recess, not really a cave, but a place where several men could hide if necessary from a search party. He came across it after being caught swimming across the river one night, a patrol in a small boat came around a bend in the river when he was still ten meters from the shore. He dove under water and swam a fast as he could towards shore. He felt the water from the waterfall hitting his back and he swam until he touched land. When he lifted his head up to take a breath he found he was behind the falls and safely out of sight of the patrol. Apparently they hadn't seen him dive, because they continued down the river without even slowing down.

Being stalked forced the young Ranger to think quickly. Pete slipped silently into one of the ravines and then did the unthinkable, he started running, not jogging, not moving quickly, running. Even six months alone in the jungle had not slowed Pete down, his blazing speed had been his hallmark on the football field and now he planned to use it to save his own life and that of his rescue party. He covered more than four hundred meters in just over a minute, putting himself way out in front of his pursuer. The running water masked his dash and once within sight of the Evac point he stopped running and quickly and quietly scaled the steep wall of the ravine and set the trap. He lay down prone on the ground under the cover of two oversized ferns and waited for the enemy to come to him. He didn't have to wait long.

The enemy sniper moved cat like along the edge of the ravine, occasionally leaning over the edge, trying to glimpse his target. He had almost gotten his shot an hour ago, but just as he was getting ready to fire the American had slipped over the edge of the ravine and out of site. It had taken him five minutes to get to the edge of the ravine and in that time the American had disappeared. This was no ordinary American, he had been tracking this sniper for two days, never even seen him until an hour ago. Then he was gone again like a puff of smoke, fading into the dense undergrowth. He was sure the enemy had continued down the ravine, he had been steadily heading that direction for a full day now. But where could he have gone? The bottom of the ravine was more rocky than the surrounding jungle and had less cover, yet the man was not there. It was getting brighter inside the forest as the sun rose steadily higher, the Russian sniper found a treewell created when a huge tree had given in to the soft soil and a heavy wind and tumbled over the edge of the ravine. Here he would rest and listen, the American couldn't stay hidden forever.

Pete had watched the man approach to nearly two hundred meters from his position and then settle into the depression on the rim of the ravine. He would be hard pressed to get a good shot at the enemy from where he lay, if he did it would probably be because the other sniper had just shot one or more of the rescue team. He needed to get to the team in time to warn them and then come back for the kill. Pete silently slid backward until his feet hung just over the edge of the ravine, then he slowly lowered himself down by clutching a vine that snaked its way up the side of the chasm. By staying tight against the side of the cliff he went unseen by the enemy. When he felt his toes touch the bottom, he felt relief, rappelling via a vine is not what it is cracked up to be. He pressed himself against the side of the cliff and moved steadily downstream. After rounding a small bend in the creek he was free to move more quickly again. He arrived at the desired location, where the three streams met and became invisible, blending himself into the underbrush and ferns. Here he would wait for his rescue.

Chapter 46

The SEALs had made their way around the enemy camp and were now directly across the river from the waterfall. Captain Miller called his team together and whispered, "that's it boys. A couple hundred meters up that little stream is where our package is supposed to be."

"I sure as hell hope he's there, these bugs are drivin' me nuts," replied Chief.

"Quit yer bitchen Chief, we ain't even started to get into the real bugs yet," quipped Faulk.

"Yeah but the worst part is the snakes, man I hate snakes," laughed Vargas knowing full well Faulk's absolute fear of snakes.

"Shut up E, you know I hate snakes!" Faulk shot back.

"Enough," Miller snapped, "let's just get this guy and get the hell outta here. Chief move upstream a little and check the river, I don't want to be half way across and find an enemy gunship bearing down on us."

"Yessir," came back Chief's immediate reply.

"Eric, you head back towards that VC camp and make sure no-one's decided to make a patrol this way during the heat of the day."

"Captain, what if they're comin', what do you want me to do?" Vargas asked the obvious question.

"Stay hidden and try to signal us, if we have to engage you can flank them and cut them to pieces," was Miller's reply.

Vargas spun from his resting position against a tree and moved quickly north towards the camp the team had just recently skirted. Twenty minutes later he returned with good news, "no movement from the camp, looks like a siesta boss."

Chief returned a moment later with equally good news, "excellent," was the Captain's one word reply. He gave a hand signal and all four men slipped into the brown stained water. The first few feet were only knee deep, but then it quickly got deeper and soon the men were swimming and trying not to be swept downstream. All four were remarkable swimmers, to be a SEAL that was an absolute requirement, and they made quick work of the 30 meter wide river. Once on the other side they labored up the opposite bank, no small feat considering it was nearly vertical and slick. Once over the lip of the cliff they quickly made their way along the swift moving stream. The rocky nature of the terrain made traveling easier, but Miller worried that they were too exposed.

A couple hundred meters later and Chief raised his hand to signal "halt". He crouched low and waited for Captain Miller to ease up beside him. "This is it sir, the package should be right here," Chief whispered.

"Roger that Chief, but where is he? Set up a perimeter and lets wait for him to come to us," the Captain answered back in a whisper.

Using hand signals Miller had Faulk cross the stream and take up position with his back to the cliff, here he was able to watch both up and down stream. The captain next positioned Vargas five meters south along one of the tributaries, and Chief moved a similar distance up the other tributary. All three men did their best to hide amongst the large rocks and small bushes that lined the streams.

Pete watched all of this from a point not two feet from Captain Miller's backside. The captain had nearly sat on Pete when he moved up beside Chief, in fact Pete had pulled his rifle back towards himself just in time or Miller would have stepped right on it. Pete couldn't help but chuckle at the situation. His laugh was so soft, just barely audible, but Captain Miller swore he heard something and began scanning the area intensely. This made Pete laugh even more, and the Captain was beginning to think he was hearing things.

"Sergeant Peter Lucas, U.S. Army sir, glad you could make it," Pete whispered so softly Miller could barely make it out.

"Where are you sergeant?" Miller replied in a manner that lead Pete to believe he was not amused.

"Right below you sir."

Miller snapped his head down towards his feet and could now make out the barrel of Pete's rifle and the oversized scope that sat on top of it. His eyes followed the rifle into the bushes, but he still couldn't really see the man hidden there. Instead he just spoke in the general direction. "Ready to move out soldier? We got a boat to catch."

"I've got company up the cliff, I was waiting for you guys to show up before I dealt with him in case I have to expose our position with a shot," Pete whispered.

"My men can handle him, what's his twenty?" Miller answered using the Navy term for position.

"Negative sir, you guys are the best in the world at what you do, but this guy's a world class ghost. He would take them all before they knew what hit 'em." Pete's reply rankled the proud SEAL.

"I suppose you can take this guy out?" Miller asked.

Pete did not respond. The captain was now getting even hotter, he looked down and just stared blankly at the ground. The rifle was gone, and so was Pete. He had been just feet away and backed away without the captain even knowing it. The roaring stream had covered the soft scraping of the ground as his feet inched him back away even as he was conversing with the SEAL team leader. Pete managed to cross the stream just below Lt. Faulk make his way up a small side ravine and head back upstream towards the sniper he knew would be soon getting active again.

Miller signaled Chief, Vargas and Faulk and they all converged at the captain's position. "OK, this Shadow says he has a sniper tracking him," Miller started.

"When did you get this info Cap?" asked Lt. Faulk.

"Just now, he was right there a minute ago," Miller motioned to the spot on the ground where the rifle had been.

"No way boss, you feeling OK?" Vargas asked while grinning widely.

"This guy is scary, I never did actually see him, but I talked to him and he went to take out the sniper. Let's move into the bush a little and wait, I'm pretty sure he'll be back soon."

"Seriously Captain, you alright? There's no way that guy got past us, talked to you and then got past us again. That just didn't happen. No way!" Chief complained.

"Holy shit!" Faulk had moved into the bushes Pete had used as cover and found the telltale signs of someone lying flat in the brush. "He was here alright, and he was here when we got here, waiting for us."

"That's right Lieutenant, now let's get hidden and wait for Houdini to make another appearance," Miller ordered. The SEAL team moved slowly into the bush, each of then looking where they stepped to make sure they weren't going to step on the guy they had come to rescue.

The Russian sniper had waited and still not seen any sign of the American. Major Kolskoff was right to fear this American he was extremely skilled, but Igor Stanislov considered himself to be the best in the world. He had 30 confirmed kills to his credit and had trained numerous Vietnamese snipers himself. He knew he would have to go down into the ravine to pick up the trail again. The problem was that this would put him in the open, exposed. But Igor was confident he had not been detected by the American, after all not once had the American even changed course to try and flush out someone on his tail. No, this American was pretty good at hiding but he didn't know he was being followed. So at 1330 he slipped over the edge of the ravine and began searching for signs of the American.

It didn't take long, he quickly found footprints that followed the stream. Something was wrong with the footprints though, at first he couldn't figure out what it was. Then suddenly he realized, but it was too late. Pete's knife entered the man's back just below the third rib and angled upward into his enemy's heart. Death was quick and silent, Pete's hand had coved the man's mouth and muffled his cry of pain. Igor Stansilov had realized too late that the footprints were all going downstream except one, Pete had doubled back on his own trail. The SEALs would have appreciated Pete's method of killing if they had only known, but this kill would remain undocumented. Pete wasn't happy about killing, it was a matter of necessity that's all.

Pete took a second and looked around to make sure the sniper was alone, nothing moved and even the stream seemed to hush for a moment. Satisfied, Pete retrieved his rifle from the nook in the cliff he had hid it in and headed back downstream to meet up with the SEALs. He moved quickly now, certain he wasn't being watched or trailed. In less than two minutes he reached the fork in the streams and instantly picked one of the SEALs out of the background cover. He stared directly at him and motioned for the team to come out of hiding. Chief had a cold chill run down his spine when Pete instantly picked him out of the underbrush. Was he that obvious? Or was this guy just that good?

Captain Miller gathered his men and met Pete by the stream. "Captain Robert Miller U.S. Navy SEAL," he introduced himself while extending his hand to Pete.

"Captain, Sergeant Peter Lucas U.S. Army, we meet again." Pete spoke so softly the others had to strain to hear.

"This is Chief, Master Chief Holcolm that is, Seaman Eric Vargas and Lieutenant Mac Faulk," Captain Miller introduced the rest of the team. They didn't offer to shake Pete's hand and he returned the favor. Captain Miller could now tell why the Army wanted this guy back so badly, the others didn't recognize the value of such a weapon but the captain understood completely.

"From now on I'm under your command sir," Pete stated flatly.

"Yes you are soldier, now lets move before Charlie finds our ride and spoils this party. Chief take the point, lets get back across the river and to the boat before dark, I like our chances on the river after dark a whole lot better." Captain Miller spoke in a whisper, the Shadow had a way of impressing quiet on everything and everyone around him.

The team moved out with Chief on point and Lt. Faulk bringing up the rear. The river was only a few hundred meters away and they reached it without incident, once there Chief studied the cliff for the best way down. He finally turned to Pete and asked, "What do you think?"

Pete answered quietly, "jump."

"What? You crazy grunt, its gotta be fifty feet at least. What if there are rocks under the water?" Chief asked incredulously.

"There weren't any there the other day, but if you have a better way I'll follow" Pete answered.

"Captain what do you think?" Faulk asked.

"Soldier are you sure about the rocks?" the captain asked.

"Yessir, and once you hit the water swim back under the falls. There is a hollow behind it that can hide us until we're all down. Then we can swim across in two teams with the others providing cover." Pete answered.

"OK boys we jump," Miller said, then turned to Pete with a serious look and threatened him. "If one of my team gets fucked up in this stunt, you'll answer to me, understand."

"Understood, sir." Pete's reply was steady and unwavering.

Chief and Vargas went first, stepping off together and plunging the fifteen meters into the dark water, they both surfaced quickly and swam back under the falls. Next to go was Faulk, he hesitated a second then stepped off. Before the Captain could jump Pete grabbed his pack and pulled him away from the lip. The captain reacted immediately and threw Pete onto his back and prepared to pummel him. Pete put his finger to his lips to signal silence. The captain hesitated, his fist cocked and ready to strike. Then came the unmistakable sound of an engine.

A patrol boat came slowly down the river from the south, on board were five VC. They carried automatic weapons but were chatting and not really paying any attention. The boat slowed in front of the waterfall and several of the men seemed to be staring at the top. Apparently they were just enjoying the view, because after several seconds the boat accelerated again and headed on down the river.

"Son, this coming out of nowhere and grabbing me shit has got to stop or I'm gonna end up killing you!" Miller scolded Pete.

Pete just smiled and rolled out from under the captain. He got to his feet and scanned the river for signs of any other boats. When he was sure, he stepped off the cliff and plunged into the river with the Captain right beside him. After swimming back under the falls the two were helped out of the water by the rest of the team.

"Man, that was close. I thought you guys were gonna jump right into that damn boat!" Vargas yelled over the roar of the falls.

The captain cast a knowing look at Pete and said, "Let's move or we'll never find that boat of ours after dark."

Chapter 47

Colonel Morgan had already called Admiral Hunt three times and was just about to make it four when his phone rang. "Colonel Morgan," was how he answered it.

"Mitch," it was his ex-wife Katherine. She hadn't called in months and he really wasn't in the mood to talk to her now.

"Kath, I'm really busy right now."

"Mitch, I'm dying," she whispered into the receiver.

"What? What do you mean you're dying?"

"The doctors say I have cancer, that I have less than six months," she was crying now.

Mitch Morgan's head was spinning, "what the hell, I'm, I'm." He couldn't find the words and just stammered.

"I just wanted you to know, I never stopped loving you. I just couldn't live with you anymore," Katherine had regained her composure.

"I will always love you Kath, you know that. Have you gotten a second opinion?" He asked, knowing the answer even before he asked the question. Katherine was very thorough and rarely made rash decisions. She had been his rock for years, until she just couldn't take the separation when he was overseas and the drinking when he was home.

"Three, I've had three doctors examine me. They all agree, its too far along."

"I'll come out to see you soon, if that's OK with you that is?" He asked almost pleading.

"I'd like that, I'm at my mom's place. Let me know when you're coming and I'll have the police waiting," she joked.

"You would, wouldn't you!" He chuckled. "It's nice hearing from you Kath, I just wish there was something I could do."

"That's OK Mitch, I'm coming to grips with it. The Lord has a plan and I will find out what it is soon enough," she replied softly.

"OK, OK, I'll call you with my schedule tomorrow. Missy has gone for the day and I don't know where I'm supposed to be unless she tells me," he answered.

"Sometimes I think Missy was sent by God to keep you in line Colonel," she joked again.

"Damn strait, hon"

"Goodbye Mitch, I hope to see you soon," she ended the conversation and hung up the phone.

Mitch Morgan stood there holding the receiver until a loud dial tone came blasting from the speaker. With that he slammed down the phone and went back to pacing. His mind even more cluttered, his emotions ripping him apart. Why would any supposed loving God take an angel like Katherine and leave a miserable wretch like him on earth? He couldn't get his mind around the thought, it just didn't seem right.

Tony and Tracy had settled into a routine, he would pick her up from work and take her home or to a late night movie. After they were in her apartment they would talk about their day and the latest news. Even though it was the wee hours of the morning, they seemed to not notice the time and hours would pass. The relationship wasn't physical, at least not yet, but it was growing very serious. Tony was due to be discharged within the month and he wanted to move back home to Ohio. Tracy had nothing to hold her back, so when he asked her to join him, she immediately accepted. Tony called Joy to give her the news.

"Mom, I'm coming home," he said into the receiver, a smile a mile wide across his face.

"You have another leave, that's great!" Joy's excitement came right through the phone.

"No mom, I mean I'm coming home for good. My discharge will be official in about three weeks."

"Oh my God Tony, that is the best news I've had since you came back to us!" Joy nearly screamed into the phone. "I'll let everyone know, we'll have a big party here at the house."

"Mom I'd rather not have the party if that's OK, I just want to come home," Tony replied.

"OK, if that's what you want. But you know everyone's gonna be here whether or not you want them." Joy spoke the truth and Tony knew it. His family was tight, and this was a special occasion, not that the Lucases needed a special occasion to get together. In fact they gathered most every weekend at one house or another for a birthday, anniversary or holiday.

"Mom," Tony hesitated for a second then added," I'm bringing someone with me."

"Any friend of yours is welcome Tony, you know that."

"This isn't just a friend mom, her name is Tracy and I think she's gonna stay around awhile," he added.

"You mean she's moving here with you," Joy said making a statement not asking a question. "Where is she going to stay son?"

"Don't know for sure yet, but she's a nice girl mom. I wouldn't put you out, but she needs a new start as much as I do."

"So you're bringing home a stray, people aren't pets Tony, they don't always appreciate the help." Joy cautioned.

"I know mom, but Tracy won't be a problem, I'm sure of it. She's a hard worker and has her own place now, so she'll get a place of her own right away. Well, as soon as she gets a job that is. Trust me mom, you're gonna like her, I do."

"Well that is as good a reason as any son, if you like her she must have something going for her." Joy said calmly. "You tell Tracy I'm looking forward to meeting her."

"I will, but do me a favor mom don't ask her about her family. She's had a rough couple of years, just let her tell you when she's ready, OK?"

"She's in good company if she's had a rough couple of years, but I'll save the interrogation for later," Joy joked.

"Thanks mom, I've gotta go, love ya," Tony said as he hung up the phone.

The SEAL team crossed the river and re-entered the jungle the same way they had come three hours before. The wind had shifted and the smell of a campfire filled their nostrils. The VC camp was still in place and apparently going nowhere fast. Captain Miller knew there would be patrols out now and his team moved slowly and carefully forward. Chief took the point as always, but he had to share the position with the new kid. Pete wasn't used to having this many men with him and he had to force himself to work within the group. To keep from taking the lead away from Chief, he slowed down and soon ended up near the back of the team.

However this just managed to alarm the SEALs and they all slowed down. The team assumed he had sensed something was wrong. Pete was used to taking days to cover a hundred meters, so the slow pace didn't concern him one bit. Captain Miller had an entirely different take on the situation.

"What's up Sergeant?" the captain whispered to Pete.

"Nothing, I'm just trying to stay in the middle. I don't want to cause any trouble sir," came Pete's reply.

"Shit soldier! We all assumed you had a reason for slowing down, were losing time here," Captain Miller snapped. "Chief, pick it up. We need to get to that boat in less than two hours."

Chief instantly picked up the pace and the team surged forward into the thick and nasty. The path he took was in Pete's mind dangerously exposed and made the Shadow very nervous. Captain Miller was directly behind Pete now and could tell the Ranger was very tense. Pete constantly swiveled his head and seemed to be tentative when moving. This wasn't the man the Captain had watched come through the ravine to meet up with his team an hour before. Something was definitely bothering the "Shadow", as he was called.

As a Navy SEAL the captain had learned more than most how to assess a situation, and as they moved along he was getting more and more nervous himself. He watched the young ranger and tried to follow his gaze. Shortly a pattern began to emerge, Pete paid great attention to areas of obvious ambush points and where it seemed human activity may have altered the landscape. He relaxed when the jungle seemed most untamed. He seemed to be listening very intently to the trees and bushes, gauging the impact the team was having on the birds and animals. As he watched his package an appreciation of this young soldier's skills began to develop.

The team skirted the VC base and began to head down river towards their hidden boat. Pete had sped up now and was once again just behind Chief. The terrain was familiar to Pete, he had been here less than a week ago. The landing zone with dead American soldiers was now less than five kilometers northwest of their current position. This area worried Pete, the enemy was thick here and the way filled with danger. Pete noticed the sign at the last second, reached for Chief and just caught his sleeve. The telltale sign of a trap, a straight line on the jungle floor, sat inches from Chief's left foot. If he had taken one more step it would have been his last.

The captain saw Pete grab Chief and hurried to their position, the other two men squatted down where they stood and scanned the surrounding forest. "What do you have soldier?" Miller asked.

Pete just pointed to the ground. Both SEALs looked at the forest floor and at first didn't see anything but leaves and tree roots. After a second of intense focus Captain Miller could se it too, Chief however was clueless. He shifted his weight and began to step with his right foot. Captain Miller grabbed him by the shoulders and restrained him. Chief instantly relaxed and let the Captain control him. His puzzled look spoke volumes.

Captain Miller let go of Chief and joined Pete who by this time knelt down next to the trip wire. Pete carefully exposed a short section of the wire and then followed it into the jungle. Two meters inside the thick jungle he found the trigger, a bent over sapling stretched almost to its breaking point, the wire looped very delicately over a stick that was being used as a release pin. Step on the wire and the pin is pulled, setting the sapling free to snap back into its upright position. Pete and the captain followed the wire to the other end and found a series of explosives wired in sequence. This trap would blow up a twenty meter section of the trail, killing everyone and everything in its path.

The team stepped carefully over the trip wire and continued on their way. For the first time in his career Chief backed off and let someone else take the point. Pete led the team through the dense undergrowth, the SEALs were getting slashed by the plants and devoured by the bugs but not one complaint was spoken. Each of them now realized that this was the best way to get out of Charlie's back yard alive. Pete stopped two kilometers later and motioned the captain forward.

"Captain, I'm not privy to where you guys hid your boat," he whispered.

"About two hundred meters further and you will come across a small side stream, the ride is hidden on the far bank in a small eddy," Miller whispered back.

"Roger, I think the light will hold about another twenty minutes, can you find your way there from here?" Pete asked.

"It's time to get outta here sergeant, you can stay with us the rest of the way," Miller answered. He didn't want to lose the package this close to the boat.

"I want outta here as much as you do sir, but that patrol boat we saw at the falls is docked at the VC camp. If you fire up your motor, they're gonna be right on our asses in no time."

Chapter 48

Captain Miller had been thinking about the same thing earlier, but had came to grips with having to try and out run the enemy. "We will have a little head start, I think we can out run them back to our support. Once the other boats join us, Charlie will abandon the chase forthwith," Miller stated confidently.

Pete looked concerned but nodded his acknowledgement and turned back towards the front of the team. In less than twenty minutes the team was at the boat and preparing to set off. Faulk, Chief and Pete made quick work of clearing the brush and vines from the skiff and Vargas took his position at the helm. Captain Miller and Lt. Faulk pushed the boat out into the center of the small stream and turned it around so that it was facing back towards the main river. They each expertly lifted themselves onto the gunwale on either side and climbed aboard. Vargas fired up the engines and put the boat in gear. The deafening sound of the boats engines hurt Pete's ears, he reached up instinctively and covered them with his hands. He had found a small area rearward of Vargas where the rear deck began and the cockpit ended. It formed a sort of natural seat and Pete settled in.

Captain Miller and Lt. Faulk watched out the rear of the boat, both hoping that nothing would interrupt the widening vee shape made by the boat's wake and the onrushing darkness. Chief manned the cannon on the front deck, scanning back and forth from bank to bank. A distant light soured the Captain's mood, the patrol boat both he and Pete had feared was in hot pursuit. To the SEAL's dismay it seemed to be gaining on them. Miller moved to the cockpit where Vargas held the wheel and shouted over the din.

"Does this piece of shit have anything more to give?" He yelled while gesturing towards the oncoming enemy.

Vargas pushed hard on the throttle and the boat responded with a slight surge, "that's it boss, that's all she's got!"

"Shit, get ready we may have to out maneuver him," the Captain yelled back.

Pete had followed the discussion and turned around to face the light that grew brighter by the moment. The enemy was still quite a distance off, but they would catch up in a few minutes at this pace. He lay down prone on the rear deck and opened the lens covers on his scope. The light was bright and it made it very difficult to see anything clearly. The bouncing of the boat added to the confusion he was seeing through his right eye. He concentrated harder and could finally make out several shapes on the enemy vessel, the driver was hidden by something and would not be a viable target. He did see something that peeked his interest however, a large round object mounted sideways on the rear deck.

"Stop the boat!" he yelled, or at least he thought he yelled. In fact it was just above a whisper and no one else heard him. "Stop the boat!" he screamed this time.

Vargas spun his head around and looked at the young ranger, but made no attempt to slow the boat down. Captain Miller also looked at Pete, he didn't think that anyone could shoot accurately in the dark, let alone from lying on the deck of a boat. He did however know that he had to figure out something quick or he was headed for a bad ending. He decided that turning around and fighting beat being blown out of the water from behind.

"Bring us around E, let Chief have a whack at them," the Captain shouted.

"Aye Aye Cap," Vargas answered and spun the wheel hard to port. The boat leaned hard into the turn and was traveling so fast that it nearly ran aground before it made the full turn. Pete who was lying flat on the deck nearly flew off, he managed to hook his left foot into the cockpit well and keep from sailing into the river. But he was now facing downstream and away from the enemy.

Chief; on the other hand was facing strait at the oncoming patrol boat and locked in with his 20mm cannon. The enemy opened up with a heavy gun and the bullets began splashing in the water in front of the American boat; the distance between the two sides getting shorter exponentially with each passing second. Chief opened up with his gun and raked the bow of the VC boat, causing them to turn away slightly. The gunner on the VC boat adjusted to the turn and raked the Americans broadside. Faulk hit the deck in agony, blood gushing from a wound in his right thigh. Captain Miller rushed to his side and administered pressure to the wound. Pete was once again in position as the enemy boat passed behind the Americans.

He aimed and fired.

"How the hell did you miss?" screamed Vargas. "They were almost on top of us!"

Pete didn't respond, he merely chambered another round, aimed again and fired a second time. The first bullet had not missed; in fact it had been a perfect shot. Piercing the round external gas tank just below the port connecting it to the fuel line. The second shot hit the man manning the deck gun in the head killing him instantly and causing him to fall backward. The gunner held onto the deck mounted gun as he fell, squeezing the trigger all the while. Bullets split the air wildly as the gun lurched first nearly upright, then the barrel abruptly snapped back down as the mans' death grip finally gave way. The final shot struck the bow of the Vietnamese boat and ricocheted off of the steel plating and then slammed into the left arm of the patrol's commanding officer.

Captain Miller had grabbed the grenade launcher from the starboard gunwale and fired a salvo that landed on the rear deck of the enemy vessel. The explosion ignited the gasoline rushing from the ruptured fuel tank and the ensuing secondary explosion obliterated the entire boat killing everyone left alive on board.

The heat from the blast seared Pete's face and forced him and Seaman Vargas to turn their heads quickly. In a matter of seconds nothing remained above the waterline but burning gasoline on the waters' surface. Vargas gunned the engines and turned the boat back downstream. Chief grabbed the radio and called ahead to the waiting escorts. He made sure they had a medic ready and that they were busting their asses to join up as soon as possible. He may have used his captain's name to get a more rapid response, but none of the team would ever admit it.

The escorts appeared right on time at the confluence of rivers and a medic was transferred onto the SEAL boat. The three American vessels roared downstream toward DaNang without any further enemy contact. Soon the boats were alongside a Marine transport ship, and the SEALs and their package were transferred on board. Captain Miller and Seaman

Vargas carried Lt. Faulk to sickbay. There a team of Marine doctors and nurses took over, it would take surgery but Mac would be OK. The rest of the team and Pete were transferred one more time via chopper, this time to the USS Kittyhawk. Once on board Pete was ushered onto the bridge to meet Admiral Hunt.

Pete looked entirely out of place. He was still wearing his filthy, torn and worn camo suit. He was filthy, and hadn't bathed in several days. Most of the Navy personnel looked at him with disdain and some with pity. He didn't belong with the spit and polish of the US Navy. Captain Miller however stood proudly beside him, he knew what the others did not, this, was a real fighting man.

The Admiral approached and Pete, Captain Miller, Seaman Vargas and Chief Holcolm all snapped to attention. The admiral looked at Pete and smiled a knowing smile; he understood what it meant to be Special Forces. He returned their salutes and said, "Captain Miller, well done."

"Thank you sir," the captain replied.

"That will be all captain, I need a moment with our guest."

"Aye, Aye, sir," The captain and his team saluted and retreated from the bridge. They headed for their quarters for a much needed shower and then sleep.

Pete stood at attention waiting for the admiral to speak. He was tired too and desperately wanted a shower and long snooze. He was nearly out on his feet when the admiral finally began speaking. "Sergeant Lucas, I understand you are the best the Army has to offer, that true?"

"I do my best sir," Pete answered flatly.

"I'm sure you do son. Colonel Morgan is a friend of mine, he asked for my help in getting you out. Took a lot of grief to get you back, hope you're worth it." The admiral was obviously not happy about the rescue, a SEAL wounded to save a grunt. "I am a Special Forces guy, I see the Special Forces being more and more important in the future. I hope you appreciate everything that was done to get you out son."

"Yessir, I do sir." Pete answered.

"The lieutenant here will show you below, we'll put you in sickbay to start out. The docs will check you out and make sure you're not going to contaminate my ship. Then we'll get you something to eat, and find a way for you to get back to your unit." The admiral didn't show any signs of outward emotion, he finished his statement and then motioned to a Lieutenant.

Pete was lead through a maze of corridors and down several flights of stairs. He was hopelessly lost in no time. He just tried to focus on the lieutenant and follow him, but men kept cutting between them and rushing here and there. Just when Pete thought he had lost his escort, the lieutenant waved to him and ushered him into sickbay. A Navy doctor took one look at Pete and scowled. He pointed to a small door, above which was a sign, "shower". Pete stepped inside and the door was closed behind him. He stripped out of the only clothes he had worn in the past three months. They literally fell apart when they hit the floor. He stepped into the shower and the hot water soothed his aching body. He was in the shower for almost a half an hour when the knock came.

"Sergeant Lucas, front and center" the doctor called.

"Yessir, one minute sir." Pete said, while shutting off the water. He quickly toweled off and dressed in the Navy blues left for him on a bench in the shower room. He exited the shower room and entered the large main room of sickbay. It was very bright with lots of stainless steel and bright white linens. It took a second for Pete's eyes to adjust; afterward he spotted the doctor waiting by a hospital bed and walked over to it. The ship was heaving with the sea, and he nearly lost his balance.

"Don't have your sea legs yet soldier?" smiled the doctor.

"Nossir, I haven't ever been on a ship at sea before today" Pete answered shyly.

"Well, I'd say you would get used to it but I understand you won't be here that long."

Pete was told to remove his shirt and when he did the doctor gasped. He had never seen anything like it; the welts and scars on Pete's body were everywhere. There were countless rings where bloodthirsty leeches had attached themselves. After gorging on his blood, they had simply dropped off to digest their meal and wait for the next donor to come along. The doctor found scores of worms and other parasites in and on Pete's skin. He and two nurses spent several hours extracting them all and dressing the open sores they left behind. Pete was embarrassed when they worked on his buttocks and groin areas, but the nurses were very professional and businesslike. After the medical team finished with this monumental task, the doctor had Pete lie on the bed. In moments he was asleep and didn't wake for fourteen hours.

Admiral Hunt decided to punish his friend the Colonel and make him wait a while before contacting him. He didn't get to wait long, Colonel Morgan made his fourth call just an hour after Pete had arrived on the Kittyhawk.

"Admiral, any word on my man?" came the inquiry.

"Yes Colonel, we got him. He's on board right now. Docs are giving him the once over, I can't afford an outbreak of disease on my ship." The admiral responded dryly.

"Excellent, I owe you one Admiral,"

"Yes you do Mitch, one of my SEALs got hit."

"Shit, your man gonna be OK?" Morgan asked more out of being formal than really caring.

"He'll be fine, thanks for asking. Your man is a bit of a runt isn't he?" Hunt replied.

"Don't underestimate him Lindsay, he's about as good as there is," Morgan's pride coming right through the receiver.

"We'll get him cleaned up and back to his unit ASAP."

"Thank you sir, Morgan out."

Colonel Morgan hung up the phone and then picked up the receiver again, he held it for a minute and then placed it back on its hook. He wanted desperately to call Tony and tell him the news, but it wouldn't be right. Instead he just shouted, "Missy!"

Missy James opened the outer door and stepped into the Colonel's office. She had been nervous and nauseous for two days. She knew Pete was in trouble and that the Colonel was uptight and that just added to her state. She entered his office on the verge of crying. She left sobbing tears of joy. Colonel Mitch Morgan had broke the rules to let her know first of Pete's recovery. She couldn't have been more appreciative if she had to, she understood that he had bent the rules for her and she would not readily forget it.

Chapter 49

Admiral Hunt requested Captain Miller join him in his quarters the next morning and over a breakfast of eggs, ham and a biscuit washed down with fresh orange juice, he asked the Captain to assess the "undersized" soldier he had rescued. Miller responded quickly and without worrying about being subtle, "never been around someone who could simply disappear like that," he said. " I almost stepped on him and still never actually saw his face when we first made contact, I take it he was in country a long time because that guy had gone native."

"You think so?"

"Yessir, did you see what he looked like? He had become part of the damn jungle. He saw stuff I would have missed for sure, we would have all been blown to smithereens if he hadn't spotted that trap." Miller said and then took a huge forkful of eggs. "That guy shot a guy dead, one shot, while lying on the deck of a rocking, moving boat with the guy he shot on another rocking, moving boat at 100 meters like it was nothing."

"So if we get this Special Operations Force going I have been pushing for I should try and get him on the team?" asked Hunt.

"He would be my first pick, don't get me wrong Admiral I love my guys, and I consider myself the best warrior there has ever been, but the guy the Army calls the Shadow scares the shit out of me." Miller added. " and I'm not scared of anything."

"Interesting", was all Hunt said in reply.

Pete awoke after his long sleep hungry and thirsty. He was lead to the mess hall and he ate heartily. The Navy's food was a whole lot better than the food he had gotten at Firebase Scout. He still wasn't used to regular fare like beef and pasta, but he decided he could get used to it real quick. While he was eating a Lieutenant came up to him and asked his name.

"Sergeant Peter Lucas, sir"

"Sergeant, I'm Lieutenant Fox, it's my job to reunite you with your unit. You will be put on a chopper to DaNang, from there you'll catch a transport to Saigon. Its my understanding your unit ships stateside in two days." He said smiling.

"I'm going home sir?" Pete asked almost in disbelief.

"You're going home, soon."

"Thank you sir, how do I find my chopper sir?" Pete asked pleadingly.

"I'll be back in ten, be ready and I'll take you up to the flight deck."

"What about my gear sir? I can't leave without my weapon!" Pete pleaded.

"It's stowed topside, we'll retrieve it on our way." The Lieutenant replied.

The Lieutenant left and several sailors nearby started talking about how they wished they were headed home. Pete smiled to himself, it would be nice to be home. He hadn't dared even think of going home until now. He thought of Missy and his mom, of Tony and Uncle John. He caught himself grinning from ear to ear and quickly changed to a more serious look. It would be rude to show obvious glee for his good fortune while these men were still thousands of miles from everything and everyone they loved. But inside he continued to smile, his thoughts racing from bean fields to his mom's fresh bread to Missy's beautiful face. A sudden thought ruined the entire mental party, "what if she isn't waiting for me?"

Pete was now concerned, what would he do if she wasn't there? He suddenly realized that she meant more to him than he could ever have imagined. He hadn't had a chance to even write in months. "Why should she wait? She probably just thinks I'm running around with some girl over here," he thought to himself. He became sullen and dejected. The lieutenant returned and escorted him topside, he recovered his weapons and pack from a locker just off to the side of the deck and then headed out onto the flight deck. There he found Captain Miller and Admiral Hunt waiting for him. He saluted and approached them along with Lieutenant Fox.

"Sergeant Lucas, it has been an honor," stated the captain and he reached out and shook Pete's hand.

"Yes sir, it has been an honor," Pete replied.

"Sergeant, give Colonel Morgan my regards when you see him and tell him I will collect on his debt," Admiral Hunt smiled.

"Yessir, I'll relay the message sir," Pete answered.

"Go home son, I have a feeling I'll be seeing you again," the Admiral responded.

Pete saluted and turned towards the waiting chopper, Lieutenant Fox helped him get settled in and the chopper lifted off of the deck and spun left, dipped slightly towards the water and then healed forward as it sped towards DaNang. In less than thirty minutes Pete was standing on the tarmac next to a cargo plane headed for Saigon. Two hours later he was exiting the plane onto the tarmac in Saigon. At the far end of the runway were several tents. As he began walking towards the tents, several MPs approached him.

"Where are you headed sailor?" one asked.

Pete had forgotten he was wearing the Navy blues, "I'm Sergeant Peter Lucas, U.S. Army Ranger!" he shouted over the roaring engines of an incoming plane.

"You're out of uniform soldier, explain yourself!" the MP yelled back.

"I was picked up by a team of SEALs and transported to the USS Kittyhawk, they gave me some clean clothes and a ride here. That's my unit down there," he pointed to the tents.

"We'll see, come with us," responded the MP.

After a few minutes and some heated words from Major Lipinski, the MP's relented and allowed Pete to rejoin the Rangers at the end of the runway. Before he did, he was issued some new fatigues and boots. He was lead to a storage locker where his other gear had been stowed, he picked up his weapons, helmet and pack. Only then did he approach his unit where he was met at the entrance to the makeshift camp by Lieutenant Roth. The lieutenant met his salute with one of his own and then promptly shook his hand and the party was on. The rangers had been looking for a reason to go wild and this was as good a reason as any. One of their own coming back from the dead, or at least they saw it that way. None of them had a clue as to what Pete had done, or where he had been. Many asked over the course of the next two days but Pete always found a way to change the subject or deflect the question. He realized he was getting good at not talking about it, and that was just fine with him. The faces of the men he had shot would never leave his mind, he would see them in his sleep the rest of his life.

The party roared right up until it was time to leave, and even continued on the plane until Major Lipinski ordered the men to calm down. He was getting concerned for the safety of the flight crew, and finally got the men to ease up. Once they did it was only minutes before the whole lot was asleep, except for one. Pete sat silently looking out the window, he could see the ocean below and the sun above. The silence seemed to sooth him, all of the noise and chaos from the party had made him tense and uneasy. The soft rumble from the engines reminded him of the hum of the insects in the jungle. He would always love the jungle, it was as much his home as the farm was.

Missy waited a full day to tell her mom the news, she knew what she was going to do but it took time to build up the courage. She told her mom her intention to get married to Pete as soon as possible, she would even propose if she had to. Pete would be stateside for at least eight months before his next tour of duty. That would be enough time to plan and hold a wedding. Emma James was happy for her only daughter, but deep inside she worried about Missy's life with a soldier and how her husband Earl would take the news. He had experienced life as a military man in the Marines during the Korean War and it had left a strong distaste for the military and the government in general. He never talked about what he had seen or done on the Korean peninsula, but Emma knew it must have been terrible.

Missy hadn't waited even two minutes after Colonel Morgan had given her the news before calling Joy Lucas. The two women laughed and cried together over the phone for nearly five minutes. After hanging up Joy made the one call she had dreamed about for six months.

"John, this is Joy," she said as calmly as she could. "He's on his way home."

"He's OK right? It's just the end of his tour right?" John nearly pleaded on the other end of the line.

"Yeah, he's fine. Missy just called. He'll be in Honolulu on Wednesday and San Diego on Friday. She says he'll be back in Kentucky Saturday morning sometime." Joy added.

"Thank God!" he replied simply.

"Yes sir, thank God indeed. I want to be there when he gets back, but Tony's due in Friday night," Joy answered. " I can't be in two places at the same time."

"Does Tony know Pete's coming in? If he did, I'll bet he'd want to be there too. I know one thing for sure, I will damn well be there!" John shouted with his excitement taking over from his attempt at being subdued.

"Can you try and get a hold of Tony, see if he knows about Pete. I need to make the rest of the calls. Tony's party will have to wait, it'll be much sweeter having them both back!" Joy's own voice betraying the enthusiasm she was feeling.

"I'll call Tony, you alert the rest of the tribe (John's common phrase for the extended Lucas family)."

"OK. Let me know what you find out," Joy said and hung up the phone.

John still standing in the kitchen where the phone hung on the wall screamed to his wife, who was in the front room of their farmhouse. "May, Pete's coming home!"

"John Lucas, don't you say that unless it's true," May hollered back.

"As I live and breath Momma, he's already in the air on his way to Saigon. He'll be back in Kentucky Saturday morning sometime!" John exclaimed having made his way to the archway separating the two rooms, a smile a mile wide on his face.

May burst out in tears and a moment later John joined her on the sofa, both crying and laughing at the same time. The pure joy they were experiencing was wiping away the months of worry that had sat firmly on their shoulders. A few minutes later John got up and headed back to the kitchen. He picked up the phone and dialed Kentucky. He wasn't able to reach Tony, but instead left a message for him to call as soon as possible.

Tony was busy helping Tracy pack up her tiny apartment. Everything she owned would easily fit in the back of Tony's pickup. The couch Tony had slept on the night he met her actually belonged to a friend, and he helped her return it. The only piece of real furniture she owned was an old sleigh bed her father had built her before he left. The rest was just clothes, pots and pans, and other odds and ends. Once Tracy's stuff was loaded up, they hopped in and Tony drove to the base. He passed through the main gate and headed directly to his quarters. He had already gotten his release papers, the official paperwork would come in the mail later. He pulled up and hopped out just as Missy came out of the door.

"Tony, I thought I missed you," she started. Then she noticed Tracy in the passenger seat and got a little uncomfortable.

"What's up Missy? We're just grabbing my gear and heading home," he replied.

Missy regained her composure somewhat, although she kept sneaking glimpses of Tracy out of the corner of her eye. "I wanted to be the one to tell you, Pete's coming home! He's already on his way! He'll be back here Saturday morning!"

"Wow that's fantastic! Crap, I'm headed for Ohio now." Tony's joy tempered a bit by the realization.

"It's just a couple of days, can't you hang around here?" Missy asked while looking straight at Tracy.

"We just cleared out her place, and I'm not supposed to even be here now. The guards gave me thirty minutes to collect my gear. I guess Morgan hasn't gotten over our little spat just yet."

"I'll work on the Colonel, you'll be welcome Saturday I promise. I think it would mean a lot to Pete," Missy said adding a pleading look at the end.

"I'll try, but I can't promise anything. We're pretty much homeless at this point," he said motioning towards Tracy.

"Do I get to meet her?" Missy finally had to ask.

"Oh I'm sorry, Tracy come here a minute I want to introduce you to someone!"

Tracy stepped out of the truck and walked slowly and uneasily to where the other two were standing. She was 5'8" tall, with long legs and a fit athletic build, her long hair pulled back in a ponytail. This was Tony's new girlfriend and she was stunning. Missy flashed red with jealousy for a moment, but took a deep breath and it passed. She smiled at Tony's new girl and Tracy smiled back.

"Tracy, this is Missy James. Missy this is Tracy Tucker." Tony said. "Missy is dating my brother Pete, and she came here to tell me some great news. Pete's coming home Saturday!"

Tracy instantly responded," that's great!"

"There is one problem," Tony interjected. "He's coming here and we're headed for Ohio."

Tracy could see the conflict on Tony's face. He wanted desperately to be away from the base and the Army, but he wanted just as badly to see his little brother. She thought for a moment and then came up with an idea. "Well why don't we head up into the land between the lakes for a couple of days of camping and come back down Saturday morning for Pete's arrival?"

"Perfect, I love camping!" Tony exclaimed and gabbed Tracy and gave her a quick kiss.

Missy again flashed red and quickly excused herself, she wasn't sure what was going on but her instinct told her she wasn't quite over Tony yet. She hadn't even thought much of Tony for the past few months. No daydreams, no dreams at all. So why was she suddenly jealous of Tracy. All she could do was hope that once Pete was home her love for him would eliminate any thoughts of Tony once and for all.

Tony collected his gear and headed for the truck. A sergeant caught him and handed him a message, "Call home ASAP, Uncle John." He loaded his stuff into the back of the truck and quickly exited the base. He headed into the land between the lakes, the area of Kentucky sandwiched between Kentucky Lake and Lake Barkley formed when the TVA dammed the Tennessee River during Roosevelts spending spree to pull the country out of the Great Depression, and later the

Army Corps of Engineers dammed the Cumberland River nearby to even out the elevation of the two bodies of water. Tony soon found a small country store along the side of the road and eased the truck to a stop in front. While Tracy went inside and bought some food, a tarp and an ice chest, Tony headed to a pay phone at the corner of the parking lot.

He dialed the operator and placed a collect call to his uncle, "Uncle John it's Tony is everything OK?"

"You get the word?"

"Yeah, Pete's coming home! Sorry you had to hear it from somebody else but I just found out about an hour ago." Tony shot back. The excitement in both men's voices plainly obvious, their shared knowledge and worry now fading into irrelevance.

"Your momma told me, so no harm done. You gonna be there Saturday? I know you were planning on heading home today."

"Yeah, I'll be there. Tell mom I'll be a couple of days late," Tony joked.

"You can tell her yourself, she plans on being there too. Better be clean shaven and have your Sunday best on."

"Not much chance of that I'm afraid, Tracy and I are going to camp for the next two nights. She had already moved out and I was basically kicked out, so we don't have anywhere to go. But she suggested camping and it sounded good to me," Tony's voice carried his happiness strait through the phone to a smiling John.

"OK, we'll see you Saturday son," John replied and hung up the phone, not knowing who Tracy was but thinking he must have been supposed to know her.

Tracy heard the end of the conversation and asked, "who was that?"

"My Uncle John, he and my mom and probably a bunch more of my family are coming down to welcome Pete home!" Tony said laughing.

Tracy looked as though she might get sick. "Shit Tony, after camping for two days I'll look like hell. I can't meet your whole family like that! Christ this is just great!" She was pacing back and forth and about to cry. Tony walked up and held her fast. He pulled her in against his chest and looked her strait in the eye.

"I'll get us a hotel room Friday night. You can get all dolled up and look beautiful for Saturday." He said smiling.

"It's too expensive, you can't afford it," she cried, tears now streaming down her face.

"I'll manage, making you happy is more important to me than money. Besides I have two years of back pay waiting for me in Ohio. Now let's get moving. We need to have camp set up before dark, and I'm getting hungry!"

Chapter 50

Pete and the rest of his company landed at Hickman
Airfield on the island of Oahu and were given 24 hours of leave
to de-compress before boarding their plane to San Diego. This
time Pete accepted an offer to join some guys on a trip to the
fabled Waikiki Beach. They hired a taxi to take them from the
western end of the small island down the coastal highway into
Honolulu and then on down to Waikiki. The guys poured out of
the taxi, Pete paid the tab, and they set off walking along the
beautiful sand beach. They were all wearing the only clothes
they had, Army issue green shorts and T-shirts, which while not
being uncommon on an island overwhelmingly dominated by
military bases still made them impossible to miss. An attractive
young woman wearing a tie-dyed t-shirt and bikini bottoms

walked right up to Pete and asked with a smug look on her face. "Killed any babies lately?"

Pete just stared at her.

"Your disgusting and should be ashamed of yourselves", she continued.

Pete shook his head and walked past her, not giving her the satisfaction of even saying a word. Coming home wasn't going to be a hero's welcome that was for sure. He slowed down and let the other guys walk ahead of him, it had occurred to him he hadn't even considered what he would do next. He was enlisted for another three years but after that would he stay in the Army or, or do what? Lost in thought he bumped into a man with long blonde hair carrying a surfboard toward the ocean.

"Easy soldier" came the reply.

"Sorry man, wasn't paying attention" Pete apologized.

"No worries, just get back from Nam? the surfer asked.

"Yeah" Pete replied bracing for the insult to come.

"Its tough man, did two tours in 66 and 68 myself, stay strong man, you'll get through it" he said smiling.

"I'm not sure which way is up at the moment, just kinda drifting" Pete admitted.

"Been there man, ended up just drifting around catchin' waves and getting drunk, finally ended up here. Got a small shack on the north shore, teach tourists to surf, life's good now, but it was a bitch for the first couple years. Nightmares and shit, it fades over time if you don't dwell on it. What unit?"

"101st, Charlie company"

"Holy shit, airborne? Serious shit my friend. Hang loose man?"

"Roger that", Pete said and watched as the surfer jogged into the water, then launched himself onto his board and began paddling out to the surf line.

The rest of the guys had reached the far end of the beach and were heading back his way, so Pete just plopped down onto the soft sand and stared out towards the ocean. The sound of the waves soothed his soul, this was a good place to relax he thought. Once the guys reached his spot, he stood and followed them to a beach bar where they ate dinner and had a few rounds of drinks. Pete had never had an ounce of alcohol before that night and afterwards decided he could do without it for quite a while. The next day he boarded his flight to the mainland with a pounding headache and a bad case of nausea.

Chapter 51

Pete's success was greeted with a wry smile by Elmore Craft, he didn't hold out hope that the war in Vietnam could be won by shooting a few Generals but he did want to make sure his counterpart in the KGB knew that he had the capability to exact a price if necessary. This was a global chess match, Vietnam was not going to end well but there were many other pieces in play and he intended to keep those pieces from being taken by the Soviets and whenever possible take a few of theirs.

Kolskoff began to suspect his personal assassin wasn't coming back when he received a cable from Moscow stating that the American Shadow was being returned to the United States. Their man inside the Pentagon had intercepted a message from Colonel Morgan to his superiors confirming the Shadow completed his mission and was recovered successfully. Kolskoff was upset at losing Igor but not enough to lose sleep over it, now if he could just get re-assigned anywhere, anywhere but Siberia that is.

The transfer in San Diego to an Army transport that would take the rangers home to Fort Campbell was routine and the guys boarded the last leg of the journey worn out and excited at the same time. Many of them had wives and kids waiting for them, others girlfriends and family, Pete wasn't sure anyone even knew he was coming, except Missy probably, maybe. He watched and listened as the other guys grew more and more excited, he was happy to be going home but he missed the jungle too. He thought about his guardian angel, the tigers, the birds, and the bugs, rats and fleas. Maybe home wasn't that bad after all.

The End

Made in United States
Orlando, FL
05 June 2023

33822738R00307